By

Larry Buege

Gastropod Publishing
Marquette, Michigan

All rights reserved. No part of this book can be reproduced or transmitted in any form or by any means, electronic or mechanical, including photocopying, recording, or by an information storage and retrieval system without permission in writing from the publisher—except for reviewers who may quote brief passages in a review.

This book is a work of fiction. Names, characters, places, and incidents are used fictitiously. Any resemblance to actual events or persons, living or dead, is entirely coincidental.

Other books by Larry Buege

Miracle In Cade County (Mystery/Love Story)

Cold Turkey (Political Satire)

Super Mensa (Techno-Thriller)

Chogan and the Gray Wolf (Native American)

Chogan and the White Feather (Native American)

Chogan and the Sioux Warrior

Chogan and the Winnebago Merchant

Published by Gastropod Publishing, Marquette, Michigan
Copyright © 2013 by Larry Buege

Library of Congress Control Number: 2013940334
ISBN: 978-0-9892477-4-0

Prologue

Summer 1898

Camp 13 was typical of the many squalid lumber camps scattered across what timber barons called the northern woodland paradise. Woodland it was—paradise it was not. Paradise was a figment of their ad agency's perverted imagination and could only be found in the logging companies' recruiting brochures. To be sure, Michigan's Upper Peninsula did offer large tracts of virgin timber begging to be cut, but they were garnished with cedar swamps and peat bogs teeming with carnivorous black flies and marauding squadrons of maladjusted mosquitoes. That alone was sufficient to repulse the more sagacious individuals. Consequently, Camp 13's personnel roster flaunted the most despicable degenerates money could buy. Leaving their families in the dingy slums of Sweden and Finland, they came to America to pursue a better life in the New World. Despite their deprivation, the immigrants were a hard-working lot with an American dream of reuniting their families as soon as financial restraints would permit; after which, they would leave for the more subdued life of farming in Lower Michigan or Wisconsin.

This squalor was not for lack of adequate opportunities for physical improvement, but due to the fact this was a *man's camp*. Unfettered by the influence of female constraints, the men were free to mold their maleness into the highest levels of social degradation, achieving heights unseen in prior civilizations. It was this lack of feminine input that allowed the camp to survive without a formal name. Real men knew Camp 13 was a totally adequate designation and easily placed on any map or chart. A formal name would be superfluous and a wasteful use of human creativity. After twelve to eighteen months, the trees would be reduced to stumps, and the men would move on to camp 14, leaving behind an unnamed barren tract of land the wilderness would quickly reclaim for its own. Women, on the other hand, were not biologically capable of withstanding the void left by an unnamed camp and would be compelled by uncontrollable outbursts of hormonal activity to create an appropriate appellation, no matter how brief the camp's existence.

This masculine utopia was not without problems, which was the reason for Charles Farnsworth's current existence at the camp. During the preceding three months, output had fallen precipitously, prompting Smith, Rice, and Homburg, partners in the Boston-based lumber company which owned Camp 13, to send their foremost trouble shooter to correct the situation. At least that was Farnsworth's assessment of his transfer to this God forsaken land. Being caught naked in Mr. Homburg's bedroom closet had nothing to do with the transfer. Farnsworth was optimistic that a timely reversal in camp productivity would free him from this barbaric bondage; he would gladly trade his soul for a ticket back to Boston.

Born to a wealthy Boston family, Farnsworth had become accustomed to the finer attributes of life, a life style he had no desire to relinquish, and a life style not offered in abundance at Camp 13. With the help of his influential father, Farnsworth had successfully avoided the draft as well as the unsavory inconveniences of service in the Civil War; but eventually, he had felt compelled to serve his country regardless of the consequence. He, therefore, accepted a commission as a second lieutenant on April 13, 1865, four days after Lee surrendered at Appomattox,— there was no sense joining before he was assured which side was winning. He resigned his commission six months later. Throughout the years following the Civil War, Farnsworth continued to promote himself until he had reached the rank of colonel. He would have gone for general, but the military exploits of generals are well defined in history books, whereas the military prowess of a colonel is limited only by one's imagination, and Farnsworth could be quite creative.

Col. Farnsworth was a widower of nineteen years, his wife having died during the birth of his only child, Abigail. Farnsworth never remarried, and since work allowed little time for domestic responsibilities, Abigail was raised by committee with her Aunt Harriet chairman of the board. She now attended a small, but prestigious, college for women in Boston.

Farnsworth hadn't been in camp long before he identified the cause of the slowdown. The large number of lumberjacks walking with short, timid steps as well as the long lines at the latrine could mean only one thing—the camp was suffering from dysentery. Local sentiment favored Porkchop, the one-eyed camp cook, as the source of this affliction, and several of his fellow employees were currently in the process of correcting the situation.

Farnsworth sat at his desk in his crudely constructed office. It was one of two such wooden structures in camp, the other being the latrine. Living quarters and the mess hall were constructed of canvas draped over wooden frames. Through his office window, he could see Porkchop, black patch over right eye, in a quasi-fetal position clinging to an overhanging branch of a tall white pine. Below, two Finlanders and a Swede were coaxing him down with axes. They would've had more help had not the rest of the crew been queuing up at the latrine. Being only a two-holer, the line moved slowly. As one lumberjack came out, another went in. The lumberjack coming out immediately returned to the back of the line. With the tree two feet in diameter, Farnsworth gave Porkchop twenty minutes at best. They would need a new cook, the fourth cook in six months.

Fortuitously, in front of him was one Maggie O'Tool applying for the position of cook, if one were to be available. At five-foot-ten, her muscular frame confirmed she was no stranger to hard work. Her red hair was non-provocatively tied in a bun, and her skin was too dark for pure Irish. Farnsworth speculated she might have some Indian blood. "So you want to be a cook?" Farnsworth inquired. Her crude appearance didn't instill him with enthusiasm. "Got any experience?"

"Five years," Maggie replied, chewing on a large wad of tobacco, her teeth stained. A small amount of red saliva drooled from the corner of her mouth. Several front teeth were missing, and Farnsworth could see large dental cavities bathed with red spittle. She spit the excess juices into the spittoon beside Farnsworth's desk. Only a small dribble lingered along the rim of the spittoon before migrating south.

"It does appear we'll need a cook," Farnsworth said, as he checked the progress outside his window. Only the two Finlanders were left; the Swede, yielding to his biological needs, was waiting in line with the others. "We've been having some problems with dysentery in the camp, and it appears our current cook may be incapacitated in the near future."

"Boiling water," Maggie offered.

"Nope, it appears to be tar and feathers," Farnsworth replied, still eyeing the situation outside.

"No, for the dysentery. Water from rivers and ponds has bad spirits that must be driven away. Boiling water makes the evil spirits unhappy. An Indian chant while circling the pot forces them up into the heavens."

"You saying we have dysentery because of evil spirits?"

"Works every time. Learned it from an old Ojibwa medicine man."

"When can you start?"

"I can start now, but I'll need an assistant."

The office door burst open revealing a frantic camp foreman. "The men are going to kill Porkchop," Dutch said between gasps for air. Spying Maggie, Dutch tipped his hat. "Good evening, Miss." It had been six months since he had seen a woman. Somehow, he remembered women being more attractive. Dutch turned to Farnsworth. "The men have gone mad. They plan to kill Porkchop."

"Tell them we have a new cook, and bring Porkchop in here."

At six-foot-four and two hundred forty pounds, Dutch could crack heads with the best of the lumberjacks, which was why he was foreman; but he had doubts about this assignment. His sentiments leaned toward tar and feathers.

"Job's yours for ten days," Farnsworth offered. "I'm not one for voodoo or Indian chants, but if the food's edible and the dysentery's gone in ten days, the job's yours for good."

A crashing noise confirmed the falling of the white pine, and Farnsworth could hear footsteps racing toward his door. The door opened wide. Dutch pushed the cowering Porkchop through the opening and slammed the door behind him. He applied the wooden crossbar, locking the door, just as the vigilantes arrived en masse.

Porkchop sat on the floor mute, his left eye glassy, his right eye patched. Years before, Porkchop's eye had been punctured by the proverbial sharp stick from a falling tree. With poor peripheral vision on the right side, he was considered a danger in the woods. With no cooking experience, he was a danger in the kitchen as well.

"Porkchop, come over here and meet our new head cook," Farnsworth said.

"I ain't working for no woman," Porkchop replied.

"She has cooking experience and may take some heat off you."

"I ain't working for no woman," Porkchop repeated, assuming no one heard him the first time.

Farnsworth walked over to the corner of the room where Porkchop was organizing his defense should the vigilantes break through. "Listen," Farnsworth whispered to Porkchop. "This will only be for ten days until the men cool down. All you have to do is let her think she's the boss."

"I ain't taking no orders from no female," Porkchop whimpered more to himself than to anyone else. Porkchop conceded that the tobacco-chewing, muscle-bound female was less dangerous than the howling mob outside the door. He would soon realize it was not by much.

Camp 13 was bounded on three sides by a large creek that meandered lazily around the northern edge of the camp. A quarter mile north of camp, the land sloped downward toward the creek and into a large ravine. The surrounding trees had been harvested, leaving only stumps as a reminder of their previous glory. At the nadir of the ravine, the creek widened into a three-acre beaver pond. This immaculate beaver pond was the engineering marvel of one overzealous beaver whose lodge protruded above the water near the far shore. The edge of the pond was sandy and the slope gradual, luring many a lumberjack into skinny-dipping on hot summer Sundays, their only day off.

It was also the source of camp water, which Porkchop now hauled in daily by buckboard wagon. Maggie boiled the water in fifty-gallon drums while extolling the gods with Indian chants. She was the object of ridicule, but in three days, the dysentery subsided.

With the conquering of the dysentery, life at Camp 13 returned to its normal mundane drudgery. The day started with breakfast at six, consisting of flapjacks, eggs, bacon strips, and fried potatoes. Meals were plentiful, as the work was hard and energy quickly consumed. The men begrudgingly had to admit Maggie could cook; and Porkchop learned to take orders from a woman. Porkchop stood three inches shorter than Maggie, and since he was no longer exposed to manual labor in the woods, had grown soft. Conventional wisdom was that Maggie could take him two out of three falls. The rest of the lumberjacks also knew better than to cross Maggie. Her Irish temper was legend, and several hapless individuals discovered a meat fork was a great equalizer.

Food and other staples arrived in camp daily by wagon. Since there was no adequate means of storage, salted meats such as sides of bacon and hams were the mainstay. The buckboards also provided mail, frequently in several languages. Tuesdays were laundry pickup days for those isolated few interested in personal hygiene, the laundry being returned the following Thursday. Every Friday saw the arrival of a stagecoach carrying the payroll and an occasional passenger or two. Thus was the routine at Camp 13.

Farnsworth had easily adjusted to the mundane routine. Yes, boring was good, he decided as he did his ambulatory camp inspection with his foreman, Dutch.

"Yo, boss man."

Farnsworth turned toward an overly energetic, eight-year-old, Indian youth running in his direction.

"You got laundry?" Running Squirrel asked.

Running Squirrel had arrived in camp unannounced three months earlier. Farnsworth, finding him to be a cheating, lying, and conniving capitalist, took an instant liking to the lad. Within two weeks of his arrival, Running Squirrel had launched a laundry business with himself as CEO. For two bits he would pick up laundry, transport it to his crew of Indian women and have it returned clean and dry within three days.

"There's a bag of dirty clothes inside my office. Help yourself." Farnsworth flipped him a quarter. Running Squirrel insisted on advance payment.

"Does the big banker coming Friday have big money?" Running Squirrel asked, mentally calculating the various ways a rich banker could be separated from his money.

"There's no banker coming Friday," Farnsworth replied. "I'd certainly know if there were."

"Ah, excuse me, Colonel," Dutch interjected. "This telegraph message arrived a couple of hours ago. Been meaning to give it to you."

Farnsworth opened the telegram. The Boston office had telegraphed it to Green Bay. From there, a buckboard transported it to camp with the regular mail.

Dear Col Farnsworth STOP John D. Bigsby III and his son-in-law Albert Hodgman representing the Chicago Bank and Trust will be arriving Friday June 17 STOP They will be evaluating camp operations in reference to pending bank financing STOP Please extend all camp courtesies STOP

"Damn," Farnsworth muttered to himself. He preferred stronger language but didn't wish to corrupt the young mind before him. He was unaware Running Squirrel had already been corrupted in three languages. He didn't have time to baby-sit VIPs nor was he in the mood to tolerate their pompous demands.

Such visitors weren't unusual, but they were a nuisance. They would conduct a charade of inspecting the camp, asking questions that could have been answered by mail. After a day or two, they would give the camp their blessing and proceed to the real reason for the visit—hunting or fishing. During their forays into the wilderness in search of big game or bigger fish, they would invariably get lost. It would be Farnsworth's responsibility to pay Chief Thunder Head and Chief Red Weasel to find them. Farnsworth had discovered all adult male Indians held the rank of chief, much like auctioneers held the honorary rank of colonel. The true meaning of chieftain had long since been lost.

Farnsworth hadn't given much thought concerning his treatment of the arriving dignitaries, but indifference seemed as good as any. He would have Dutch erect a sleeping tent, but would go no further. He originally planned to pitch the tent downwind from the latrine. He later decided this would be vindictive and not within his current policy of indifference. The tent was moved to a more fragrant location. Farnsworth would flaunt his indifference by being preoccupied with more important matters and unable to greet the bankers when they disembarked from the stage. He would decide later what were the more important matters. Having them seek him out would firmly establish the pecking order early in the game.

As fate would have it, Farnsworth was walking across the compound with Dutch when the stage arrived. The driver brought the coach to a halt at Farnsworth's feet, making it appear he had purposely come to greet the visitors. No sooner had the coach come to a stop than a balding man occluded the doorway with his corpulent frame. Thick, wire-rim glasses magnified his eyes, and his nose was turgid and wrinkled like a sun-dried prune. Farnsworth estimated him to be in his fifties. His three-piece suit and soft hands might be appropriate in a corporate boardroom, but definitely out of place in a lumber camp; trouble had arrived.

"Col. Farnsworth, I presume." Bigsby offered in more of a statement than a question, his fat cigar bouncing with each syllable. Bigsby clumsily stepped down from the coach and would have fallen had it not been for Farnsworth's quick reflexes. Had Farnsworth more time to assess the situation, Bigsby would have been picking himself off the ground.

"And you must be John D. Bigsby III." Farnsworth hoped for the sake of humanity there wasn't a Bigsby IV. "This is my foreman, Dutch. He handles our day-to-day operations."

"And this is my able assistant and son-in-law, Albert Hodgman," Bigsby said, completing the introductions as a frail, bespectacled individual stepped into the doorway of the coach. He tipped his hat but didn't speak, having learned over the years to defer all conversation to his father-in-law. His disembarkment from the coach was slow, but more elegant than his boss's. He didn't appear any more capable of coping with a wilderness environment than Bigsby, definitely a case of the blind leading the blind.

Farnsworth was unprepared for what followed. As Hodgman stepped down, a new figure filled the doorway. Her face had soft features that were perfectly symmetrical. Her long, dark hair rested quietly on her shoulders, and a snug dress augmented her generous chest. Forty-two and one-half pairs of eyes were immediately focused on this rare spectacle while testosterone levels surged to heights not seen in recent camp history.

"Shut your mouth, you're drooling," Maggie told Porkchop. She punctuated the statement with a jab of her meat fork into Porkchop's posterior, but Porkchop's posterior was totally anesthetized by the high testosterone level and he felt no pain.

The young lady appeared to float in slow motion as she climbed down the two steps to the ground. Her chest slowly rose and fell with each step. Forty-two and one-half pairs of eyes slowly rose and fell in unison. Her feet finally hit *terra firma* with the hemline of her dress provocatively well above her ankles.

"Hi, Daddy," the teenage girl said as she gave Farnsworth a big hug.

"Abigail, what are you doing here?" Farnsworth stared at his daughter; his problems with the bankers now seemed trivial.

"Didn't you get my letter?"

"Excuse me, Col. Farnsworth," Dutch interjected. "Been meaning to give you this telegram. It arrived yesterday."

Dear Daddy STOP Will arrive at camp 13 on June 17 STOP Will stay for one week STOP Love Abigail STOP

"Your Aunt Harriet let you come?" Farnsworth asked.

"She had no problems with it after I told her it was all right with you."

"Well, it's not OK with me. I'm sending you back." A multitude of complex situations flashed though Farnsworth's mind, none of them good.

"It's for a school project. I need to interview some immigrants, so I can write a report for my sociology class on how different ethnic groups adjust to life in America. If I have extra time, I can help you here in camp. Won't that be fun?"

"No, that won't be fun. The men aren't used to having women around. You won't be safe."

"But Aunt Harriet said you have a woman cook."

"Unless you're good with a meat fork, you're hardly in the same league. Besides, this is a man's camp. The men won't like having a woman around." He really had no choice, Farnsworth decided, but he would send her back on the next stage.

Farnsworth couldn't have been more wrong about the camp's acceptance of Abigail. After three days of interviews, she had been propositioned in four languages, five if you count sign language. She also had all the information she needed for her class, allowing her to devote her energy toward camp improvement. It was obviously in need of a woman's touch.

Bigsby and Hodgman were less of a problem. They asked a few intelligent questions and observed the camp operations for several days before moving on to their prime objective. Farnsworth, hoping they would opt for fishing, was disappointed when they uncased a couple of expensive, European-made, hunting rifles—not a good choice.

"You run a taut ship, Farnsworth, my boy. A very taut ship," Bigsby reiterated. "I see no problems with the financing. We finished our evaluation earlier than expected; so I thought I'd take the boy hunting. He's never been in the north woods, you know," Bigsby said, pointing to his twenty-nine year old son-in-law. Hodgman, looking pathetic, offered no rebuttal.

"Have you considered fishing? We have some fine fishing streams, and there's less chance of getting lost following a stream," Farnsworth suggested.

"I've got my compass." Bigsby patted his breast pocket. "No way we're getting lost."

How many times had he heard that before? Farnsworth wondered. "Don't shoot any Indians. They're friendly in these parts. Might even be of some help."

"I won't shoot them first; but if they give me any trouble, they'll be in for a surprise."

Farnsworth conceded defeat as the bankers headed out the door and into the morning sunshine. If they were to be lost in the woods, at least they would have a nice day.

Farnsworth hadn't finished musing over problem #1 when problem #2 walked through the door in the form of an exasperated foreman. Farnsworth was wondering if he would ever see Boston again.

"You've got to do something about that daughter of yours," Dutch demanded. "She's taking over the camp. Yesterday she had men hang a sign over the camp entrance. Camp 13 is now Camp Sunshine. She told the men you approved it. This morning at breakfast, there were wild flowers on the tables. Flowers on the tables! If this gets out, we'll be the laughing stock of the lumber camps."

"I'll take care of it," Farnsworth replied, although he had no plan in mind. "I'll talk to her." He could see Dutch wasn't reassured. "We have another problem. Bigsby and Hodgman left on a hunting expedition."

"They'll be lost by noon." Dutch had little sympathy for bankers, feeling they should be part of the food chain—the lower end of it. He could see Farnsworth didn't share his views.

"We'll need a search party. If you see Running Squirrel, tell him I need to talk to him."

"That won't be hard. I hear he's looking for you with dollar signs in his head. He says he has a proposition for you. Beware of that kid. When he has dollar signs in his head, they're usually your dollars."

Dutch walked out the door as the eight-year-old capitalist walked in. Farnsworth could see it was one of those revolving-door mornings. He was already getting a headache.

"Morning Boss," Running Squirrel announced with way too much enthusiasm. "I understand your daughter's leaving soon."

"Not soon enough."

"Give her a break...She's a good influence on your men. Some of them are washing laundry twice a month now. Laundry business is up forty percent. You talk her into staying longer and ten percent is yours. I think white man call it 'kickback.'"

"Not a chance. I've got another problem, which may provide some financial reward." Farnsworth had the young capitalist's undivided attention.

"You mean the lost bankers?"

"They aren't lost yet."

"They will be."

"Find Thunder Head and Red Weasel. Have them round up the hunters at the end of the day. There's five bucks in it for you guys."

"It's seven bucks for hunters," Running Squirrel replied.

"What do you mean seven dollars? You only charge five dollars for lost fishermen."

"Fishermen don't shoot," Running Squirrel explained. "Chief Thunder Head won't do it for five...not after what happened last time."

"That was an accident."

"That may be so, but it took an hour to remove the bird shot from his rear when he rescued that quail hunter."

"What did he expect? He was hiding behind that bush with only his partridge feathers protruding above the branches. What was he doing anyway?"

"Hey, bears aren't the only ones who do it in the woods. Seven bucks for hunters; that's the best I can do."

"OK, seven bucks," Farnsworth grudgingly agreed. It would be money well spend if he could get them out of the woods and back to Chicago without further complications.

"Times two hunters, that'll be fourteen dollars in advance."

"Fourteen! It's the same amount of work for two as for one."

"Yes, but there're two guns. Won't be able to talk them into it for less."

Running Squirrel was just learning to read and write, thanks to the influence of Jesuit Priests; but his math skills were superb. His brain worked like a cash register. He had no difficulty calculating percent profit and cost overruns. Damn those Jesuits, Farnsworth thought to himself. "OK, it's a deal."

"Can they spend the night in the woods?"

"Won't hurt them any," Farnsworth judged. The thought of the bankers spending a cold, miserable night in the woods raised his spirits. Maybe it will even rain.

***

Chief Thunder Head stood quietly at the edge of the stream, fishing pole in hand. This was his favorite pool, which always produced impressive brook trout, a fact confirmed by the stringer of trout by his side. This was his pool. He hadn't even told his best friend, Chief Red Weasel. Some things in life aren't to be shared, and this was one of those personal secrets. The pool, which was two miles downstream from camp 13 (now Camp Sunshine), had steep banks making accessibility difficult. That was why no one had found it, Thunder Head mused.

Thunder Head crouched low to reduce his silhouette; movement was minimal. He made no sound, lest he scare the fish. There was one large brook trout he had been after for several days. Today would be the day. Today he would add that trophy fish to his stringer. Even Red Weasel would be envious. He could see the fish inspecting his bait. Victory was his.

"HI, UNCLE THUNDER HEAD," Running Squirrel yelled from the top of the embankment.

"Damn," Thunder Head muttered as he watched the fish take off with a splash. "What are you doing here?" He tried to give his nephew his best evil-eye look, but it was countered by a childish grin.

"I was hoping I would find you here, oh great warrior and mighty chief of the Ojibwa."

"Flattery will get you nowhere; I'm broke."

"I'm not here for your money. I have a lucrative proposition for you," Running Squirrel said with a hurt look.

"How come every time you have a lucrative proposition, my wallet gets thinner?"

"Col. Farnsworth has a couple of bankers who'll be lost in the woods by nightfall. He wants you and Chief Red Weasel to round them up and bring them back. It's worth five bucks."

"They hunters or fisherman?"

"Well...they might be fishermen," Running Squirrel said without much conviction.

"I knew it. They're hunters. I don't do hunters, not after last time."

"These are deer hunters with rifles. White men are poor shots. They wouldn't have gotten you last time without a scatter-gun," Running Squirrel cheerfully pointed out. "Tell you what; I'll give you the whole seven dollars, and won't even make a profit, just because of the risk involved."

"Would that be fourteen dollars for the two of them?"

"No, Col. Farnsworth was adamant about that. He says it's the same amount of work since they'll be together. They're wealthy bankers," Running Squirrel continued, "with big money. You and Red Weasel should be able to get big tips."

"That's Chief Red Weasel to you. You need to pay more respect to your elders."

"When do I get to be a Chief?" Running Squirrel asked. "And I want to change my name to something more masculine, something with some bite like Snake Eyes. Running Squirrel sounds like a kid's name."

"Hate to burst your bubble, kid; but you are a kid."

"But I'm almost nine."

Thunder Head wasn't listening. He was mentally counting the possible tips. "Can we let them spend the night in the woods?" A cold, damp night in the woods always increased the tips.

"No problem; Col. Farnsworth thinks it'll be good for them."

I could use some folding money, Thunder Head thought to himself. Maybe I could get that new fly rod I've been wanting.

"Chief Red Weasel and I will have them back by morning."

***

Thunder Head quietly slipped into the deerskin lodge and waited until his eyes adjusted to the dim light. His wife, White Dove, was folding laundry. The lodge squatted on the north shore of Moose Lake. Someday he would build a log cabin; White Dove had always wanted a cabin overlooking the lake.

"Chief Thunder Head bring home many fish," Thunder Head proclaimed.

"How come you never bring home a turkey? I'm getting tired of fish every night," White Dove moaned without looking up from her work.

"Turkeys aren't indigenous to the area. By the way, I won't be home for supper."

"What do you mean; you won't be home for supper. Who's going to eat those fish?" White dove glared at the smelly fish with disgust. She would've preferred a turkey.

"Smoke 'em. They'll keep. I'm going hunting with Chief Red Weasel."

"That'll be three times this week."

"What can I say? We're hunter/gatherers. I hunt—you gather."

"I wish you wouldn't hang out with Weasel so much."

"That's Chief Red Weasel to you. He's a noble Ojibwa warrior chief."

"Don't give me that. You all think you're noble warrior chiefs. Your nephew came by this morning. He's talking about becoming a chief. He wants to change his name to Snake Eyes. Says it's more masculine. I've seen some snakes, but I could never tell a masculine snake from a feminine snake. By the way," White Dove continued, "he's looking for you. I'd hide your wallet."

"Already talked to him. He wants me and Chief Red Weasel to find some lost bankers."

"You got a gig to find two bankers? We can use an extra ten spot. They are fishermen, aren't they?"

"Well…sort of," Thunder Head mumbled.

"They're hunters. Don't you ever learn? I'm not plucking any more bird shot out of your behind."

"That was an accident. Running Squirrel says both bankers have thick glasses, and everyone knows white men can't shoot."

"That last one had a pretty good shot pattern," White Dove pointed out. "But fourteen bucks will come in handy."

"Seven bucks," Thunder Head said. "Running Squirrel says Farnsworth will only pay for one, since they'll be together."

"You're being conned by your nephew again."

"He wouldn't do that. I'm his favorite uncle."

"Running Squirrel would send you to the cleaners, leaving you with nothing but a belt buckle if he could make a quarter."

"Running Squirrel says the bankers have big money, and Farnsworth's letting us leave them out overnight. We'll get a big tip. And there's a trophy buck that's been eating at my apple pile I can sell them for another ten spot. They don't like to go back empty handed.

***

Thunderhead crawled toward his bait pile from downwind. When he was within one hundred yards, he could see the twelve-point buck, as he had expected. He could've gotten closer, but that would have taken the pleasure out of using his new Sears and Roebuck four-power scope. When he retold the quest to Red Weasel, the distance would be three hundred yards. He could see the buck easily through his gun sights. Carefully, he placed the cross hairs over the chest. He had learned to avoid headshots, since white men place deer heads on walls as part of their worship activities. Thunder Head squeezed the trigger, and the animal immediately fell to the ground. Retrieving an arrow from his pack, Thunder Head stuck the point deep into the wound. White men expect deer to be shot by bow and arrow. If he had to hunt with a bow and arrow, he would have starved years ago.

When Thunder Head returned to the lodge, White Dove was still folding clothes. The laundry business had picked up since Abigail's arrival.

"What are you doing here? I thought you went after the hunters," White Dove asked.

"You don't expect me to go in these duds, do you?" Thunder Head replied, referring to his red flannel shirt, Levi pants, and leather boots. "White men give bigger tip if I go 'Injun.' Have you seen my buckskin pants?"

"If you'd hang them up, they wouldn't get lost."

After a thorough search of the lodge, Thunder Head found his pants hidden in a pile of clothes by the corner.

"I hate wearing these buckskin pants. I don't know how our ancestors survived in these. They always chaff me in the crotch," Thunder Head muttered mostly to himself.

"If you'd wear underwear like white men, it wouldn't happen."

"How do you know what white men wear under their pants?"

"I do their laundry, don't I?"

"Next time you do Farnsworth's laundry, save me a pair of his underwear. He's my size. White man have saying, 'You don't know a man until you walk a mile in his underwear.'"

"Shoes, you idiot. Walk a mile in his shoes."

Thunder Head slipped on his moccasins and adjusted his headband. He debated the merits of one feather verses two. He decided on two.

"And don't think you're using my lipstick. Last time you and Weasel used it for war paint, you made a mess."

"I'll be back first thing in the morning." Thunder Head slipped out the door on his way to meet Weasel.

***

Thunder Head and Weasel had no trouble finding the bankers' trail. Being the better tracker, Thunder Head took point and let Weasel carry the twelve-point buck. Weasel wasn't the sharpest arrow in the quiver, but he made a good pack animal.

The trail weaved through the woods in a pretzel pattern with the trail frequently overlapping itself. Thunder Head took the fresher path at each junction and by dusk had overtaken the two bankers. They were sitting in a clearing attempting to start a fire. Hodgman was striking two sandstones together in a vain attempt to make a spark. Bigsby, being more sophisticated, had constructed a bow and spindle. The spindle was made of green wood.

"We have to get between them and their guns and establish rapport before they have a chance to blast us," Thunder Head whispered to Weasel. Weasel wasn't fond of the "we" stuff. Both guns were leaning against a tree ten feet from the hunters.

"Go for it," Weasel whispered back. "I'll keep you covered."

"What do you mean, you'll keep me covered? We don't have guns."

"You make the introductions, and I'll simulate the guns," Weasel replied, holding his hand out with index finger pointing and thumb up in a simulated pistol.

"You're totally useless, Weasel, you know that." Thunder Head crept to a point half way between the hunters and their guns before he stood up in front of two startled hunters and raised his right hand. "How, we come in peace." Thunder Head had no idea what "how" meant, but white men expected Indians to say that. He did his best to speak in broken English; white men expected that also.

"We hunt long time. Much tired. We share fire?" Thunder Head asked in his worst English.

"We hunt long time also. We chase big buck deep into woods," Bigsby replied in broken English—Indians only understand broken English.

"You lost?" Thunder Head asked, knowing full well the answer.

"No lost. Camp six miles to the south," Bigsby replied, pointing to the east. Thunder Head figured the camp was a quarter mile to the west. "Daylight too short. Spend night in woods and return to camp in morning," Bigsby continued. "Me show son-in-law how to start fire without matches."

"Me help," Thunder Head said as he plucked two rifle cartridges from Bigsby's vest. Thunder Head extracted the bullet from the first cartridge with his teeth and poured the gunpowder over the kindling wood. He likewise removed the bullet from the second cartridge and poured a small trail of gunpowder from the kindling wood to the cartridge. A pointed stone was placed against the primer cap at the rear of the cartridge. Placing his left moccasin over the shell and stone to immobilize the two, he tapped the stone with a second stone. With a soft poof and a large flash, the kindling wood became an instant campfire. Thunder Head estimated a week for the flash burn on his foot to heal. He knew there was a reason he hated moccasins.

It took a moment for Bigsby and Hodgman to recover muscular control of their drooping mandibles. Bigsby was the first to gain enough control of his jawbone to put it to use. "I always liked that trick," Bigsby said. "I was planning to show Hodgman that trick next if he were unable to start the fire with the stones."

Weasel set the twelve-point buck on the ground, making sure the head and antlers were in full view of the bankers and the arrow in the chest wound clearly visible. He then stood motionless with arms crossed in his best imitation of a cigar store Indian. Weasel spoke excellent English, but remained mute during these negotiations—something about a political statement. Thunder Head never did understand. He had learned long ago not to try to understand Weasel. Weasel's logic was far too shallow for understanding.

"Nice buck," Bigsby said. "Not as big as that fourteen pointer we were chasing."

"Feed many women and children," Thunder Head replied. Let the negotiations begin.

Thunder Head and Weasel cut off two large venison steaks, placed them on wooden roasting sticks, and began heating them over the campfire, making sure the bankers were downwind from the aroma. It was obvious they hadn't brought food or overnight equipment.

"That venison sure smells good. I'll give you a dollar apiece for those steaks," Bigsby offered. Thunder Head and Weasel pretended to think about it for a moment before passing over the roasting sticks in exchange for the folding money. They cut another two steaks for themselves.

"Trouble with those big bucks is the meat can be pretty tough," Bigsby said while chewing a mouthful of venison. "Not as tender as a young doe or fawn."

Thunder Head nodded in agreement, his mouth also full.

"I suppose a good hunter like you could easily replace that buck with a couple tender does."

Thunder Head reckoned he could.

"Those men back in camp don't get much fresh meat. They'd appreciate some venison, even if it were tough," Bigsby speculated. "Tell you what; you seem to be a nice guy. I'll give you eight dollars for that buck, and you can replace it with a couple of tender does."

"How about you give me ten dollars, and I not be nice guy," Thunder Head countered.

"Deal," Bigsby said as more folding money was exchanged. Thunder Head began to pull the arrow from the wound. "Why don't you leave the arrow there?" Bigsby asked. "I want the men back at camp to give you credit for the kill."

With the meal over, Thunder Head and Weasel opened their bedrolls and prepared for sleep. Both had pads to protect them from the hard ground. Thunder Head detested sleeping on the ground. It was so uncivilized.

Bigsby and Hodgman, without bedrolls of any type, elected to stay up a bit longer and keep the fire going. Thunder Head and Weasel made sure they didn't sleep too close to the fire, knowing a white man's fire would be too hot to get near.

"The fire should keep away the timber wolves," Thunder Head said as he winked at Weasel. Hodgman immediately began collecting more firewood.

The sky was clear. Thunder Head expected a cool night with heavy dew. The bankers were already huddling around the fire with one side of their bodies too hot and the other side too cold. A miserable night made for better negotiations.

The night went quickly for Thunder Head and Weasel—too quickly for Weasel who would have preferred to sleep-in. The sky in the east was a brilliant red as the sun began to rise. The bankers didn't notice. They were semi-comatose and staring at the glowing embers with bloodshot eyes. Time for final negotiations.

"Ah, it's a good day to be alive," Thunder Head said as he stretched out. Bigsby and Hodgman weren't so sure. "I guess it's time we get back to our village." Thunder Head began rolling up his bedding in preparation for leaving. Panic stricken, Hodgman began hyperventilating. The thought of being stranded in the forest was more than he could handle. Bigsby was more confident, knowing money solved all problems.

"I wrenched my shoulder chasing that fourteen point buck," Bigsby said, "and Hodgman, here, isn't the athletic type. Think you could carry the buck back to our camp for another ten dollars?" Bigsby asked in a euphemism for "show us the way home."

"Our wives are expecting us home early this morning."

"Twelve bucks"

"Weasel's wife can get ugly if he isn't home on time."

"Fifteen bucks"

"Deal," Thunder Head agreed as money was exchanged.

The campsite was a quarter mile from Camp 13, and Thunder Head could have gotten them back in fifteen minutes, but decided to take a circuitous route to give the bankers their money's worth. After two hours of walking, the foursome arrived at the beaver pond north of camp. The bankers became more invigorated upon finding familiar territory.

"We can carry the deer from here," Bigsby said, not wanting to be seen led back to camp by Indians. He had his pride.

Weasel dropped the buck on the ground. Even pack animals get tired. The two Indians shook hands with the bankers before leaving them—with thinner wallets.

Once the Indians were out of sight, Bigsby removed the arrow from the deer and tied the deer's front legs and hind legs together. Then, using a long pole, the two triumphant hunters carried the deer into camp safari style.

Farnsworth could see the arrival of the great white hunters from his office window. He estimated ten minutes before Bigsby would burst through the door to brag about his exploits. That would give him time to deal with his hysterical foreman. Farnsworth hadn't yet elucidated the current problem confronting

Dutch, but he assumed it had something to do with his daughter—these days it usually did.

"We have a total work stoppage," Dutch was saying.

"So why aren't the men working?"

"Because your daughter told them they needed a bath and that you had approved it."

"I see," Farnsworth replied even though he didn't.

"They're heating water in fifty-gallon drums for men to bathe in. Now the men are expecting Abigail to take her turn." Dutch didn't add that he wouldn't mind watching that spectacle himself.

"Try to hold on for one more day. Abigail will be leaving on the morning stage. Then we'll get back to our normal routine." Dutch didn't seem convinced but did leave to make the best of a bad day.

The office door had hardly slammed shut when Bigsby reopened it. "Boy, did we have an adventure." Bigsby waved the arrow in the air. "Those Indians aren't as friendly as you would make one believe. Five of them attacked us and tried to steal our trophy buck. They shot several of these arrows at us. None of them came close. I knew you wanted to keep peace in the area, so we didn't shoot them. I did shoot the feather off the chief's head. The rest ran in terror."

Farnsworth hoped Bigsby was exaggerating about shooting the feather. If it were true, he'd never get Thunder Head's help again.

"You sure no one was injured?"

"We only fired one shot, and that was cleanly through the feather. The Indian was only a hundred yards away. It was hard to miss."

"We returned late because we saw this large buck. The sun was setting, so we had to track it in the dark. About midnight we found the deer and broke off for the night. Unfortunately, we didn't have any matches with us. Did I ever show you how to start a fire with two rifle shells?"

Farnsworth wished he had a quarter for every time he heard the rifle shell story.

"I understand you'll be leaving tomorrow morning?" Farnsworth asked, trying to shorten the banker's oration.

"Yes, got to get back to work. Can't spend the entire summer shooting Indians and hunting deer. But now, I think I'll catch a quick nap."

***

It was Abigail's last night in camp. Tomorrow she would be leaving for Boston. It had been an exciting week. Still, she was glad it was almost over. It was approaching July, and even Michigan's Upper Peninsula can get hot in the summer. She hadn't had a bath since her arrival. The basin and washcloth only rearranged the sweat and grime. With the days muggy and the nights hot and sweaty, sleeping was difficult. Tonight was no exception. A short walk in the cooler air outside her tent might be therapeutic, she decided.

The air outside the tent wasn't much cooler; but it was a clear night, and the stars were breathtaking. No lanterns were visible in any of the tents; apparently, everyone was asleep. Abigail walked north, as if pulled by some unseen force. Maybe she would have one last look at the beaver pond. During her stay, she often sat on a stump overlooking the pond and watched the beaver ply his trade. He never rested and continuously worked on his dam.

Visibility was less than twenty feet, but the path created by the buckboard wagons were easy to follow. Within minutes, she had reached her favorite stump, but the beaver pond was obscured by darkness. She would have to be content counting stars. To the north, the bright trail of a shooting star caught her eye. Would it bring her luck? She felt lucky tonight.

As Abigail watched for more shooting stars, the blackness lifted like a veil and a sudden increase in light illuminated her surroundings. To the east, a full moon was rising, bathing the entire ravine in the moonlight. She could now see the pond clearly. At the far side, the beaver lodge protruded above the surface of the pond like a giant turtle shell. She could see white ripples from the beaver's wake at the west end of the pond where he was diligently at work.

Abigail walked to the edge of the pond. Taking off her shoes, she placed her right foot into the water, finding the water warm and refreshing. With reduced flow, the water had quickly warmed up in the summer sun. She walked along the edge of the pond, allowing her feet to play in the water. The water was enticing.

Abigail returned to where she had left her shoes on the sandy shore. One by one, articles of clothing fell to the sand until she stood naked in the moonlight.

The water beckoned her. Abigail waded out until the water was up to her hips. Leaning forward, she let the ground beneath her feet drift away, and she quietly breaststroked into deeper water. It felt like a great cathedral where only whispering was allowed.

Abigail decided to explore the beaver lodge while the beaver was at the far end of the pond. After a minute of swimming, Abigail reached the lodge. She grabbed one of the protruding sticks and pulled herself up. The stick held, confirming the sturdiness of the structure.

The lodge was a disappointment, nothing more than a pile of sticks and mud. The opening had to be hidden below the water's surface. Standing at the top of the lodge, Abigail let the water drip from her nakedness. It felt good, and she savored the moment. From the top of the lodge, the entire pond could be seen. It was like an amphitheater and she was on center stage. The stump-covered hill in front of her was her audience. Due to her present nakedness, she preferred the stumps to a live audience. Not wishing to further annoy the beaver, Abigail dived into the depths of the water. She would swim under water for as long as her breath would last.

The beaver had been ignoring his human visitor—he had better things to do. Having seen her sitting on her stump many times during the day, he considered her harmless. She was hardly a great swimmer by beaver standards, but more graceful than the occasional lumberjack who came to swim. Her swimming was unproductive and wasteful of time and energy, very unbeaver like. To each his own, he decided.

Neither Abigail nor the beaver observed the arrival of another visitor to the beaver pond. A large grizzly bear had come to quench his thirst. The bear drank his fill, but his curiosity was piqued by the smell of Abigail's perfume. He had never encountered that smell with lumberjacks. He walked toward the smell until he came to the pile of clothes. Sniffing them a few times, he decided they were, indeed, the source of the strange odor.

The large predator at the water edge finally caught the beaver's eye. Well protected by his watery domain, the beaver had no concern for his own safety. At this point, his only concern was for the safety of his human visitor. The bear had a special interest in her removable pelt. Unable to shout a warning, the beaver sounded the alarm the only way it knew. He lifted his tail high above the water and slapped down forcefully against the water as he swam for the cover of his lodge.

Chapter One

25 Years Later

Spring does not come early in Michigan's Upper Peninsula, and the spring of '23 was no exception. The first of May found the snow in the woods still a foot deep, and large drifts were abundant in open fields. Yoopers, as the natives of the U.P. refer to themselves, were just emerging from their quasi-hibernation and beginning to stir. It had been a long, hard winter, and snowshoes had been the only reliable means of transportation. Still, the Yoopers were a happy lot—they didn't know any better. They were unaware that in lower Wisconsin, people were picking wild flowers, and snowdrifts were a distant memory. True Yoopers never left the U.P. Having been told by other Yoopers this was God's country, they felt no desire to wander.

One individual who should have known about God's country was the local Methodist preacher. He had arrived the previous spring, marveling at the beauty of the Upper Peninsula with its trees, wild flowers, and beaver ponds. For reasons unclear to native Yoopers, he departed during a lull in a major winter storm, taking nothing with him other than the clothes on his back and the snowshoes on his feet. Inspection of his parsonage revealed a daily journal filled with increasingly depressive entries. The final entry was the day he left where he stated the snow snakes were coming after him, and he would make a run for the Wisconsin border. A search party found snowshoe tracks heading south, but the tracks were lost in an approaching storm.

A request to the bishop for a replacement fell on unsympathetic ears, and the members of the Bare Creek Methodist Church were encouraged to survive the best they could until spring when Bishop Johnson would consider appointing a new pastor. He had assigned five pastors over the previous two years—none lasted more than six months. The last appointee was now weaving baskets in a downstate sanitarium, and the mere mention of Bear Creek would send him slithering into the fetal position which he would maintain for days at a time while babbling about demon-possessed beavers and premature purgatory. Any new pastor would have to be expendable. The bishop also felt it impractical to relocate a new minister in midwinter.

No one ever came to the U.P. in the wintertime. At Bear Creek, no one *came* to town in the summer time. They might pass through the town or be forced to spend a night in the hotel above the Snake Pit Saloon, but no one *came* to Bear Creek. There was no reason to come to Bear Creek, as nothing ever happened at Bear Creek. But the Yoopers who lived there didn't care—they didn't know any better.

Bear Creek, located above the Wisconsin border in Michigan's Upper Peninsula, does offer the usual amenities. It has the Bare Creek Cafe and the Snake Pit Saloon, now allegedly dry with prohibition. There is also the Bare Creek Gazette and the Bare Creek Hardware and Feed store. For those unfortunate travelers stranded in Bear Creek, there is lodging available at a reasonable price above the Snake Pit Saloon. It may not be quiet or clean, but it is the only hotel in town.

The occasional itinerant who does wander through Bear Creek is often confused by the spelling of the town's name. On all maps the town and creek are spelled "Bear Creek" whereas the sign at the edge of town and the names of many of the businesses refer to it as "Bare Creek." The locals attribute this discrepancy to the beaver pond incident. According to local legend, in June of 1898, when Bear Creek was nothing more than a temporary lumber camp, the nineteen-year-old daughter of a wealthy timber baron mysteriously disappeared at the beaver pond just north of town. A search, conducted in the light of the full moon, revealed only the pile of Abigail Farnsworth's clothes and the footprints of a large grizzly bear.

The formal report concluded her encounter with the bear had been her demise; therefore, the town and surrounding river were named Bear Creek. Townsfolk remained convinced Abigail was alive and well and could occasionally be seen running naked through the woods chased by the large carnivore. On warm summer nights during a full moon, she would return to the beaver pond searching for her clothes. If one were lucky, he or she might catch a glimpse of the naked Abigail standing on the beaver lodge as the full moon rose to illuminate the pond. Totally embarrassed, she would dive into the water and disappear. It was this legend of the naked Abigail Farnsworth searching for her clothes that gave the town its name.

During the summer months, the rising of a full moon was a major social event, with the entire population of Bear Creek gathering on the hillside overlooking the dam in great anticipation. Below, the beaver pond would be obscured in darkness, but as the full moon rose to illuminate the pond, mothers covered the eyes of small children; and men strained their eyes hoping to catch a glimpse of the naked Abigail before she would dive into the water's depths and disappear. Weeks later, men would still be discussing her beauty while women folk took pity in her plight.

The mayor of Bear Creek was one P.C. Taylor, who was also owner and manager of the Bare Creek Cafe. No one seemed to know what the P.C. stood for, and P.C. wasn't volunteering any information. He had lost his right eye in his youth while working as a logger and now wore a black patch over the eye. P.C. was elected mayor as a joke, having been nominated by Silas Kronschnabell during a drunken brawl. The job had no salary since the town had no taxes or other means of income. P.C. took the job seriously and strutted around town in his three-piece suit, frequently looking at his pocket watch, which always registered quarter past one. Occasionally he would cut a ribbon at an opening of a new store; but for the most part, he spent his time with his best friend Chief Red Weasel. Since the retirement of Chief Thunder Head, Weasel was the senior Indian Chief in the area, and the two heads of state had many a summit meeting down at their favorite fishing hole.

P.C.'s wife, Maggie, managed the cafe quite nicely without his help, and that was fine with her. She did have their seventeen-year-old daughter to assist with some of the chores. Some say Maggie had been a real firebrand in her youth before she got religion. Now she was president of the Ladies Aid Society at the Bare Creek Methodist Church, and her old zeal was directed against liquor and wild women, both of which could be obtained in ample quantities at the Snake Pit Saloon—despite prohibition.

Early May found the morning cool even by Yooper standards, forcing the Bare Creek Economics Club to pay homage to the potbelly stove in the front of the Mel Barker's Hardware and Feed Store. Located in the center of the store, the potbelly stove, now glowing hot, made the room more hospitable, one of the reasons members of the Bare Creek Economics Club gathered at the Hardware and Feed Store each morning. Mel couldn't remember the last time they discussed the local economy, but the name gave the group respectability and purpose, unlike the Methodist Church's Ladies Aid Society, which everyone knew only met for gossip sessions.

Silas Kronschnabell, proprietor of the Bare Creek Gazette, called the Bare Creek Economics Club to order. Frenchie, a young French Canadian, was in the process of beating P.C. Taylor at checkers despite P.C.'s ill-conceived efforts to cheat. A small wager made the game worthwhile. Both players felt cheating was a finely honed skill, adding a new and stimulating dimension to the game. The outcome depended as much on cheating skills as expertise in the fundamentals of the game. Except for Frenchie, the club members were in their fifties.

"We may have a problem," Mel said when the meeting began. "Silas thinks that new preacher is arriving today."

"May already be here," Silas confirmed while he lit his pipe from a burning splinter of wood taken from the potbelly stove.

"Anyone know anything about him?" Mel asked, looking around at the others.

Silence

"Name's Rudy Hooper," Silas said as he nursed his newly lit pipe. The tobacco was reluctant to catch but finally glowed reddish-yellow. Puffs of white smoke belched from the pipe with each breath, rising upward in graceful swirls before dissipating into the air.

"Think he might be young and impressionable?" Mel asked. "If he is, the women could easily manipulate him."

"Can't have him going off on local social crusades." Silas's head was now shrouded in smoke. "Perhaps we need to approach him before he meets the women." Silas chewed on the pipe stem in a moment of deep thought. "Last thing we need is a self-righteous preacher telling us what to do."

"I don't take no orders from no preacher," P.C. pointed out, in case anyone was unaware of his policy on taking orders. P.C.'s momentary distraction from the checkerboard was all Frenchie needed to furtively replace one of his kings P.C. had surreptitiously removed several moves earlier.

"He could come down hard on liquor and the 'Ollies.'"

The 'Ollies' being referred to were Polly, Molly, and Dolly. They had arrived in town simultaneously and now resided in the hotel above the Snake Pit Saloon. The fact they had no last names or visible means of support led the ladies in town to speculate they might be "Soiled Doves" and a threat to the moral fiber of Bear Creek.

"Hey, the 'Ollies' are an important town resource." The conversation now had Frenchie's undivided attention. Frenchie, at age twenty-two, was the youngest of the group. Rumor had it he had been chased out of Quebec by a jealous husband, barely escaping with his life. The French Canadian was a slow learner and was one of the first to welcome the three 'Ollies' upon their arrival. If today was Thursday, tonight would be Molly.

"We're church elders," Mel reminded the others. "I say we push for converting the heathens in New Guinea and feeding the starving children in China. That way the church can feel righteous without meddling into our personal affairs."

Mel Barker, the most impulsive of the group, was a self-proclaimed hero of the Spanish American War and had fought with Teddy Roosevelt at San Juan. He would be happy to tell about it if someone were careless enough to ask. During the Great War he tried to enlist but was informed he was too old. He continued to harass the recruiter until the recruiter gave him a steel helmet with the assignment of guarding the northern coast against an invasion from Canada. Previously, he had considered Canada a friendly neighbor. Obviously, the recruiter was privy to information unknown to Mel. The Great War had been over for several years, but Mel continued to watch the northern front and would continue to do so until relieved of duty. His steel helmet and an old flintlock were always at the ready.

"Mel's right," Silas agreed. "The situation in New Guinea and China is critical. We need to place their welfare above the petty social concerns of our small community. We need to bend the ear of this new preacher before the women corrupt him."

***

Meanwhile, over at the Bare Creek Cafe, Maggie Taylor called to order a special meeting of the Ladies Aid Society. About six to eight of Bear Creek's more influential ladies were sitting around the tables sipping tea. It was ten o'clock in the morning, and the breakfast trade had come and gone. The Cafe was noted for its fine food, but the clean tablecloths and fragrant flowers discouraged real men from loitering. Most of the men had gone to work or wandered over to Mel's hardware store for meaningful discussions about politics and the weather, leaving the Cafe the domain of women. Jennifer, Maggie's daughter, was busy in the back room washing the last of the morning dishes.

"I assume you're all aware the new Methodist preacher will be arriving today." Maggie paused for emphasis as she sipped her tea.

"And none too soon," added Trudy, the wife of Mel Barker and church organist. "We could use a little moral leadership around here."

"Silas came home Saturday night with alcohol on his breath, and I know he's getting it from that Snake Pit," said the wife of the Bare Creek Gazette editor. She poured more tea into her cup. "The Snake Pit needs to go dry or we shut it down." Heads nodded in agreement.

"Let's not forget those three women above the Snake Pit," Maggie said. "Our men can't handle that kind of temptation. They don't have our moral strength." Again there were nods of agreement.

"I think the first order of business for our new minister is to confront those ladies—and I use the term loosely—to determine their intentions in this town," Trudy said as she stood up for emphasis but then, feeling foolish, quickly sat down.

"That's an excellent idea," Agnes agreed.

"All in favor of having our new minister confront those women?" Maggie asked.

"Aye"

"That's what he gets paid for."

"Aye"

"Let's go for it."

"Aye"

"Motion carried," Maggie proclaimed. "Meeting adjourned."

***

Rudy Hooper sat on his porch swing and admired the view. He had been apprehensive about his appointment to the Bare Creek Methodist Church, feeling the bishop may have followed a vindictive impulse because of some disparaging comments Rudy had made concerning the character of the bishop's wife. He expected a run-down parsonage in some God forsaken land filled with tsetse flies and cannibals. Instead, he was sitting on the porch swing of his parsonage overlooking a scenic beaver pond. He could see the white wake left by the beaver as it swam toward his lodge at the far side of the pond. He would become good friends with the beaver. After all, he was one of God's creatures. I think I'll name him Luther, Rudy decided. Yes, that would be a good name.

The inside of the parsonage was a mess. Rudy's predecessor left in a hurry. According to the bishop, the previous minister was still hospitalized because of a lengthy illness; the bishop refused to elaborate further. Rudy wished the bishop had been more forthright about the previous pastor's medical condition. Rudy was very susceptible to diseases and didn't wish to experience a similar fate.

Rudy wasn't one to savor someone else's ill fortune, but God must have been smiling on him. If the previous pastor hadn't taken ill, Rudy might not have received such a plush assignment in this rural paradise.

He would clean the parsonage later. For now, he would enjoy the view and recuperate from his long journey. The only disappointment was the lack of indoor plumbing. An outhouse located downhill from the parsonage and half way to the beaver pond would have to do. It would be a cold walk in the winter snow, but he was looking forward to that first snow. Each snowflake was unique and one of God's many wonderful creations.

At the bottom of the hill a thirty-foot wide section of flat land extended out to the edge of the pond. He would turn that into a garden. He had always wanted a garden. He would grow carrots and peas and maybe some corn. Gardening would provide a relaxing hobby to help him unwind at the end of the day.

Rudy, now twenty-eight, was still single. He had met Miss Right on several occasions but lacked the social skills to take her from Miss Right to Mrs. Hooper. Asking young women to sit with him on some deserted hillside to watch the stars seemed inappropriate for a man of the cloth. He wasn't shy. He had no trouble talking to women in meetings or in comforting the bereaved, but when it came to small talk with eligible women, his palms got sweaty, and his mind became void of intelligent thoughts.

Rudy was not one to stop women cold with his good looks. At six foot one and a hundred and sixty pounds, his slender frame resembled a rough-sawn fence post. His dark brown eyes were recessed into the head more than one should expect, and a full beard hid a scrawny jaw. The fact that he cut his own hair didn't enhance his image. Some strands were longer than others, and his hair was never combed. Despite his appearance, most people found him to be a warm, compassionate person. Wasn't that what being a pastor was all about?

Above all, Rudy was an optimist. He was confident this would be a good year and his stay in Bear Creek enjoyable. He decided to document his first year in a journal, which he could someday read to his grand kids, should he ever have grandchildren. He thought he would include the activities of his nearest neighbor, Luther, in his journal. Grand kids would like that.

May 2, 1923. Today is my first day in Bear Creek and the beginning of my journal. I am captivated by the beauty that is visible from my porch swing. The parsonage overlooks a beaver pond, and I can watch the engineering marvels of a beaver I have named Luther. I am fortunate to have such an interesting neighbor as Luther. Tomorrow I will start work on a garden by the edge of the beaver pond. I expect an exciting year.

Closing the cover of his journal, Rudy sat back to watch the beaver. He was sad to note Luther walked with a slight limp.

***

May 2nd was like any other day for Luther. As usual, he had awakened early to begin work on his dam. Luther came from a long line of over achievers who passed on a strong work ethic; it allowed little time for rest. He inherited the Bear Creek beaver dam from his granddaddy who built the dam over twenty-five years ago. It was a responsibility he didn't take lightly. Today's project involved shoring up a weakened segment of the dam that had been leaking water. A large pile of branches and mud had been set-aside for the repair. He could have worked faster without his gimpy front leg, a result of an industrial injury in Luther's youth when a tree he had been cutting fell on him—he had failed to allow for windage. Now he was an experienced woodsman, and such an accident would be unthinkable.

It was mid-morning, around 7 a.m., when Luther noticed the human sitting on the porch. Humans, Luther had discovered, were lazy animals, and this one was no exception. The human was wasting a good portion of the morning daydreaming. For the most part, they were a harmless species, and Luther was willing to let them continue in their slovenly ways.

Due to their unpredictable antics, humans could be entertaining. When Luther was just a lad, his Granddaddy told him many humorous human stories. Some were just too funny to be true. His favorite story happened when Granddaddy wasn't much more than a youngster himself. He was homesteading the area and building the current beaver pond. There were humans in those days too. Well, one evening when Granddaddy was working late, a female came to the pond. Like the current human, she would sit on a stump and waste the time away. This time, she shed her removable pelt and went for a swim in the moonlight. Very awkward swimmer, Granddad used to say. Anyway, she was playing in the water like those childish otters, when a huge grizzly bear came along. Each time Granddad told the story the bear got bigger. Granddad said he wasn't the least bit frightened, since he could swim circles around any old grizzly bear; but the bear had an interest in the human's removable pelt. Granddad looked about; the human couldn't be seen. He assumed she was swimming under the water. Granddad figured a good slam on the water with his tail would warn her no matter where she might be. Granddad lifted his tail and smacked it against the water. But his tail never hit the water. You see, the human was coming up to the surface, and his tail came down splat on her tail. At least it would have hit her tail if she had one. Luther liked best when Granddad described how the human's gruesome scream sent shivers down Granddad's spine. She took off running across the water with only her ankles getting wet. That ol' grizzly bear was so scared he also took off running. Granddad figured that bear didn't stop until it was clear into the next county. When Granddad got to this part, he would go through the motions of running across the water. It was so funny! Well, I guess you'd have to have been there. Enough daydreaming, he was getting to be as bad as those humans, Luther decided as he returned to the dam repair.

***

As his first order of business, Rudy called a meeting of the church Trustees for a walk-through tour of the church and parsonage. The Trustees were responsible for the maintenance and mechanical upkeep of the church's physical property. It was a good place to start his orientation to his new assignment. Silas Kronschnabell, chairman of the Trustees, was waiting at the church when Rudy arrived.

"You must be the Rev. Rudy Hooper," Silas said, pumping Rudy's hand. "I'm Silas Kronschnabell, chairman of the Trustees." Silas had planned to take immediate control of the meeting to firmly establish the church's pecking order. After sizing up the new minister, he assumed this would be an easy task. Rudy's scraggly, unkempt appearance didn't instill an immediate feeling of authority. Silas had been hoping the new minister would possess more backbone than what was apparent on first impression. It was a personality flaw the church women would use to their advantage. This new minister could be a problem.

"We have a nice church here," Silas said. "We may be a rural church, but we take seriously world problems such as hunger in China and converting the heathens in New Guinea." Silas was prepared to elaborate further, when the other two members of the Trustees arrived.

Silas introduced the new pastor to the Widow Watson, local schoolteacher and Sunday school superintendent, and P.C. Taylor, church custodian. After handshakes were exchanged, the tour of the church began.

"Our church is about fifteen years old, but in good physical shape," Silas began as he assumed command of the small group. "We have seating for sixty people, although the average attendance is closer to forty." The Widow Watson and P.C. Taylor tagged along behind the chairman of the Trustees.

The Widow Watson was really Alice Watson. Alice and her husband, Carl, arrived in Bear Creek five years previously, Alice to teach in the one-room schoolhouse and her husband to pursue a writing career. Carl had been seeking a secluded romantic paradise conducive to writing. The romantic seclusion proved to be too much for Carl, who became quite depressed during the first winter, finally succumbing to the grippe in late February. Alice remained at the school more for lack of alternatives than for love of the locality. At twenty-six, Alice was still attractive, and it was well known in Bear Creek that she was on the prowl for a second husband if a suitably intelligent specimen could be found. In Bear Creek that was wishful thinking.

The Widow Watson studied the new preacher as they walked through the church. Not much to look at she decided, but he did have a college degree. She tried to imagine him clean-shaven with a decent haircut. He would be scrawny, but good cooking would put some flesh on his frame. Maybe more flesh would improve those deep-set eyes. Alice had never seen a fat man who did his own cooking. It was also obvious he was unable to dress himself. The sweater vest clashed with his pants, and that tie didn't match anything. Yes, the tie would have to go. It would take a lot of work, but he might be salvageable. She would be willing to clean him up.

As the group approached the organ, Alice slipped in between Silas and the new pastor, firmly attaching her arm inside his elbow. "Let me show you our organ." Alice pressed against Rudy's shoulder. "It's a pump organ. You pump it with your feet. It provides excellent sound."

Rudy felt his throat begin to tighten.

"The organ has one problem." Alice pulled Rudy toward the organ. "High 'C' doesn't work. Trudy, our church organist, thinks a mouse damaged the reed."

"Can it be fixed?" Rudy asked. At the moment, he was more concerned with Alice's shoulder pressing against him. He wished she wouldn't do that.

"So far it hasn't been necessary. Trudy inserts a 'La' or 'Da' or whatever sound best fits the music in place of high 'C.'"

"The mouse situation is under control," P.C. said. As church custodian, P.C. considered the church his personal domain. He worked hard at his duties providing one hundred and ten percent effort with at least sixty-five percent return. "I've obtained the services of a tomcat who's an excellent mouser. The mice will be eradicated in no time."

Rudy wasn't fond of this remedy. He didn't like mice, but he liked cats even less due to his allergy. It may be power of suggestion, but Rudy's eyes were beginning to water. Fortunately, he wouldn't have to spend long periods in the church, and he would make it clear to the cat that it wouldn't be welcome at the parsonage.

Rudy felt a tug on his elbow as the Widow Watson directed him toward the church bell tower. Rudy, preoccupied with the grip on his elbow, barely heard when the Widow Watson explained that the bell tower was over sixty feet high, and the bell weighed over fifteen hundred pounds. It was the largest bell in the Upper Peninsula, clearly out of proportion to the size of the church. The bell was a gift of a wealthy Chicago banker by the name of John D. Bigsby III, who had been a frequent visitor to the area on hunting and fishing trips. Bigsby wanted the bell audible in the countryside; and indeed, it could be heard in distant cabins over five miles away. He hoped the bell would help lost hunters find their way back to Bear Creek. Bigsby had never been lost, but was concerned for the less knowledgeable woodsmen.

Rudy looked up at the huge bell. A wooden ladder along the wall of the bell tower extended up to the bell. Rudy hoped climbing that ladder wasn't part of his job description. The rope to the bell was looped back on itself at the bottom with the lower end of the rope eight feet short of the floor.

"That's to prevent children from riding the rope," Alice said, as if she could read Rudy's thoughts. "Once the bell's in motion, kids can hang on to the rope and ride as high as ten or twelve feet. We thought that was a bit dangerous."

"At fifteen hundred pounds, it'll even pull me up," Silas said.

Rudy walked toward the side of the bell tower to better view the bell, but his feet slipped with each step; a slimy layer of bird droppings covering the floor. He was about to make a comment when a well-fed mouse ran between his legs, heading toward the pump organ. A plump, tiger-striped tomcat was in pursuit. Rudy lifted a leg to yield the right-of-way and slipped to the floor, landing on hands and buttocks. The flock of pigeons at the top of the bell tower, agitated by the noise, sent down a shower of additional droppings. Rudy decided it was best to keep his mouth shut.

"We're really sorry about this." Silas helped Rudy to his feet. "We need to do something about those pigeons."

"I'll take care of them," P.C. said without additional thought.

Silas Kronschnabell and the Widow Watson, with no practical suggestions of their own, left P.C.'s statement unchallenged. The one-eyed church trustee didn't impress Rudy with his abilities. If he were to handle this problem as he did the mouse, Rudy expected to find a vulture lurking in the bell tower by morning. Rudy tried to visualize the size of vulture droppings. He didn't think it would be a pleasant sight.

Due to his stained clothes, Rudy cut short his tour. He had seen enough for one day. His eyes were red and itchy, and his nose was beginning to run. It was definitely that cat and not the power of suggestion.

***

May 3, 1923. Today was another uneventful day. I didn't get to the garden, as I had planned. It may still be early for planting, but I had hoped at least to turn over the soil. Luther is constantly working on his dam. He makes me feel guilty whenever I take a break. He acts like he's disappointed in me. I'm sure it's only my imagination. Still, it's nice having him as a neighbor.

I had a tour of the church today with the church trustees. The church is nothing special but will be adequate. The church bell is huge. I am not sure if I have seen a larger bell. It was a gift from a wealthy Chicago banker. The church has a nice pump organ, although it has been damaged by mice. The church custodian has obtained a cat to live in the church, hopefully, to resolve the mouse problem. I don't like mice, but due to my allergies, I prefer them to cats. I am stuck with both of them for a while. I will name the mouse Sodom and the cat Gomorrah after the two cities of sin in the Bible. The story can be found in Genesis, Chapter 19. (Rudy felt he should give references to Biblical quotations for the less scholarly of his future readers.) *I have decided as soon as Gomorrah takes care of Sodom, I will take care of Gomorrah.*

Sodom and Gomorrah aren't the only animal problems in the church. We have a large flock of pigeons nesting in the bell tower. P. C. Taylor, our church custodian, says he will get rid of them, since they are very messy. I don't know how he's planning to do it. P. C. has a black patch over his right eye, and his appearance doesn't overwhelm one with confidence in his abilities. He's mayor of Bear Creek, so I'm sure he's more capable than I give him credit.

***

Gomorrah arched his back to stretch out those muscles that had yet to wake up before stepping out of the collection plate where he had been curled up for his afternoon nap. He arched his back one more time in case he had missed a muscle. Naps were always followed by an inspection of his food dish. It was full as usual, which met with Gomorrah's specifications. Gomorrah's life as official church mouser was quite predictable, but Gomorrah had no complaints. It was better than his existence before he had been shanghaied from the streets of Bear Creek by that one-eyed human. He had no desire to spend another Upper Peninsula winter in the cold panhandling for food. At the church he had a multitude of warm places to sleep and all the food he could eat. For this, all he had to do was chase mice.

After one week of mouse chasing, Sodom asked Gomorrah to meet for peace talks. Gomorrah didn't see any need for peace since, with his size, the advantage was his; but he was willing to listen out of idle curiosity. They met at the corner of the organ near a hole into which Sodom could take refuge should Gomorrah try to pull a fast one.

"Do you have tenure in your job?" Sodom asked Gomorrah. Gomorrah had no idea what tenure was; he assumed he did not.

"I get a warm place to sleep and all I can eat. That's all I need," Gomorrah replied.

"And how long do you think that'll last after I'm gone?"

"I don't know." Gomorrah hadn't really given it much thought; but now that he did, the answer became apparent. Although Sodom was only bite size, he did have a head on his shoulders.

"I'll tell you. As soon as the mice are eradicated from the church premises, you'll no longer be needed, and you will find yourself out in the cold. I don't need to tell you how cold it gets in the winter, do I? You'll have to find your own food."

"What do you suggest?" Gomorrah asked. Sodom wasn't painting a pretty picture.

"Mutual coexistence."

"What's that?" Sodom was using those big words again.

"We have a truce," Sodom said. "You'll have to chase me occasionally when humans are watching to prove you're still doing your job, but you never catch me. Otherwise, we ignore each other."

"What's in it for you?"

"All I want is peace of mind and the crumbs from your food dish."

Gomorrah figured one mouse couldn't eat much, and food was plentiful. At his age, chasing mice wasn't as much fun as it had been. Given a choice, Gomorrah preferred a nap. "Deal," Gomorrah said after a moment of thought.

The armistice worked well. Gomorrah had more time for his naps, which were now interrupted only by meals. The one-eyed human even created a hole in the wall covered by burlap, allowing Gomorrah access to the outside world. Gomorrah still fancied himself as God's gift to female felines everywhere and spent many a night in amorous pursuits. After two months the opening had to be enlarged to accommodate Gomorrah's growing corpulent frame. Sodom thought Gomorrah's name should be changed to Goliath.

***

Chief Red Weasel sat at the end of the dock with his bare feet dangling in the water. He absentmindedly nursed a fishing pole while his bobber lazily rode the small ripples in an otherwise calm

Moose Lake. Down below, a worm was taking swimming lessons. For Red Weasel, fishing was now only a means of relaxation and not an obsession. If he were to need fish for subsistence, he was fully capable of filling his stringer with minimal effort. As it was, he still had several perch and walleye dangling from his stringer.

Life at the Moose Lake Lodge was relaxed these days with only an occasional client. In earlier years, the lodge had been bustling with activity with a multitude of wealthy clients seeking hunting or fishing adventures in the Upper Peninsula wilderness. Weasel started the lodge with his best friend and partner, Chief Thunder Head, at the urging and financial backing of their mutual friend, John D. Bigsby III. Bigsby, an influential and wealthy banker from Chicago, provided a steady stream of wealthy clients. Thunder Head was the brains of the partnership and had a knack for pampering the clients while giving them the impression they were roughing it. After a week of hunting or fishing at the lodge, they all left happy and with thinner wallets. Over the years Thunder Head and Red Weasel accumulated large sums of money, which Bigsby helped invest in the stock market. The funds were now managed by Bigsby's son-in-law, Albert Hodgman. Hodgman assumed Bigsby's position as a vice president in the Chicago Bank and Trust upon Bigsby's death and mailed a healthy dividend check to Weasel the first of each month.

Thunder Head retired three years earlier and moved to Arizona, which he felt would be better for his rheumatism. He was tired of shoveling snow during the long winters. For Weasel, the Upper Peninsula would always be home. He didn't think he could adjust to life in an Arizona trailer park. He would miss the tall pines and the abundant lakes and streams that were a part of his heart and soul.

After Thunder Head's retirement, business began to deteriorate. Weasel was an excellent guide, but he didn't have Thunder Head's business acumen, and the clients dwindled. That was fine with Weasel. He no longer needed the money, and the peace and quiet was greatly appreciated. The only visitor these days was Bigsby's son-in-law, Albert Hodgman, who viewed the lodge as his personal retreat. He often brought his wife and kids. Weasel and his wife, Water Lily, had no children and were quick to become surrogate parents to the Hodgman's two young girls.

Water Lily spoiled them the best she could. Since they were both in the tomboy stage, they were eager students in the way of the woods, one of the few areas where Weasel excelled.

Weasel's reflexes took command when his bobber disappeared beneath the water's surface. His pole bent downward as an irritated walleye displayed its displeasure at the hook being set. The result of the confrontation was a forgone conclusion, and Mr. Walleye was soon added to the stringer. Weasel had just re-baited his hook and thrown out his line when he heard noise behind him.

"Morning, Chief," P.C. called to his best friend.

"Hello, Mayor," Weasel replied. Although they were best of friends, they addressed each other with formal titles as would any chiefs-of-state. Weasel could see P.C. Taylor came equipped with a fishing pole and a can of worms.

Taking off his shoes, P.C. dangled his feet in the water. It was one of the pleasures he shared with Weasel. Conversation was minimal. Good friends don't feel obligated to have continuous and meaningful conversations. The sharing of each other's presence was all that was required. But there was no silence. A loon could be heard calling from across the lake, and a chickadee was scolding them from a nearby spruce. A bullfrog hiding among the lily pads provided the bass section of the orchestra. It was never silent at Moose Lake, and neither fisherman would have it any other way.

"Ever hear of squab?" P.C. finally asked Weasel.

"Nope, can't say as I have," Weasel replied.

"Ain't nothing more than a pigeon," P.C. explained after a moment.

"Mighty fancy name for a pigeon. Guess I like pigeon better. Can't see why people have to change the names of things that already have perfectly good names." That was about as philosophical as Weasel ever got. Weasel assumed P.C. had a purpose to this conversation but didn't wish to rush his friend. He rightly figured P.C. would get around to it in his own good time.

P.C. pulled out his pocket watch and opened the cover. It was quarter past one as usual. "Can't rightly say I heard much about it either until a year ago when I read about it in one of Maggie's fancy restaurant magazines. It appears you can cook an ordinary barn pigeon and serve it under a glass lid. It fetches a pretty price in those fancy restaurants."

"Is that a fact?" Weasel replied, not sure if he should be impressed.

"That's what the article said. Now I've eaten barn pigeons before, and they ain't all that bad, but I don't think they're any better than quail or duck. The key is you have to call them squab. Otherwise no one will pay big bucks."

"I still don't see how calling a pigeon a squab will make it taste any better even if you do serve it under glass," Weasel protested.

"It doesn't. It's just the kind of people who go to these fancy restaurants aren't as smart as we are," P.C. pointed out. "There's a lot of money to be made in pigeons. We can pluck the pigeons and the customers at the same time."

Weasel could see this conversation was leading to one of P.C.'s moneymaking schemes. Neither of them was hurting for money, but P.C. could never pass a chance to get something for nothing. Weasel was always dragged into P.C.'s projects, because you never say no to a friend.

"I happen to know the Methodist Church's belfry is filled with pigeons," P.C. continued. "All we have to do is climb up the ladder some night with a flashlight. One of us shines the light in the pigeons' eyes, and the other plucks them up and puts them in a tote sack. Pigeons are blinded by the light. Catching the whole flock shouldn't take more than five or ten minutes. We can sell them at the Bare Creek Cafe and split the profit."

Weasel wasn't convinced there was money to be made, even if you did call them squabs, but it wouldn't hurt to help his friend catch some pigeons. It sounded easy enough.

***

Rudy leaned against his shovel and surveyed his garden. It was only twenty by forty feet, but it still took the better part of three days to turn the soil over and prepare it for planting. The area had been covered with sod, and the roots ran deep, as did the dark, rich topsoil. His muscles ached from the hard labor, but it was a good ache. There were times when he wondered if it was worth it, but now that it was done, he had no regrets. Once he had turned over the soil and broken the clods, he raked out the grass and other organic debris. He would use this for a compost pile.

Rudy and his friend, Luther, worked side by side, albeit on different projects. Much as Rudy hated to admit it, Luther put in longer hours. Every time Rudy looked up, Luther was at work shoring up his dam. Luther had increased the height of the dam by a foot, and the water now flowed over the dam only in a small segment near the middle of the dam. Luther was a good role model. People could learn a lot from him. But Rudy had worked hard too. He hoped his hard work over the last several days would be pleasing to Luther. For some reason, he needed to please Luther. He had this feeling of oneness with Luther as if they could feel each other's emotions. That was silly, he decided.

Rudy leaned against his shovel while he let his mind wander and his muscles recuperate. Luther looked over at him, and the guilt returned. Luther was a hard taskmaster. It was just as well, since he had seeds to plant. The season was short in the U.P., and he needed to plant those seeds if he were to harvest the fruits of his labor.

Rudy planted the corn in perfectly straight rows. He assumed, and rightly so, that corn grows best in perfectly straight rows. Next, he planted pole beans. They would need something to climb on; he could provide that later. The season was too short to grow peppers and tomatoes from seed, so he planted six inch potted plants he had purchased from Mel Barker's Hardware and Feed store. Mel planted from seed early in the spring. They grew well in his small greenhouse behind the Hardware and Feed store. Mel assured him they were disease free, and even a fool could get them to produce large quantities of big, ripe tomatoes and peppers. Rudy didn't consider himself to be in the fool category and expected even greater rewards for his labor.

***

The day was like any other day for Luther. Work started at sun up and ended at sundown. If there were any moonlight, he would work into the night. Today's project was the same as yesterday and the same as tomorrow. He would continue to shore up and expand the dam. Over the last several weeks, he had increased the height of the dam by a foot, although the water continued to pour through a small gap in the center of the dam. Today, he would fill that gap.

Work would have been easier if it hadn't been for his gimpy leg; he worked harder to make up for the defect. Care of such a large dam was a great responsibility for a lone beaver, and it left no time for frivolous pursuits such as socialization or relaxation. This was why Luther had never taken a mate. He didn't have any patience with the weaker sex. If a beaver couldn't carry his or her share of the load, he or she wouldn't have a place in Luther's world.

Luther was dragging a large branch through the water toward the gap in the center of the dam when he caught sight of Rudy leaning on his shovel. Rudy had been working harder than normal over the last three days, although Luther could see no purpose to his actions. He still had that character flaw and would periodically lean on his shovel to daydream, but what can you expect from a human.

***

It was late in the day when Rudy finished the last of the planting. It felt good to be done. Rudy leaned on his shovel, taking a few minutes to rest and admire his work. He could see Luther working on his dam. Doesn't he ever quit? Luther gave him that guilt look, but it wouldn't work this time. Rudy had finished his work. Even the Lord rested after his work was done. It was fortunate a beaver hadn't created the world, or we would never have gotten Sundays off. Rudy wondered if that was a sacrilegious thought.

There was one project left to do; you can't have a garden without a scarecrow. This wouldn't be work. It would be like planting your flag on Mount Everest after a difficult climb. It would be the crowning glory of his achievement. It would be a proclamation to the world that there was a garden here, and it was his.

Rudy tied two poles together in a shape of a cross. He liked the symbolic significance. It was then firmly planted into the ground and dressed in some of Rudy's old clothes. The body was fleshed out with straw and the head covered with a straw hat. Rudy didn't know if scarecrows worked. The fact that birds were already using the outstretched arms as perches didn't instill him with confidence. Still, it was a beautiful scarecrow.

***

The sun had set, but a quarter moon illuminated the beaver pond, providing light to finish the day's work. Luther noted Rudy put in half a day and quit before dusk. It was just as well since Luther could see no results of Rudy's labors other than that ridiculous "man on a stick." He did tear up the ground some, but the weeds would grow back in a matter of weeks, returning the soil to its previous state.

By contrast, Luther's progress was noticeable. The gap in the center of the dam was narrow, and Luther would soon close the gap with a few strategically placed sticks packed with mud. After two hours of work in the moonlight, the gap was filled, and the water ceased flowing over the dam. With no place for the excess flow to go, the water began backing up. By morning, the feet of the scarecrow would be soaking in six inches of water.

***

P.C. found Weasel waiting at the church door. Fortunately, they had both managed to sneak out of their houses without the knowledge of their wives; wives would never understand such a complex operation. Since there was no electricity in Bear Creek, any light had to be provided by kerosene lantern or flashlight. P.C. preferred the flashlight because of its focused beam. They also had six-foot lengths of rope to tie their waists to the ladder once they reached the top. This would allow use of both hands. P.C. and Weasel weren't a couple of fools.

P.C. opened the door, and the two comrades-in-arms entered the church. The belfry was off to the left through a small corridor. Within seconds the Bear Creek Commandos were standing at the base of the tower. P.C. shined his light in the direction of the bell. The flashlight's limited beam failed to illuminate the bell or the pigeons. Nervous cooing from the rafters above confirmed the presence of their prey.

"You have better eyesight, Chief. I'll let you go first."

Weasel wasn't flattered by the honor, but neither was he a coward. He took the flashlight without comment and started up the wooden ladder. P. C. followed several feet behind him. The tower was sixty feet tall, requiring several minutes to reach their objective. Once they reached the top, the nervous cooing changed to flapping wings as the pigeons jockeyed for better positions on their perches. Unable to see in the darkness, they didn't attempt to fly.

"OK, I'm at the top," Weasel whispered to P.C. "I can shine the light on them, but how are you goin' grab them? There's only room up here for one of us."

P.C. paused to rethink his operational plan. While P.C. was deep in thought, Weasel explored the surroundings with his flashlight, finding numerous pigeons roosting in the belfry. One of the pigeons, pushed off his perch by an adjacent bird, was in the process of retreating from the noise and light. With a perch no longer under its feet, the pigeon flew into the darkness looking for a new perch. The floundering pigeon, finding nothing to grab with its feet, bounced off the wall twice before obtaining a precarious grip on the bridge of Weasel's nose. It dug its claws deeply into the soft flesh to secure its perch. Due to the downward slope of the Chief's facial appendage, the pigeon was unable to maintain its center of gravity and flapped its wings in Weasel's face in a vain attempt to maintain balance.

"Get that bird off of me!" With good judgment yielding to instinct, Weasel dropped his flashlight to brush away the pigeon with his right hand. It took three seconds for the flashlight to fall sixty feet. The Bear Creek Commandos heard a crash below and became engulfed in darkness.

"What the heck you doing, Chief? Turn on the flashlight."

Weasel didn't have time to respond. He was in mortal hand-to-wing combat with a vicious, saber-tooth barn pigeon. In the darkness, the pigeon was unable to find a more suitable perch and refused to ease its grip on Weasel's nose. Weasel, mustering the inner strength of a noble Indian warrior, continued to bat at the assailant with his right hand while his left hand hung tenaciously to the ladder. If only he had taken the time to tie onto the ladder with his rope, he would have had the use of both hands. Then it might have been an even fight. He was now at a decisive disadvantage since his formidable foe had use of all four appendages and Weasel had use of only one. It was the ultimate battle of man against beast: the Great Winged Warrior vs. the Noble Indian Warrior Chief.

Flailing around with his right hand, Weasel found the rope to the bell and grabbed hold. It was two inches in diameter and appeared solid. Using the rope for additional support, Weasel shifted his weight to the rope, hoping to attack his assailant with his left hand. A surprise attack from the opposite flank might give Weasel that tactical advantage he so desperately needed. But the rope gave way under his weight, and the bell began to rise. With his full weight now on the rope, Weasel commenced a twelve-foot round trip ride through the darkness. Earsplitting gongs punctuated the extremes of each trip. P.C. deduced from the moans interspersed with whimpering that his friend was in trouble. Weasel's location, however, was a bit of a mystery. First, he sounded above P.C. and seconds later he would call from below. P.C. reached out and felt Weasel's body as he traversed his twelve-foot excursions. On the third pass, P.C. lunged for Weasel's feet. He didn't lead Weasel sufficiently and grabbed the rope instead. The pull on the rope plucked him from his perch adding more momentum to the bell, which rang out with increased enthusiasm.

***

Maggie looked at her bedroom clock. It was 3:30 in the morning, and her mind was still semi-comatose with sleep.

"P.C., wake up, the church bell is ringing. There must be something wrong." P.C. didn't respond. "P.C., wake up!" She reached over, but the other side of the bed was empty. The remaining fog in her brain immediately dissipated, making the sound of the church bell more resounding. The church bell would only be used at this time in the morning for major emergencies or disasters. With P.C. missing, it was most likely the latter. "I hope he isn't with Weasel," she mumbled. Weasel was a nice enough man, and his wife, Water Lily, was a delight; but when P.C. and Weasel got together, it was nothing but trouble.

"The church bell's ringing," Jennifer said as she walked into the room from the adjacent bedroom.

"Your Pa's gone."

"He isn't with Red Weasel, is he?"

"Get dressed. We're going to the church."

***

Mel Barker awoke with the sound of the church bell's first gong. He remained in bed stroking his graying beard for a moment of deep thought. "It's the Canadians. The Canadians are invading!" Mel informed his wife. Trudy was somewhat deaf and hadn't heard the church bell. She immediately assumed Mel was having one of his flashbacks. She knew she shouldn't have given him that apple pie before bedtime. Once fully awake, she also heard the bell. A fifteen hundred pound bell is hard to ignore.

Mel grabbed the steel helmet he had hanging on the wall for just such an occasion. He only wished Teddy Roosevelt and the Roughriders were here. If they were, they wouldn't need additional help. As it was, the best he could do would be to hold off the Canadians until help arrived. Being the only man in town with military experience, it would be up to him to provide the leadership. Mel placed the strap of his powder horn over his head and grabbed his flintlock. The powder in the powder horn was over twenty years old, but he took pride in keeping his powder dry. It wouldn't fail if he needed it.

"Wait for me!" Trudy called out. She wasn't convinced of the Canadian hypothesis, but knew the church bell wouldn't be ringing without a good reason. Not wishing to be left alone during a time of crises, she put on a housecoat, wrapped a red scarf over her curlers, and followed Mel out the door.

***

"Silas, wake up!" Agnes demanded. "The church bell is ringing."

Silas Kronschnabell woke to find Agnes straddling his hips while shaking his shoulders. He always thought his wife was a bit too theatrical. Once fully awake, he had to agree that, indeed, the church bell was ringing, the significance of it being at the moment unclear. As editor of the Bare Creek Gazette, it would be his duty to investigate. Agnes, not wishing to miss any excitement, was getting dressed.

***

Rudy was the first to arrive at the church. He had a kerosene lantern, but it wouldn't penetrate the darkness of the bell tower. The bell had ceased ringing, and the church was quiet.

"What's going on?" Silas asked when he arrived on the scene.

"We're being invaded by the Canadians," Mel answered as he followed Silas into the church.

"What Canadians?" Rudy asked. "I don't see any Canadians."

"Who rang the bell?" Silas was starting to sound like a newspaper editor. Most of the town had now arrived at the church, but no one was willing to "fess up."

Silas, who was the only citizen with the foresight to bring a flashlight, aimed the beam up into the bell tower. It wouldn't illuminate the top of the tower, but it did reveal one and a half pairs of eyes peering down at them from the darkness.

"What's that?" Rudy asked. He was beginning to wonder if tonight was a typical evening in Bear Creek. He had been told it was a quiet community.

"The pair of eyes gotta be a coon," Silas reckoned. "I have no idea what the one-eyed critter is."

Rudy wondered if only one eye of a vulture would be visible at a time.

"We'll soon find out," Mel proclaimed. Before anyone had time to reason with him, Mel raised his flintlock to his shoulder and pointed the barrel in the general vicinity of the top of the bell tower. Mel wasn't noted for going half way on any project, and tonight was no exception. He had been overzealous in placing black powder in the flash pan, and when the flint struck metal, the resulting flash singed the beard on the right side of his face leaving curly stubs and a foul smell of burnt hair. A large cloud of black smoke bellowed from the muzzle of the gun. The projectile missed its mark; Mel hadn't been much of a marksman in the Spanish-American War either. It was hard to miss a fifteen hundred pound bell, however, and the musket ball bounced off the inside of the bell, ricocheting several times within the bell before it was spit out, hitting the back of Weasel's hand. The energy of the musket ball was, for the most part, spent, and the lead ball failed to penetrate the skin. There was still enough energy remaining to make Weasel's hand wish it had been elsewhere. Weasel was unable to hold the rope any longer and began sliding down the rope, colliding with his comrade. Giving in to the demands of gravity, the two continued their descent down the sixty-foot bell tower until they ran out of rope eight feet from the floor. They fell the last eight feet unassisted, encouraged only by gravity.

The pile of arms, legs, and other assorted body parts left more questions than explanations. For most of the sleepy spectators, the sight of P.C. and Weasel together was explanation enough, and the crowd began to disperse.

"What are you two trying to do?" Maggie asked. There wasn't much sympathy in her voice.

P.C. could see Maggie's lips moving, but the sound had been turned off. "YOU HAVE TO TALK LOUDER. I CAN'T HEAR YOU." The only sound P.C. could hear was the sound of the bell, which logic told him, had ceased ringing ten minutes earlier.

Knowing there was one language he would understand, Maggie grabbed P.C. by the ear and ushered him toward the exit; the interrogation would have to wait until morning. P.C. offered no resistance and followed Maggie out the door.

Weasel, likewise, was still hearing the gonging of the bell and couldn't comprehend any of the conversations emanating around him. Assuming that this was a white man's problem, he slithered out the side door. He would have enough trouble explaining this to Water Lily in the morning. He wasn't looking forward to that encounter.

"Can someone please tell me what's going on?" Rudy inquired. No one offered further explanation.

"Where are the Canadians?" Mel asked as he reloaded. The stubs of facial hair on the right side of his face were still smoking.

"That was P.C. and Chief Red Weasel," Silas pointed out. Need he say more?

Weasel had made good his escape, and P.C. was being escorted from the church; therefore, no further insight could be obtained until morning. Within minutes, Rudy was standing by himself in bewilderment at the base of the bell tower. His eyes were beginning to burn. Beside him sat Gomorrah surveying the mess. "And they call us dumb animals," Gomorrah muttered to himself.

***

Water Lily heard noise coming from the direction of the bathroom. She lit the kerosene lamp at her bedside. Weasel wasn't in bed beside her.

"Is that you, Weasel?"

Weasel arrived in the bedroom doorway fully clothed, his nose covered with Band-Aids.

"Where've you been?"

"Humph," was the only reply. Water Lily assumed any explanation would have to wait until morning.

***

May 9, 1923. I have now been here a full week. I had expected Bear Creek to be a small, quiet community; but this appears not be the case, at least for this week.

The Yoopers, as they refer to themselves, have a unique lifestyle and many strange customs, some of which may take time getting used to. For instance, during the night, I was summoned to the church by the ringing of the bell. The whole town turned out for the occasion in a matter of minutes. I believe it was some sort of civil defense drill in case we are invaded by Canadians. I always considered the Canadians a friendly lot, but then I am new here. Anyway, P.C. and this Indian fellow by the name of Red Weasel – I am told he is an Indian Chief – were up in the top of the church belfry in the dark. (You couldn't get me up there in the daylight.) They must have been lookouts as the church steeple is the highest point in town. Mel Barker is head of the civil defense team, and when he signaled the all clear by firing off his rifle, both P.C. and Red Weasel came sliding down the rope rather smartly. I can now see how P.C. Taylor got to be Mayor. There is a lot more to him than meets the eye.

The congregation is treating me well. Yesterday, the Widow Watson brought over an apple pie. This is the second pie she has given me this week. I think her real name is Alice Watson. She is definitely a good cook. She teaches in the local school and is also the Sunday school superintendent. I am sure I will be working closely with her in the future.

The only downside to the week was my garden. I had worked hard plowing and tilling the soil. It must have taken me the better part of three days. I had the garden all planted including several tomato and pepper plants. The next day I found the garden flooded with water. It appears Luther, in all his energy, had increased the size of his dam causing the water to overflow onto my garden. The pepper plants and tomatoes are all ruined, and the seeds may have been washed out, so I will have to replant.

Now I do love Luther dearly, but he has to learn that man is in charge. "God said unto them, Be fruitful and multiply, and replenish the earth, and subdue it: and have dominion over the fish of the sea, and over the fowl of the air, and to everything that creepeth upon the earth," Genesis 1:28. Luther definitely falls under "everything," and therefore it is my responsibility to subdue and have dominion over him. Tomorrow I will dismantle some of the dam to bring the water level back to its previous level. I will do it at night when he isn't observing since I cherish his friendship. I am still optimistic I will have a fruitful garden by fall.

Rudy closed his journal and leaned back in his porch swing. He enjoyed sitting on his porch where he could watch over his dominion. Yes, he would have a good summer.

Chapter Two

Rudy thumbed through the Sears and Roebuck catalogue. He was amazed at the variety of items available by mail, more important than ever now that he was living at the fringes of civilization. For many people, the Sears and Roebuck catalogue was the only link to the outside world. Orders could be placed at Mel Barker's Hardware and Feed Store, and the merchandise would be delivered in seven to ten days.

Only limited sunlight filtered through the crescent-moon shaped opening in the outhouse door. Rudy was thankful he had been blessed with keen eyesight, allowing him to read the catalogue's fine print. The outhouse was quiet and free of distractions, which encouraged his mind to wander. Several of his best sermons owed their origins to such moments of inspiration. Today he was under no such pressure. His Sunday sermon was complete and his garden ready for replanting. His mind drifted aimlessly as he scanned the catalogue. He didn't intend to make a purchase, but he enjoyed flipping through the pages.

Several hornets buzzed overhead, a reminder of the hornet's nest he had inherited with the outhouse. He had considered aggressive action on several occasions, but, lacking a safe eviction plan, the matter was tabled. Rudy studied the nest at the apex of the outhouse; it was definitely larger than the previous week.

Rudy's fingers reached the farm section where the pages resisted further flipping as if by divine intervention. There it was — an apple tree. Rudy read the fine print, "hardy to northern states." He had to have that apple tree. The price was two dollars. For twelve dollars, he could have six trees. He could have a small orchard. He could be the Johnny Appleseed of the Upper Peninsula. The work would be limited. Once he planted the trees, he could sit back and watch them grow. Rudy tried to visualize how they would look from his porch. If he remembered right, apple blossoms were white. Yes, they would look pretty in the spring. It would be a long-term investment; he might not be in Bear Creek to see fruition of his project. Still, it would be a small legacy he could leave for future pastors.

Rudy considered the men who had come before him, paving the way for his present ministry. Father Marquette and Bishop Baraga came to mind. They were the original pioneers serving God in this area when the Upper Peninsula was really primitive. Bishop Baraga traveled so much during the winter, he was known as the snowshoe priest. Maybe he would name the apple orchard after Bishop Baraga. The Bishop Baraga Memorial Apple Orchard, it had a nice professional sound.

First thing in the morning, he would stop at Mel Barker's store and order the trees. He had to be in town anyway to meet with the Ladies Aid Society. Since he had received a special invitation, he felt obligated to attend. It would be a chance to meet the women of the church.

In the afternoon, he would replant his garden. The misunderstanding with Luther was a thing of the past. He had removed a large section from the center of the dam, allowing the water to recede to its old boundaries. Not wishing to be seen by Luther, he had done it during the dark of night; he still valued his neighbor's friendship. Rudy could dismantle faster than Luther could rebuild. Luther was the harder worker, but God had given man the superior mind, and man would always come out on top. It was God's intent that man should have dominion over the earth and all its inhabitants. Rudy had no intention of doing otherwise.

***

Luther surveyed the breach in his dam. How could this happen? It was not uncommon for a storm or flash flood to wash away even a well-built dam, but there had been no such storm or flood. A structural defect in the architectural design could cause the dam to collapse. That would be a devastating blow to his ego and was, therefore, quickly dismissed. Luther took pride in his work. He never cut corners and always used the proper ratio of sticks to mud. Luther walked across the top of the dam. The remainder of the dam was strong, without evidence of any wear or deterioration. He swam under water to check the footings. They, too, were solid.

The breach in the dam was a major disappointment, but Luther was not one for self-pity. He had only one option: rebuild the dam. This time he would increase the ratio of sticks to mud, making it even stronger. His pride was on the line.

***

The Ladies Aid Society met promptly at ten in the Bare Creek Cafe. It was more convenient than the church, and the cafe offered the advantage of coffee or tea for those who wished to partake. Eight of the ladies were already present and sipping tea when Rudy arrived. He was running late. Filling out the forms for his apple trees had taken longer than he had expected. With a bit of luck, the trees would arrive within the week.

"Good morning, ladies." Rudy found a chair at the edge of the group. Since he was a guest and not a member, he preferred to remain on the sidelines.

"Good morning, Reverend Hooper. It's so nice of you to join us today," Maggie said as she opened the meeting. "Girls, do we all know the Rev. Rudy Hooper, our new minister?" They all nodded in agreement. There were no secrets in a small town like Bear Creek. Rudy was offered coffee or tea; he chose coffee.

"Trudy, will you read the minutes of the last meeting?" Maggie asked. This was followed by the treasurer's report and several small committee reports. Rudy had never seen a group of women that wasn't over organized. The meeting was boring, but pleasant. Rudy relaxed at the edge of the group. He didn't need the spotlight and did his best work quietly on the fringes without recognition.

"And now for the new business."

Rudy, hearing little of the meeting, allowed his mind to wander. Nice cafe, he was thinking. He liked the woodwork. The place was clean and had a pleasant atmosphere. Evidence of a woman's touch was everywhere.

"I am sure, by now, Reverend Hooper is well aware that our church is an active church, and we are not afraid to address the social concerns and sins that are so prevalent in our world."

The sound of his name brought Rudy back to reality. "Why yes, I understand the church has been active in converting the heathens in New Guinea and feeding the starving children in China."

"Yes, and there are sins and social concerns that need to be addressed much closer to home, in fact, in this very town."

The rest of the ladies nodded in agreement. Rudy, uncertain of the direction the conversation was heading, tightened his grip on his chair's armrest. Hopefully, this wouldn't be a long meeting.

"You may not be aware, but this town has a drinking problem," Maggie continued.

"I thought alcohol was illegal."

"Yes, but we have people who would break the law and encourage our men to become intoxicated. I am referring to that Snake Pit Saloon!" Maggie said, pointing to the establishment across the street.

Rudy heard murmurs of agreement from the ladies of the group. They were now staring at him. He was no longer on the edge of the group; he was center stage. "I wasn't aware of that," Rudy replied, loosening his shirt collar. It was beginning to get warm in the cafe.

"It's that Chief Snake Eyes who's responsible," Agnes pointed out with her customary zeal. "He runs the place."

"But he has the support of all the men," Trudy said.

"And don't forget those three women," Maggie added.

"What three women?" Rudy wasn't sure what the three women had to do with hard liquor. It was definitely getting warm. Rudy felt a droplet of sweat trickle down his forehead.

"Polly, Molly, and Dolly," replied several voices almost simultaneously.

"They live above the Snake Pit," Maggie said. "They moved into town three months ago and have no jobs or other means of support."

"What are their last names?" Rudy asked.

"THEY HAVE NONE!" came the chorus from the back.

"I see," Rudy said, although he didn't. "What do you want me to do about it?" Rudy suspected he might not be happy with the answer.

"You need to talk to them and then run them out of town," Agnes said. She was never one for half measures.

"Have they done anything illegal?"

The women looked around at each other, trying to figure out what that had to do with the conversation.

"The Bible clearly teaches the need for patience and forgiveness." Rudy suspected this wouldn't be one of his better sermons. "Has anyone talked to them?"

The ladies could see Rudy was bringing up more irrelevant questions and totally missing the point.

Rudy looked at his pocket watch, announced he had an appointment for which he couldn't be late, and politely excused himself. The appointment wasn't until the following morning, but he still didn't wish to be late.

"I don't think that preacher's going to be much help," Trudy said after Rudy departed. "Typical male."

"Then we'll find a way to handle this problem ourselves," Maggie said. She had no particular plan in mind.

"I have an idea," Agnes informed the ladies. A diabolical smile crossed her face.

***

Rudy felt relief upon leaving the meeting. He was not unsympathetic with their concerns; he just wasn't qualified to resolve their problems. Aggressive confrontations were not his forte. That was what he liked about his garden; it was non-confrontational. There was the minor issue with Luther; that he could overlook. That problem was solved; it was time to forge ahead.

Forging ahead was what he planned to do. He had decided some of the tomato and pepper plants were salvageable and had replanted them. With luck, they would still grow to produce fruit.

The seeds were a different matter. Many of the seeds had eroded away. There was no telling if any of them were still good, or where they would sprout up if they did grow. Rudy had decided to re-seed his garden. If any of the seeds grew in inappropriate places, he would pull them up as weeds.

Rudy looked over at the beaver pond and felt a moment of guilt. Luther was repairing the large gap in the dam. Rudy wondered if Luther knew who was responsible for the damage. It was God's will, not his. It was God who placed man in charge of "all living creatures."

***

The following day Silas Kronschnabell called a special meeting of the Bare Creek Economics Club. As usual it was held in Mel Barker's Hardware and Feed store where everyone met each morning, whether there was a special need or not. P.C. and Frenchie were playing their routine checker game. Frenchie was more proficient at cheating and, therefore, slightly ahead. P.C. figured he could catch up if someone would only divert Frenchie's attention.

"I heard the women have conned Rev. Hooper into helping them dry up the town," Frenchie said as he jumped one of P.C.'s pieces. They all enjoyed an occasional nip or two of the spirits and had a vested interest in the operation of the local pub. Prohibition had formally dried up the saloon, but kegs of beer were regularly smuggled in from Milwaukee on Mel Barker's supply wagons. For the right price, such spirits were still available in the Snake Pit Saloon; use the back door please. Women were not encouraged to visit the saloon; and for the most part, they preferred the cleaner tables and atmosphere of the Bare Creek Cafe.

"As I understand it, he turned them down," Mel replied. "At least that's what Trudy says."

"I liked that man from the beginning," Silas said. "The man has spunk."

"They aren't going after our liquor," Mel continued. "According to Trudy, they're going after the 'Ollies.' She wouldn't reveal the plan."

"We can't let them do that!" Frenchie said. P.C. took advantage of Frenchie's distraction to pull ahead in the checker game.

"We need to find out what the plan is," Mel said.

"I can tell you what the plan is." All eyes were on Silas. "They plan to raid the Ollies' apartment, take pictures and names of any visitors, and I'm to print the pictures and names in the Bare Creek Gazette."

"You're going to do what?" several voices asked in unison.

"Have you ever tried to say no to my wife?" Silas asked. Silas did have a valid point.

"We gotta do something," Frenchie pleaded, momentarily forgetting his checker game. P.C. crowned two more kings.

"Hold on. It won't be that bad," Silas said in his defense. "Agnes has to get the camera from me, right?" Everyone was in agreement. Silas had the only camera in town. "We'll, therefore, know in advance which day they plan to make the raid. We simply notify all the men in town; and when they make their raid, I'll print a picture of Polly, Molly, and Dolly sitting in rocking chairs, knitting socks for the orphans in China."

All present agreed such a plan might work and tensions eased. It was a small town; notifying all the men on short notice wouldn't be difficult.

"There won't be much lead-time. You guys will have to work fast. I assume Agnes will be watching me, so I'll use the code word 'rain.' If I say it looks like rain on Saturday, the raid will occur on Saturday," Silas explained. "Don't let this leak out to the women, or it won't work. It may also be best if Rev. Hooper didn't know. He appears to have a character flaw—he's honest." Silas had found this a common flaw among pastors. "He couldn't lie if his soul depended on it. If the women got hold of him, there's no way he'd keep it secret."

***

The apple trees arrived earlier than expected. Since the merchandise was perishable, Mel personally delivered them to the parsonage, a courtesy Rudy greatly appreciated. The trees were four to five feet in height with a small burlap-covered ball of dirt enclosing the roots. A slip of paper attached to each tree provided planting instructions. Rudy carefully studied the directions including the fine print. Twelve dollars was a lot of money on his salary. He could ill afford errors. Each hole was to be two feet in diameter and one foot deep. Immediate planting was recommended. Rudy had no intention of doing otherwise.

Rudy, dominated by his obsessive-compulsive personality, planted the trees in a straight row with each tree precisely twenty feet apart. They had to be planted such that their shadows wouldn't rob his garden of valuable sunlight, yet still be visible from his front porch. A good view of the apple blossoms in the spring was paramount.

It took twenty minutes to mark off the locations, and prepare the first hole. Rudy leaned against his shovel to admire his work. He had no doubt his twelve dollars was well spent. When he closed his eyes, he could visualize the mature trees clustered with big, red apples.

As usual, Luther was working on his dam. Rudy estimated the dam would require further dismantling in another day or two. He had discovered it slowed repair if he threw the dismantled sticks downstream, allowing them to float away. If he cast the sticks to the side, Luther would quickly incorporate them into the dam.

Enough daydreaming, Rudy began digging the first hole. He had a measuring stick to ensure the holes were, indeed, two feet in diameter and one foot deep. Nothing would be left to chance. Within an hour, all six apple trees were planted in a perfectly straight line with perfect size holes. Rudy felt the satisfaction of a job well done.

***

Maggie Taylor, Trudy Barker, and Agnes Kronschnabell met at the Bare Creek Cafe as a subcommittee of the Ladies Aid Society. Security was of utmost concern, and it was agreed that only those ladies involved in the operation should know the details.

"I think we should make our move on Friday," Maggie suggested. As the self-appointed, alpha female, Maggie assumed leadership of any group.

"That'll work for me," Trudy said. "How about nine o'clock? By nine o'clock, the men will be all liquored up at that Snake Pit Saloon and looking for adventure. It'll give us a long list of names to print in the paper."

"You think Silas can keep his mouth shut?" Maggie asked.

"Good point," replied the wife of the Bare Creek Gazette editor. "Much as I love him, Silas can't be trusted. I'll need lessons on working the camera. That can be done a few hours before our mission. After that, I will be on Silas like fleas on a bear. He won't go anywhere without me until just before nine o'clock. Then it'll be too late."

"After Friday, Polly, Molly, and Dolly will be history," Trudy proclaimed. The assessment was unanimous.

***

Rudy was pleased to find his new orchard plainly visible from his porch swing. The trees were small, but they were no longer dormant and sported a few green leaves. The trees would become more conspicuous over the years. They were a welcome addition to the view from his porch.

As usual, Rudy had finished his sermon early in the week. His apple trees were planted, and his garden re-seeded, giving him time to sit on his porch swing and enjoy the good life. Next time Rudy saw Bishop Johnson, he would have to thank him for the pleasant assignment. He did feel badly about the previous pastor's illness, but his loss was Rudy's gain. As long as the medical problem wasn't contagious; Rudy was easily susceptible to illnesses. With the exception of his allergy to Gomorrah, Rudy had been healthy so far. Rudy knocked on wood.

He might even be putting on some weight. The desserts the Widow Watson had been bringing over were taking their toll. Rudy munched down on a chocolate chip cookie, one of Widow Watson's latest gifts. Yes, life was rather pleasant at Bear Creek.

The only thing that bothered him was the recent meeting with the Ladies Aid Society. Rudy wished he were more aggressive during such confrontations. If he had more character, he would have volunteered to pay a visit to Polly, Molly, and Dolly; not necessarily to run them out of town, but to say hello and maybe invite them to church services. Rudy knew this would never happen.

***

"Can you show me how to use your camera now?" Agnes asked.

Fridays were busy for the editor of the Bare Creek Gazette, but he had learned early in his marriage that you don't keep Agnes waiting. "What exactly do you want to do with it?"

"We need to take a picture of an entire room."

"Then you'll need the wide-angle lens." Silas replaced the normal lens on the camera with a special wide-angle lens. "This lens will give you plenty of coverage."

"Show me how to shoot the picture. I can't see anything," Agnes said, her head buried under the black cloth at the back of the camera.

"And you won't as long as the cover is on the lens." Silas's patience was already wearing thin. "Once you remove the cover, you can see the picture from the back. It won't be very bright, which is why we use the dark cloth to cover your head."

"That seems easy enough." Agnes said. Silas removed the cover, allowing full view through the camera lens. "Everything is upside down. Will the picture look the same as what I'm seeing here?"

"It'll still be upside down, but otherwise it should look exactly the same as long as you don't move the camera. If it's out of focus, twist the lens a bit to refocus the picture."

"But how does this take the picture?"

"Once the camera is properly aimed and focused, you remove this glass plate." Silas pulled out a square piece of frosted glass from the side of the camera. "This is where the image you were just looking at was displayed. We now replace this glass with a sheet of film and we're all set. The film is covered with a piece of sheet metal to prevent it from being exposed. Don't remove this until you're ready to take the picture, or you'll fog the film. Place the lens cover back on and remove the piece of sheet metal. Now you're ready to shoot the film."

"This is easy." Agnes's head was still under the cloth. "Can I take pictures for your paper?"

"NO!"

"Is this all I need to know?" Agnes asked as she extracted her head from under the hood.

"Just about," Silas continued. "When you're ready to take the picture, remove the lens cover to expose the film for about two seconds. Replace the cap, reinsert the protective piece of sheet metal, and you're done."

"What if there isn't much light?"

"In that case you'll need a flash." Silas retrieved a one-foot square piece of sheet metal with a spindle on the bottom for holding. "This is what we use for a flash. Place one scoop of magnesium powder on the top and insert this five-second fuse. Take the cover off the lens, light the fuse and when the flash is over, place the cover back on the lens."

"Gotcha. No problem."

"This magnesium stuff is dangerous. Use only one scoop and keep it away from your hair when it goes off, or you'll be wearing a wig in the future. And don't look at the flash. It'll blind you at short distances."

"You'll have to excuse me now. I have to go over to the hardware store to see if my shipment of printer's ink has arrived. You can continue playing with the camera, if you want," Silas said, grabbing his hat.

"Let me go with you. Are you sure I can't work with you on the paper?" Agnes begged.

"YES, I'M SURE!"

***

Mel was checking inventory when Silas arrived with Agnes in tow. "And how are the Kronschnabells this afternoon?" Mel asked. Mel had developed an impressive five o'clock shadow on the right side of his face, but it would require several months to catch up with the full beard on the left side. Since Mel was sensitive about the flintlock episode, the irregularity in facial hair was not mentioned.

"We're doing well," Silas replied. "Although I'm afraid it might rain tonight."

"Is that a fact?"

"Can you check to see if my printer's ink has arrived? I'm trying to get as much work done this afternoon as I can, because it might rain tonight."

"I believe it did come in. Let me check." Mel returned with a large box of printer's ink. "That'll be a dollar ninety-five."

Silas paid the money and picked up the package. "Did I mention it might rain tonight?"

"Yes sir, yes sir, I believe you did."

Silas walked out the door with Agnes in hot pursuit.

***

"Hello, Frenchie. It looks like rain tonight."

***

"Good afternoon, Mr. and Mrs. Olson. Fine day today, but I'm afraid it'll rain tonight."

"I must be sure I carry my umbrella," Mrs. Olson replied.

"Thank you for the information. We don't want to get caught in a storm," Mr. Olson added with a wink.

***

"Looks like rain tonight, Amos."

***

"Hello, Rudy. How are you today?"

"Fine, thank you."

"Yes, it looks like rain tonight."

Rudy looked up at the sky. There wasn't a cloud in sight. How do these Yoopers do that, he wondered. He would have thought it was going to be a nice evening. The garden and apple trees could use the rain. He shouldn't complain.

***

Luther, as usual, was hard at work repairing his dam. As of late, he found work frustrating. Normally he enjoyed his work; he could see the results of his labors. During the last week, it seemed he was getting nowhere. A stubborn section of the dam kept washing away. He had tried several different designs to improve the strength without success. At first, the debris was scattered around the hole in the dam, which is unusual for water damage. It did make repair easier since he could recycle the branches. Lately, however, the sticks were washed down stream. This was more consistent with water erosion.

Luther wasn't one to wallow in despair. Hard work overcomes all problems. He would just have to work harder, maybe put in some overtime. Luther worked late into the evening. It was well past dusk when Luther dragged the last of the apple trees toward the breach in the dam.

***

Rudy arrived in the alley behind the Snake Pit Saloon two hours after sunset. After a cursory search in the dark, he found the wooden stairs leading up to apartment 2-B where Polly, Molly, and Dolly lived. Rudy had made a commitment earlier in the day to pay a visit, but he had been braver then. He was always braver in daylight. It was too bad the apartment was in the rear of the building. The apartments toward the front were accessed from the street where there was light and people, making it safer for young ladies.

Rudy explored several reasons for not climbing up the stairs—none were valid. Was he doing this because it was the right thing to do, or was he reacting to the Ladies Aid Society? He wouldn't stay long. He brought some Christian literature. He would invite them to the church services and give them the literature. He wouldn't have to step inside. No, he wouldn't go inside the apartment. Just invite them to church and give them the literature. Mission accomplished.

Rudy started up the steps. Maybe they won't be home. If they weren't home, it wouldn't be his fault. He had tried. Rudy was disappointed to hear voices behind the door of apartment 2-B. He would hand them the literature and leave, he reminded himself.

Rudy softly knocked on the door, hoping it wouldn't be heard. He was greeted by further disappointment, when he heard footsteps heading for the door. He would just give them the literature. He wouldn't go inside. The door opened wide revealing Dolly's well-built frame.

"Why, Rev. Hooper, this is a surprise. Look girls, it's Rev. Hooper. Come on in." Dolly grabbed him by the elbow and escorted him to an overstuffed chair. "You don't mind if we call you Rudy do you?" Dolly asked, not waiting for a reply.

"This is convenient," Polly said. "We just made some chocolate fudge brownies with walnuts in them. It's a new recipe, and we could use a man's opinion."

Rudy had to admit he was partial to chocolate. "With walnuts did you say?"

Polly produced a large platter of brownies. The aroma alone was enough to make Rudy salivate. He picked one of the larger pieces from the platter and took a bite, letting his tongue massage the brownie to better absorb the chocolaty flavor. He crunched on one of the walnuts to appreciate its texture and then looked up at the Ollies who were awaiting his verdict. "Not bad," Rudy proclaimed.

"Did you make these, Molly?" Rudy asked, looking at Dolly.

"I'm Molly."

"I'm Polly."

"I'm Dolly."

Rudy hoped he now had the names straight. "Never did catch your last names."

"We...ah," Polly began to explain.

"We're orphans," Molly said.

"Yes, we're orphans," Polly confirmed.

"We never knew our real parents," Dolly added. "We were left at the orphanage door and raised by the Sisters of Mercy."

"That's terrible." Rudy felt duly touched. If only the women of the church knew this...

"We might even be sisters, but we'll never know."

Rudy didn't think they looked much like sisters. Dolly was a blond, Polly was a brunette, and Molly was a redhead. He felt this could change on a weekly basis.

"What brought you to Bear Creek?" Rudy asked.

"We're collecting data for a men's magazine," Polly replied.

"Yes, we interview men for the magazine," Molly added.

"But please don't tell anyone. We want to keep that quiet, or it would bias our data," Dolly said.

"Wow, I wish I could tell the women about this. I'm sure it would change their viewpoint, but I'm a man of the cloth and trained to honor confidentiality."

***

Maggie, Trudy, and Agnes crept up the back stairs. Agnes, as official photographer, carried the camera and tripod. Trudy carried an umbrella. She heard it might rain. At the top of the stairs, they paused. Agnes opened the legs of the tripod and silently positioned the camera in front of the apartment door. The focus was set for ten feet.

"It's dark, so we'll use a flash," Agnes informed her cohorts. She passed the flashboard to Maggie. "Hold this." Agnes placed a scoop of magnesium powder on the board. "It's pretty dark here; maybe we should use two scoops." A short fuse was placed into the powder. Checking to ensure the lens cap was in place, Agnes removed the protective shield from the film. They were ready.

"Timing is everything," Agnes informed the others. "When I light the fuse, we'll have five seconds to remove the lens cap and get the door open. If the door's locked, we'll have to break it down. It looks pretty flimsy. I think the three of us can break it down without problems. And don't look at the flash or it'll blind you."

***

"Actually, the reason I came here is to invite you ladies to our church," Rudy said. "We have a nice little church that is quite active in world concerns. We are presently working to convert the heathens in New Guinea and feed the starving children in China."

"Having been brought up in an orphanage by the Sisters of Redemption, we are Catholic, but since there's no Catholic Church in Bear Creek, we would feel privileged to attend your church," Dolly said. Polly and Molly nodded in agreement.

"I thought you said it was the Sisters of Mercy?" Rudy asked.

"Did I?"

"The order changed when we were eight," Polly said.

"Converting the heathens in New Guinea and feeding the starving children in China sounds like a worthwhile project," Dolly said. "We would be honored if you would accept a small donation to your project." Dolly dipped into her purse and pulled out a five-dollar bill.

Rudy reached for the money, but heard a crash and was instantly blinded by a flash of light. It was like Saul on the road to Damascus, Acts chapter 9, or was it chapter 10? Rudy felt confused. But Saul was blinded because he had persecuted the Lord. Rudy hadn't persecuted the Lord, had he? Maybe he was going to have a divine revelation. That was it; this was a spiritual event. Was he about to have a vision? Rudy's world was beginning to spin. He reached out, but nothing was there. He began to fall. He was falling through space.

Rudy looked up into the eyes of an angel. The face was out of focus, but it had to be an angel. She had long, blond hair. It had to have been made of Golden Fleece. She was smiling. He would be OK. The angel was talking to him, but he couldn't hear the words. Rudy squinted his eyes, and the angel gradually came into focus. It was Dolly!

"What happened?" Rudy asked.

"You tripped and hit your head on the coffee table," Dolly replied.

Rudy looked around him. He was lying on the floor with his head resting in Polly's lap. Molly was holding a cold steak over his left eye. Rudy looked up at Polly, but her face was obscured by her chest. He began to feel uneasy. His current position on the floor with his head in Polly's lap had to be unprofessional, at least for his profession. He tried to get up but it only aggravated his splitting headache. His left eye was swollen shut and was now becoming discolored.

"I better return to the parsonage."

"Do you think you'll be OK?" Dolly asked. "We can walk you home."

"No, I'll be fine," Rudy replied. "A walk in the cool air will do me some good."

Rudy staggered to his feet. With an Ollie at each elbow, Rudy took a few steps, finding his legs in working condition.

"I'll be all right," Rudy said with a little more conviction. "I want to thank you for everything. I'll make sure the five dollars is put to good use."

Rudy walked toward the door. That was strange, he thought. The hinges to the door had been ripped off. He hadn't noticed that on the way in. They really should get that fixed. Ladies weren't safe without a strong door they could lock.

The walk back to the parsonage in the cool air gave Rudy time to think. Sometimes he worried too much about his health, but the flash of light and momentary blindness were real. Did he have a seizure? He wondered if the previous pastor developed seizures. Could there be some environmental hazard at the parsonage? When he reached the back door to the parsonage, he found a large bowl of plum pudding. It was one of Widow Watson's bowls. That was nice of her. Rudy placed the plum pudding on the counter and sat in his chair.

His eye was swollen shut. Rudy assumed it would be black and blue for several days, perhaps longer. How would he explain this to his congregation on Sunday when he couldn't explain it to himself? Little did he realize by Sunday, everyone in Bear Creek would know—except for Rudy.

***

Silas emerged from the dark room with several 8 X10 glossy pictures.

"Well, here are your pictures," he said to Agnes. "I made several copies for you. Nice profile of Rudy." It would have been better, Silas thought, if Rudy had combed his hair. "Dolly also turned out pretty well." He handed the pictures to Agnes. "You want this printed on the front page?"

"Ah, shut up," Agnes replied.

"Why is Rudy giving Dolly five dollars?" Silas asked, but Agnes was already out the door.

***

The following morning the Ladies Aid Society met in another emergency session to discuss their sting operation. Emergency meetings were becoming routine. Agnes passed copies of the picture around the room.

"Our cover was blown," someone said.

"Impossible," Agnes replied. "Only three of us knew the day and time. Once Silas was informed, I watched him like a hawk. There was no way he could have informed the others."

"Do you think Hooper was involved in this?" Trudy asked.

"No, Rudy has this character flaw—he's honest." Maggie had found this to be a common flaw among pastors.

"I heard he invited the Ollies to church," Trudy said.

"Don't expect me to sit next to them," Agnes said.

"Why is Rudy giving Dolly five dollars?" someone from the back wanted to know.

***

It has been another strange week here in Bear Creek. It appears I am coming down with a strange illness, which I believe to be a brain disorder since it causes flashing lights, loss of coordination, and confusion. It has given me a severe headache, although this could be from the fall and the injury to my left eye. I am not optimistic about my future, but if it is God's will, I will accept it. I wish the Bishop had been more forthright about the previous pastor's illness since the illnesses we have may be the same.

I had a chance to meet the Ollies. They turned out to be lovely ladies. It is not well known in town, but they were brought up in an orphanage. They were left at the orphanage steps as babies and don't even know their last names. They are now gathering data for a men's magazine. I invited them to our church services, and they said they would come. Dolly gave five dollars toward converting the heathens in New Guinea and feeding the starving children in

China. They are much misunderstood. I think the townsfolk would like them better if they would only take the time to get to know them.

This week I planted six apple trees. It cost me twelve dollars, which is a lot of money on my salary. I had great hopes for having an apple orchard. Yesterday, all six of them were cut down. I found tooth marks on the tree stumps. Now, I didn't see who did this, but I only know one beaver in this area. That Luther is taxing my patience, and I will have to put a stop to this, even if it means an end to our friendship. There are limits to what a man will endure.

Rudy closed the cover to his journal and went to bed.

Chapter Three

The hardware and feed store was void of customers when Rudy arrived Monday morning to buy some paint. Rudy thanked the Lord for small favors; he wasn't in the mood for socializing. He was still self-conscious about his black eye even though the swelling was down and his vision was back to normal. Most people accepted his explanation of the fall, and that was fine with him. He didn't mention the circumstances surrounding his injury. Some things are better left unsaid. He also didn't mention the flash of light or his seizure. Since he had no similar attacks for several days, he was hoping the brain tumor was in its early stages. Was that too much to ask? He had many projects to complete before he became incapacitated. He wasn't looking forward to his final days, but if that was God's will, Thy will be done.

"Morning, Rudy. How ya doing today?" Mel climbed down from his stepladder after proclaiming the shelf he had been stocking adequate.

"About as good as can be expected," Rudy replied. "I need some paint."

"Any particular color?"

"A quart of white and a quart of red will do fine." Rudy could see the facial hair on the right side of Mel's face was filling in. "I need to paint the outhouse."

"If I remember right, the previous pastor never did paint that outhouse. I'm surprised the wood hasn't rotted." Mel scratched a recalcitrant itch on the right side of the face. "It's a good thing you came in this morning. We close early when there's a full moon, you know."

"Why's that?" Rudy asked out of politeness.

"Considered a holiday in these parts," Mel said. "The town shuts down early. That's only during the summer months."

Rudy hoped this wasn't some pagan ritual or moon worship. He had heard such practices were common on the fringes of civilization. He didn't feel like pursuing the conversation. "Can you add a couple of paintbrushes to that order?"

"No problem." Mel grabbed two brushes from the shelf. "Oh, by the way, those vitamin supplements you ordered arrived today. You aren't sick are you?"

Thank the Lord; they've arrived. "I'm doing fine, thank you." *Considering his condition, Rudy wanted to add. Vitamin supplements won't cure a brain tumor, but they might postpone the inevitable.*

"No doctor around these parts, but Maggie can stitch cuts, deliver babies, and she's good with herbal medicine. If you get sick, give her a call. She'll fix what ails ya."

"No, really, I'm fine. How much do I owe you?"

"That will be two dollars and ninety-five cents."

***

If Jennifer were a swearing woman, which she was not, she would have sworn Frenchie had twice as many hands as she did. No sooner had she parried one probing hand than she would be confronted with two more. It was hard to convince Frenchie she was not that kind of a girl; after all, she was brought up a lady. Frenchie? Well, he was just brought up. Kissing was different. Even ladies were allowed an occasional kiss, and Jennifer had gained considerable expertise in that social event over the last year. The current kiss was approaching a minute when Jennifer and Frenchie came up for air.

"Why don't you tell your parents and be done with it?" Frenchie asked after they had recovered their breath. "Then we wouldn't have to hide in the choir loft."

"It's not that easy." Jennifer replied. "You know Ma's temper."

Frenchie had to admit, Maggie did have a quick temper—at least that's what he had heard.

"I don't want to spend the rest of my life sneaking around the choir loft."

"I don't like it either," Jennifer replied. "I was hoping Ma would learn to like you, but your reputation with the Ollies hasn't helped. I'm not fond of that myself."

"What do ya mean? The Ollies thing was your idea. You said people wouldn't suspect us if they thought I was chasing the Ollies."

"But it's different now. People think you're some sort of superhuman sex machine."

"Really?"

"That's nothing to be proud of."

If people in Bear Creek were observant, which they weren't, they would have noticed Frenchie wasn't spending time with the Ollies, as was the current consensus, but was sneaking out of town on evenings and weekends to work on a cabin he had been building. He had purchased two forty-acre parcels north of town, which he hoped to turn into a potato farm. It would be too late to plant this year, but he expected his first crop the following year. The cabin could house a small family.

It was true Maggie was not fond of Frenchie, not only due to his reputation as a womanizer, but because he was a foreigner and a Catholic. If given enough time, she could find additional reasons to justify her displeasure. The fact that he was attending the Methodist Church didn't make him less Catholic, nor did his perfect English make him less French; he still had an accent. To say Maggie was set in her ways was an understatement. From her viewpoint, the only proper attitude for any American was English, Republican and Protestant, preferably Methodist.

"What if your Ma never likes me? We might never get married. Fifty years from now, we'll still be sneaking off to the choir loft to steal a kiss. By then we'll be gray with false teeth and hearing aids."

"Stop making fun of me." Jennifer playfully pushed him away. "You know I'll marry you as soon as it's possible."

"You really mean that?"

"Yes," came the soft reply.

"Then I'll pick you up Thursday at midnight. Leave a note for your parents and climb out your bedroom window. I'll get a ladder. By Friday night, we can be in Green Bay where we can find a justice of the peace to marry us. Maybe your parents will like me better after we're married."

Jennifer looked into Frenchie's eyes. They were soft and kind, but there was also strength and determination. They were the eyes of the man she loved.

"OK, I will be ready."

***

Rudy debated the merits of pacing himself to obtain a few more productive days or pushing himself to make the most of the time he had left. Since he didn't have the patience to delay a worthwhile task, he decided on the latter. Rudy, therefore, disregarded his health and attacked the outhouse project. To increase lighting and provide better ventilation, he enlarged the crescent moon. Several knot holes provided additional lighting. Rudy had excellent eyesight, but the flashing lights might foreshadow future visual impairment. He painted the interior white to augment the light filtering through the hole in the door. Still apprehensive about the hornet's nest, Rudy covered the crescent hole with a slab of birch bark and painted in darkness, assisted only by a flashlight.

The outside of the outhouse was a separate problem. This would be visible to the world, or at least the Bear Creek portion of the world, and needed to cater to the esthetic tastes of the local community. The simple shed appearance couldn't be altered, but Rudy accented the roof with an old weather vane in the shape of a rooster perched on an arrow. He discovered it tucked away in the parsonage attic. When placed at the peak of the roof, it gave the outhouse a bucolic look. The exterior walls were painted bright red with black trim. Rudy found the black paint in the church basement—it didn't appear anyone else would use it. He could have chosen more subdued colors, but the outhouse was a part of his life, a part that deserved no shame.

After three hours, Rudy stepped back to admire his work. He took pride in his humility but found humility challenged by the most perfect outhouse. He figured four hours for the paint to dry in the summer breeze.

Rudy climbed the hill to inspect the view from his parsonage swing. The red outhouse with its black trim stood in bold contrast to the greens and browns of the landscape, and the weather vane provided the ultimate artistic touch. In the background, Rudy could see Luther working at his dam. He had not repaired the center of the dam, although the rest of the dam was now much taller. That was fortunate; at the moment, Rudy lacked the energy to dismantle the dam. Rudy collapsed onto the porch swing with the satisfaction of a job well done.

Relaxing in the swing was a welcome relief from the hours of painting. Rudy didn't care what Luther thought; the rest of the day would be devoted to relaxation. P.C. would be over later in the afternoon to fix a broken hinge on a closet door; after which, Rudy planned a long soak in his bathtub with a good book.

***

Luther had given up on the center of the dam, at least for now. He had nothing against hard work, but he liked to see the fruits of his labors, and he was getting nowhere with his current efforts. Even with stronger materials and a multitude of design changes, the center continued to falter. If he could see it crumble, he might have a better understanding of the mechanics involved; but it always collapsed at night. That was rather odd, he thought.

The decision to postpone work on the center of the dam was a practical one. After a day or two, he might have better insight. This didn't mean Luther would sit around and do nothing. No sir, a respectable beaver never dawdles. Luther diverted his attention to the rest of the dam, which appeared to be holding up well. It was refreshing to see progress again, as the dam grew larger in height. If only he could patch the center, he would have a respectable dam.

***

Rudy waited an hour before giving up on P.C. The porch swing was relaxing, but couldn't compare with a tub of hot water and a good book. The hot water would soothe his aching muscles. Scraping off a few layers of dirt wouldn't hurt either.

The tub was a P.C. original, consisting of an old watering trough fitted to wheels, allowing the tub to be wheeled into the kitchen for filling with water. The parsonage plumbing, also designed by P.C., defied imagination, although it seemed to function adequately. P.C. had erected a 500-gallon water tank twelve feet off the ground with copper tubing leading into the kitchen where a valve turned on the water. A large cast iron pipe carried the wastewater from the sink to an outside sump.

Rudy dipped a toe into the water to test the temperature. The water had to be heated on the stove, making temperature control an unreliable art at best. Ah, perfect temperature, Rudy decided.

Preparing for a bath required military precision. The tub was positioned between the stove, where a large pot heated water to re-warm the tub as needed, and the kitchen table, which sported an assortment of bathing accessories consisting of a towel, reading material—today he would read *Meditations of Saint Augustine*—and a bottle of his secret indulgence, bubble bath.

Rudy didn't know why he felt guilty about the bubble bath. Maybe because it had no practical use, or was it because it was indulged solely for the carnal pleasure of being engulfed in soapsuds. Rudy didn't know which, but it felt too good not to be a sin. He purchased the bottle before coming to the Upper Peninsula. Once the bubble bath was consumed, there would be no replacement. It wasn't an item he could casually order at the Hardware and Feed Store. He would miss it when it was gone.

The hot water worked quickly, and Rudy's aching muscles began to relax. He eased his head back into the water, allowing the soapsuds to engulf his head, sparing only his face. For the better part of twenty minutes, he lay motionless in the water before surfacing to indulge in his book. Yes, this was utopia and like all utopias, time stood still and yet it did not, as the afternoon grew into evening.

It was a quarter past six when he heard the knock on the door. That must be P.C., Rudy decided. He was several hours late, but Rudy had asked him to fix that hinge several times. He was happy P.C. had finally come to fix it.

Rudy climbed out of his paradise with bubble bath still clinging to his face. Grabbing the towel from the table, he wrapped it around his skinny waist—it wrapped around twice. The knock on the door repeated itself. "I'm coming, I'm coming," Rudy replied.

***

Jennifer knocked on the parsonage door and waited for a response. When no response was forthcoming, she rapped again. This time she heard a muffled voice from behind the door. The door finally opened revealing Rev. Hooper wrapped in a towel. His beard and hair were covered with soapsuds resembling the mane of an albino lion. Jennifer noted the washboard ribs. Clearly, Rudy was not single by accident.

"Hi, Reverend Hooper. How are you today?" Jennifer asked, trying to ignore his appearance.

"I'm fine, thank you. I was expecting your father."

"Sorry. He won't make it today because of the holiday."

"Holiday?"

"No one told you? Everyone gathers down by the beaver pond during a full moon. It's a local holiday. All of the businesses close. The townsfolk have been doing that for years."

"I guess Mel did mention something about that this morning." Over Jennifer's shoulders, Rudy could see the entire population of Bear Creek gathered on the hillside overlooking the pond.

"Actually, the reason I'm here is to see if we can borrow some salt. Ma needs it for her potato salad. She was hoping to avoid running back to the cafe."

Rudy disappeared and returned in seconds with a saltshaker.

"Why don't you join us? It's a lot of fun."

"Maybe I will," Rudy replied. "I suppose I should put some clothes on."

It took Rudy only a few minutes to rinse the soapsuds from his face and climb into some clothes. Since the party was in his back yard, he felt obliged to attend and was soon mingling among the crowd. It reminded him of the county fairs of his childhood. Kids and a few adults were swimming in the beaver pond while others played catch or horseshoes. Tablecloths covered the ground as the women prepared picnic lunches. Rudy didn't understand the rationale behind the full moon, but he knew a good party when he saw one.

Rudy tried his hand at horseshoes (he lost) as well as softball with the kids before he sat back on the hillside to watch the townsfolk at play. He was glad he had painted the outhouse earlier in the morning as it was in frequent use. He may have to do something about the knotholes in the walls. Some of the children were using them for unauthorized education. Mrs. Olson had just exited the outhouse and was looking for a switch to further the lads' enlightenment.

***

Sodom didn't normally venture far from the church. After all, he was a church mouse and not a field mouse, but he could make an exception for a full moon. The food at the church wasn't bad, mind you; but the buffet spread out on the grass during a full moon was a sight to be seen. It was like a twenty-course meal; you take a bite here or nibble there and move on to another location. Yes, Sodom wouldn't miss this for the world.

The tall grass provided excellent cover, allowing Sodom freedom to maneuver. He first sampled Agnes Kronschnabell's spread and found the ham and cheese sandwiches superb. Next was a quick stop at Maggie Taylor's. She had the best rolls in town.

The last stop was Mrs. Olson, who was noted for her macaroni and cheese. You haven't lived until you have had some of Mrs. Olson's macaroni and cheese. It was baked to perfection with a thick crust of cheddar cheese melted over the top. Just thinking about it made Sodom's mouth water. It might be a bit heavy for a daily diet since he was watching his cholesterol; but for a special occasion such as a full moon, he would indulge.

Sodom was disappointed when he arrived at Mrs. Olson's spot; she had yet to spread the picnic buffet for him. That was OK. He would help himself. The food was stored in a wicker basket, making climbing easy. At the top, covering the basket, was a red and white checkered towel. Sodom poked his head under the towel and tumbled into the basket. It was dark inside. Even for a mouse, it was difficult to see, but he could smell the macaroni and cheese, and what a smell it was. Mrs. Olson had outdone herself this time. With the poor visibility, Sodom would have to rely on his keen sense of smell.

It had to be somewhere under the tablecloth. Sodom tunneled under a layer of the soft fabric. The folded tablecloth was like a maze, and he soon became lost within the folds. Persistence would eventually pay off. He had to be close. The aroma was intense.

"Whoa, who's rocking the boat?" Sodom clung tightly to the tablecloth as it whipped through the air. "This is not good!"

Mrs. Olson was shaking out the wrinkles in the tablecloth and would have shaken out Sodom if not for his tight grip. It was fast becoming a delicate situation. Like any red-blooded American mouse in a tight spot, Sodom headed for the nearest hole, which in this case happened to be Mrs. Olson's sleeve. He had scampered up to the right shoulder before realizing he could be trapped. He needed an exit posthaste.

Sodom ran back and forth across Mrs. Olson's chest looking for an exit, while Mrs. Olson methodically thumped her chest Tarzan style, eventually forcing Sodom down the left sleeve where he fell to the ground and disappeared into the grass.

***

From his vantage on the hillside, Rudy could observe all of the townsfolk. He enjoyed watching the various ways people entertain themselves. Take Mrs. Olson for instance, Rudy could see her perform some sort of ritualistic self-flagellation by beating her chest. He had heard this kind of behavior was common among Yoopers. Sometimes they would sit in a steamy sauna, and then jump into snow banks and whip each other with birch boughs. He didn't think he would ever understand Yoopers.

"And how is Reverend Hooper this evening?"

Rudy looked up at the Widow Watson. She had arrived with picnic basket in hand. "I'm fine, Mrs. Watson. And how are you?"

"Oh, do call me Alice."

"Only if you call me Rudy."

"Have you eaten yet?" Alice asked.

"I'm afraid I didn't plan in advance," Rudy explained. "It's no real problem. I can easily find something to eat at the parsonage when I get hungry."

"Do you like fried chicken and potato salad? I have more than I can eat."

"I can't impose upon you," Rudy said apologetically.

"Don't be silly; you won't be imposing. Grab a corner of the tablecloth," Alice said. Rudy could see Alice had slipped into her authoritarian, schoolteacher mode, and he wisely grabbed a corner of the tablecloth as commanded. It was obvious he would be sharing Alice's fried chicken, and there would be no further discussion.

Alice produced table settings for two from her picnic basket. That was odd, Rudy thought. It was as if she had planned for two people. Rudy hoped he wasn't taking someone else's place at the picnic. There was also enough fried chicken to easily feed two hungry people.

Rudy gave the meal his best blessing and sat at the edge of the tablecloth to begin the meal. He had expected the Widow Watson to sit opposite him. Instead, she sat beside him, shoulder to shoulder. Rudy wished she wouldn't do things like that. It could give people the wrong impression. Fortunately, the Widow Watson was able to carry on the conversation without input from Rudy other than an occasional nod. The fried chicken and potato salad were excellent and plentiful. It was a good excuse for not talking—he couldn't talk with his mouth full, could he?

They had eaten their fill and still there was chicken and potato salad left over. It seemed like a lot of food for one person to prepare for herself, but that was Rudy's good fortune. The tablecloth was folded and replaced into the picnic basket, leaving the two of them sitting on the hillside overlooking the beaver pond. Dusk was approaching, and a few brave stars were venturing forth in preparation for ruling the night. Only the silhouettes of people could be seen, making them unrecognizable. Rudy felt some relief; if he had to sit so closely to the Widow Watson, at least no one could see him. The darkness brought additional distress as Alice's shoulder increased its pressure. He was trapped. There was no escape. There was no way he could take his leave without hurting her feelings. After an excellent picnic dinner, that was the last thing he wished to do.

"It sure is a beautiful evening," Alice said.

"It sure is." Rudy could think of nothing more to say. His mind refused to function.

"Rudy, I hate to part with your company, but you may want to sit with the men while there's still light to find them. It's traditional for the men to sit together when the full moon rises."

Rudy thought it strange for the men and women to be segregated as the full moon rose. He would have thought it would be a perfect time for a little romance; but then, what did he know about romance. Still, it was as good an excuse as any to escape from his current dilemma. Rudy thanked the Widow Watson for her delicious fried chicken and politely made his exit.

Rudy found a group of men off to his right. In the darkness he could still recognize P.C., Frenchie, and Silas. Others he recognized only by voice. It was already too dark to see the beaver pond.

"Is this your first full moon at Bear Creek?" Frenchie asked.

"Yes, it is," replied Rudy. "Mel told me about it this morning, but I never dreamed it was such a big occasion. I've had a lot of fun."

"The best part is yet to come," Mel Barker said. "Wait until the full moon rises. You have never seen such beauty."

"Really?" Rudy had seen full moons before, and yes, they were pretty, but he never got this excited.

"According to Silas, the moon'll rise at 10:26," Frenchie said. (Silas owned the only almanac in town.) Several people looked at their pocket watches with their flashlights and confirmed the moon should rise in ten minutes. P.C. looked at his pocket watch. It was a quarter past one.

"If you don't know what you're doing, you'll miss everything," Frenchie said. "You know your way around the beaver pond, don't you?"

"Yes, I guess I do," Rudy replied, not sure if he understood the point.

"You have to stare at where you think the beaver lodge is. If you aren't staring at the lodge when the moon comes up, you will miss everything."

Rudy found the directions strange. One would think there would be more beauty looking at the moon as it rose, but then this was his first full moon at Bear Creek, and he would do as directed. He was sure he knew where the beaver lodge was even in the darkness. "OK, I'll stare at the lodge."

A couple of watch checks confirmed the rising moon was only minutes away. There would be no further time checks. A flashlight could ruin someone's night vision. It became deathly quiet as everyone in the town of Bear Creek stared into the darkness at the beaver lodge. Rudy found it almost spooky.

At precisely 10:26 the full moon rose on cue, filling the ravine with moonlight. The beaver lodge was now clearly visible.

"Did ya see her?" Mel asked.

"What a gorgeous body!" Frenchie exclaimed.

"See who?" Rudy asked.

"Abigail," Silas answered.

"Who's Abigail?" Rudy was now totally confused.

"Abigail Farnsworth. On full moons she comes down to the beaver lodge looking for her clothes."

"Why does she need clothes? Is she naked?"

"Yeah, isn't that great!"

"You mean we've been sitting here all evening just to see a naked lady?" Rudy seldom lost his temper, but he could feel his adrenaline begin to rise.

"Sometimes it's a waste of time, since she dives into the beaver pond as soon as she sees us on the hillside. If you aren't looking at the right spot, you miss everything. I suppose you can't blame her," Silas said.

"I can't believe you men would take advantage of such a young innocent girl!" Rudy could feel the makings of his Sunday sermon. "As for me, I don't wish to be a part of this any longer." Apparently, it was over anyway; people were starting to leave. Rudy headed back to his parsonage still stewing about the events of the night.

***

The Bear Creek residents weren't the only ones taking advantage of the full moon. Luther, who had been forced into seclusion most of the day, was making up for lost time. Now, Luther didn't mind if humans wished to waste their time, but when they interfered with his work, it became personal. Luther had been unable to get a lick of work done with all those humans swimming in his pond, skipping stones, and otherwise being a generalized nuisance.

He had been increased the height of most of the dam by two feet, but there was no advantage to increasing it further unless he solved the problem at the center of the dam. That was receiving his current attention. He decided to use larger sticks that were interwoven for greater strength. Smaller sticks were used for the gaps. Both were cemented together with mud and grass. When completed, the dam should be stronger than needed, but Luther was taking no chances. In the past, the dam faltered during the night, but tonight it appeared to be holding. There was no evidence of deterioration, and the gap in the center of the dam was slowly succumbing to diligent work. By three in the morning, it was complete. Luther climbed to the top of the dam to survey the results of his labors. He was pleased to find the pond expanding rapidly. With a feeling of great satisfaction, Luther returned to his lodge for some well-earned sleep.

***

It was Saturday morning, and Rudy was finding it difficult to extract himself from bed. He was still brooding over the "Abigail" episode of the previous night. It wasn't that he really believed a naked girl was relentlessly chased through the woods by a grizzly bear, nor did he feel any of the townsfolk believed it. It was the principle, and even more so the fact he was drawn into that voyeuristic episode.

Rudy plucked a thermometer from his nightstand and slipped it under his tongue. Taking his temperature was now a morning ritual. Although he had no recent symptoms, he didn't want to be caught off guard and felt daily monitoring of his temperature might give him early warning of any relapse.

Sunday's sermon had been completed earlier in the week, but would have to be postponed. Tomorrow the congregation would get a piece of his mind. It was time to take off the gloves and let them know how he really felt. Several Scriptures came immediately to mind. Yes, he would be standing on the Scriptural high ground.

Rudy removed the thermometer from his mouth and was disappointed to note it read 98.8. That was one tenth of a degree higher than yesterday, clearly a trend. He wouldn't let that get him down; he had work to do. He decided to put the thermometer back into his mouth for a second opinion. It still registered 98.8.

Rudy pried himself out of bed and slid into his pants while his toes wiggled into a pair of slippers in preparation for his morning trip to the outhouse. Still half asleep, he headed for the front door. The morning air felt like a cold, wet rag against his face, partially arousing him from lingering shrouds of sleep, but his eyes, morphed into thin slits, vigorously protested the dawn's early light. Rudy stared through the thin slits at the beaver pond in disbelief. During the night, it had grown into a lake. Rudy was now fully awake. The water's edge came almost to the parsonage steps. He could fish from his porch swing—not that he cared to. In the center of the pond, a wooden structure floated aimlessly. It was painted red, and attached to the top was a cast-iron rooster perched on an arrow.

"That's it. Luther has to go!" Rudy wasn't sure how he would do it, but he was sure Luther was history, even if Rudy had to dismantle the dam by hand. Now calm down, Rudy told himself. He didn't need too many problems at once, not in his condition. He would calmly dismantle enough of the dam to get the water level back to normal; he would calmly finish his sermon for tomorrow; he would calmly repair the outhouse, and then he would DRAW AND QUARTER THAT BEAVER!

***

Gomorrah waddled over to his food dish for his early morning breakfast. A Saturday night of carousing around was enough to work up an appetite in any tomcat, and Gomorrah was no exception. Feeling benevolent, Gomorrah left a few crumbs for Sodom. His growing frame was testimony that Gomorrah wasn't in the habit of leaving many crumbs.

Once his fat cells were refurbished, Gomorrah searched for the perfect place to nap. The aching pain in his joints reminded him he was no longer a youngster. Although he had considered cutting back on his nightlife, he didn't wish to disappoint his harem. He had responsibilities, you know. After a nice nap he would be rejuvenated and ready for his next meal or maybe another night on the town. Since he no longer fit in the offering plate, that was out. It had been one of his favorite spots. The concrete floor, he decided, was too cold. Finally, he settled on a nice cozy spot under the pulpit. After circling a few times, he settled down for his nap.

***

By Sunday morning, Rudy's anger had hardened into resolve, and he looked forward to the church service with anticipation. It might not be a popular sermon, but it needed to be said. Converting the heathens in New Guinea and feeding the starving children in China was a noble cause, but sometimes the sins of the local community needed to be addressed.

Rudy took his normal seat in the chair behind the pulpit. The pews were starting to fill. He was pleased to see all three Ollies sitting in the third row. The rest of the congregation had given them lots of space, as the surrounding seats were unoccupied. Also empty were the front rows; after all, this was a Methodist church. At the organ, Trudy Barker was playing some introductory music, taking care to add the appropriate "La" or "Da" in place of the organ's missing high "C." Rudy had to admit she did a good job at it.

The service opened with the hymn *Bringing in the Sheaves,* followed by the offering. From experience, Rudy found it preferable to have the offering first if he were giving a controversial sermon. After receiving the offering, Rudy stepped up to the pulpit. With the exception of the front seats and the seats around the Ollies, the church was full. P.C., sitting in the second row, appeared to be in deep meditation or already asleep. Rudy assumed the latter. In the fourth row he could see Mrs. Olson glaring at some boys in the back who had shot a spitball at Sarah Peterson but had hit Mrs. Olson in the neck by mistake. The service was starting off normally.

"The book of Genesis tells the story of two cities of sin. I am referring to the cities of Sodom and Gomorrah," Rudy began his sermon.

"Hold on a minute. You never mentioned that when you named us," Sodom protested from his hole in the back of the organ, but no one was listening.

"The inhabitants of Sodom and Gomorrah were sinners because they worshipped the flesh and reveled in the nakedness of women."

"He isn't comparing Bear Creek with Sodom and Gomorrah, is he?" someone whispered.

"And there are other cities that have sinners. Sinners who likewise revel in sex, nakedness, and carnal pleasure."

"Surely there are more important issues to address, such as converting the heathens in New Guinea and feeding the starving children in China," Silas muttered to himself.

"The Bible states: *Thou shalt not commit adultery*, Exodus 20:14. And what is adultery?"

He expects us to explain adultery to him, Agnes wondered?

"I will tell you, and I quote: *Ye have heard that it was said by them of old time, Thou shalt not commit adultery, but I say unto you, that whosoever looketh on a woman to lust after her hathe committed adultery with her already in his heart,* Matthew 5:27." Rudy's eyes were starting to burn. *That other Gomorrah must be close by.*

I would rather have our men preoccupied with sex than to be occupied with it, Maggie thought. *I'm more concerned with those Ollies than any imaginary Abigail.* Maggie gave a glaring look at the Ollies.

"There are those in this town who are sinners and have lusted in their hearts. Do you know what happened to the sinners in Sodom and Gomorrah?"

Mel assumed they were about to find out.

"They were smitten by the Lord." Rudy's eyes were beginning to water. *Where was that cat?*

"Hey, this is getting good." As official church mouse, Sodom had heard many sermons, but this was one of the best.

"The Lord rained upon Sodom and upon Gomorrah brimstone and fire from the Lord out of heaven, Genesis 19:24."

What's brimstone, Jennifer wondered?

"If the sinners in this community continue in their lust of carnal activities, there will be thunder, and there will be lightning, and there will be hell fire! And they will be smitten like the sinners of Sodom and Gomorrah!" Rudy pounded his fist on the pulpit for emphasis.

The congregation squirmed in their seats—all except P.C., who was still meditating.

The pounding on the pulpit awakened Gomorrah from a restful sleep. *How can a cat take a catnap with all that racket? If he can't sleep, he may as well eat.* Gomorrah arched his back to stretch out his muscles as he surveyed his surroundings. He was surprised to find the legs of the minister standing behind the pulpit. Stepping out from under the pulpit, Gomorrah rubbed his back against Rudy's legs.

"I beg of you sinners. It's time to repent." Rudy could feel that cat rubbing against his legs, and tears began flowing down Rudy's cheeks. *It was not the time to have an allergic reaction.*

This has got to be the best sermon I've heard yet. I would give him a 7.5 on delivery, 8.6 on content, and 8.2 on relevancy, Sodom calculated. *He would have given him a higher score on delivery,* but he thought the tears were too melodramatic. Sodom climbed to the top of the organ for a better view.

I never realized he felt that strongly, Silas thought as he watched the tears roll down the minister's cheeks. The entire congregation was now fidgeting in their seats—except for P.C.

Rudy's nose began to itch. He didn't need to start sneezing now; he was about to make his summation. The best part of his sermon was yet to come. He had worked too hard on the closing segment to have it ruined by that stupid cat.

Sodom arrived at the top of the organ only to be met by the glare of a rabid organist.

"There's that horrid little mouse that has been chewing the reeds to my organ," Trudy mumbled through clinched teeth. Taking the hymnal in her right hand, she swatted at the transgressor while her left hand accidentally hit the organ's keyboard forming a perfect "C" chord. P.C., aroused from his meditation, immediately stood up and began singing *Amazing Grace*. The rest of the congregation, wishing to end an unsettling sermon, recognized opportunity when they saw it and quickly joined P.C. in the closing hymn.

"Wait, I'm not done," Rudy protested, but it was too late. The congregation had now been joined by Trudy at the organ. Totally ignored by everyone, Rudy closed his Bible and sat down.

***

This has not been one of my better weeks here in Bear Creek. I sometimes wonder if I am reaching anyone at all. Thursday, the citizens of Bear Creek gathered down by the beaver pond in hopes of seeing a naked lady. Local legend has it that a teenager by the name of Abigail Farnsworth disappeared down by the beaver pond twenty-five years ago. I am not sure I understand all of it, but apparently she is chased naked through the woods by a grizzly bear, and on nights with a full moon, returns to the beaver pond to look for her clothes. I don't know if anyone actually believes this; however, it sets a bad example for the youth of Bear Creek. I addressed the subject in today's sermon, but I don't think it went over well.

I am also at my wit's end with this beaver thing. He is relentless. It is like the story of the hare and the turtle. He never rests and plods along endlessly, sometimes working day and night.

I am now firmly convinced the only reason Noah had a flood was because he left two beavers outside.

On the brighter side, I have had only minimal symptoms from my brain tumor; although, I am starting to get a fever. Yesterday it was up to 98.8, which is a recent all-time high. I expect the early stages of the disease process to be quite subtle and easily overlooked if I am not observant. Rudy closed the cover of his journal and decided to take a nap. His head was throbbing, a subtle reminder of his ever-present brain tumor.

***

The soft sand under the horse's hooves muffled the sounds of the horse and buggy, and the only noise that purloined the silence of the night was the pounding of Frenchie's heart as the buggy converged on the Bare Creek Cafe. The commitment in his heart didn't lessen the anxiety in his stomach. His only source of comfort was that he and Jennifer would soon be off for Green Bay to be married.

Frenchie stopped short of the rear of the building lest a neighing horse accidentally announce his coming. A ten-foot wide alley separated the cafe from the Bare Creek Gazette building. A small candle burned in an open window above the cafe. That would be Jennifer's bedroom. According to Jennifer, there would be a ladder left on the ground next to the cafe. Frenchie was pleased to find it as promised, although some mental calculations concluded it would be three feet short of reaching the window. A fresh wave of anxiety sent shivers through his body. He had come too far to be denied now.

Frenchie found a three by four foot wooden box at the rear of the cafe that contained two barrels of garbage. The box had been built to deny wild creatures the pleasure of its contents. It was just over three feet tall and might provide the extension needed to reach Jennifer's window. Frenchie dragged the box toward Jennifer's window.

The box groaned with any movement, forcing Frenchie to slowly inch the box along its intended course. Even though the street was free of people, Frenchie feared the noise would arouse someone's curiosity.

Frenchie aged several years by the time he positioned the box under Jennifer's window, and he was sure he had the beginning of a good ulcer. He waited in the shadows until convinced that, although the ulcers were real, the townsfolk were still asleep. Climbing up on top of the box, he raised the ladder, placing its base on the box. The top of the ladder reached the window ledge with room to spare; his plan might work after all. Seconds later, Frenchie arrived at Jennifer's window.

"I thought you would never make it," Jennifer whispered as she pulled her lover into her bedroom.

***

"Pa, wake up!" Maggie commanded, but P.C. was a heavy sleeper and his one eye refused to open. "Wake up; someone's breaking into the cafe!" Maggie repeated as she shook her husband.

"Not tonight dear, I have a headache," P.C. mumbled, then rolled over and went back to sleep.

"Pa, I'm serious. Someone's trying to break into the cafe." Maggie shook P.C. more vigorously to press home her point. "I've been hearing noises. Go check it out." Maggie rustled out of bed and lit a kerosene lamp.

Against his better judgment, P.C. crawled out of bed. It was obvious he would get no rest until he went downstairs and checked the cafe. "OK, OK, I'll check it out."

"Take your scatter-gun with you. I don't want you to get hurt." Maggie handed P.C. his double-barreled shotgun that normally hung on the wall.

"If ya don't want me to get hurt, why don't ya let me go back to bed?" P.C. asked as he accepted the shotgun and grabbed some shells from the dresser. "You probably had a bad dream."

P.C. slipped into some slippers and headed toward the stairs. He didn't bother to dress further, feeling his nightcap and full-length, white nightgown would be sufficient attire for this inauspicious occasion. His black patch over the right eye was in stark contrast to the rest of his wardrobe.

With his scattergun in his right hand and a lamp in his left, P.C. checked the rooms of the cafe one by one. He checked the front door and found it locked. He checked the back door. It, too, was locked, but just outside, a horse and buggy patiently awaited its owner.

"Now that's strange," P.C. mumbled to himself as he opened the door to investigate. The horse was still lathered and hadn't been waiting long. He could see nothing missing or out of place behind the cafe. "Wait a minute. Someone stole our garbage cans! That's stooping mighty low."

P.C. set the lamp on the ground. He could clearly see the trail left by the garbage box. Cocking both barrels, P.C. followed the trail until he came upon the box resting under Jennifer's window. A ladder on top of the box extended up to his daughter's window. "The swine is after my daughter!" P.C. growled as he began climbing the ladder.

***

"Quick, I hear someone coming," Jennifer warned Frenchie. "Hide in this closet."

"But I don't want to hide in the closet. Let's get out the window and on our way."

"Don't argue with me." Jennifer shoved Frenchie into her closet.

"Are you OK?" Maggie asked upon entering the room. Maggie raised her lantern for a better view of the bedroom. Her other hand firmly gripped a meat cleaver that she kept in reserve for such occasions. She had learned over the years that a meat cleaver was superior to a two-pronged meat fork. It may not have the range of Pa's scattergun, but it still got everyone's attention. "We heard noises."

"I didn't hear any noises," Jennifer lied. "You must've been dreaming."

"Well, maybe so. Just the same, I have your Pa downstairs checking the cafe to make sure no one's breaking in." Could it have been just a dream, Maggie wondered?

Maggie, feeling reassured, relaxed the grip on her meat cleaver until scraping noises emanating from the window again heightened her vigilance. When the twin barrels of a shotgun protruded through the window, she shifted into combat mode. "They're after my baby!" Maggie raised the meat cleaver and was on her way to decapitate the assailant when a familiar black eye patch followed the shotgun through the window.

"What're you doing out there, Pa?" Maggie asked.

"Someone used a ladder to break into Jennifer's room."

"You must have scared them off," Jennifer suggested. "I didn't see anyone."

"Just the same, I'm checking the entire house." A thorough search under Jennifer's bed revealed some well-entrenched dust bunnies, but no villains. P.C. moved his attention toward the closet.

"Move out of the way," P.C. told Jennifer who was standing defiantly in front of the closet. "I need to check the closet." Jennifer made no attempt to move.

"No one's in there. I would've seen them."

P.C., pushing Jennifer aside, opened the closet door to reveal a cowering Frenchie hiding behind a flimsy, pink negligee.

"It's Frenchie…You pervert!" P.C. stuck the shotgun into Frenchie's ribs.

"What are you doing here?" Maggie wasn't sure she was going to like the answer.

"Want me shoot him, Ma?" P.C. took his best aim at Frenchie, but every time he closed his left eye to sight down the barrel, Frenchie disappeared.

"Don't you dare shoot Frenchie," Jennifer ordered.

"And why not?" P.C. asked while he tried to maneuver around Jennifer for a clean shot.

"Because we're getting married."

"What do you mean you're getting married?" Maggie asked. "You hardly know Frenchie."

"That's not true. We've been seeing each other for over a year."

"With all the time he spends across the street with those Ollies, when did he ever find time for you?"

"That's not true either. He doesn't even know the Ollies. That was my idea. I figured if you thought he was spending his time with the Ollies, you wouldn't suspect he was seeing me. You just don't like Frenchie because he's French and Catholic."

"Well, he is French and Catholic." Maggie couldn't think of a worse combination.

"There's nothing wrong with being Catholic. They're good Christians. No worse than we are. Pa was raised Catholic, and there's nothing wrong with him!"

To say there was nothing wrong with Pa was being charitable, but Maggie had to admit it had nothing to do with being Catholic. She did have a fair number of Catholic friends, and they were good people. Maggie wasn't sure what she had against Catholics, other than the fact she had always placed them on the same level as Democrats. Maggie had a strong opinion on everything and hated to be confused with facts.

"Frenchie and I are leaving for Green Bay where we're getting married. We plan to live in the cabin he built north of town. In the spring we'll plant some potatoes and maybe have a milk cow and some chickens. Nobody is going to stop us from getting married."

"I guess I did see a cabin going up north of town," P.C. said. "Right nice looking cabin too."

Maggie looked at her daughter, now standing defiantly in front of the closet. It was obvious she had no intention of backing down. She was a pillar of strength and determination with a fire in her eyes Maggie had never seen before. Her daughter was in love. It reminded her of another young woman in a logging camp many years ago. She, too, had that same intense fire in her eyes as she defended her man. When they got married, they didn't have any land or cabin. All they had was love, the same intense love her daughter now possessed.

"My mind's made up," Maggie declared, "No daughter of mine is running off to be married by any justice of the peace. If you want to get married, it'll have to be a proper church wedding with a white wedding dress and with your Pa in a tuxedo and the whole works—and that's final."

"Oh Ma, I love you!" Jennifer gave her mother a big hug. There were tears in Jennifer's eyes that freely drained down her checks; there were also tears in Maggie's eyes. In Frenchie's eyes were the twin barrels of a twelve-gauge shotgun.

"Does this mean I don't get to shoot him?" P.C. asked.

"Of course not," Maggie said. "You don't want to shoot your future son-in-law."

P.C. always did like Frenchie, although he wasn't sure about having a son-in-law who cheated at checkers, but then it might be fun to wear a tuxedo. He had never worn a tuxedo. As mayor of Bear Creek, he should have a tuxedo. He could wear it at ribbon cutting ceremonies and other official events.

"Does this mean we're engaged?" Up to this point Frenchie had correctly assumed it had been a private family discussion and his opinion wasn't being solicited.

"It's after one in the morning and no time to be discussing wedding plans," Maggie informed the group. P.C. checked his pocket watch, which confirmed it was a quarter past one.

"I think it's time for everyone to go back to bed. Tomorrow we can make wedding plans," Maggie suggested.

Frenchie headed for the window to make good his escape. The shotgun was making him nervous.

"You may use the front door," Maggie said. "And in the future when you come courting my daughter, I expect you to use the front door like a proper gentleman caller."

"Yes ma'am," Frenchie replied, tipping his hat.

"I'll show him to the door." Grabbing his hand, Jennifer dragged a bewildered Frenchie down the steps toward the front door. As they stepped out of sight of her parents, she wrapped her arm around Frenchie's waist, pulling him against her. They were finally going to get married.

Maggie returned to her bedroom. From the front window, she could see two lovers kissing in the moonlight. It was a prolonged kiss. Yes, her daughter was in love. She had been a beautiful child and now a woman. Maggie had always known she would grow up and leave to start her own family. Still, it was hard to accept.

Maggie placed her trusty meat cleaver on her bed stand and crawled into bed. P.C. was already in bed, having returned his unloaded shotgun back to its rack on the wall. Maggie lay in bed quietly in deep thought for a minute or two before rolling over toward P.C. She placed her arm over his chest and laid her head on his shoulder. After a few more minutes of thought, she whispered into P.C.'s ear, "I love you." But it was too late; P.C. was already asleep.

Chapter Four

Excitement is a rare commodity in Bear Creek, and the news of the local debutante's pending marriage spread quickly. It was a welcome source of fresh gossip, and the merits of the match were discussed in depth at tea parties, afternoon luncheons, and late-night poker games. The Bare Creek Gazette covered the story in great detail with accompanying pictures by the Gazette's ace photographer, Agnes Kronschnabell. Interviews with major participants as well as opinions from the man-on-the-street saturated the front page, pushing the birth of Olie Olsen's five kittens to page two.

No wedding invitations were issued as it was assumed all inhabitants of Bear Creek would not only attend but also participate in the planning—at Maggie and P.C.'s expense of course. Since Jennifer was their only child, expense was not an issue. The wedding reception would consist of an ox roast with potato salad and rolls from the Bare Creek Cafe. If weather permitted and townsfolk weren't too full of potato salad, a friendly softball game might be in order.

As usual Maggie took charge of the fine details like a seasoned general. She ordered a white wedding dress for Jennifer along with tuxedos for P.C. and Frenchie. A robin's-egg blue dress was currently under consideration for herself. This would be the wedding Maggie never had; nothing would be left to chance.

Unfortunately, major military campaigns cannot obtain favorable objectives based solely on the skill and expertise of generals, and there comes a time when generals must place their faith in their lieutenants. General Maggie, therefore, called a meeting of the Taylor family's voting members to secure any loose ends. Since Frenchie was technically still on probation and not a true member, his presence wasn't encouraged.

As with most of the Taylor family meetings, it was held over breakfast after the routine breakfast trade had come and gone. Sandwiched between breakfast and lunch, this was a quiet time at the Bare Creek Cafe. P.C. was eating his usual two fried eggs with hash browns and toast. Per his tradition, he ruptured one of the egg yolks, allowing the yellow fluid to flow out lava-style, which was then dammed up with a barricade of hash browns. Only after P.C. had exhausted all avenues of entertainment was the meal consumed. P.C. detested family meetings, preferring a good checker game over at the Hardware and Feed Store. He was three dollars behind, for the week, and hoped to get even with Frenchie before the weekend. Maggie and Jennifer were discussing wedding dresses, and it was obvious his opinion wouldn't be in great demand.

"Pa, what do you think of this robin's-egg blue dress?" Maggie asked as she held up a picture in the Sears and Roebuck catalogue, but then didn't wait for a reply.

"I think it would look good on you," Jennifer answered for P.C.

"Then that's the one I'll order."

"What about the food for the reception?" P.C. was always more concerned with practical aspects of life.

"We're having potato salad, homemade rolls, and the meat from the ox roast," Maggie replied.

"And we'll need lots of lemonade." Jennifer was partial to lemonade in the summertime.

"I've talked to the Ladies Aid Society," Maggie said. "They'll peel potatoes and make dough for the rolls, but the men will have to be in charge of the ox roast." Delegating this responsibility to the men was a major, but necessary, concession. In Bear Creek, it was an insult to suggest a member of the male sex ply his culinary skills inside a kitchen, but an outside barbecue or ox roast was a man's exclusive domain, and no self-respecting female would dare suggest otherwise.

"Roasting the ox won't be a problem." With a couple stabs from his fork, P.C. put the two eggs out of misery.

"I don't want you and Red Weasel doing it," Maggie said. "Get Mel, Silas, or some of the other men to be in charge. It'll take a good twenty-four hours to roast the ox. That's a lot of work."

"And no alcohol," Jennifer demanded. "I don't want my wedding ruined by a bunch of inebriated men."

"Alcohol's illegal. I wouldn't think of having alcohol," P.C. said with his fingers crossed under the table.

"We'll make sure the men have lots of lemonade," Maggie suggested. "It'll be hot work keeping the fire going."

***

Chief Red Weasel's head rested against his backpack as he lay at the end of his dock. A length of fishing line linked his cane pole to the bobber floating on the lake's surface. Two perch had tested the line and found it sturdy, but received immediate pardons from the Chief and were released unharmed. The hook was returned to the water bare lest another fish disturb Weasel's meditation.

Fishing wasn't on the day's agenda, but it did pass the time while he waited for his friend, the mayor. They were to meet at precisely eight o'clock, this being only a formality, since Weasel didn't own a watch, and P.C.'s pocket watch always registered a quarter past one. P.C. would arrive when he arrived, and that was fine with Weasel. Basking in the morning sun wasn't an unpleasant task, except for the sun's annoying glare. A broad-brimmed, black hat placed low over the forehead provided some relief.

"Morning, Chief."

Weasel lifted the hat from his face and looked up at the Mayor. A large burlap bag of corn was perched on P.C.'s right shoulder. "Morning, Mayor."

Without further conversation, the two men climbed into a fourteen-foot, wooden rowboat and began rowing across the lake, the bag of corn safely stowed in the bow. Except for the groaning of the oarlocks, the lake was silent as Weasel rowed the boat toward a small peninsula jutting out from the far side of the lake. P.C., sitting at the rear of the boat, dangled his hands in the water, creating small whirlpools, which slowly dissipated behind the boat.

It took fifteen minutes to reach the far side, where a hundred-yard hike led them to a clearing. P.C. set the bag of corn inside a large lean-to.

"This batch looks about ready," P.C. said as he checked a vat of foul-smelling broth. Weasel nodded in agreement.

Since the vat was too heavy to carry, the liquid was ladled out with wooden buckets and poured into an old converted boiler. A small fire under the boiler sent alcoholic fumes spiraling through copper tubing, where it condensed into an earthenware jug. P.C. took a nip of the sweet nectar to confirm what he already knew. His eyes began to water as the wave of irritation oozed down the esophagus.

"Not bad," P.C. said. He would have offered some to Weasel, but he knew the Chief wouldn't indulge. In his youth, Weasel had imbibed more than his share of spirits, some say to excess; but he had made a promise to his wife that he would give up alcohol. A promise is a promise, and Weasel hadn't touched alcohol for over twenty years; Weasel was an honorable man. This didn't mean he couldn't help a friend. After all, what are friends for?

The entire operation took less than three hours. A new batch of yeast and corn was added to the vat, and three large jugs of corn whiskey were tucked into the front of the rowboat. Weasel again took command of the oars and the small craft lurched out into the lake, heading toward the dock in front of the Moose Lake Lodge.

"I hear Jennifer is getting married," Weasel said after several minutes of deep thought.

"That's a fact."

"On July 4th?"

"Yep, it seems strange to have a man lose his independence on Independence Day."

"That's not far off."

"Little over a week."

"They grow up fast. She's been like a niece to Water Lily and me," Weasel said. "We'll need to get her something."

"Ollie Olson, down at the livery stable, has a good plow horse I have half a mind to buy them," P.C. said. "They'll need a good plow horse, if they expect to do some farming."

"That they will," Weasel said. "You know that small buckboard wagon I got back at the lodge? Never use it anymore. A good horse could easily pull it. It would take a little fixin', but a coat of red paint would make it look right pretty."

"I believe it would."

"I think I might just fix that wagon up and give it to them," the Chief decided.

"That'll make a mighty fine gift. Haven't told Ma yet. Maybe we could get a horse and wagon together and surprise our wives too."

***

Normally the Economics Club of Bare Creek met for meaningful discussions about politics, local events, and the weather, as opposed to the gossip sessions of the Ladies Aid Society, but today the meeting had been called to order for more important business.

"As you all know, Frenchie and Jennifer are getting hitched in a few days," Mel said, "and we've been given the responsibility for roasting the ox."

"Never roasted an ox before," Silas said as he lit his pipe. He could think better with a pipe to chew on.

"Seen it done once in Cuba," Mel offered. "I was with the Roughriders, and we were 'bout to storm San Juan Hill when..."

"How'd ya roast the ox?" Silas interjected in an effort to cut off the entire rendition of how Mel and Teddy Roosevelt single handedly won the Spanish American War.

"Oh, the cooks ran a rod through the ox and rotated the meat over a fire. It took the better part of a day."

"We might be able to do that." Silas took a drag on his pipe. "I have an eight-foot rod left over from that old printing press. It might work." Silas continued puffing on his pipe. It was a known fact that the rate of puffing on his pipe was directly proportional to the depth of Silas's thought. Silas was, by far, the smartest of the group, and the only one with a college education. When he was in deep thought, the rest waited patiently for his forthcoming wisdom. "I have some left-over gears we can use." Silas's head became obscured by smoke. "Yes, I'm sure it'll work, but we'll need to monitor the fire throughout the night."

"We can do that," Mel said. "We'll work in shifts."

"It'll take a lot of firewood."

"Weasel and I'll cut the firewood," P.C. offered. "Since the fire going be hot, I suggest we also provide some spirits to keep the men's spirits up."

"Can't be too obvious about the alcohol," Silas warned. "Don't want anyone getting drunk."

"Ma's providing lemonade for the people roasting the ox. Maybe we can add a little bite to the lemonade."

"Do we have any alcohol?" Mel asked. "I haven't been able to get any shipments up from Milwaukee for two weeks. Some federal guy by the name of Ness has dried up Chicago. All of the bootleg liquor in Milwaukee is heading south."

"No problem," P.C. informed the group. "Chief and I have a still producing eighty-proof corn whiskey. That'll mix nicely with the lemonade."

"Sounds good," Silas said. "If there's no further business, meeting adjourned."

***

"We have four days before the wedding," Maggie said as she opened the special meeting of the Ladies Aid Society. "We still have lots of work to do." Maggie paused to sip her tea. "Most of the work will have to wait until the day of the wedding. We'll need potato peelers and help making the dinner rolls. I'm hoping some of you can bake rolls in your own ovens."

"You can count on us," Trudy said. "We'll make the rolls."

"The potatoes we can peel ahead of time," Agnes said. "I'll be busy taking pictures for the Gazette, but the day before the wedding, I'm all yours."

"I appreciate all your help. I don't know how we would do it without your assistance," Maggie told the ladies.

"I hope we can count on the men," Trudy said. "They're not the greatest cooks."

"Silas put together a rotisserie. It should work," Agnes said, "as long as they stay sober." Memories of previous disasters flashed through her mind.

"That's not the problem it used to be," Trudy told the girls. "If what I heard is correct, the men have been smuggling alcohol in from Milwaukee on Mel's freight wagons, but that source is drying up. This federal guy has shut down the breweries in Chicago, and all the alcohol in Milwaukee is going south."

"I heard they have a still somewhere in the woods," one of the ladies said.

"Mel did order a coil of copper tubing awhile back," Trudy said. "I wondered at the time why anyone would want copper tubing."

"Either way, we can't let our guard down," Maggie warned the girls. "The cafe will be providing lemonade. We need to make sure they don't drink anything else." Maggie rechecked her list of agenda items. "I guess that's all for this meeting. Meeting adjourned."

***

"Good afternoon, Mel," P.C. said as he entered the Bare Creek Hardware and Feed store. "Can ya sell me a harness for a horse?"

"What in blazes do ya need that for? You don't even own a horse."

"Buying a plow horse for the newlyweds," P.C. replied. "Chief Red Weasel's giving them a wagon, but we don't have a harness."

"That's right nice of you two. You know that horse is goin' need some corn or oats during the winter," Mel said. "Tell you what I'll do. You back the wagon up to the loading dock the night before the wedding, and I'll fill it with corn and oats. That'll be my wedding gift."

P.C. paid for the harness and stuffed it under his shirt. He didn't want Maggie to see it before the wedding.

***

The third of July was hot and humid, at least by Yooper standards. But the sweat on the brows failed to dampen the enthusiasm of the Bear Creek citizens as they prepared for the wedding. Rudy run the participants through the ceremony several times to ensure there would be no snags or confusion during the wedding. It would be Rudy's first wedding in Bear Creek; he didn't wish to have any mishaps. After several counseling sessions with the young couple, Rudy was satisfied they were indeed in love and the marriage had a strong chance of survival. Frenchie had officially joined the Methodist Church. Rudy pointed out that Frenchie wasn't changing religions, since both Catholics and Protestants were members of the same Christian community. Rudy took pride in his ecumenicalism.

Outside the church, men constructed tables and benches, while women sat in circles gossiping as they peeled potatoes. The men began roasting the ox early in the morning. The steer had been skewered by an eight-foot iron rod and placed over a trench of hot coals. One end of the rod was attached to a set of gears and pulleys, which rotated the steer every two minutes. A large rock, hanging from a pulley at the top of a sixteen-foot tripod, provided power for the rotisserie. Every five minutes the rock had to be cranked back up to the top. It was hot work, but, with plenty of lemonade, there was no shortage of volunteers. Men lingered around the fire pit just to sip the lemonade. A large stack of firewood ensured a continuous fire.

***

P.C. and Weasel pushed the wagon up against the loading dock by hand; they wouldn't pick up the plow horse until the following morning.

"Nice wagon," Mel said from his viewpoint on the loading dock. The bright red wagon with black wheels and spokes set a pretty picture. "That'll be a handy wagon for a farmer."

"It's old, but sturdy," Weasel said with pride.

"Help me load the corn and oats," Mel said. He grabbed a burlap bag filled with corn and tossed it onto the wagon. He was joined by P.C. and Weasel; and, within five minutes, the wagon bed was overflowing with corn and oats. "We should cover it with a tarp in case it rains." The sky was clear, but who was to take chances. A large tarp was placed over the pile of grain.

"Can we leave the wagon here until tomorrow?" P.C. asked. He didn't relish the thought of moving the loaded wagon by hand.

"No problem, leave it as long as you wish."

***

It had been a long, tiring day for the inhabitants of Bear Creek, and most of the community welcomed the coming of dusk and the excuse to crawl into bed. Tomorrow would be an even bigger day. The town was exceedingly quiet except for the men at the roasting pit. They were unusually cheerful as they sipped on their lemonade.

Behind the Bare Creek Hardware and Feed store, only starlight penetrated the darkness. Critter peered into that darkness to ensure the area was safe before stepping into the alley. She would have been invisible if it weren't for the white stripe down her back. Critter wandered across the alley searching for stray kernels of corn. She was in a family way and needed the grain to nourish the growing young inside her belly. The most productive area would be the loading dock, but sometimes she found grain in the alley. She was in no hurry. Critter's meandering path eventually led to the top of the ramp, where she found a few kernels of corn. There were no piles of spilled grain, but it was nourishment just the same. She checked the corner of the loading dock, finding empty sacks, but nothing edible. She waddled toward the center of the dock and slipped under a canvas tarp that covered a pile of swollen burlap bags. Perhaps they contained food. She chewed a hole in one of the bags, which released a steady flow of golden corn. Bingo! She checked another bag; it was filled with oats. "Supper is served." Critter ate her fill and then some, until the pain in her belly confirmed she had made a glutton of herself. What Critter needed now was a nap. Critter found a good spot in the crevice between bags of corn. Sleep came quickly.

***

The morning of July 4th arrived with a bang, as kids with too many firecrackers and not enough supervision took over the town, not that anyone really wanted to sleep in on such an important day. The aroma from the ox roast flowed through the town filling every nostril with its fragrant smell. The wedding wasn't scheduled until one o'clock, but there was still work to be done. The men tending the ox survived the night. Most of them had relaxed smiles on their faces, but true to their word, none had over indulged in the lemonade. They now looked forward to a few hours sleep when relieved by the next shift.

As was to be expected, the Taylor household was filled with organized chaos. Maggie, with the help of Weasel's wife, Water Lily, sequestered Jennifer in her bedroom as she prepared to don her wedding dress. Tradition dictated that the groom not see the wedding dress prior to the wedding. Since he was safely tucked away in his cabin two miles north of town, the women decided to ostracize P.C. in lieu of the groom. That was fine with P.C. He had enough problems of his own trying to assemble his tuxedo. There were too many parts and insufficient directions. After several false starts, he managed to get the cufflinks and cummerbund in their proper anatomical locations. The bow tie was tied in a knot, which vaguely resembled a bow. After studying it in the mirror, P.C. proclaimed it good enough. The black tuxedo went nicely with his eye patch. Maybe he should have bought a tuxedo instead of renting one. A mayor should have a tuxedo for all those ribbon-cutting ceremonies. P.C would have spent more time in front of the mirror, but he had promised to meet Weasel at the Hardware and Feed store. After harnessing the horse up to the wagon, they would drive out to Frenchie's cabin and surprise him.

Weasel was waiting behind the Hardware and Feed Store when P.C. arrived. He was sporting two feathers in his headband as well as buckskin pants and all the other regalia of an Indian Chief. It was obvious P.C. felt better in his tuxedo than Weasel did in his Indian garb. Weasel preferred jeans and flannel shirts.

"Morning, Mayor."

"Morning, Chief." P.C. looked at his pocket watch. It was quarter past one, time to get going. "Shall we hitch up the horse and head out to Frenchie's place?" It was a rhetorical question; no answer was expected. "I named the horse, Charlie. I suppose Frenchie can name him something else if he has a mind to." Charlie was wearing a large straw hat with holes cut out for his big floppy ears. It took the better part of five minutes to properly attach the harness. Charlie was less than cooperative and eyed the heavy wagon with suspicion. Cooperation was finally obtained after a bribe of some sweet molasses, sugar candy.

"We need to tie down the tarp," Weasel said.

After the tarp was securely tied down, the two heads of state climbed onto the wagon and urged the horse north. Heads were held high as Weasel in his ceremonial Indian dress and P.C. in his tuxedo with stovepipe hat drove through town in the bright red wagon.

Frenchie's cabin was two miles north of town on a dirt road filled with ruts and erosions. It made for a bumpy ride. Fortunately, the seat, which was suspended on the side of a "U" shaped piece of spring steel, absorbed most of the punishment. The sacks of feed in the back, however, bounced with every bump in the road. On some sections, the large ruts would bring the wagon to a complete stop. Only after P.C. bribed Charlie with additional molasses candy were they able to proceed. P.C. wasn't sure if it was his imagination, but Charlie appeared to be stopping at smaller and smaller ruts. Fortunately, P.C. had a bag full of the candies.

***

Human voices woke Critter from a deep sleep, but she was safely secured in the crevasse between two feedbags. There was no cause for alarm. Critter returned to sleep. At least she tried to sleep. Her bed began to vibrate. Sharp jolts periodically bounced her off the feedbag. "Maybe it's time to mosey out of here." Critter waddled toward the edge of the canvas tarp, bouncing against the sides of feedbags with each bump. She tried to slide her nose under the edge of the tarp, but the tarp was lashed down. "What the..." She tried another edge. This, too, was tightly bound. She was trapped. Critter was not a happy critter. The deteriorating situation didn't help her disposition, and she was rapidly developing an attitude. "Someone will pay for this!"

***

The church grounds were bustling with activity as townsfolk completed last minute tasks. Long rows of picnic tables awaited the banquet meal. Large jugs of lemonade were scattered among the tables for those who might develop an early thirst. Over at the fire pit, a fresh crew had relieved the night shift. The ox was about to be proclaimed done, and the sweet aroma filled the air, drawing many spectators to the fire pit.

"It sure smells good," Mrs. Olson told the men. Mrs. Olson was one of the best cooks in town, and the compliment wasn't taken lightly. "It must be hot work." Mrs. Olson noted the grease dripping off the carcass and splattering on the hot coals below. "I can see where you can develop a powerful thirst," Mrs. Olson said, pouring herself a large glass of lemonade.

"Wouldn't you prefer lemonade from one of the tables?" Silas asked. "It's colder."

"Mm, this is good lemonade," she said, pouring another glass.

***

Charlie had consumed most of the molasses candies by the time P.C. and Weasel arrived at Frenchie's Cabin. Hopefully, there were enough left for the return trip, but that would be Frenchie's problem. On the return trip, Charlie would be Frenchie's horse. P.C. pulled back on the reins, bringing the wagon to a stop. Charlie was happy to oblige.

"Hey Frenchie. You ready to get married?"

"I will be once I figure out this monkey suit," Frenchie replied. Frenchie was sitting on his porch swing looking dejected. Obviously, weddings were more fun for brides. His cummerbund was wrapped around his tuxedo coat like a belt, and the black bow tie was stuffed in his shirt pocket as a lost cause. The tuxedo had far too many parts.

"We thought we would stop by and see if you needed a ride into town."

"Wouldn't mind a ride at that." Momentarily forgetting his sartorial dilemma, Frenchie walked over and inspected the wagon. "Didn't know you owned a horse and wagon."

"I don't, but you do," P.C. replied. "It's a wedding gift, the horse from me and the wagon from Chief Red Weasel."

"Well, I'll be..." Frenchie checked out the wagon in more detail and found it sturdy. The horse appeared to be about four years old and still in its prime. "I don't know how to thank you," Frenchie said as he shook their hands.

"The horse's name is Charlie, but you can change it if you have a mind to."

"Charlie sounds like a fine name to me" Frenchie examined the horse's head; he had good teeth. Charlie, unimpressed by the attention, looked around for a shade tree. He had no desire to stand in the hot sun. He also found the straw hat, which was strapped to his head by a bright red ribbon, particularly irritating, definitely not appropriate for a horse of his stature.

"He's partial to molasses candies. Try giving him one of these." P.C. tossed Frenchie a candy.

Frenchie caught the candy and offered it to Charlie, who decided that, for molasses candy, he could overlook the stupid hat. "It's a nice horse—and a beautiful wagon." Frenchie walked around the horse and wagon a second time.

"Stick these in your pocket. He'll do anything for these." P.C. threw the sack of candies to Frenchie, who placed them in his pocket.

"This'll come in handy at harvest time."

"If you want to get married, we need to be going," Weasel said. "We should unload the wagon first."

"Help me untie the tarp. You won't believe what's under here," P.C. said as the three men flipped back the tarp.

***

Jennifer and her entourage arrived at the church an hour early to allow time for last minute details. Since the room below the bell tower was at the back of the sanctuary, it was the perfect departure point for Jennifer's walk down the aisle. The church trustees had evicted the pigeons the previous week, and a screen of chicken wire prevented their return, creating a clean room below. Maggie immediately took command of the room and posted guards at the door: no men allowed, thank you. Since Maggie, as mother of the bride, would be sitting in the front row, Water Lily volunteered to help the bride start her walk down the aisle. Jennifer would carry a bride's bouquet of daisies, mums, and other flowers collected from the village flower gardens.

Outside the church, preparations continued. Women were cutting cooked potatoes for the potato salad and ovens throughout the town were baking large quantities of fresh dinner rolls. Over at the roasting pit, men were allowing the coals to run their course. No new wood was being added; although, fat dripping off the meat continued to fuel the fire. The aroma emanating from the ox was enough to convert even the most skeptic doubters. Compliments flowed freely.

"It sure smells good. I must say you men have done an excellent job," Mrs. Olson told the men. "Mighty hot work too. I know it's making me woozy, probably dehydration. Maybe I will have some more of that lemonade." Mrs. Olson staggered toward the jug of lemonade.

"Maybe you should go easy on the lemonade," one of the men warned her.

"Nonsense, I'm just dehydrated," Mrs. Olson replied, pouring another glass. "I don't feel so good."

"The wedding's about to start. Why don't you go into the church and sit down?" With a man at each elbow, Mrs. Olson was guided toward the church.

***

Maggie opened the door a crack and peered into the sanctuary; the church was filling up. A couple of men were ushering Mrs. Olson to one of the few remaining seats. That was nice of them, she thought. Everything was running like clockwork. Maggie looked at her watch. Fifteen minutes until show time.

"Is everyone ready?" Rudy asked as he entered the room.

"I think so," Maggie replied.

"Is Frenchie as nervous as I am?" Jennifer asked the minister.

"I don't know. Haven't seen him yet."

"He should have been here twenty minutes ago," Maggie said. "Have you seen Pa?"

"Haven't seen him either," Rudy confessed.

"What about Uncle Weasel?" Jennifer asked. "Where's he?"

"Let's not get upset," Maggie said. "We don't know for sure that they are together. They still might get here on time."

Jennifer didn't have any true relatives in the area, but Red Weasel and Water Lily were as close to an aunt and uncle as she would ever have. They had known Maggie and P.C. from the logging camp years and had watched Jennifer grow into womanhood. It was Weasel who had taught her to swim at the Moose Lake Lodge. It was Weasel who taught her how to find her way through the woods and how to live off the land. Jennifer could shoot a gun as well as any man and was prepared to skin a deer if needed. At this moment, she was prepared to skin both Pa and Weasel. "How could you allow the two of them to get together without adult supervision?"

***

The church grounds were deserted when Charlie arrived with the three musketeers in tow. Long rows of tables covered with potato salad, dinner rolls and jugs of lemonade eagerly awaited the banquet feast.

"Looks like everyone is inside," Frenchie said.

"Why don't you two go inside while I tie up the horse?" P.C. suggested.

P.C. unhitched Charlie as Frenchie and Weasel headed toward the church but found a scarcity of secure objects to which a horse could be anchored. He finally settled on a small post that had been hastily placed into the ground. A pair of longneck geese, obviously a wedding gift, was tethered to the pole. P.C. figured Charlie could defend himself against the geese. After ensuring Charlie was comfortable, P.C. headed toward the church.

***

Maggie opened the door a crack to view the sanctuary. It was almost full. She could see Red Weasel on the far left of the aisle. If he was here, P.C. couldn't be far off. Despite the crowded sanctuary, the seats around Weasel were vacant. Maggie knew there was racial prejudice in the community, but it had no place in her church. Weasel was sitting tall and proud in his best Indian dress, ignoring those around him.

"Weasel is here," Maggie told Water Lily. "How did you get him to dress up?"

"It wasn't easy," Water Lily replied. "If it were anyone other than Jennifer, I don't think he would have. You know how he likes his jeans."

"Where's Pa?" Jennifer asked. "We should have started five minutes ago."

Maggie was about to send someone looking for P.C. when he walked through the door. "Are you ladies ready?"

"Ugh, you stink." The assessment was unanimous.

"Minor accident at Frenchie's cabin. You'll get used to it after a while."

"Frenchie stinks too?" Jennifer asked.

"Not too bad," P.C. replied. Jennifer wasn't reassured.

"Is that why no one is sitting next to Weasel?" Maggie asked.

"Could be. He's a bit ripe."

"We need to get started," Maggie said. "I'm going in to sit down. They'll sing a hymn, and then Trudy will play the wedding march. That's your cue to walk Jennifer down the aisle."

"I'll make sure they start off at the right time," Water Lily said.

Rudy nodded at Trudy at the keyboard when Maggie took her seat in the front row, and a melodic rendition of *Rock of Ages* began flowing from the organ. Trudy now had to vocally simulate both high "C" and "F$^\#$." Apparently, the church mouse had destroyed another reed. Rudy stood up and joined the congregation singing the hymn.

At the close of the hymn, Rudy nodded at Frenchie, who was peering through a peephole in the choir room door. This was Frenchie's cue to enter the sanctuary. The essence of skunk assaulted Rudy's nostrils seconds before Frenchie assumed his position in front of the minister. It was enough to bring tears to his eyes. Rudy gave a nod toward the back of the church and P.C. in his tuxedo and Jennifer in a long white wedding dress began their walk down the aisle. It was like the parting of the Red Sea as the congregation leaned away from the aisle when P.C. walked past.

"Is this a double wedding?" Mrs. Olson wondered. Two couples were walking down the aisle. "I don't feel well. I need to get out of here," Mrs. Olson mumbled, but no one was listening.

"We are gathered here today to join the lives of two people in holy matrimony. Who gives this woman to be wed?"

"I do," P.C. replied before taking his seat next to Maggie.

The church was beginning to spin. "I gotta get out of here," Mrs. Olson whispered to no one in particular.

Agnes flipped the black shawl over her head and peered through the camera. She would only get one picture, and that she would reserve for the couple kissing at the end. They appeared in focus. It was a little dark in the sanctuary; she would need a flash. From past experience, she had found it is best to use moderation in the amount of flash powder.

"The scripture lesson for today is taken from Genesis 2:18-24: *And the Lord God said, It is not good that the man should be alone, I will make him a helpmate for him. And out of the ground the Lord God formed every beast of the field, and every fowl of the air: and brought them unto Adam to see what he would call them: and whatsoever Adam called every living creature, that was the name thereof. And Adam gave names to all cattle, and to the fowl of the air, and to every beast of the field; but for Adam there was not found a helpmate for him. And the Lord God caused a deep sleep to fall upon Adam and he slept: and he took one of his ribs, and closed up the flesh instead thereof; And the rib, which the Lord God had taken from man, made he a woman, and brought her unto the man. And Adam said, This is now bone of my bones, and flesh of my flesh: she shall be called Woman, because she was taken out of Man. Therefore, shall a man leave his father and his mother, and shall cleave unto his wife: and they shall be one flesh.*

"This completes the reading of the scriptures." Rudy closed the Bible and returned it to its place on the altar.

"Do you, Frenchie, take this woman to be your lawfully wedded wife, to honor and cherish, until death do you part?"

"I do."

"Something is definitely wrong," Mrs. Olson mumbled. Her stomach was getting queasy. "I need to get out of here."

"Do you, Jennifer, take this man to be your lawfully wedded husband, to honor and obey, until death do you part?"

"I do." Jennifer had issues with the honor and obey part; she would address that portion of the vows with Frenchie later.

***

Being tied to a post wasn't Charlie's idea of a good time. If there was a party going on, he needed to participate. Spending time with those longneck geese was like having front row seats in the wallflower section of the prom. Charlie pulled on the rope and felt a give. Another tug pulled the pole from the ground. "Let's check out the goodies at the table," Charlie told the geese. Charlie dragged the geese and post toward the tables

Stopping at one of the tables, Charlie sampled the potato salad. "Little too much mayo," Charlie decided. "It could use a bit more mustard." He checked out the dinner rolls and found them to his satisfaction. What he really wanted was more of those molasses candies. If he remembered right, that guy with the funny accent had a bag full in his pocket. Charlie headed toward the church with post and geese in tow.

The church door had been left open for ventilation. That was convenient; Charlie had trouble with doors. He stuck his head inside the doorway. "There he is," Charlie told the geese. That's him at the end of the aisle." Charlie started down the aisle, dragging the two squawking geese behind him.

"There's a horse in the church...I am not a well woman. I have to get out of here," Mrs. Olson mumbled when Charlie walked past her pew.

"Is there anyone who knows any reason why these two individuals should not be married? If so, speak up now or forever hold your peace."

Mrs. Olson slowly stood up. "I have to..."

The entire congregation turned toward Mrs. Olson, who was staring at Frenchie and Jennifer with glazed eyes.

That was just a rhetorical question. No one ever answered that in any of Rudy's other weddings. Maybe she didn't understand, Rudy thought. "Is there anyone who knows of any reason why these two individuals should not be married? If so, speak up now or forever hold your peace."

"I have to..." Mrs. Olson repeated. Then she slowly sat down only to slither onto the floor.

"She just needs some air," Silas said as he pulled her out by her shoulders. With Mel carrying her legs, Mrs. Olson was whisked from the church.

Rudy would have waited until Mrs. Olson was removed from the church before proceeding, but a plow horse was bearing down on the wedding party. He decided to speed up the service. "You may place the ring on Jennifer's finger." Frenchie removed the ring from his pocket and slipped it over Jennifer's ring finger.

By the time Charlie reached the front of the church, the geese had broken loose from their tethers and were flying low over the pews. Two boys gave chase, feeling it was their patriotic duty to apprehend the feathered fugitives. Charlie gave Frenchie a nudge, hoping for some candy, but Frenchie did his best to ignore him. "These don't look bad," Charlie decided as he munched on the bridal bouquet.

"You may kiss the bride, and I now pronounce you man and wife."

A subdued flash of light confirmed that the kiss had been immortalized on film. The flash of light and the pronouncement of husband and wife were taken as cues to evacuate the church, and the attendees ran for any available exit—they could only hold their breath so long. A class of school kids getting out for summer vacation couldn't have evacuated the building faster. Within seconds, only the wedding party remained. The wholesome odor of horse sweat freely mingled with the essence of skunk.

"Get that beast out of here," Jennifer yelled at Frenchie.

A bit testy, are we, Charlie thought? Hardly a proper attitude for the three of us to start a marriage.

Frenchie did his best to remove the horse. Unfortunately, horses don't do well in reverse, and there was insufficient room to turn around in the aisle.

Rudy could feel his brain tumor starting to flare up. He had the beginning of a nasty headache. "We need to fill out the wedding license before this is legal," Rudy informed the group. "What's Frenchie's real name?"

P.C. looked at Maggie. Maggie looked at P.C. Maggie and P.C. looked at Jennifer.

Jennifer shrugged her shoulders. "I don't know. I've always called him Frenchie. Hey, Frenchie, what's your name?"

"Claude Pierre D'Artagnan," he replied.

"I'm a D'Artagnan?" Jennifer hoped she pronounced it correctly. She had assumed she would be Mrs. Frenchie.

***

It felt good to be out of the church. Maybe the fresh air would help his headache, Rudy hoped. The ushers left the doors and windows open to remove the stench, although Rudy assumed it would take several days to remove all traces of skunk. That had to be the worst wedding he had ever conducted. But the Yoopers took it in stride, as if having a plow horse munching on the bridal flowers during the wedding kiss is a normal event. Rudy checked on Mrs. Olson, but she was napping under an oak tree. She probably needs the rest, he decided.

"Reverend Hooper, did you get something to eat?" It was the Widow Watson. She was always concerned about his nutritional welfare.

"Not yet, I just finished filling out the marriage certificate."

"Let me help you get some food." The Widow Watson grabbed Rudy's elbow and ushered him toward the tables where she retrieved two plates, one for her and one for Rudy. "Here, you'll need a roll," she told the minister. "And some potato salad."

Rudy felt qualified to carry his own plate, but that was not one of the options. He passively followed the widow's directions.

"The meat is over by the fire pit." The Widow Watson led Rudy toward the ox.

The aroma from the ox was enough to make Rudy's mouth water. He had been unaware of his hungry until the succulent odor overwhelmed his olfactory senses. Silas, wearing a large white apron, was carving the roast to the specifications of the hungry guests.

"A little roast beef?" he asked the couple.

"Put a little on each plate," Alice replied before Rudy could respond.

"Want a little more?" Silas asked as he placed a couple juicy pieces on each plate.

"Give the Reverend a little more." With plates full, the Widow Watson led her hostage toward a couple of empty seats. "We can sit here," she informed the parson.

"This roast beef is excellent," Rudy declared after smothering it with the Bare Creek Cafe's special barbecue sauce. Rudy had a fondness for good roast beef. The potato salad wasn't bad either.

"I understand the wedding couple is planning to visit the Tahquamenon Falls on their honeymoon, now that they have a horse and wagon," Alice said. Rudy had never been to the Tahquamenon Falls, but he had heard it was the second largest falls east of the Mississippi.

"That'll be a nice trip," Rudy said. "It's a nice looking wagon. Someday those wagons will be replaced by motorcars like in the big cities."

"I think they're getting ready to leave. Do you have any rice?" The Widow Watson handed Rudy a bag of rice before he had an opportunity to reply.

Jennifer carefully climbed onto the wagon seat, not wanting to rip her white wedding dress. Jennifer was no stranger to horses and could drive a team as well as any man. Managing an arrogant plow horse, would be a snap. In her right hand was a willow switch, which she felt was better than molasses candy when motivating a horse. Frenchie was confined to the back of the wagon where he would remain until he could be cleaned up and deodorized.

"Try washing him up with tomatoes," Maggie yelled up at Jennifer. "That'll remove most of the odor."

"Giddy up, horse," Jennifer commanded. The command was punctuated by a light tap of the switch.

"The name's Charlie," Charlie mumbled. Charlie lurched forward, pulling the wagon through a gauntlet of flying rice. It was the beginning of Frenchie, Jennifer, and Charlie's honeymoon.

***

Rudy sat at his kitchen table staring at his journal, which was illuminated by the light of his kerosene lamp. He could postpone documenting the previous day's wedding no longer.

On July fourth, I had the honor of uniting Jennifer Taylor and Claude Pierre D'Artagnan in holy matrimony. It was my first wedding here in Bear Creek. I would like to say it was uneventful, but that wouldn't be entirely true.

Rudy looked down at his copy of the *Bare Creek Gazette*. Silas must have worked all night to get the story out the next day. The wedding and reception had been a major event in the life of Bear Creek. There was a good picture on the front page of Jennifer kissing Frenchie. Unfortunately, Frenchie's face was partially obscured by Charlie's hat. Jennifer held a bouquet of flower stems in her left hand. In the background, one of the Maki boys could be seen chasing a white goose. No one would believe this, Rudy decided. Perhaps this should be left out of his journal.

During the service, Mrs. Olson passed out and had to be removed by a couple of men. Apparently, she had a stomach flu, as I understand she vomited quite a bit after she was carried out of the church. She felt much better after she slept several hours. This was too bad since she missed the best part of the reception.

Some of the men roasted an entire ox over open coals. Actually, it tasted quite good. After the dinner, we had a softball game with the merchants against the farmers. They must have thought I would be impartial since they let me be the umpire. The game was called after the third inning when P.C. Taylor hit a foul ball into the roasting pit's hot coals with the town's only softball. In the evening someone broke out a fiddle, and people danced most of the night.

I left early since I had a relapse of my brain tumor and developed a severe headache. I had hoped it was in remission. I don't know how much longer I have before I am totally incapacitated.

Rudy closed his journal and went to bed.

Chapter Five

Rudy's headache resolved during the night. Perhaps the tumor was still in its infancy, or was that wishful thinking. As per his custom, Rudy reached for the thermometer on his nightstand and placed it under his tongue. Now that the headache was gone, he did feel better. A normal temperature would be reassuring. He could use some good news. After remaining in bed the required three minutes, Rudy removed the thermometer and noted the temperature at 98.6. Yes, it would be a good day.

Rudy sat up on the edge of his bed, his eyes still closed, and his mind still clouded with sleep. For Rudy, waking up was a gradual process that couldn't be rushed. He found the cool water swirling around his feet particularly refreshing. He wiggled his toes and the water responded with gurgling noises. Water?...Rudy opened his eyes and tried to focus on the floor at his feet. The small ripples surrounding his feet gradually came into focus. The fog of sleep immediately dissipated, revealing a bedroom flooded with eight inches of water. In the center of the room, a bullfrog was causally doing the breaststroke, as it headed across the room.

"LUUTHEERR!"

"I'm going kill that beaver." Rudy waded out to the front porch and found the sun gleaming off a vast lake. Perched on Rudy's porch swing, a painted turtle was absorbing some of the sun's early rays. Rudy could feel the return of his brain tumor; his head was beginning to throb. He needed to sit down and collect his thoughts. Fortunately, the painted turtle was willing to relinquish its seat on the swing. He needed a plan, and it had to provide permanent relief. He couldn't keep treading water. He hated the metaphor even as he spoke it. Rudy could see Luther on the beaver dam. Even though it was over a hundred yards away, Rudy thought he saw a smirk on Luther's face. "I'm going kill that beaver!"

***

Jennifer tapped Charlie on the rump with her willow switch, and Charlie responded with a minute increase in speed. After twenty seconds, he returned to his normal plodding speed. Much as Jennifer hated to admit it, Charlie was a strong horse. Many horses would have given out by now. By Jennifer's estimate, they had traveled over thirty miles.

Jennifer was apprehensive about the impulsive honeymoon trip to the Tahquamenon Falls. She wasn't obsessive-compulsive, but she did like to plan well in advance. It was getting toward evening on their first day, and so far there had been no unforeseen problems. Mel had loaned them an old army tent to provide shelter and a place to sleep. They had cooking utensils as well as canned beans and vegetables. Frenchie had borrowed Pa's double-barreled shotgun to provide fresh meat for the table. Jennifer could think of nothing they were missing.

The road to the falls was a well-worn, dirt trail with many ruts, making for a rough ride, and they were almost as tired as Charlie. Fortunately, there was little traffic on the road. Most of the traffic they encountered was horse drawn buggies and wagons. Occasionally they would see a motorcar, but that was rare in the Upper Peninsula. Gasoline was difficult to find in the middle of nowhere, but a horse could be filled up at any meadow.

"I think Charlie's getting tired. We should stop for the evening," Jennifer said. The pecking order was evolving, and it was obvious that "to honor and obey" was a relative concept, at least in Jennifer's eyes.

"I can see a grassy area up ahead on our left," Frenchie said. "We can set up our tent there."

Jennifer guided Charlie onto the grassy clearing; Charlie was happy to oblige. The ground was flat, perfect for setting up the tent.

"Why don't you get a fire started? I'll see if I can get some meat for the stew." Frenchie grabbed the twelve-gauge shotgun and headed into the woods without waiting for a reply.

Jennifer was never one to shirk from work and immediately set about building a fire. Within an hour, she had a fire turning to hot coals and had set up a tripod to support a kettle of stew.

"I couldn't find anything," Frenchie said when he returned empty-handed. "I don't think there's any game in this area. Maybe we'll just have to eat vegetables."

"Let me have a try." Jennifer took the shotgun, a handful of shells, and headed into the woods. She returned twenty minutes later with two gray squirrels and a partridge.

"Not a bad stew," Frenchie said after devouring several helpings. He had never sampled Jennifer's cooking and was pleased to find he had married a good cook. The time spent growing up in a cafe hadn't been lost on Jennifer.

"I suppose we should set up the tent. It'll soon be dark," Frenchie said after he had cleaned up the last of the stew. The tent was an old army issue officer's tent that measured six feet wide by eight feet long. It wasn't large but provided room for two people to sleep with some extra storage space. Since neither Jennifer nor Frenchie had set up the tent previously, there was some initial confusion; but eventually, they got the tent in a semi erect condition. Darkness came early due to approaching storm clouds. With no source of illumination other than a flashlight, the couple did what most honeymooners do on their first night. They went to bed.

***

Charlie took advantage of the thick grass in the forest clearing to appease his hunger. Pulling the wagon had been hard work, and he had been given only limited time to graze. A long, fifty-foot rope tether provided room for Charlie to roam. By the time Charlie had eaten his fill, it was well after dark. In the west, lightning flashes periodically illuminated the sky.

It could rain, Charlie decided. He wasn't fond of storms. A few droplets of rain gradually changed into a drenching downpour, confirmed his prediction. Charlie found refuge under a large maple tree. It provided some relief from the rain, but the lightning was getting closer, and the leaves on the trees trembled as volley after volley of thunder reverberated through the nighttime sky. Charlie moved closer to the tree trunk, but the rain, whipped by large gusts of wind, saturated the tree leaves, negating any protection they had previously provided. "This isn't good." The thunder, now directly overhead, propelled Charlie to action. "I should discuss this with Frenchie and Jennifer." Charlie trotted over to the tent door. "Hey guys…it's raining out here." Charlie poked his head into the tent. "Did ya know it's raining outside?"

"Frenchie, that horse of yours is in our tent."

"Huh?"

"I said that horse of yours is trying to get inside our tent."

"Charlie, get out of here." Frenchie made no effort to surrender the comfort of his warm blanket.

"Is that the best you can do?" Jennifer asked.

"All right, all right, I'll handle it." Frenchie found his tee shirt and boxer shorts inadequate for the cool, damp air. Hopefully, he could quickly resolve the problem and return to his warm blanket. "Charlie, you can't come in here." Frenchie gave a push to the straw-hat-covered horse's head.

Don't they know it's raining out here, Charlie wondered?

The pressure on Charlie's head was having the desired effect, and he began withdrawing. But a clap of thunder sent the panic-stricken horse leaping toward the center of the tent. His broad shoulders, not quite fitting through the door, pulled the tent stakes free.

"The tent's coming down. Do something, Frenchie."

"What do you expect me to do?"

The tent collapsed on Charlie's head, and darkness replaced the dim light that had protruded through the tent door.

"We need to get out of here before that stupid horse of yours steps on one of us."

"Which way's the door?" It took several minutes of scratching at canvas before Frenchie and Jennifer extracted themselves from their canvas conundrum. Standing before them in the rain, was a tent shaped like a horse.

"He's going to destroy our tent. Get him out of there, Frenchie."

"How do you expect me to do that?" Frenchie's question was answered by the sound of ripping canvas, as Charlie stepped out of the tent.

"What're we going to do now, Frenchie?"

"We still have the tarp on the wagon. We can use that."

The tarp over the back of the wagon provided some relief from the rain as Jennifer and Frenchie, individually wrapped in damp blankets, huddled under the wagon. The main part of the storm had passed, leaving only a steady drizzle. Unfortunately, the coolness of the wet blanket did nothing to dampen the heat of Jennifer's temper. She chose to display her displeasure by ignoring Frenchie. That was fine with Frenchie; right now, he didn't want to know her thoughts. He assumed he would hear about them in the morning.

It was beyond Charlie's understanding why *they* were upset. A romantic camping trip to the Tahquamenon Falls was *their* idea, not his. He was the one left out in the rain, not *them*. His attempts to find relief from the rain by sticking his head under the wagon hadn't been met with much enthusiasm.

***

Rudy could still detect traces of skunk, when he entered the church. Even with the doors and windows open, it would take time for the odor to dissipate. Hopefully, it would be gone by Sunday. Rudy didn't relish the thought of conducting a church service under such conditions. He could endure the smell only so long. The only reason he was in the church was to discuss some important business matters with P.C.

Rudy found P.C. at the rear of the sanctuary trying to remove stains from the rug. The bulk of the horse droppings had been shoveled out, but some persistent stains were defying efforts to remove them. P.C., armed with a scrub brush, was unwilling to accept defeat.

"Good morning, P.C. How are things going?"

"Morning, Reverend," P.C. replied. "Some of these stains are pretty stubborn, but I think I can get 'em out." P.C. noted Rudy's soggy shoes and wet pant legs. "Looks like you been playing down by the beaver pond."

"I had to let some water out of the dam." Rudy tried to be casual about his reply. "I thought the pond was getting too large." That had to be the understatement of the year.

"That pond has gotten pretty big. You got to admire that beaver. He sure is a hard worker."

"I guess you're right." Rudy hated it when he was forced into saying something he didn't wish to say. He didn't have to admire that beaver. He detested that beaver, but Luther's days of tormenting him were numbered. It was time for drastic measures.

"You wouldn't happen to know where I could get a stick of dynamite, would you?" Rudy asked.

"What ya need dynamite for? You blowing up a stump or something?"

"Yeah." It wasn't quite a lie, Rudy rationalized. He didn't have to tell P.C. he was answering the "or something" part of the question.

"If I remember right, I think Frenchie had some he was using to bust up stumps out at his place. He might be willing to spare a stick or two."

"I only need one stick and about a foot of fuse."

"He's on his honeymoon, you know, but I'll ask him as soon as he gets back. They only plan to be gone two or three days."

"Have you heard anything from them?"

"No, but I'm sure those young'ens are having fun. It must be nice to be young and in love."

How would I know, Rudy wondered? Love and romance hadn't been a major part of his past experiences.

"I'd prefer you didn't mention the dynamite to anyone. I don't want people to worry."

"Mums the word," P.C. replied.

"Thanks, I appreciate that."

***

Dispositions had improved only slightly when Jennifer, Frenchie, and Charlie departed on the final leg of their trip to the Tahquamenon Falls. Jennifer had progressed to at least talking to Frenchie, although Frenchie found it less stressful when she didn't. They spread the tent over the back of the wagon to dry. Jennifer tried to repair the tear with needle and thread but found it difficult on the bumpy road. If all when well, they would reach the falls by early afternoon.

"I can sew this together," Jennifer said, "but it'll never be the same."

"It really wasn't Charlie's fault," Frenchie replied. "He just got spooked by the thunder."

"I just hope he realizes that geldings also make good plow horses."

"Gelding?" Jennifer had Charlie's full attention. "Frenchie, we got to hang together on this one. If it can happen to me, it could happen to anyone!"

Frenchie decided not to pursue the conversation, and the rest of the trip continued in chilled silence. By early afternoon the honeymoon trio arrived at a grassy opening near the falls. A sign announced that the trail to the falls was a one-mile walk.

"This looks like a good place to set up camp," Frenchie said, breaking the silence with a positive spin. "It's flat for the tent and has plenty of grass for Charlie to eat."

"I guess it's as good as any," Jennifer agreed. Jennifer had never been to the falls, and the excitement was beginning to overcome her irritation over the events of the previous night. "The falls is only a mile hike. Maybe we can see the falls while it's still daylight and pitch the tent later."

"That sounds good to me. I'm stiff from the ride. I could use a good walk." Frenchie unshackled Charlie from his harness and set him free to graze. "You ready to go?"

"You just can't leave that horse loose like that," Jennifer protested.

"He'll be all right. Animals are smart. He'll stay near the wagon because that's where the grass is."

"I hope you're right." Jennifer grabbed Frenchie's hand and pulled him toward the trail.

***

Milford thrashed through the underbrush. His broad, palmate antlers occasionally snagged on overhanging branches, slowing his progress, but it didn't dampen his spirits. This was rutting season, and Milford was a moose on a mission. A few recalcitrant branches wouldn't be allowed to impede his progress. He had romance on his mind. Somewhere out there in that vast Northern Michigan forest was his true love, and he must search until he found her. Motivated by raging hormones, Milford forged through the dense forest. His plodding march eventually brought him to a clearing in the woods.

Looking over the grassy clearing, Milford saw the blurred outline of a red wagon. He wasn't concerned with the blurred vision. Over the years, he had grown used to his visual impairment. With no danger in sight, Milford, the myopic moose, stepped into the clearing to inspect the wagon.

As he approached the wagon, he saw a large animal grazing on the grass, obviously another moose. Even with his poor vision, Milford could see the grazing animal lacked antlers. Could this be his true love? Milford squinted his eyes for a better look. It was love at first sight, limited as his sight might be. Milford, totally obsessed with carnal lust, trotted over to the object of his newfound affection. He would formally introduce himself before starting his courtship.

"Buzz off, bozo…this is my grass," Charlie said with his usual charm.

"Hello, my love. I have come to sweep you off your feet." Milford nuzzled up against Charlie, drenching the base of Charlie's neck with wet, slimy kisses.

"Get away from me, you imbecile!" Charlie moved away, but Milford, with lust on his mind, followed.

"Come here, my sweetie pie. We were made for each other."

"Hey, fuzz face, are you blind? Anyone ever tell you that you have a deformity on your head?" Charlie trotted off toward the edge of the clearing.

"Ah, we wish to play hard to get," Milford said as he scampered after Charlie. "Ready or not here I come."

Irritation changed to alarm, and Charlie shifted into a full gallop. Looking over his shoulder, he could see the misguided moose was still in hot pursuit. The woods at the edge of the clearing barely slowed Charlie's pace. He was inspired by the heavy breathing emanating from the galloping Casanova at his rear. Maybe he could hide behind that bush up ahead, Charlie thought, as he placed his head and forequarters behind a large bush, leaving his hindquarters fully exposed.

"We wish to play hide and seek, my love?" Even with his blurred vision, Milford could see the business end of his lover protruding from the foliage. "I can still see you, my snookums," Milford announced as he playfully nibbled at Charlie's exposed hindquarters.

"Get away from me, you pervert! I'm not your snookums!" Charlie headed into the woods in panic. "Frenchie? Jennifer? Where are you?" Charlie ran deeper into the woods, wishing only to increase the space between him and that sex-starved savage. The thick undergrowth at the edge of the clearing turned into the more open area of a mature white pine forest. Charlie's flight drove him farther from the wagon and familiar surroundings.

Fifteen minutes of unfettered flight brought Charlie to a riverbank. The river, swollen by the previous night's rain, blocked his escape. Looking down, Charlie saw the raging water swirling ten feet below. It wasn't a pleasant sight. He was caught between the raging water of the river and the raging hormones of a moronic moose. It was a difficult decision that had to be made quickly; but Charlie, with his honor to protect, had little choice. With a leap that would have impressed Butch Cassidy and the Sundance Kid, Charlie entrusted his fate to the water below. Milford, stopping at the edge of the riverbank, watched the blurred image of his true love disappear into the turbulent water. A large tear ran down his cheek.

***

Jennifer and Frenchie walked, hand in hand, down the well-worn path toward the falls. There was no rush; they were more interested in each other than the falls. They allowed other tourists to pass them by; you cannot rush those in love. The walk to the falls was only a mile, and they had plenty of time. After an hour of slow walking interspersed with brief periods of heavy necking, the honeymooners approached Tahquamenon Falls. The deafening roar confirmed they were approaching the second largest falls east of the Mississippi River. The air became cooler and filled with mist.

"How much farther are the falls?" Jennifer asked a kid who was stooping at the edge of the trail. He appeared to be collecting stones for the slingshot protruding from his back pocket.

"No more than a hundred yards," replied the kid. "You're just in time to watch the horse go over the falls."

"That'll be interesting," Jennifer replied. Children have such good imaginations. "Is it a pretty horse?"

"No, he's actually kind of dumb looking and is wearing a stupid straw hat."

"Did you say kind of dumb looking?" Frenchie asked.

"With a funny looking straw hat?" Jennifer wanted to know.

"Yeah, why?" the kid asked.

Jennifer and Frenchie looked at each other. No, it couldn't be, they both thought. Breaking into a run, the couple rapidly covered the hundred yards to the falls. The kid, with no desire to be left out of any excitement, ran after the couple, his pockets now full of appropriate size stones.

The falls were as magnificent as they had heard. The Tahquamenon River drained a watershed of over 790 square miles, and by the time it got to the falls, the river was over 200 feet across with a flow of up to 50,000 gallons per second down a 50-foot vertical drop. A large cloud of white mist rose up far above the water giving the impression of a firestorm.

Jennifer and Frenchie weren't in the mood for admiring the scenery. "Where's the horse?" Jennifer asked. She was beginning to hope this was just part of the kid's imagination.

"There he is," the kid said, pointing to the cowering plow horse perched on a small flat rock in the center of the river, less than a hundred feet from the edge of the falls. Through the mist the unmistakable outline of a straw hat could be seen covering the horse's head. The rocky perch, no more than three or four feet in diameter, barely gave harbor to the four large hooves.

"It's Charlie!" Frenchie said.

"No, it can't be Charlie," Jennifer replied. "Charlie is back by the wagon. Charlie wouldn't leave the area, you said. Charlie would stay where all the grass is, you said. Animals are very smart, you said. So what's your estimate of that animal's I.Q.?" Jennifer asked, pointing to the pathetic figure on the rock.

"I think I can get him off the rock, if I can get a good rump shot." The kid shot another stone at the horse with his slingshot. He missed, but his pockets were full of ammunition.

"What're we going to do?" Frenchie asked.

"I think we should leave him there. It serves him right."

"It'll be a long walk home."

"I suppose you're right," Jennifer grudgingly agreed. "We need some rope."

"There is a coil of rope at the ranger's station," the kid informed the couple. "It's only a short distance from here."

"Quick, go get it," Jennifer told the kid. The kid was just getting the range with his slingshot and reluctant to leave, but the authority in Jennifer's voice was difficult to ignore. He returned in three minutes with a coil of half-inch rope. Jennifer estimated the length at one hundred and fifty feet. The rope was designed for rescuing stranded humans. Would it work on a twelve hundred pound horse?

Grabbing the rope, Jennifer walked upstream from the hapless horse. "Tie this end to that tree." Jennifer gave one end of the rope to Frenchie. Jennifer slipped out of her dress, revealing a white undershirt and a pair of white baggy pantaloons that gathered in a lacy edge just below her knees.

"What are you doing?" Frenchie asked after tying his end of the rope to a tree. "You're exposing your legs in public."

"You want to walk home?" After tying the remaining end around her waist, Jennifer inspected the knot Frenchie had tied around the tree. She removed the granny knot and replaced it with a bowline. "I'm going to swim out to Charlie. If I don't make it, the rope will swing me back to shore."

"Are ya sure you can make it?" Frenchie asked.

"Only one way to find out."

Jennifer kicked off her shoes and dove into the water. She made it a shallow dive, since she was unsure of the water's depth. The water, stained red with tannin leached from the cedar, spruce, and hemlock swamps that fed the river, immediately engulfed the swimmer. Jennifer didn't fight the current, but swam across the flow. She was a strong swimmer. The lessons Uncle Weasel had given her at the Moose Lake Lodge hadn't been in vain. She needed to cover one hundred feet across the river before the current pulled her past Charlie's rocky pedestal.

Jennifer's muscles were aching from the cold Upper Peninsula water, but she covered the distance with time to spare. She coasted the last twenty feet, letting the current carry her toward the stranded horse.

"Jennifer, am I glad to see you!" Charlie said as Jennifer arrived. "We're friends, remember? Just you and me, Baby."

Ignoring Charlie, Jennifer continued her work; people don't understand horse talk. Climbing on top of the rock, Jennifer removed the rope from her waist and tied it around Charlie's neck. She tied another loop around his rump.

"OK, I WANT YOU TO PULL ON THE ROPE," Jennifer yelled at Frenchie. "ONCE WE GET THIS STUPID HORSE OFF THE ROCK, THE CURRENT WILL SWING HIM TOWARD THE SHORE."

"Who you calling stupid?" Charlie asked.

Frenchie gave a pull on the rope, but the twelve hundred pounds of horseflesh didn't budge. Even with the help of several bystanders, Charlie couldn't be enticed into the water.

"Jump into the water, Charlie," Jennifer commanded.

"And she's calling me stupid?" Charlie leaned back against the pull of the rope.

"Stupid horse," Jennifer mumbled. "This isn't going to..." Jennifer was cut off in mid-sentence as Charlie lunged into the water, a well-placed stone having found its mark on Charlie's backside. Jennifer, caught by surprise clung to his neck, while on the shore; the kid was doing a victory dance with slingshot held high.

Should have walked home, Jennifer decided. Frenchie was yelling something at her from the shore, but she couldn't hear anything above the roar of the falls that were rapidly approaching. There had to be better ways of testing the strength of a rope.

Jennifer offered a quick prayer asking that the rope would hold. God must have been listening. As the rope pulled tight, Jennifer and Charlie swung toward the shore. Less than ten feet from the falls, Charlie felt the river bottom come up to meet his feet, and he staggered up the shore with Jennifer clinging to his back. He didn't mind having Jennifer on his back. Someone had to pull her from the water. If there had to be a hero of the day, it might as well be him.

***

It was early in the morning when Jennifer, Frenchie, and Charlie headed home, hoping to make it by dusk. The Tahquamenon Falls had been pretty, but you can only spend so much time watching water fall over a cliff. Jennifer, wrapped in a wool blanket, was holding a box of tissues; she had picked up a cold during her visit to the falls.

"How ya feeling?" Frenchie asked.

"I think I'll be OK," Jennifer replied between sneezes. "It'll be good to be home in a real bed."

The return trip of any vacation tends to drag, and the return to Bear Creek was no exception. To save time, they didn't stop to eat but fixed sandwiches on the go. They didn't even stop to let Charlie graze. Charlie considered complaining, but decided it best to keep a low profile.

"Jennifer, I don't know if you noticed, but a big bull moose has been following us for the last twenty miles," Frenchie said. Jennifer looked behind them and saw a large moose with a, impressive rack following them one hundred yards back.

"Maybe we should go a little faster." Charlie increased his pace.

"Look, even Charlie is in a hurry to get home," Frenchie pointed out.

Jennifer noticed the moose had also increased his pace. "I wonder if he's going to follow us all the way home?"

***

Rudy wrapped his robe around his bony frame and headed toward his door. "I'm coming, I'm coming," Rudy shouted, as the visitor rapped on the door a second time. It was eight in the morning and unusual for anyone to come calling at such an early hour. He hoped it wasn't an emergency. Rudy opened the door to find P.C. standing in his doorway. P.C. had a reputation for being an early riser.

"Morning, Reverend, I hope I didn't wake you."

"That's OK. It was time for me to get up anyway."

"I got that stick of dynamite you requested." P.C. pulled a red cylinder out of a paper bag and passed it to Rudy. It had a ten-inch fuse protruding from one end.

"The fuse should give you fifteen seconds to get away," P.C. explained.

"I didn't expect the dynamite so soon." Rudy felt the raw power in his hand. He would soon have his beaver problems solved. A diabolical smile came to Rudy's face.

"Jennifer and Frenchie got back last night, a day sooner than expected," P.C. replied.

"Did they have a good time?"

"I'm sure they did. Jennifer picked up a cold. I guess the air is damp around the falls with the mist and all."

"I'll be working late tonight in the church. If you see a light in the church, that will be me." Rudy decided to start creating an alibi. Hopefully everyone will be in their homes later tonight and won't hear any blast coming from the ravine. If they did, Rudy wanted them to think he was at the church.

"No problem." P.C. started to leave. "Oh, by the way, Jennifer and Frenchie wanted me to give you this." P.C. handed Rudy a small package wrapped in brown paper. "It's a thank you gift for the wedding."

Rudy wasn't quite sure he deserved anything after the way the wedding turned out, but he was appreciative just the same. He opened the package and found several large steaks.

"What is this, beef?" Rudy asked.

"Nope, moose."

***

"Morning, Mel," Rudy said as he greeted his friend behind the counter of the Bare Creek Hardware and Feed store.

"You're up bright and early today. What can I do for you today?"

"Just thought I would stop by and see if my order for vitamins came in."

"You just got vitamins last week. You sure you're feeling OK?" Mel asked.

"Yes, I'm fine. Never felt better."

"If you ever do have a medical problem, talk to Maggie. She knows a lot about such things."

"No, really, I'm OK." Rudy wished he were more confident about that statement.

"By the way, I'll be working late tonight at the church. If you see a light at the church, it'll be me." The more people he told, the better the alibi. The church was at the edge of town, but a light in the church window could still be seen. The beaver pond was behind the church and downhill in the ravine. Rudy was hoping no one would notice the explosion, but a good alibi wouldn't hurt.

***

"Hello, Maggie. Just a cup of coffee and a donut."

"Good morning, Reverend. We don't usually see you in the cafe this early in the morning."

"Got a lot of work to do today. I expect to be working late into the evening. If you see a light at the church, that'll be me."

***

It was just getting dark when Rudy placed a kerosene lamp in the church window. It would easily be seen from town. He did have work he could be doing in the church, but he was too anxious for any work other than the task at hand. Tonight he would finally solve his beaver problems. Drastic problems require drastic measures.

Rudy checked the stick of dynamite again. It had a ten-inch fuse. Rudy wasn't an expert in explosives, but P.C. said it would give him fifteen seconds. That would be enough. He would need matches to light the fuse. To ensure the matches would work, he dipped them in hot paraffin. That would make them waterproof. When the match was struck, the paraffin would slough off, and the match would light. He coated several matches to be used as back up.

It was getting dark outside, but not dark enough. He didn't want to start too early; he would wait until all the townsfolk were inside for the night. Any noise would be less noticeable from inside a building.

The beaver lodge was located at the far side of the pond and about twenty feet from shore. The best avenue of attack would be from the far side of the pond. He would cross a quarter mile upstream and stage his attack from the rear.

Rudy checked the kerosene lamp to ensure there was fuel for several hours, although he expected to accomplish his mission in far less time. Rudy slipped out the side door of the church and headed upstream. The treated matches were in his right front pocket, the dynamite tightly held in his left hand. He knew exactly where he would cross the river, having been there many times before. In the daylight it would have been only a five-minute walk. The chosen point had the advantage of stepping-stones—no sense in getting wet.

Once he crossed the river, Rudy headed downstream. The river widened as he approached the beaver dam. With no path to follow, Rudy was forced to make his own way through the brush, finally arriving at the far side of the pond. The brush near the pond had all been clear-cut by the overzealous beaver, making maneuvering, even in the dark, quite easy.

There it was. Rudy could see the outline of the beaver lodge. He would have missed it in the darkness had he not known where to look, but it was definitely the beaver lodge. Everything was proceeding exactly as planned. Victory would soon be his.

Now all he had to do was wade out to the lodge and place the stick of dynamite in the entrance to the lodge, simple as that. It wasn't his intent to kill Luther, but only to destroy the lodge. He didn't know if Luther was in the lodge. If he happened to be in the lodge and were to be killed, that wouldn't be Rudy's fault. It would be an act of God. He couldn't interfere with an act of God, could he? The thought of Luther's demise brought a smile to Rudy's face.

Rudy rolled up his pant legs and began wading toward the beaver lodge. He had gone less than three feet, and the water was already up to his knees. This wouldn't work, he decided, returning to shore. It was only a momentary setback. He wouldn't be denied his victory. He would merely have to change his plan of attack. It was totally dark, and no one was around. He would swim out to the lodge.

In less than a minute Rudy had shed his clothes, and was swimming toward the lodge. The stick of dynamite was clutched in his teeth along with several wax-coated matches. Within seconds he was standing on the beaver lodge. Water dripped from his naked body, but the dynamite and matches were dry. All he had to do was place the dynamite in the lodge entrance and swim clear of the blast. Military commandos couldn't have done a better job. Victory was his.

Looking around, Rudy was unable to find the entrance to the lodge. It hadn't occurred to him that the entrance would be underwater. Only a minor problem Rudy decided when no entrance was found. He would place the charge in a large crevice in the lodge foundation, that would be sufficient. He was pleased to find several to choose from. He selected a crevice that ran particularly deep into the structure of the lodge. This would be a good one, he decided.

The cool night air was giving Rudy a chill as the water dripped from his body, but this didn't dampen the enthusiasm for his mission. He felt around on the lodge until he found a small piece of granite that had been encased in the mud of the lodge. The surface was rough, perfect for striking a match. His mission was almost completed. The match lit on the first strike, obviously a good omen. The fuse also ignited without problems. Rudy had expected the fuse to burn like a sparkler, but it merely glowed, as the fuse grew shorter. He had fifteen seconds. Victory was indeed his.

This was a moment to savor. It was a moment of triumph. Rudy stood proudly on the beaver lodge with the stick of dynamite held high. He was Moses parting the Red Sea. He was Joshua at the Battle of Jericho. He was Samson destroying the Philistines with the jawbone of an ass. He was Rudy Hooper standing naked on a beaver lodge holding a stick of dynamite with a fuse that was getting perilously short. Maybe it would be wise to get on with business and save his victory dance for later. In the darkness no one could see him anyway.

A full moon rose above the horizon in the east flooding the ravine with moonlight as Rudy was about to place the charge in the crevice. Simultaneous "Oh's" could be heard from 152 men, women, and children as if they had just seen a particularly pleasing display of fireworks. Sitting on the hillside on the far bank, the entire population of Bear Creek was staring at the beaver lodge!

Rudy stared back at them for a few seconds as he tried to think. He supposed he owed them some sort of explanation, but no convincing argument came to mind. Maybe he should lead them in a short period of prayer, but that didn't seem appropriate under the current circumstances either. Looking up at the stick of dynamite in his outstretched right hand, he noticed the fuse was within a fraction of an inch of the charge. Maybe it would be best to deal with his congregation after he addressed the immediate problem of the dynamite in his right hand.

Rudy wasn't a coward, but neither was he a fool. From the minuscule length of fuse, Rudy estimated only seconds before the dynamite ignited. He cast the stick of dynamite high into the air and dove into the dark water.

***

The citizens of Bear Creek had always claimed to see Abigail during the full moon, but it was just a brief glimpse. Now in front of them was the naked Abigail Farnsworth boldly standing on the beaver lodge. It wasn't just a fleeting image, as she stood there in the moon light with her arms outstretched for over ten seconds before she dove into the water.

Except for the initial interjection of astonishment, the townsfolk sat on the hillside in total silence. They had assumed Abigail was nothing more than a legend. It had been nothing more than an excuse for a town party. How then were they to explain the naked figure on the beaver lodge?

The silence didn't last long as a mighty flash of lightning illuminated an otherwise cloudless sky. This was followed by a massive clap of thunder. They had reveled in sex, nakedness, and carnal pleasure; and now they were about to be smitten by the Lord like the ancient cities of Sodom and Gomorrah. Brimstone and fire from the Lord would soon rain down upon them from heaven. Armageddon was upon them. They had ignored Reverend Hooper's sermon and had sinned in their hearts. They had worried too much about converting the heathens in New Guinea and feeding the starving children in China when they should have worried about local sinners.

The townsfolk sat silently for a moment or two and then, as if signaled by an orchestra director, began running toward town and the safety of their homes. The men led the way followed by women with children scooped up under their arms. Mel Barker, in his haste to lead the women and children to safety, accidentally stepped on Gomorrah's tail. Gomorrah had been wandering among the crowd to check out the local action. As Mel's full weight came down on Gomorrah's tail, Gomorrah let out a howl only a cat with its tail in a ringer could make. The howl reverberated between the walls of the ravine dispelling any doubts that the four horsemen of famine, war, pestilence, and death were galloping down upon them. Within minutes, the hillside was barren except for picnic baskets and blankets left behind by the revelers.

***

Luther emerged from the comfort of his lodge. He heard what appeared to be thunder and needed to check the dam to ensure that a flash flood from a summer storm hadn't caused any damage. He was surprised to find only solitude. The sky was void of any clouds, and a full moon brightly illuminated the pond. There were no signs of any pending storm. Luther swam toward his dam. It was in good shape except for the vandalism created by that human. He had done a fair amount of damage, but Luther figured he could repair it in a day or two. He would start repairs first thing in the morning. Luther finished his patrol and returned to his lodge. He could find nothing to explain the loud noise. As he was about to enter his lodge, he noticed something peculiar. In the center of the pond a lone, hollow reed protruded above the water. That was strange he thought, but not enough to warrant investigation. Luther returned to the safety of his lodge.

***

The following morning the Economics Club of Bare Creek met as usual. Conversation was held to a minimum, and then only in low whispers. P.C. and Frenchie were playing their usual game of checkers. Neither player felt an urge to cheat, making for a dull game. Although it wasn't mentioned, Abigail Farnsworth was on all their minds. Prior to the previous evening, they had believed Abigail was nothing more than a legend. It was true they all lied about seeing the naked youth during the full moon vigils, and they all assumed the rest had also lied about seeing Abigail. Now that they knew Abigail did exist, they wondered if the others had been seeing her all along.

The silence was finally broken around noon by Silas Kronschnabell. "You think Abigail lost much weight since last year?" he asked.

"I believe you're right," Mel agreed. "She seemed like she was just skin and bone."

"I remember her having a lot more flesh when I saw her last year," P.C. lied.

"It almost looked like she had some facial hair," Frenchie added. "I suppose she's no longer a teenager. Reckon she would be about forty-four now."

"Anybody have any idea where the lightning and thunder came from?" Mel asked. "There wasn't a cloud in the sky."

Everyone looked at Silas for an educated answer. Silas leaned back in his chair and withdrew a pipe from his pocket, as well as a pouch of tobacco. It was obvious they weren't about to receive a simple answer. Silas took his time packing his pipe with tobacco and tamping it down. He retrieved a match from his shirt pocket and struck it against the sole of his shoe. A cloud of blue smoke soon engulfed Silas's head as he settled into deep thought. The members of the Bare Creek Economics Club, knowing better than to rush Silas when he was in deep thought, waited patiently for an explanation.

"I'm not totally convinced what we saw and heard was lightning," Silas said in a slow deliberate tone. "You need clouds and a storm to produce lightning."

"If it wasn't lightning, what was it?" Mel asked.

"It could have been a meteor," Silas said. Everyone nodded in agreement. "But if it were a meteor, we should have seen a streak of light not a point flash." That made sense to everyone. "Unless the meteor was coming straight at us, in which case it would give the illusion of being stationary." That was logical, everyone agreed. "But then the flash should have lasted several seconds as the meteor burned up in the atmosphere, and there wouldn't have been an audible bang." Again there were nods of agreement. "Unless the meteor hit the earth."

"What if the meteor hit the earth, there would be a bang then, wouldn't there?" P.C. asked.

"If the meteor was coming straight toward us and hit the earth, we wouldn't be currently discussing this issue." Silas waited for the laughter to subside. "Nope, I don't think it was a meteor."

"OK, it wasn't lightning and it wasn't a meteor, then what was it we saw and heard?" Mel asked. It was obvious Mel was beginning to lose his patience.

"I have no personal experience with this, but I have read about a phenomenon called mass hallucination."

"What the heck is that? Are you saying we're all crazy?" Frenchie asked. Up to this point, Frenchie had been listening quietly, "I'll take umbrage if you're trying to insinuate I'm a lunatic." Other members of the Economics Club were also getting agitated. All except for P.C. who was trying to figure out what umbrage meant.

"No, it doesn't mean anyone is crazy. The way I understand it, if you have a high expectation of an event happening, the mind may fill in the void, making the individual think that event actually happened." Silas took another puff on his pipe. "If everyone is expecting the same event to occur, they may all have the same hallucination. This would be reinforced by other observers."

"So the flash of light and bang were caused by mass hallucination?" Frenchie asked as he tried to sum up in one sentence what Silas said in several paragraphs.

"I didn't say that," Silas admonished. "Mass hallucination would explain the apparition, since we were all hoping to see Abigail Farnsworth." Silas took several drags on his pipe to let his statement sink in. P.C. still hadn't figured out umbrage and now he had apparitions to worry about. "The flash of light and bang couldn't be mass hallucination because no one was expecting that."

"Then what the heck was it?" everyone asked in unison.

"I have no idea," Silas replied.

***

By early afternoon, influential women of Bear Creek began gathering at the Bare Creek Cafe. Throughout the morning they had waited for brimstone and fire as well as further bolts of lightning to rain down upon them from heaven. With no additional catastrophes noted, they had come to the conclusion that the lightning bolt from the previous night had only been a warning shot, and if they repented their sins, they might yet be spared.

"I suppose we're all here for the same reason," Maggie said as she opened the impromptu meeting. "It appears the Lord has noticed the sins that are being committed in our community."

"I think last night was a wakeup call for us solid citizens to work harder to eliminate all the sex, alcohol, gambling and other sins in our community," Agnes said. "We need to do something about those Ollies." Agnes was still burning from the outcome of her last sting operation.

"We need to do something about the flagrant flow of alcohol in this town," Trudy added. "Look what happened to Mrs. Olson at Jennifer's wedding."

"I thought that Ness guy in Chicago had dried up all the alcohol?" Maggie asked.

"He has," Trudy replied. "I don't think the alcohol is coming from Milwaukee. I think the alcohol is coming from a still out there in the woods."

"If there's a still out there, we need to destroy it," Agnes said. "It takes a lot of time and energy to run a still. If the men folk are running a still, all we have to do is watch them closely; they'll lead us to it."

"What about poor Abigail?" Jennifer asked. She had been clearing tables, but was still able to eavesdrop on most of the conversation. "What did we see last night?"

"I think we can all agree we saw something last night," Maggie said, "but I'm not quite sure what I saw."

"No one could live naked in those woods for twenty-five years," Trudy said. "That's only a legend."

"But we did see something, didn't we?" Agnes asked. "What if she does exist? I think we need to do something for her." It was obvious Agnes had decided on a course of action, and no one would be able to dissuade her from her endeavor.

"And what do you think we should do for her?" Maggie asked.

"At the very least, I think we should find her something warm to wear."

"And how do we get the clothing to her?"

"Maybe we could leave some warm clothing on the beaver lodge at the next full moon. Silas has an old coonskin coat he wore when he was going to Northern Normal School. Maybe I'll give that to her. That'll keep her warm."

"You're going to give away Silas's college coat, the one with the Northern Normal School embroidered on the back? He won't be very happy."

"He'll never miss it."

***

Rudy had a sleepless night and woke with a throbbing headache. He didn't bother to take his temperature. He had to make a decision. Previously he had hoped to remain at Bear Creek until his failing health prevented further service to the community. Now he wondered if he were providing any moral leadership to the community at all. It would be difficult to stand behind the pulpit and proclaim the higher ground. How could he ask them to be morally just after what he had done the previous night in front of men, women, and children?

Rudy walked into the kitchen to brew a cup of coffee. Maybe the caffeine would help clear his mind. It was difficult to think with his sleep deprivation and splitting headache. Rudy placed the coffeepot on the stove and walked to his porch while he waited for the coffee to brew. He could see Luther diligently repairing the dam as if nothing had happened. Rudy estimated the dam would be repaired in another day or two. Maybe it was time to admit defeat. He had been bested by a beaver.

Rudy returned to the kitchen to find his coffee through percolating and poured himself a cup. He had made it unusually strong; he needed the extra caffeine boost. It wasn't until he finished his second cup of coffee that his mind began to clear and the appropriate course of action became obvious. It was imperative that he write the bishop and request an immediate replacement. The congregation at Bear Creek deserved better. It was difficult to admit failure, but it was something he needed to do.

Rudy sat down at his desk to begin his letter to the bishop. He didn't elaborate on the details but merely cited poor health and spiritual bankruptcy. It was simple and to the point. Rudy signed the letter and placed it in an envelope. He would mail it later in the afternoon.

Rudy picked up his journal. He needed to add a few words of explanation in his journal, although he wasn't sure why. The journal was to have been a documentary of his first year at Bare Creek Methodist Church, but he had been here only a few months and was leaving as a failure. It would hardly be a document he would like to share with his grandchildren. What grandchildren, he wondered. He was a failure in that arena too. Rudy read some of his early entries in the journal. The entries were filled with promise and hopes for the coming year. He even had praises for Luther. How could he have been so stupid and naive?

Today I must reluctantly note that I have decided to terminate my position here at the Bare Creek Methodist Church. I had hoped to serve a full year, but due to my medical condition as well as other personal reasons, which are best not documented, it has been necessary to request immediate relief from my duties. I have sent a letter to the bishop to this effect and hope to receive a response within the next two weeks.

Rudy closed his journal and stared at his coffee, which sat unmolested on the table. This could be the last entry in his journal.

Two weeks passed without a reply and then three and four weeks. Rudy was disappointed when, after four weeks, he had received no reply from the bishop. He had also expected acrimonious comments from the congregation, but to his surprise, not one individual mentioned the incident at the beaver pond. Even more strange was that church attendance was up fifty percent, and the offering was up seventy-five percent. Rudy would never understand Yoopers.

At the next full moon, few people turned out for the community observance. Agnes, true to her word, placed Silas's coonskin coat on the beaver lodge. A search of the area the following morning found no trace of the coat. Agnes was convinced Abigail had found the coat. It only convinced an irritated Silas Kronschnabell that his coat was now a permanent part of the Bare Creek beaver dam.

Chapter Six

September 2, 1923

Dear Reverend Hooper,

It is with great regret that I received your request for a replacement based on medical and personal reasons. You were not specific concerning the nature of your problems, and I pray they are not serious or long term.

As for your replacement, I will be unable to provide a replacement minister for the Bare Creek Methodist Church until late spring. If you are unable to continue in your current capacity due to personal or medical reasons, this office will understand. The position at Bare Creek has been vacant several times in the past with minimal loss of religious integrity, and I assume the congregation can again survive without a minister if this becomes necessary.

On the other hand, any additional time you can serve at the church will be greatly appreciated.

May the Lord be with you,

Samuel Johnson
Bishop Samuel Johnson

Rudy stared at the letter for several minutes. It had been four weeks since he sent his request to the bishop, and the reply now came as a surprise. The passage of time hadn't diminished Rudy's feeling of moral inadequacy nor had it reduce his desire to step down, but he had no wish to leave the church pulpit vacant. He had to admit the congregation had been very supportive and forgiving. Even after Rudy informed them of his decision to seek a replacement, many members expressed disappointment. No one mentioned the episode at the beaver dam, and church attendance has never been greater.

Life at Bear Creek was otherwise unchanged. Every morning Rudy demolished a section of the dam, and by the following morning, the damage was repaired. Few people showed up for the full moon in August, and that was OK with Rudy. Agnes had placed Silas's favorite coonskin coat on the beaver lodge, as a gift for Abigail. The following morning the coat was gone making Agnes quite pleased. Silas was not as pleased and firmly convinced that his coat had been incorporated into the structure of the dam. Knowing Luther, Rudy was inclined to agree with Silas.

Rudy laid the letter on the kitchen table and reached for his morning cup of coffee. The brain tumor with its occasional headaches was really just a nuisance. Was he quitting out of personal embarrassment? Was he giving up because the going was tough? Scriptural passages about other Christians with far greater adverse situations came immediately to mind. His problem with Luther wasn't as serious as when Daniel faced the lions, although it had to be close. Rudy saw Luther as being more of a Goliath. Luther seemed invincible; but, like Goliath, Luther had to have an Achilles' heel Rudy could use to his advantage if he could only find it.

Rudy finished his coffee and placed the empty cup on the table next to the letter. Bear Creek was a major test of his faith. He wasn't a great minister, and the people of Bear Creek deserved better, but he had to be better than nothing, and if his health permitted, he would continue until a more qualified replacement could be obtained in the spring. Until replaced, he would do his best to serve his congregation in Bear Creek.

Tonight he was to meet with the Widow Watson to discuss the beginning of Sunday school. Alice Watson was the one and only schoolteacher in Bear Creek and, because of her teaching background and experience, was naturally appointed to the position of church school superintendent. It was Rudy's understanding she was excellent at both positions. Both the church and secular schools had been out for the summer, leaving Rudy little familiarity with either program. He was looking forward to the evening's discussion. Besides, Alice promised coffee and cookies. Rudy had found the Widow to be an above average cook.

***

The morning was cool even by Yooper standards, forcing Mel to fire up the potbelly stove to take the chill out of the autumn air. He expected the day to warm up once the sun rose higher in the sky; Mel always had been an optimist. The Farmer's Almanac was predicting the winter of '23 would be a hash one, and Mel feared an early winter. Even an optimist must defer to the Farmer's Almanac. P.C. and Frenchie had returned to their cheating ways at checker, both feeling cheating was a finely honed skill, which added a new and stimulating dimension to the game. Except for the checker game, little was happening at the routine meeting of the Bare Creek Economics Club, and members were sitting around in abject boredom.

"What this town needs is some good, old-fashioned excitement," Mel said after spending ten minutes watching a spider spinning a web over a pitchfork that was hanging on the wall. "We never have a bank robbery or have a citizen abducted by aliens."

"Don't have a bank in town," Silas reminded Mel, "and no self-respecting alien would be caught dead in Bear Creek. Even they think Bear Creek is too dull." An alien abduction did have possibilities, Silas decided. As editor of the Bare Creek Gazette, Silas was always on the lookout for quality news.

"I'm willing to help build a bank and throw in a couple of bucks if you can find someone with the energy to rob it." Mel wondered if spiders ever got bored spinning webs.

"How about a M.A.C.H.O. night?" Silas suggested.

"What's a M.A.C.H.O. night?" Frenchie asked.

"It stands for Men Advocating a Completely Hedonic Outing," Silas replied. "It's a night dedicated to male bonding, where we shed the shackles of domestic servitude and rise up as free men, free of the banal bondage of boring bleakness, free of the malignant microcosms of the maladroit mainstream, free of the..."

"Basically we sit around, play cards, and have a nip or two of P.C.'s corn liquor," Mel said, cutting short Silas's soliloquy. Since prohibition, the only available liquid entertainment came from P.C.'s still, which by necessity was hidden in the deep woods, far from the prying eyes of their self-righteous wives.

"I suppose we could meet at the still," P.C. suggested. "There's a good place for a bonfire, and with a few lanterns in the trees, we'd have plenty of light for playing poker."

"Are you talking about spending the entire night?" Frenchie asked.

"Unless the liquor runs out," Mel replied.

"I'd have to check with Jennifer first."

The members of the Bare Creek Economics Club looked at each other. This boy needs help, they decided. Silas walked over to Frenchie and placed his arm around Frenchie's shoulder.

"Look at it this way," Silas suggested. "Jennifer loves you, doesn't she?"

"Yes, I guess she does."

"If she really loves you, she'd want you to have a good time, wouldn't she?"

"I suppose so."

"Even though Jennifer would prefer that you come with us, she would be under great pressure from the rest of the women, misguided as they may be. Women are good people, mind you, but they're obsessed with this perverted sense of morality that stymies their imagination and creativity, limiting the wholesome appreciation of life. Without men they would have absolutely no fun at all, which is why they marry us. These malignant moral values are forced upon unsuspecting girls in their formative years when they're still young and impressionable. That peer pressure can be unbearable. We know; we're married to them. You'll actually be doing Jennifer a favor by not telling her. You really do love her, don't you?" Silas took out his pipe and filled it with tobacco.

"Of course I do."

"If you really love her, it's your duty not to tell her and avoid placing her in an awkward position." Silas lit the pipe and took a drag, producing a cloud of blue smoke.

"I have to tell her something. Can't just not come home."

"You and I are going to Marquette to check on the market for potatoes," P.C. suggested. "That'll cover both of us."

"I have to go to Escanaba to see about parts for my printing press," Silas decided.

"I may have to be out of town at a hardware convention in Green Bay," Mel added.

"Are ya sure this'll be all right?" Frenchie asked.

"If you really love your wife, it's the only option," Silas said. "We do it all the time, and we love our wives."

"I guess you guys have more experience in this area than I do."

"Then it's settled. We'll meet at the still next Friday," Silas said. "It might be wise to arrive at different times. We don't want to draw undue attention."

***

Rudy adjusted his bow tie and knocked on the door. He checked his notes for the third time, finding them folded in his Bible where he found them the last two times he had checked. It was unlikely he would need his Bible, but he liked to be prepared in case a scriptural question should arise. That was silly, he thought, surely the highly educated Widow Watson would have her own Bible.

When Rudy received no response, he knocked again and the Widow Watson opened the door. He was surprised to find the Widow rather formally dressed for such a routine visit. Alice was wearing a tight pink sweater that accented her feminine features. A light blue skirt conservatively extended down to the ankles completing her wardrobe. Around her waist, was a white apron suggesting she had been working in the kitchen. Rudy was pleased to see the ankles were covered. He wasn't enthused with the newer fashions that exposed the lower limbs almost to the knees. Rudy was convinced those new liberal fashions would eventually lead to a decadent society. With Alice so formally dressed, Rudy was glad he decided to wear his bow tie.

"Reverend Hooper, you are punctual," the Widow said as she greeted the pastor. Rudy didn't mention that he had been waiting outside until his pocket watch said exactly seven o'clock.

"Good evening, Mrs. Watson," Rudy said, tipping his hat.

"Come in, and do call me Alice. Mrs. Watson sounds so formal."

"I always thought Alice was a pretty name." Rudy hated small talk. This was strictly business, he reminded himself. He was only here to discuss the Sunday school program, after which he would take his leave.

"Please have a seat. I have some cookies that have to come out of the oven."

Rudy stepped into Alice's living room. He found it cozy. It definitely displayed a woman's touch. Pressed up against the far wall and sandwiched between two end tables was a light brown couch. An ornate walnut coffee table with a plate glass top rested on a woven throw rug in front of the couch. The coffee table gave the appearance of a family heirloom. Facing the couch was an overstuffed chair, which clearly had seen many years of use. Rudy decided on the couch and sat down near the left end table. The end table was covered with Sunday school material. Obviously, Alice had been spending time planning for the start of Sunday school.

"Here are some cookies hot from the oven." Alice placed a large platter of cookies on the glass top of the coffee table. Another trip to the kitchen produced two china cups and a silver coffeepot. Steam from the spout confirmed that the coffee was still hot.

"You sure can cook," Rudy proclaimed through a mouth-full of cookies. A few cookie crumbs were already accumulating in Rudy's black beard. Rudy had expected Alice to sit in the overstuffed chair facing him. Instead, she sat down beside him, her knees firmly pressed against his.

"Let me pour you a cup of coffee. It'll help wash down the cookies." The Widow poured a cup for Rudy and then filled her cup. "I hope you don't think I am too forward, but I made something for you today." Alice extracted a small silk pouch, which had been stashed under her wide black belt. Rudy could see the initials R.H. embroidered on the front. "It's a coin pouch,"

Alice explained. "Pull on these two loops and the pouch closes." Alice passed the gift to Rudy and watched his eyes for a reaction. She wasn't disappointed.

"Why, thank you." Rudy opened and closed the pouch several times. The two draw string loops each had a large bead at the end to make for easy grasping.

"They're easy to make, and I had some extra material."

"That was thoughtful of you."

"Really, it was nothing. I have a foot operated sewing machine that sews the pouch together within minutes."

Rudy plucked a few coins from his pocket and inserted them into the pouch. He was pleased to see them disappear as he pulled the drawstrings apart. In the excitement of his new toy, he had totally forgotten the pressure against his knee. He didn't notice as the thigh-to-thigh contact increased until the Widow Watson's hip pressed tightly against his. Returning to reality, Rudy rearranged his position, but the flank attack continued, crushing him against the end of the couch. There was no further room to maneuver.

"You said you had some ideas for the Sunday school?" Rudy asked.

Alice took a sip of her coffee and returned the cup to its saucer on the coffee table. "I was thinking of starting off with the story of Noah and the flood."

Noah must have had beaver problems also, Rudy decided.

"The flood story is something I think the kids can understand."

Rudy's mind began to drift. I really have to do something about that Luther, Rudy thought, but no solutions came immediately to mind.

"Maybe we can have the children make an ark out of papier-mâché."

That's what I need, an ark instead of a parsonage. Then, if the water gets too high, the ark will just float around the pond. I would need a small rowboat to get to shore.

"Of course we would have to explain cubits and other details to the children."

I wonder if people would laugh if they saw me building an ark. It would be best if I didn't call it an ark. I could call it a barge. Rudy liked that idea.

"Then we'll explain the reason for the flood was that God wished to punish the many sinners throughout the world."

What sin did I do to deserve Luther, Rudy wondered. It would have to be a large sin for the Lord to severely punish me with such a great plague as Luther.

"Is there anything I left out?" Alice asked.

"Huh?" The question brought Rudy back to reality.

"Do you have any suggestions?" Alice repeated.

"No, it sounds good."

"I have a picture of the ark we can use as a model. It's somewhere in one of these magazines."

Alice, her left arm resting on the top of the couch behind Rudy's head, leaned over to obtain one of the magazines lying on the table beside Rudy. As she did, her tight pink sweater brushed across Rudy finally coming to a rest firmly pressed against his chest.

"I think it was in this magazine," Alice said, flipping through the pages with her right hand.

Rudy pushed back into couch, his mind totally obsessed with the chest tightly pressing against him. He could feel the sweat accumulating on his palms. He exhaled some air to minimize the physical contact, but the grip tightened like a boa constrictor coiling around its prey.

"I know it's in this magazine." Alice continued to thumb through the pages.

Rudy exhaled more air, but the serpent wrapped another coil around his chest, and again the slack was eliminated as the Widow continued with her two-pronged attack.

"Here it is," Alice proclaimed, with a finger pointing to a picture of the ark.

Rudy could feel the coils squeezing every ounce of breath from his lungs. He was beginning to get dizzy. Although he could feel his pounding heart pushing up against the pink sweater with each beat, the ever-tightening coils of the pink python cut off blood flow to the brain. He could no longer breathe. The room was beginning to spin. Death was imminent.

"Are you O.K.?" Alice asked after she retrieved her magazine and returned to her upright position. Beads of sweat covered Rudy's forehead. "You look awful pale."

"Must be a touch of the flu," Rudy replied. "Maybe I should go home and get some rest."

"Do you want me to walk you home?"

"No, I'll be fine. I just need some rest." Rudy grabbed his hat and coaxed his body to an upright position. "I would like to thank you for your hospitality and also for the coin pouch."

Alice ushered Rudy to the door. "We must get together again to discuss the rest of the Sunday school program."

"I'm sure we will," Rudy said, heading for the safety of the exit.

Alice watched Rudy disappear into the darkness and then sat down to place an entry in her diary.

Today Reverend Hooper came to visit and discuss the Sunday school program. I think he likes me. He complimented my cooking several times and really liked the coin pouch I had made for him. He even seemed to have a little twinkle in his eye when I suggested we meet again to discuss the Sunday school program. I guess I will have to invite him over more often.

***

Rudy sat down at his kitchen table and opened his journal.

Tonight I met with Alice Watson to discuss the forthcoming Sunday school program. The day was otherwise uneventful.

***

"Good morning, girls," Maggie said as she opened the September meeting of the Bare Creek Methodist Church's Ladies Aid Society. "I'm now going to turn the program over to Trudy who has a neat idea for a church fund-raiser."

"The other day I was thinking of ways we could raise money for a coal furnace." Trudy stood up to speak, feeling it added more authority to her statements. "As you all know we only have a wood burning stove to heat the church, and that doesn't heat the basement at all. It makes it very cold for the children in Sunday school. I'm, therefore, suggesting we have a potato sausage sale."

"Potato sausage? What's that?" Agnes asked.

"It's made of chopped onions and potatoes mixed in with ground beef and pork. Add some salt and pepper, stuff it into some animal casings, and presto, you have potato sausage."

"How do you expect to make any money with the potato sausage, sell it to ourselves?" Agnes wasn't totally convinced.

"No, of course not. That would be silly. What good would it do to make potato sausage and then sell it to ourselves? We sell it to our husbands."

"Maybe they won't buy the sausage."

"They will if we tell them to."

"But our husbands won't know how to cook the potato sausage after they buy it," Mrs. Olson pointed out.

"We'll have to cook the sausage, but by then we'll have their money."

It all made sense when Trudy explained it that way.

"We have a sausage stuffer at the cafe that will fill the casings with sausage," Maggie informed the ladies.

"I think it's a great idea," Mrs. Olson decided.

"All in favor?" Maggie asked.

"Aye."

"OK by me."

"Let's do it."

"I'm for it."

"Motion carried."

"When is a good time?" Agnes asked.

"Friday would be a good time for Jennifer and me," Maggie said. "Pa and Frenchie will be in Marquette checking on the potato market for next summer. Might as well do it when they're not around."

"Friday is good for me also. Mel has to go to a hardware convention in Green Bay."

"Silas will be in Escanaba checking on parts for his printing press."

"That's convenient. All of our husbands will be gone at the same time," Trudy noted.

"That's too convenient," Maggie said.

"What about you, Mrs. Olson?"

"My husband will also be out of town."

"I smell a rat," Maggie said, summing up the feelings of all present.

"What do you think they're up to?"

"Probably a night of gambling and hard liquor."

"They're not meeting anywhere in town."

"I have a feeling if we find where they're meeting, we'll find their still."

"I think you're all wrong," Jennifer said. "Frenchie would never lie to me. If he says he's going to Marquette to check on the potato market, then he's going to Marquette to check on the potato market."

The members of the Bare Creek Methodist Church's Ladies Aid Society looked at each other. This girl needs help, they decided. Agnes walked over to Jennifer and placed her arm around Jennifer's shoulder.

"Look at it this way," Agnes suggested. "Frenchie loves you, doesn't he?"

"Yes, a course he does."

"If he really loves you, he'll expect you to use your best judgment to care for his needs. Men cry out for guidance and stability. They do best in a structured environment. That's why they marry us."

That's not why Frenchie married me, Jennifer thought. He had other things on his mind—and he didn't need any guidance either.

"They don't have the internal strength to fight off temptation like we do," Agnes continued. "It's up to us to provide that moral guidance they so desperately crave. It's not that men are bad, they just don't know any better."

"Well, I guess you women have been married longer than I have." Jennifer wasn't convinced, but didn't feel up to further argument.

"The bottom line is men are children that never grew up. Their hearts may be in the right place, but they can't be trusted." The rest of the women nodded in agreement.

"Where do we go from here?" Maggie asked, returning to the problem at hand.

"I say we follow them and see if they lead us to their still," Trudy suggested. "Then we smash the still and take no prisoners!"

"It would be best if only a small group tailed them," Agnes said. "Maybe Trudy and I could tail them and come back for the rest of you after we find their still."

"Everyone in favor of Agnes's motion?" Maggie asked.

The motion passed unanimously.

***

Rudy didn't get many presents other than an occasional chicken or moose steak, and a gift such as a coin pouch was a memorable event. He had taken the coins out several times just so he could return them to the pouch and watch them disappear when he pulled the drawstrings. He was particularly fascinated with the closing mechanism. It was simple, but effective.

Rudy pulled two kitchen chairs together so the upright posts of the chair backs were four inches apart and carefully looped one of the drawstrings over each post forming a bridge between the chairs. With two fingers of each hand, he gently opened the pouch. The silk was stiff and light, remaining open after Rudy released his grip. Standing above the coin pouch, he dropped pennies into the pouch. The first penny missed, falling to the floor. The second, third, and fourth were right on target and sank into the money pouch. To Rudy's disappointment, the pouch opening slowly closed as the weight of the coins pulled down on the purse strings. By the time he got to the fifth penny, the opening was much too small, and the fifth penny fell to the floor.

Rudy stared at the pouch; the gears within his mind began to turn. "I wonder..." Rudy removed the pennies from the pouch and replaced the pouch between the chair posts making sure the pouch was wide open. He took out his pocket watch and dropped it from ten inches above the pouch. The watch hit the bottom with a soft bounce and then disappeared as the weight in the pouch pulled the drawstrings taut. Rudy removed the watch and repeated the experiment. Again, the watch hit the bottom and disappeared when the opening to the pouch closed. A third time produced similar results. A diabolical smile crossed his face, the same smile he always got when he thought he might get the best of Luther.

***

Rudy knocked on the door and was about to knock a second time when the Widow Watson appeared.

"Why, Reverend Hooper. This is a pleasant surprise. Please come in."

"No, I really can't stay, and I do apologize for coming unannounced."

"Heavens no, you're always welcome here."

"I was wondering if I could ask a favor." Rudy was beginning to regret his actions, but he was a desperate man. Desperate men will do anything.

"I would be more than happy to help you any way I can."

"You don't have to do it if you don't want to."

"What's the favor?"

"If you say no, we can still be friends."

"I'll be glad to do it."

"It's really too much to ask of you. I don't know what came over me."

"That's what friends are for."

"It was a dumb idea, and I am sorry I wasted your time. I should be going before I waste more of your time."

"WHAT IS IT YOU WANT ME TO DO?"

"Would you make me a laundry bag similar to the coin pouch?" Rudy finally blurted out.

"That sounds simple enough." Alice was expecting a more complex task, given the prolonged introduction to the request.

"I have the materials." Rudy offered Alice a length of clothesline and a large piece of burlap.

"I can find better material than burlap." Alice was not impressed with the coarse material being offered.

"No, it has to be super strong. I'm hard on laundry bags."

"I suppose I could do it out of burlap if you insist."

"Can you make it three feet deep with a two-foot diameter opening?" Rudy asked.

"That's a good size laundry bag."

"I have a lot of laundry."

"It won't look pretty," Alice said.

"It doesn't have to be pretty, just strong and functional. Maybe you could sew the seams twice to increase the strength."

"I could embroider your name on the bag. That would make it more personal," Alice said.

"If you really want to embroider something on the bag, you could do *Deliver me from mine enemies*. That's Psalm 59." Rudy sometimes even impressed himself with his Biblical recall.

"I can have it done by tomorrow. Is that soon enough?" Alice asked.

"That would be fantastic," Rudy said. "I have to get going, but I'll stop by tomorrow."

"I'll bake some more cookies then." Alice watched as Rudy walked back toward the parsonage. He does like me, she decided.

***

It had long been rumored that the elusive still was located east of town. Based on this information, Agnes and Trudy posted their lookout on a rocky outcrop overlooking the only road leading east. From their lofty perch, they could observe any travelers who might ply the road below. If they were wrong and the still wasn't east of town, they would know within the next half-hour. Mel was scheduled to leave the hardware store for his meeting in Green Bay forthwith.

They weren't disappointed. A dark shadow could be seen slinking along the edge of the road. From their distant viewpoint, it was impossible to identify the scoundrel, but he was obviously up to no good. Like a common criminal, he frequently looked over his shoulder to ensure he wasn't being followed.

"There he is." Agnes said, pointing to the figure walking on the road.

"Let me take a look through Mel's telescope." Trudy lifted a telescope to her right eye. According to Mel, the telescope was given to him by Teddy Roosevelt himself. The story became more embellished with each telling.

"It's Mel all right. I would recognize that scraggly beard anywhere," Trudy said. The right side of Mel's beard had grown considerably since it was singed during Mel's bell tower incident, but had yet to match the longer whiskers on the left.

"Watch him and see where he goes,"

Mel continued east for three-quarters of a mile before turning north into the woods. A tall white pine marked the point of his departure from the road.

It took ten minutes for Agnes and Trudy to descend from their rocky lookout to the road below. By the time they arrived, Mel was gone. A trail did lead into the woods, splitting frequently into a maze of sub trails.

"What do we do now?" Agnes asked. "He could've taken any of these trails."

"We wait," Trudy replied. "There'll be others."

"At least we know the conclave is east of town."

"We need to hide," Trudy said. "When the next lying varmint comes along, we'll follow him until he leads us to the others."

"It won't be easy following him without being seen."

"Not to worry. I haven't been listening to Mel's war stories for nothing."

Trudy, finding a small mud puddle left over from a recent rain, scooped up some of the dark mud and carefully smeared the gooey mess over her face and hands until her skin was totally darkened.

"Ugh, surely you don't expect me to cover my body with that filthy dirt?" Agnes asked, as she watched in disgust. "There is no telling what kinds of bugs and creepy organisms are crawling in that mud."

"The girls are depending on us," Trudy said, smearing mud on Agnes's face.

"They're still going to be able to see us.

"That's because we're not done yet." Trudy cut some branches from a small bush, sticking them in her shirt, under her belt, and any other place that would secure the branches. A few vines were added to the ensemble to give a little variety. Agnes did likewise, and the two ladies disappeared into the foliage.

"The key is to freeze and not move if someone is looking at you," one bush said to the other bush.

The two camouflaged commandos didn't have to vegetate long before the next fugitive from female fetters arrived on the scene.

"That has to be Silas," said Bush Number One.

"Don't move. Let him walk past us," commanded Bush Number Two. "OK, let's follow him," Bush Number Two whispered when Silas passed the brush pile.

The brush pile watched as Silas continued down the path, turning right at a fork in the trail.

"Freeze!" Bush Number One whispered, and Bush Number Two immediately froze. Silas had turned around and was staring at the brush pile. Seeing nothing out of place, he returned to his brisk stroll.

***

Silas made no attempt to conceal that he was renting a horse from Ollie Olson's livery stable. After saddling up, he headed back into the center of town instead of heading directly toward Escanaba. He was careful to stop and say hello to any friends along the way, especially women folk, letting them know that, indeed, he was on his way to Escanaba. After much fanfare, he rode off to the west only to circle around behind the livery stable where he returned the horse with a wink to Ollie. Where he was going, he wouldn't need a horse.

Silas gave the town a wide berth as he circled around to the road leading east. He continued down the road until he came to a branch lying on the road. It was nothing more than a twig that had recently been broken free from its attachment. Most folks would have ignored it, but Silas turned down a trail suggested by the broken end of the twig. He came to a fork in the trail, and another broken twig pointed toward the correct path.

This is easy, Silas thought. Agnes didn't suspect a thing. It's amazing how naive women can be. It just proves the natural superiority of men over women. That's why women should never have been given the right to vote. The female mind doesn't have the capability of complex thought, which is why they're always outwitted by men.

Silas thought he heard some noise behind him and turned to look. He would have sworn that bush had moved. It must have been the wind, but none of the other bushes were moving, and he didn't feel a breeze. Maybe it was a small bird moving among the branches. Either way, it was none of his concern, and he turned back to the trail.

It was a three-mile walk to the still, and by the time Silas arrived, it was already starting to get dark. Mel, P.C., and several other men had arrived earlier and had set up a table consisting of wooden planks across sawhorses. The trunk of a white pine had been cut into sections, which were being used as stools. Let the drinking and card playing begin.

Should be enough corn liquor to keep them going deep into the night, Silas decided after surveying the operation. There were several vats of finished product waiting to be sampled while other vats, containing fermenting corn syrup, awaited their turn at the still. A fire under a copper kettle confirmed that the still was in full operation. The flickering light from the fire cast shadows that danced on the bushes at the edge of the clearing. If one didn't know better, one would swear the bushes were moving. Silas filled his mug with corn whiskey and headed for the table. "Deal me in," he informed the others.

***

"We were right," Agnes told the hastily assembled group of women. "They're partying at their still."

"There were several vats of finished whiskey as well as two vats of corn syrup waiting to be distilled." Trudy scratched at her neck. She wished they had been more selective in choosing the leaves and vines to stuff into their shirts. She was hoping the itching was from the mud remaining on their faces and necks, but she feared the worst.

"The trail is marked by fresh cut branches with the cut end pointing in the correct direction," Agnes informed the crew. "It's on the other side of Moose Lake."

"I suggest we meet back here in thirty minutes with flashlights and axes," Maggie suggested. "First we destroy the still, and then everyone is in charge of collaring her own husband."

***

By midnight, a good portion of the male citizens of Bear Creek had arrived at the party, requiring the addition of several new poker tables. Greenbacks were passed freely back and forth as the participants, now well lubricated with the one hundred proof corn whisky, bet on trivial hands.

The fire under the copper kettle provided warmth for those with an occasional chill, but failed to provide adequate light for serious poker players. Therefore, kerosene lanterns hung from the trees along the periphery of the card tables. Neither the light from the fire nor the light from the lanterns penetrated into the depths of the surrounding woods, providing safe haven for any stalking predators. A wary observer, however, would have noted the occasional flicker of a flashlight. A wary observer would have noted the unexplained snapping of a twig. A wary observer would have heard the low whispers protruding from the darkness. But there were no wary observers to provide advance warning. There were no wary observers to sound the alarm before the predators pounced upon their prey. The predators slowly but methodically closed in upon their quarry. There would be no escape. They would give no quarter.

A soprano voice yelled, "Attack!" and a dozen Amazons wielding axes, hatchets, and sledgehammers descended upon the panic stricken men. The still and wooden vats of fermented produce were the first to go, as axes changed the vats into kindling wood and the copper still into scrap metal.

"It's an ambush, run for your lives!" one of the more sober men yelled out. "It's every man for himself!" Men scattered in every direction.

Many people would find it difficult to navigate through the woods in the daylight even when sober. It can be more difficult at night when the finely honed skills of the northern woodsman are mitigated by the influence of one hundred-proof corn whisky. Needless to say, clunking noises could be heard as hard heads ran into harder trees. Other fugitives howled as they became entwined in briar patches, and moans could be heard coming from every corner of the periphery. The predators, with flashlights in hand, followed the moans until every generic husband had been subdued by the ear and returned to center stage for prisoner exchange. Once all of the women were reunited with their inebriated spouses, the long trek home began. Penance would begin in the morning.

***

Rudy checked the burlap laundry bag. The seams were doubly sewn as he had requested. It wasn't a work of art, but it was sturdy and that was what counted. Embroidered on the side of the bag was the inscription *Deliver me from mine enemies*. Rudy pulled on the clothes line drawstrings, and the opening to the bag closed just like his coin pouch. It would work, Rudy convinced himself.

Rudy began digging the hole fifty feet from the edge of the beaver pond. He made the hole two feet in diameter and four feet deep. It took twenty minutes to dig, but like all labors of love, time went fast. A wooden stake was inserted into the ground on each side of the hole. Rudy placed a loop of each drawstring over a stake and set the bag in the hole. To his horror, the bag collapsed under its own weight. It wasn't going to work. He had to make it work. Rudy found four small sticks and placed them in the opening of the bag in a tic-tac-toe configuration. It formed a square and not a circle, but it held the bag open. It would work. Rudy covered the hole with a few more twigs and leaves, totally concealing the opening. It was baited with fragments of wood taken from the dam.

Most of the wood was placed beyond the trap, but a small piece was carefully placed over the hole itself. Now all he had to do was wait.

***

Silas tossed a peeled potato into the stainless steel pot filled with water. The members of the Bare Creek Economics Club who surrounded the pot cringed in pain as the noise of the splash echoed throughout the church basement. From the quality of his headache, Silas assumed he must have had a good time the night before. He reached into the bag beside him to retrieve a fresh potato. There were many more to peel.

"I don't know why we have to peel all of these potatoes," Frenchie said.

"That's the way life is," P.C. informed his son-in-law.

"Have you seen how they make the sausage?" Frenchie asked. "They grind up pork and beef and mix in potatoes and onions. Then they stuff it into cow guts. What idiot is going to buy that stuff?"

"We're the idiots who'll buy it," Mel said.

"Well, I'm not going to buy any of it," Frenchie informed the group.

"How's the potato peeling coming?" Jennifer asked from the door to the church kitchen where the women were busy stuffing the sausage. "We need more potatoes. We're expecting to sell a lot of sausage. We're doing so well, we've decided to make this an annual event. Frenchie, be a dear and buy five pounds of sausage, O.K.?" Jennifer returned to the kitchen without waiting for an answer.

"Five pounds? I suspect the fine for the rest of us will be closer to fifteen pounds," Mel said.

"They're letting him off easy because it's his first offense," Silas decided.

"How come we are doing all this?" Frenchie asked.

"It beats three weeks on the couch. You do the vice, you pay the price. If you get caught on a M.A.C.H.O. night, you got to pay the dues."

"How often do you have M.A.C.H.O. nights?"

"Once or twice a year."

"Do you always get caught?"

"Shucks no!" Mel said indignantly. "Why just four years ago—or was it five years ago?"

"I think it was five years ago," Silas said. "It was just after the end of the Great War."

"Anyway," Mel continued, "P.C. and Red Weasel made this fishing raft out of four army surplus inflatable boats by building a wooden platform over them. It was so big you could've danced on it."

"Mighty fine raft at that," P.C. said.

"We hung lanterns from corner posts and built a canvas canopy in case it rained. We added a few tables for cards, and bingo, we had a perfect M.A.C.H.O. platform."

"The women didn't find out?" Frenchie asked.

"Oh, they found out all right," Mel said, "but they couldn't do anything about it. We were a quarter mile off shore."

"We must have partied until three in the morning."

"Yeah, that's when P.C. added more kerosene to the lanterns."

"The kerosene wouldn't have caught fire if it hadn't been for that stogie Mel was chewing on," P.C. pointed out in his defense.

"Then what happened?" Frenchie asked.

"Well, inflatable rafts don't do well around fire," Silas said, "and the wooden platform didn't do much better."

"Did they ever find Hank Heikkinen's body?" Mel asked.

"Someone thought they saw him in Montreal. Maybe he's still alive and hiding from his wife."

"At least he doesn't have to peel these stupid potatoes," Mel said, tossing another peeled potato into the pot of water.

***

The sun was rising in the east when Luther headed out for his daily inspection of his watery domain. The fall sun didn't rise as early as it did in the summer, and the shorter days cut into Luther's productivity, a situation Luther found particularly irritating. Even at high noon, the sun remained low in the sky with minimal penetration into the depths of the beaver pond. This early in the day, inspection of the dam's submerged portion would be useless. That would have to wait until later in the day.

Luther was obsessive-compulsive when it came to his dam. Every bit of the dam would be inspected and a damage assessment made before repairs were begun. Some wear and tear was expected. What made him irate was the vandalism. That part of human behavior was difficult to tolerate.

Luther had found humans to be lazy beasts, and for the most part, they could be safely ignored. They preferred to daydream or socialize rather than pursue hard work. It was amazing they accomplished anything. Many times, he had seen humans sitting around doing nothing but talking, definitely very unbeaver like.

Now, it is not as if beavers are antisocial. There is a time and place for everything. At one time Luther had even considered taking a mate, but he had his priorities and there was little time to find a proper companion. Not any mate would do. He wouldn't fall for some young thing with a pretty pelt, no sirree. Any mate would have to carry her weight. Running a beaver dam is a full time job, requiring hard, physical labor, definitely not the place for the weaker sex.

Luther climbed up on the dam to continue his inspection. He could see small leaks throughout the dam. Small leaks were inevitable and had to be expected. Even the best of dams wasn't totally watertight. What concerned him most was a section at the center where the water was gushing over the top. That human had been at it again. Luther limped toward the gurgling water. The breach in the dam was six feet wide and a good foot in depth, Luther decided as he estimated the damage. He checked the damage from several angles including an underwater inspection. The footings were sound. That would reduce repair time. Luther calculated the material list; he would need a fair amount of branches and mud and maybe some stone. He reckoned about six beaver-hours of labor. He should have it done by noon.

First, he would need sticks and branches. That two-legged varmint had been throwing the material from the dam downstream where it was washed away, forcing him to use new material. Climbing to a high spot on the dam, Luther stood on his hind legs to locate the best source of wood. Much of the surrounding brush and trees had already been used.

"Eureka! Am I living right or what," Luther said to himself as he spied a pile of debris on the pond's south shore. "I'll have the dam repaired in three hours tops."

Luther dove into the water and headed toward the south shore. His nose formed "V" shaped ripples in the water, but he swam silently. His gimpy leg worked flawlessly in the water, but then, it didn't have to bear weight. As he pulled himself onto the shore, the discomfort returned.

Most of the dam fragments were in a pile seventy-five feet from the pond. Dragging branches down to the pond would be time consuming, but it was quicker than fresh cut. "There's a small twig the human had obviously dropped. I'll get that one first and then go back for the others." Luther reached for the twig, but the ground under the twig opened up under his weight, and he began to fall. "What the hey!" Luther tumbled onto his back. He could momentarily see the sky through the small opening until that too was swallowed up by the hole.

"I got the beaver! I got the beaver!" Rudy sang to himself as he danced a little jig on his porch. He had been watching Luther for the better part of two hours, but it seemed like days. Victory was his. He'd gone against Goliath, and his stone had found its mark. The Lord had delivered him from his enemies. At last he had dominion over the fish of the sea and over the birds of the air and over every living thing that moves upon the earth. Orderliness had been returned to the earth, and the earth was again dominated by man, as God had intended.

Rudy lifted the bag out of the hole to reveal a writhing burlap bag filled with one very irritated beaver. It was just as well beavers couldn't talk. Rudy didn't think the Lord would be impressed with such language. Rudy stared at the squirming bag in disbelief. He may have lost some battles, but he had won the war and that was what counted. Now he had to dispose of the beaver. Killing Luther was out of the question. It was one thing to blow up a beaver lodge, but to purposely kill Luther would be murder. He would relocate him to a rural section of the county. That would be the Christian thing to do. He would turn him loose five miles from town.

The five-mile walk took two hours, but Rudy found it enjoyable. He was reminded of his victory with every bounce and wiggle of the burlap bag tied to the end of the six-foot pole, which was draped across his right shoulder hobo style. A few fluffy clouds occasionally obscured the sun, but for the most part the sun shone brightly, bringing out the reds and purples of the autumn leaves. There was something about the smell of freshly fallen leaves that reminded Rudy of his childhood when he would jump into piles of newly raked leaves. Yes, it was a good day for a walk.

Rudy assumed he knew five miles worth of church hymns. When he had sung each song once and whistled the verses he couldn't remember, he stopped to pardon Luther. It gave him a feeling of power to hold Luther's fate in his hands, but a pardon is good. Rudy was not vindictive, and forgiveness and redemption are major tenets of Christianity.

Rudy had expected Luther to run for the safety of the oak and aspen forest when the bag was open, but Luther slowly waddled out limping on his bad leg. Rudy wondered if the leg was painful. Luther had always limped, but it never occurred to Rudy that it could be a source of discomfort. Luther waddled the fifty feet to the edge of the woods. He didn't look back until he reached the base of a large oak at the border to the woods. Only then did he turn to look back at Rudy. Rudy swore it was an *et tu Brute* look. He stared at Rudy for a moment or two and then disappeared into the woods. Rudy wished him well. Somehow, the victory isn't as sweet once you have seen the vanquished. It was a long solemn walk home.

***

It has been an interesting week. I met with the Widow Watson this week to discuss the new Sunday school program. It looks like she has it well under control. She made me a nice coin pouch, which closes automatically with a pull of the drawstrings. She says they are simple to make, but just the same it is a nice gift. I hope she isn't reading too much into our relationship.

She made a similar style laundry bag out of burlap, which I used to catch Luther. I turned him loose five miles west of town. I hope I did the right thing, but I really needed to get rid of him. He had such a forlorn look on his face when I released him. I hope he will be able to care for himself in the woods; he is a wild animal after all.

This week the women of the church held a potato sausage sale to raise money for a new church furnace. It apparently was quite successful although they only earned half the money needed. I was surprised the men volunteered to help. They peeled the potatoes while the women mixed the ground potatoes, onions, and meat together and filled the casings. I bought five pounds. I hope it is good.

On a sadder note, it appears Agnes and Trudy got into some poison ivy, and their faces and arms are covered with blisters. They are treating it with a pink lotion Maggie made for them. It sure looks uncomfortable. They must have gotten it raking leaves. I hear there is a lot of poison ivy around here. I also noticed several men with scratches on their faces, and some even have a few bruises. They didn't say how they got them, and I didn't think it was my place to ask. Yoopers can be strange at times.

Chapter Seven

Mornings arrived early for Jennifer and Frenchie, and the first of October was no different than any other day in their mundane lives. Their potato farm wouldn't produce income until the following summer, requiring Jennifer to continue her work at the Bare Creek Cafe while Frenchie continued his employment at Olie Olson's livery stable. Both employers expected early arrivals from their employees. That didn't make crawling out of bed any easier on cool autumn mornings when the warmth of the bed with its feather quilt encouraged tardiness. The only heat in the two-room log cabin came from the wood-burning stove in the front room, and little of that managed to find its way to the bedroom. By morning, the wood stove would be down to a few glowing coals begging to be fed.

The wind-up alarm clock arrogantly awoke promptly at six; too promptly, Frenchie thought. The alarm continued to announce the coming of morning until the spring unwound causing the clanging to wither and die. Frenchie waited for Jennifer to get up and feed the stove, as he knew she would. Jennifer was a quick riser, a trait Frenchie didn't wish to discourage. If he procrastinated long enough, he could arise to a warm cabin. This particular morning, she was slower than usual.

"Jennifer, it's morning."

"Humph."

Maybe he would have to be the first one up after all, Frenchie feared. He extended his right foot out from under the quilt to test the temperature. The foot recoiled in horror to the protection of the warm quilt. "It's cold out there," Frenchie said, hoping Jennifer could take a hint.

"Humph."

Obvious, she didn't intend to be the first one out of bed. "Why don't you stay in bed until I get the heat going?" Frenchie suggested, hoping for a guilt effect. The guilt trip didn't work either, forcing Frenchie to make the ultimate sacrifice. Frenchie headed toward the bedroom door, which led to the front room where the starving wood stove waited for its morning feeding. As he reached the doorway, he was slammed to the floor by a stiff-arm and body check that would have made a college running back proud. Jennifer continued through the living room and out the front door. When Frenchie caught up with her, she was leaning over the porch railing staring at the previous night's dinner.

"I think the potato sausage we had last night went bad," Jennifer said.

"I don't know. I thought it tasted pretty good," Frenchie replied. "You know, the potato sausage looks about the same coming back up as it did when we stuffed it into those cow guts—maybe a bit soupier."

Any recalcitrant tidbits of sausage still lingering in Jennifer's stomach quickly surrendered in the face of Frenchie's observations, creating a new wave of gastrological gymnastics.

"I don't feel well."

"Maybe you ought to stay home. I can stop by the Cafe on the way to work and let your mother know."

Jennifer offered no rebuttal and passively headed back to bed. "Tell Ma I'll be in tomorrow. This can't last too long."

"Here's a bucket you can keep by your bed."

"I think I'm all right. I won't need it if I just lie in bed."

"Actually, I thought the potato sausage was pretty decent. I was a bit skeptical when I was the women stuffing that slimy stuff into the cow innards," Frenchie said. Jennifer made a lunge for the bucket. "Let me add some wood to the fire before I leave. It'll keep you warm for most of the morning."

***

Frenchie could have walked the two miles into town but decided to take the wagon; he needed to stop at the store for supplies. Besides, Charlie could use the exercise. Normally, Frenchie found the ride into town relaxing, giving him time to think. Charlie knew the way and little guidance was needed; although, without encouragement, the trip could become time consuming since Charlie had a pronounced aversion to sweat.

It was strange only Jennifer was sick. If it were the potato sausage, they should both be sick, Frenchie mused. There were many possible causes for Jennifer's illness, most of which weren't serious. She should be better in a day or so. He did have a childhood friend who had a similar illness, ending in a painful death. The doctor called it a ruptured appendix. Frenchie was only eight at the time, but he still had memories of his best friend moaning in pain. That was years ago. Today, a surgeon would remove the appendix, and the patient would do fine. But a trip to a surgeon in Marquette would take the better part of a day. A patient with appendicitis could be dead before arriving in Marquette. The more Frenchie thought about Jennifer's illness, the worse it seemed to be.

Charlie arrived at the cafe in record time, sparing Frenchie the effort of planning Jennifer's funeral. Charlie had been more energetic, ever since he discovered that cute little filly down at the livery stable. He saw no need for stopping at the cafe and was quick to show his displeasure when Frenchie ran into the cafe to inform Maggie of Jennifer's illness.

P.C. was tormenting two sunny-side-up eggs, as was his custom this time in the morning. He had a double helping of hash browns on the side. This was more than his usual, but he had work to do. A skunk with a litter of kittens had taken up residence under Weasel's tool shed, and P.C. had promised to help deliver the eviction notice. It would be a delicate operation, but well within their capabilities; they weren't a couple of dummies.

P.C. was about to mount a flank attack on his hash browns when Frenchie arrived at the Cafe. "Is Ma around?"

"She's in the kitchen," P.C. replied as he prepared his hash browns for the coup de grâce.

"Morning, Frenchie," Maggie said as she came through the kitchen door. "I thought I heard your voice. Why don't you sit down; I'll fix you a couple of eggs."

"Jennifer's sick," Frenchie said. He sat down as suggested. Frenchie had learned Maggie's suggestions were tantamount to an order. "She's been vomiting all morning. Maybe the potato sausage we had last night was bad," Frenchie suggested. That was better than appendicitis.

"I thought the potato sausage was good," P.C. said.

"You'd eat anything," Maggie countered. "You didn't get sick did you, Frenchie?"

Frenchie shook his head, no.

"Then it can't be the sausage."

"Do you think it's serious?" Frenchie asked.

"Nah, she'll be OK. She just picked up a bug. She'll be better in a day or two. In the meantime, I'll need some extra help around the cafe. Do you think you could help?" Maggie asked, looking at P.C.

"I promised the Chief I'd go fishing with him," after we evict the skunks, P.C. thought. "We don't want to start an international incident." P.C. thought it best not to mention the skunk; Maggie had a tendency to worry.

He wouldn't be much help anyway, Maggie decided. "Can you ask Water Lily if she could help out for a few hours?"

"I'll head right out there and ask her."

Maybe he had overreacted, Frenchie decided. Maggie wasn't concerned. Just the same, Frenchie would see if he could leave work early.

***

Luther didn't look back until he reached the edge of the woods. He could see that human standing at the edge of the road staring at him. What did I ever do to him, Luther wondered? There was no time for circumspection. Luther was stranded in unfamiliar territory without any knowledge of his whereabouts. Where was he to go from here? The only world he had ever known was the Bare Creek beaver pond. He had never built a dam from scratch; although he had no doubt he was capable of such an endeavor.

Luther wasn't one to feel sorry for himself. His current situation presented immediate and serious problems. There would be no time for self-pity. Luther's foremost problem was his personal safety. A beaver is agile in water and in times of danger, can disappear under water for minutes at a time. He can sleep comfortably in his lodge, which can be accessed only from its below-the-water entrance. On land, beavers are easy prey for fox, wolves, and bobcats.

Luther limped into the woods. He needed to find water, and he needed to find it quickly. Instinct suggested he would eventually cross a stream or lake, as water was plentiful in Michigan's Upper Peninsula. It may not be adequate for his needs, but it would provide limited protection from predators as well as increase his mobility. Luther could move quickly in water, but walking through the dense undergrowth was difficult and exhausting. Fortunately, it was early in the day; he would have several hours of daylight before nocturnal predators ruled the night. Despite the risks, he would travel well into the night if need be. He couldn't afford to rest until he had reached the safety of water.

It was almost dusk when Luther detected the faint smell of water; he was getting close. The gurgling noise of a small brook soon became audible. Within minutes, Luther was soaking his sweaty body in the cool water of a small stream. It was too small for his needs, not even deep enough to swim, but it was still water. He would follow it downstream where it would enlarge with the addition of other small streams. Eventually it would provide sufficient water flow for a proper beaver dam. If nothing else, it was easier walking down the stream than forcing his way through the undergrowth. The limited water depth provided buoyancy, reducing the weight on his gimpy leg.

***

The early October morning was cool, but not cold; still Weasel decided it was time to break out his autumn attire consisting of the routine summer jeans and flannel shirt with the addition of a brown quilted vest for added warmth. A coonskin cap replaced his black, broad-brimmed hat and feathered hatband. Water Lily had made the cap by hand with the design taken from a picture of Davy Crockett. Weasel was impressed with anyone who could "kill a bear when he was only three." The cap proved practical for the U. P. weather since the fur lining could be pulled down over his ears when the weather got nasty. That wouldn't be the case today. The vest was already proving too warm, and from the clear sky, Weasel reckoned it would be even warmer by afternoon, unusual weather for October. After five minutes of splitting wood, the vest was discarded.

"Morning, Chief," P.C. announced on his arrival. The Moose Lake Lodge was about three miles north of town and, with P.C.'s short legs, a good hour walk. He extracted his pocket watch from his shirt pocket. It was a quarter past one. He had made good time.

"Morning, Mayor. That's where they are," Weasel said, pointing to the large tool shed. "A polecat and three young kittens have set up housekeeping under the shed."

To prevent wood rot, the wooden shed had been built on a series of short concrete pillars, elevating the structure off the damp ground. Weeds growing around the structure reduced the flow of light in the crawl space. P.C. peered into the darkness. He could see ten feet at the most. A black skunk would be difficult to see even with its white stripe.

"How ya going to get them out?" P.C. asked.

"Goin' smoke them out. Wind's coming from the west. Figure we can build a fire along the west side of the shed and cover it with wet leaves. The wind will blow the smoke under the shed and flush them out. We just need to stand by with buckets of water to make sure the shed doesn't catch fire."

P.C. could see his friend had a well thought out plan, as he had expected. "Sounds easy enough."

***

Critter, awaked by the sound of splitting wood, opened a sleepy eye. "How is anyone supposed to sleep with all that racket?" Critter was a little testy, having been up all night seeking food for herself and her litter of three. Foraging for food in the forest was an exhausting process. It would have been more productive to reap the spoils behind the feed store, but Critter had selected the crawl space under the shed for its quietness. It was to be a better environment for raising her brood, and it was—until now. Whoever was responsible for the noise had no respect for nocturnal animals.

Critter waddled to the edge of the crawl space to investigate. Standing in front of the shed was a short, pudgy man with a black patch over his eye next to a tall, skinny, darker-skinned individual wearing a dead coon on his head. "Not those two again." Critter still had distasteful memories from last summer's encounter. For some reason, the intruders were making small pieces of wood out of big pieces of wood. Critter wasn't one to hold a grudge. As long as they left her alone, she could overlook the noise...at least for now.

***

"Ya think we split enough wood?" Weasel asked as he surveyed the fruits of their labors. A large pile of kindling wood paid tribute to the sweat on their bodies.

"Should be enough there to flush them out."

Small piles of wood were placed every five feet along the west side of the tool shed while buckets of water waited on standby. A pile of wet leaves was also at the ready.

"When she comes out, she'll have an attitude, so keep your distance." Weasel checked the wind. It was still coming from the west.

Neither Weasel nor P.C. had ever been a Boy Scout, and the patience required for an artistically initiated fire wasn't one of their virtues. Therefore, copious amounts of kerosene were splashed over the kindling.

"Shall we proceed, Mayor?"

"I do believe we are ready, Chief."

Weasel struck a match against the zipper of his jeans, and within minutes, five small fires lined the western wall of the shed. "Make sure the building doesn't catch." Weasel's warning was hardly necessary with such a well-planned operation. The wet leaves created large columns of white smoke as planned, but the smoke rose unmolested toward the sky. The wind had subsided. "The wind will pick up," Weasel assured P.C.

After several minutes, P.C. consulted his pocket watch; it was now a quarter past one. The fire was beginning to burn through the damp leaves, and the smoke was starting to diminish. A new layer of wet leaves was added.

"Ya know, we don't have to rely on the wind," P.C. said after checking his pocket watch for the third time. "We could tie a rope to some burning pine branches and pull it under the shed. Leave it there long enough to smoke out the critter and pull it out before the building has a chance to catch fire."

That's what Weasel liked about the Mayor; he was always thinking. "How we going get the rope under the shed in the first place?"

"I can crawl under the building from the other side and pull the rope through. It's dark under there, but I reckon I can see six feet ahead of me. That'll be more than enough to avoid any encounters with that skunk."

"Sounds like a workable plan to me. I'll fetch some rope."

At five foot two, P.C. was far from the largest man to walk the earth, but Maggie's cooking had provided a more than adequate waistline. As P.C. slithered under the shed, his backside scraped against the underside of the building. It was a close fit, but it wasn't tight and in no way an obstacle to the ultimate goal.

"Can you see anything?" Weasel asked as he played out the rope.

"I can see six or eight feet. A flashlight would have been nice."

"Don't get too close to that polecat."

P.C. found Weasel's comment insulting. He wasn't born yesterday. The shed was large; P.C. reckoned about twenty by thirty feet.

"Think I'm 'bout half way there," P.C. said after he had crawled ten feet. A quick search revealed no evidence of the skunk. P.C. pressed on but felt resistance. Increased effort was rewarded with a ripping sound.

"I think my pants are caught on a nail," P.C. informed his colleague at the other end of the tether.

"Can you get it loose?"

"Maybe." P.C. reached for the offending nail, but there was no room for maneuvering, and every movement caused increased tearing of his trousers. He had no desire to ruin a good pair of britches. "I can't reach it."

"Can you take your trousers off?"

P.C. reached for his belt buckle but found it firmly pinched against the ground. "Can't seem to get to the belt buckle either."

"Hold on, I'm coming in."

At six foot one, Weasel was taller than P.C. but had a slender frame and easily slipped under the shed. With his eyes unaccustomed to the darkness, visibility was nil. "Talk to me, and I'll follow your voice."

"It's starting to get smoky in here," P.C. said. "I think the wind's picking up." Large puffs of smoke billowed through the crawl space confirming P.C.'s suspicions and reducing visibility to inches.

"I should be close to you." Weasel continued toward the choking sounds emanating from the interior of the crawl space. "Let's get you loose and get out of here."

P.C. reached out blindly for his friend, grabbing a large, furry tail. This must be the Chief's coonskin cap, he wishfully told himself. He considered it a bad omen when the tail began to rise.

P.C. and Weasel exited the crawl space almost simultaneously, with P.C. minus his trousers; he knew he should have worn underwear. With bodies reeking of essence-of-skunk and lungs filled with smoke, the two comrades-in-arms took to their legs in a foot race toward the salvation of Moose Lake. The longer legs of the Chief carried him to a first place finish with the Mayor in hot pursuit. They crossed the finish line at the end of the pier with a couple of less than elegant splashes. Mosquitoes and black flies evacuated the area as the two aromatic heads surfaced for air.

"I think the wind picked up," Weasel confided to his friend. His coonskin cap was drenched with water, and the tail draped over his left eye. With his right eye, he could see flames licking up the side of the shed with insatiable hunger. It was already too far gone for a couple of buckets of water to make a difference.

"That was a mighty nice shed."

"It leaked some and there were a few rotten boards," Weasel countered, practicing the speech he would give his wife. "It wasn't worth all that much." Now if he could only convince Water Lily.

"Hey, look." P.C. pointed to a black and white furry ball and three smaller ones waddling away from the fire.

"We did it!"

"Look at them run! They won't come back to that tool shed again."

P.C. and Weasel exchanged high fives for a job well done.

P.C. and Weasel sat in the water and watched the flames spread across the top of the shed. Weasel had several cords of firewood stored in the shed, and he expected the blaze to continue throughout the afternoon.

"I suspect we should burn our clothes," Weasel suggested after a bit of thought. "We'll never get the smell out." With only his shirt to spare, P.C. had little to sacrifice.

"We may have to air out some ourselves before the smell is gone," P.C. said. "Maybe we can get in a bit of fishing this afternoon." He had told Maggie he would be fishing; it wouldn't hurt to bring home a couple large walleye. After burning the rest of their clothes, they could air out on Weasel's rowboat and maybe catch a few fish.

Fortunately, fate was smiling as an unusually warm autumn sun radiated down upon the daring duo who, clothed only in their epidermis, developed sunburns in places difficult to explain to inquisitive wives as they floated in their small rowboat. Their nude bodies were draped across the boat like wet dishrags. Conversation was held to a minimum, since neither individual felt compelled to provide idle and meaningless conversation. Cane poles cantilevered over the water while bobbers drifted with the small current. On the shore, the shed continued to burn with abandon. Life just didn't get any better than that.

"Ya know, Chief, I don't have any clothes."

"That's a fact," Weasel replied, thinking P.C.'s nudity should be obvious.

"I mean, I got nothing to wear home."

"Suppose that does present a problem."

"Think I could borrow some clothes from you?"

"Don't think any of my clothes would fit you. Your waist is a mite larger than mine." Weasel pondered the situation for a moment or two. It did pose a bit of a dilemma. "Could wear one of Water Lily's skirts. She's fairly wide at the hips."

"Might work," P.C. agreed.

"She has a buckskin skirt that's quite loose."

"Is that the one with the leather thong fringe along the bottom? Always did like that skirt."

"Yes, I think that would be perfect for you."

Now that another one of life's major problems was solved, the two heads-of-state returned to the pleasantries of daily life at Moose Lake. With the ends of their cane poles firmly restrained between their toes, they patiently awaited the arrival of a hungry walleye.

***

Work at the livery stable was difficult, since Frenchie couldn't clear Jennifer's illness from his mind. He was relieved knowing Maggie wasn't unduly concerned. Still, his mind wandered back to his childhood friend who died from a ruptured appendix. His illness started out as nausea and vomiting with abdominal cramping, but his illness didn't get better. His condition deteriorated until he died in severe pain. His death had left a deep scar in Frenchie's mind that now come back to haunt him.

It is hard to clean manure out of stables when your wife could be dying from appendicitis. The more he thought about it, the more he convinced himself of a dour outcome. Olie Olson finally suggested Frenchie take the rest of the day off. He wasn't getting much work out of him anyway.

"A little faster, Charlie." Despite Frenchie's urging, Charlie declined to be rushed. Charlie picked up the pace on his own once they came closer to the barn; therefore, Frenchie didn't press the issue. In the distance, Frenchie could see dark, bellowing smoke coming from the direction of Moose Lake. Weasel must be burning some brush, Frenchie surmised.

Jennifer was up and walking about when Charlie arrived at the cabin. Maybe her illness had resolved. Frenchie had to admit he sometimes overreacted. She certainly looked like her normal self, unlike a person dying from a ruptured appendix.

"How ya feeling? You look better than this morning."

"I think whatever I got is about over. I ate some carrots and apple cider without any problems, and I haven't vomited since noon."

"Since you were sick today, I've decided to fix supper. I picked up the fixings for a big ol' mess of goulash."

Jennifer made a dash for her oak bucket.

***

"Ma, I'm home, and we'll have fish for supper," P.C. announced as he entered the back door of the cafe.

Maggie turned to find the Mayor of Bear Creek clothed only in boots, buckskin skirt, and black eye patch. She rightly assumed he was wearing nothing under the skirt. A unique blend of fish, smoke, and skunk oil assaulted her nostrils. In P.C.'s right hand was a stringer of walleyes he was proudly holding up for review. Maggie decided she didn't want to know.

***

Night fell early, but night always falls early in the deep woods where the receding sunlight fails to penetrate the thick foliage. Luther would have preferred an additional hour or two of daylight; that was not to be. Nighttime belonged to the fox, coyote, and the bobcat and not to a wayward beaver far from deep water. The small stream Luther had found was too shallow to provide adequate protection, but it offered hope and direction. The stream would widen if Luther follow it downstream. Luther pushed on into the night. The stream widened and increased in depth, although not enough to provide protection. Wading along the stream was easier than forging through the dense undergrowth, but still exhausting. Finally, Luther was forced to seek rest in the brush alongside the stream.

Luther awoke to sunlight filtering down through the trees. He had survived the night. He wouldn't always be that lucky. He needed to find deep water before the end of another day. He pushed forward with his characteristic zeal. In many areas, the water was deep enough to swim, propelling him downstream with increased momentum until the creek widened into a small pond.

The pond appeared out of place for such a small stream. A cursory inspection revealed a pile of brush obstructing the mouth of the stream. Chisel marks on the tree branches confirmed the work of a beaver. Poor quality work, Luther decided. The location was all wrong. There wasn't enough water flow to support a proper dam, and the sides of the riverbank weren't adequate to provide boundaries. Granddad used to say the three most important aspects of dam building were location, location, and location. Here the water flowed over the land only to be absorbed by the porous soil. This was the work of an amateur. It was the quality Luther might have created in his youth, when he was still inexperienced, but not fitting for a seasoned craftsman.

Luther climbed the riverbank to further evaluate the pond. The trees around the pond had been cut, obviously by the same beaver that had created the dam. At the far end of the clearing, Luther saw a small beaver working on a six-inch diameter poplar. Luther limped over for a closer look. Luther wasn't impressed by her shiny pelt. That was the problem with females; they expected instant respect just because of a slick look or fancy pelt. Luther wasn't one to be impressed by such superficial attributes. If a beaver couldn't cut wood or create a proper dam, then he or she didn't deserve respect. Luther wouldn't be swayed by skin-thin beauty. The fact that she was totally ignoring him while she worked on the small poplar was even more irritating.

For lack of anything better to do, Luther stepped up to a similar size poplar and commenced cutting. If nothing else, he could show this young female the proper way to cut a tree. Within seconds, Luther was throwing wood chips in all directions. Coincidentally, the larger chips seemed to be thrown in Fancy Pelt's direction, an action Fancy Pelt continued to ignore.

Not to be outdone, Fancy Pelt sent a few choice chips in Luther's direction, making sure some of them hit that arrogant intruder square on the head. This was her turf, and no outsider was going to come in and take over. She could cut down trees with the best of them. For good measure, she increased the rate of chip dispersal.

How dare she think she could out-chip him on tree cutting. Luther attacked his tree with renewed vigor. Wood chips flew in all directions as the two beavers plied their trade at an ever-increasing pace. The six-inch trees that should have taken twenty minutes to slay fell almost simultaneously in less than fifteen minutes. She did have a head start, Luther rationalized as he waddled off. Still, she didn't do too badly — for a female.

***

Jennifer was already hugging her favorite bucket when Frenchie's alarm clock announced the advent of another morning. If his sleep clouded brain was accurate, this must be day five, and his wife was no better than day one. If anything, she was worse. Frenchie climbed out of bed hoping his math would prove wrong once his mind cleared, but it only increased his concern. It couldn't be the potato sausage; that would have been out of her system by now. If it were just a bug as his mother-in-law suggested, she should be getting better. This left only one possibility—appendicitis. He could deny it no further. He needed to face the facts; Jennifer was seriously sick and needed immediate help.

"How are you feeling?"

"I still feel..." Jennifer started to reply, but a gastric eruption forced her head back into the bucket.

"I think I know what's wrong with you," Frenchie said. Jennifer looked up from her bucket with an exhausted expression. "You have appendicitis."

"Appendicitis?"

"I've seen it before when I was a kid. One of my friends had it. He had lots of vomiting and abdominal cramping just like you."

"What happened to your friend?"

"Today, a surgeon takes out the appendix, and the patient does quite well," Frenchie replied. He didn't answer her question, but the look on his face told Jennifer everything she wanted to know.

"I'm going after your mother. She'll know what to do."

"Hurry," came the echo from inside the bucket.

"You stay in bed. I'll hitch Charlie up and be right back with your mother." Frenchie headed out the door.

It took three minutes to hitch Charlie up to the wagon. "Come on Charlie, Jennifer has appendicitis and is goin' die if we don't hurry," Frenchie climbed onto the wagon seat.

That was all Charlie needed to hear. Jennifer was family. She was in danger, and it was up to him to save the day. Charlie took off at a gallop. Fortunately, few wagons were on the road, and what few were, gladly moved to the side when they saw a plow horse with wagon in tow bearing down on them at a full gallop. The two miles into town were covered in less than fifteen minutes. Frenchie was almost thrown from the wagon when Charlie dug in his hooves bringing the wagon to an abrupt halt in front of the cafe.

P.C. and Rudy were eating breakfast when Frenchie burst into the cafe. The Ladies Aid Society was scheduled to meet later that morning to discuss ways to raise money for the new church furnace. They had the hundred and fifty dollars from the potato sausage sale, but another hundred and fifty was still needed. With winter just around the corner, Rudy felt he should attend the meeting. It provided an opportunity to eat breakfast at the cafe, which was always better than his own cooking.

"Where's Ma?" Frenchie blurted out as he entered the cafe. "Jennifer needs help. I think she's dying from a ruptured appendix."

Maggie returned from the kitchen with Rudy's bacon and eggs in time to hear Frenchie's statement. "What kind of symptoms is she having?"

"She's been sick for five days, and it's not getting any better. Everything she eats comes back up. I think it's appendicitis."

"Appendicitis is nothing to trivialize. P.C., you're in charge of the café. Frenchie, let's head out to the cabin. Reverend, you may want to come too."

Conversation was held to a minimum as Charlie made the return trip again in record time. Appendicitis brought fear into the minds of the knowledgeable at its mere mention. It could be cured by surgery, but surgery was a risky procedure at best and only available in larger cities. If the appendix ruptured, there was nothing in the medical armamentarium that could stem the course of the insidious infection. The patient died a painful death. No one verbalize these fears, but the fears were there just the same.

If surgery were necessary, it would require hours of travel by horse and wagon over bumpy and sometimes impassable roads. Often the patient arrived dead at the surgeon's doorstep.

How does a man of the cloth minister to such a dying individual, Rudy wondered. This was the part of his profession he found most distasteful. It was something for which no seminary could prepare its students, yet every congregation assumed their minister knew just the right words to say. Why else had Maggie requested—no demanded—he come. She was right, of course. This is where he should be, even if he had no idea what to say or do.

Charlie was wheezing and covered with lather when they arrived at the cabin; he had earned his day's keep. Frenchie decided he would reward him with some of his favorite molasses candies. He would have Jennifer make them from her special recipe. What was he thinking? She could be dead by morning.

"Make sure you keep Charlie hitched up. We may need him shortly," Maggie grabbed her medical bag containing her thermometer, stethoscope, and an assortment of herbs and other folk remedies.

School trained physicians were a rarity in the rural areas of Michigan's Upper Peninsula and normally found only in the larger cities. As a result, many communities had individuals who took it upon themselves to provide rudimentary health care to the local citizenry. Maggie was one of those, and a good one at that. She was the one who delivered the babies and sewed up the lacerations. She had a potion for most simple ailments, many of which were old Indian folk cures. Maggie wasn't one to overestimate her abilities and was quick to refer a patient to a physician in Marquette City when needed. This might be one of those cases.

They found Jennifer in her bedroom sitting on her bed with her favorite bucket between her legs. She had a worn and exhausted look on her face, the result of many days of misery. Her expression improved only slightly at the sight of her mother.

"Hi, Honey, we're going to fix you up." When Maggie said "we," it didn't include Frenchie or Rudy; they were quickly dispatched when they tried to follow her into the bedroom.

Frenchie began pacing across the front room. This was when he should provide words of assurance, Rudy thought. But the words didn't come. What do you say to someone who was about to lose his wife? Rudy felt so inadequate. Rudy offering a small prayer, but it sounded simple and unpolished, unlike the more professional prayers he had composed in seminary. When he was in seminary, he was given proper time to prepare and compose the prayer before offering it up for evaluation. At the end of the prayer, Frenchie crossed himself. It was hard to remove the habits of his Catholic upbringing. When no one was looking, Rudy crossed himself also, just in case Catholics knew something he didn't. Rudy figured he could use any edge he could get.

Maggie emerged from the bedroom after a fifteen-minute evaluation. In the bedroom Jennifer continued her vigil over her bucket.

"Is it appendicitis?" Frenchie asked.

"No," Maggie replied.

"Well, is she going to get better?"

"Eventually"

"What do you mean, eventually? How long will that take?"

"About nine months."

"You mean..."

"Congratulations. Now if you would be so kind as to give me a ride back into town, I have a meeting with the Ladies Aid Society. We're trying to find a way to obtain money for the new church furnace. Just give Jennifer soda crackers and keep the house well ventilated to reduce food smells. She'll get better."

"I'm going to be a father!" Frenchie gave Maggie an unexpected hug. He pumped Rudy's hand, and then decided to give him a hug also.

His prayer must have worked, Rudy decided, or maybe it wasn't even necessary. In situations such as this, Rudy felt it best to give the Lord the benefit of the doubt.

"Guess what, Jennifer; I'm going to be a father!"

Jennifer looked up from her bucket only long enough to give Frenchie a glaring look. It was hard to share his enthusiasm, now that she knew who was responsible for her current misery.

***

The Ladies Aid Society meeting was underway when Maggie arrived back at the cafe. Agnes was chairing the meeting, and they were discussing various possibilities for raising money for the new church furnace.

"How's Jennifer?" Trudy asked. "We heard she was sick."

"She's not really sick, but it appears I'll soon be a grandmother."

"Congratulations."

"When's she due?" one of the ladies asked.

"Late April or early May."

The ladies immediately began counting fingers. When they reached the ninth finger, there were smiles and nods of approval.

"We haven't been able to come up with any good ideas for fund-raisers," Agnes told Maggie.

"I don't see why the responsibility has to fall on us," Trudy said. "We raised a hundred and fifty dollars on our potato sausage sale. I think the men should have a part in this. They should be responsible for the other half." There were nods of agreement around the room.

"They're a part of our church too," someone else said. More nods of agreement.

"I suppose it wouldn't hurt to ask them," Maggie said as she took over the leadership of the committee. "We could still help if needed. We don't want the men going off and doing something unsupervised."

"I want to make that a formal motion," Agnes said with her characteristic enthusiasm.

"Second"

"All in favor?"

"Aye"

"I'm for it."

"Me too."

"Let's go for it."

"Motion carried. Meeting adjourned."

***

It has been another stressful week in Bear Creek. For a while, it looked like Jennifer D'Artagnan had appendicitis. Jennifer is the young lady I married to Claude Pierre D'Artagnan last July, but everybody calls him Frenchie. Jennifer had been sick for five days, and Frenchie thought it was appendicitis. Fortunately, it turned out to be morning sickness. It appears she is pregnant. Just the same, she gave us all a pretty good scare.

Jennifer's mother asked me to accompany her out to Jennifer's cabin when it appeared she might die. I feel so inadequate in such situations. Frenchie was beside himself, and I couldn't think of anything to comfort him. What do you say when you think a loved one is dying? Other than offering a simple prayer, I pretty much sat there in silence. This community needs someone better than me. They need someone who can find the words to console the suffering and the wisdom to know what actions to take during a crisis. I am counting the days until my replacement comes in the spring.

Rudy closed his journal and stared at the wall.

Chapter Eight

The unusually balmy weather of October was not to last, but then no true Yooper expected it would. There was, therefore, no disappointment when the frigid winds of November brought an abundance of snow as well as subzero temperatures that quickly froze lakes and slow moving streams. Several feet of snow inundated the countryside and billowed up into large drifts that rendered roads impassable. Pedestrian traffic was limited to well-worn paths. Life, as exemplified by the normal routines of summer, had come to a screeching halt.

The advent of winter wasn't a new concept for Yoopers, who quickly made the adjustments essential for winter survival. Wheels were removed from wagons and the wagons refitted with skis, allowing the wagons to travel over the top of the crusty snow; pantries were stocked with emergency provisions to tide the inhabitants through the more tumultuous storms; and snowshoes hung by entryways for easy access. Life was harsh during the winter months, but life went on.

Winter can last five months or more before a spring thaw arrives to provide relief from the snowy confinement. For those individuals who accept this confinement unconditionally and remain secluded in the confines of their humble homes, depression and cabin fever were frequently the ultimate rewards. True

Yoopers saw winter as another phase of daily life and planned their social activities to take advantage of the chilly opportunities winter provided.

One such activity, much to Rudy's delight, was ice-skating. Every Saturday afternoon, and sometimes on weekdays as well, the Bare Creek beaver pond became the epicenter of Bear Creek's social life. Snow was shoveled to the edge of the pond where crudely constructed benches provided relief for the weary. For the non-weary who preferred to demonstrate their skating skills, music was provided by P.C.'s wind-up victrola, which played the best of out-of-date records.

Rudy wasn't much of an athlete, but skating was one of the few activities in which he excelled. Having been raised along the shore of a downstate lake, he had spent many a wintry afternoon skating or playing hockey with other neighborhood kids. His long legs and spindly frame made him a natural on the iron rails. It was, therefore, with great pleasure that Rudy discovered Bear Creek's major winter attraction—the neighborhood ice rink.

Rudy spend every available moment skating circles and pirouettes around the Bear Creek beaver pond. The second Saturday of November was no exception, and with his Sunday sermon finished, Rudy headed down to the beaver pond for an afternoon of skating. He was pleased to note P.C. had already arrived and his victrola was playing a spirited waltz. Music added a new dimension to skating that encouraged the skater to display his or her best form. Rudy was normally a modest individual, mostly due to lack of appropriate talents to flaunt. This wasn't the case with skating, and Rudy was more than happy to strut around the ice rink with a black top hat and a white scarf that flowed with the wind.

Rudy sat down on the crude bench to apply skates to his feet while the victrola exhorted the skaters gliding over the ice. Several kids were debating over who would wind the victrola. There was never a shortage of labor to keep the victrola wound.

"Afternoon, Rudy," Silas said as he skated over to Rudy's bench for a rest. He was joined by Agnes, who was looking for any excuse to catch her breath.

"Good afternoon, Silas, Agnes. And how are the two of you doing this afternoon?"

"It's a little bit chilly," Silas replied. "It would be better if I had my coonskin coat."

"Oh, hush up already. Abigail needs it more than you do. You wouldn't want her exposed to this kind of weather without something warm to wear, would you?"

"Hogwash," Silas replied. "Abigail's a legend, a figment of your imagination."

"She was Charles Farnsworth's daughter. I've even seen a copy of her birth certificate," Agnes said with too much hostility for Rudy's liking.

Rudy finished strapping on his skates and headed onto the ice. He had no intention of being dragged into a family dispute. Silas still hadn't forgiven Agnes for leaving his favorite fur coat on the beaver lodge. Abigail Farnsworth was an interesting piece of folklore, but a legend just the same.

Most of the Bear Creek citizenry were happily sliding along on their skates, Rudy was pleased to note. There was no satisfaction in showing off one's skills without an attentive audience. Rudy skated a few circles around the ice to warm up his skates and loosen his muscles. To show style and confidence, he clasped his hands behind his back, telling the world he had no intention of falling. It was also important to stand tall and straight with his black, stovepipe hat jauntily set low on the forehead. As he picked up speed, his white scarf flowed freely in the wind. Rudy looked out of the corner of his eye to see if townsfolk were watching; they were.

It was time to show his stuff. With his hands still behind his back, Rudy coasted on his right skate, his left leg held high behind him and his back gracefully arched. After he skated through a small circle, he topped it off with a tight pirouette. As he opened up into a straight path, he felt a warm mitten grab his left hand.

"Hello, Rudy. It's a lovely day for skating." The Widow Watson skated effortlessly alongside Rudy, an accomplished skater in her own right.

The waltz was still playing on the victrola. Apparently, it was a favorite of the lad currently in charge of winding the machine. Seizing the opportunity, Rudy spun around facing Alice. With his right hand firmly placed on the small of her back, Rudy waltzed her in and out of the admiring crowd. Weaving around the social skaters was easy, but a spirited hockey game was in progress among several of the youth who felt social skating wasn't aggressive enough for their tastes. Several times Rudy had to take evasive action to avoid a misguided puck or pursuing hockey player. On several of those encounters, Alice would have fallen had it not been for the steady arm around her waist. They waltzed several laps around the pond in time to the music.

"I think you've gotten me all tuckered out," Alice confessed after the third circle of the pond. "I need a rest."

Swinging around beside Alice, Rudy guided the exhausted schoolteacher toward the bench for a well-deserved rest.

"Rudy, aren't you tired?" Alice sat on the bench to catch her breath. She had hoped Rudy would do the same.

"I'm just getting the old legs loosened up."

Rudy tipped his hat at the Widow Watson and headed back to the ice rink. On the ice, he was bold and self-confident. On the ice, he could be courageous, but idle conversation with the opposite sex was terrifying. Rudy skated onto the center of the pond in search of people to impress. He made a few flawless circles, skating forwards and then backwards. He tried to present his best casual bored look while he performed intricate moves on his icy stage.

"Pretty fancy skating, but I bet you can't play hockey," taunted one of the youngsters, as he ushered a hockey puck toward the opponent's goal.

That was the wrong thing to say. Rudy scanned the rink for an unused hockey stick. He found one protruding from a snow bank at the edge of the pond. Without losing stride, Rudy plucked the stick from the snow bank and headed onto the ice in search hockey action. A net had been placed at each end of the pond, and a teenager was currently bearing down on the net at the far end, his stick coaxing the hockey puck ahead of him. It was the same youth who had made the taunting comment.

Putting his skates into high gear, Rudy took after the lad, quickly closing the gap. With one sweep of his stick, the puck was transferred to Rudy's stick as he swooped past the astonished teenager. Revenge is sweet.

"Hey, give back our puck!"

"Come and get it." Rudy made a tight U-turn, allowing the former puck owner to overshoot him. The two hockey teams immediately combined into one, and ten irritated skaters took after a common foe. But it wasn't as easy as first assumed. The man with the stove pipe hat and white scarf easily weaved in and out of their midst. Just for the sake of show, Rudy passed the puck between the legs of a bewildered pursuer only to skate around the individual to retrieve the puck from behind. Can he play hockey? He would show them.

After five minutes of weaving and bobbing in the cat and mouse game of keep away, the hockey players were no closer to retrieving their puck than they were in the beginning, and the puck thief showed no signs of tiring, even though the young hockey players, at half his age, were huffing and puffing. Rudy, noting his opponents were slowing down, decided they had learned their lesson. With one good slap shot, Rudy sent the puck screaming across the ice and into the net at the far end of the pond.

That preacher sure can skate, Agnes told her husband as they sat on the bench watching the display. But Silas wasn't listening. He was lost in thought; the gears deep in his mind were grinding away. He had momentarily forgotten how miserable he was without his favorite fur coat.

***

"We have a problem," Silas said as he gained the attention of the members of the Bare Creek Economics Club. Heads turned toward Silas for further clarification. Silas took out his pipe and began filling it with tobacco. Why can't he light his pipe before he gets everybody's attention, several people wondered? There would be no rushing Silas once he began preparing his pipe; the men waited in silence. Within minutes, white curls of smoke began to rise from Silas's pipe as he sat back in his chair.

"We have a problem," Silas reiterated for emphasis. "It appears the women folk have stuck us with the responsibility for raising an additional hundred and fifty dollars to purchase the new church furnace."

"How we going to do that?" Mel asked.

"They say they raised half the funds with their potato sausage sale, and it's up to us to obtain the other half," Silas continued, ignoring Mel's question.

"If I remember right, we did most of the work," Frenchie indignantly pointed out.

"That sounds like a lot of money," Mel said.

"Every year we play hockey with the Pine Stump Junction Economics Club, right?" Silas asked.

Everyone nodded in agreement.

"If we were to place a little wager on the outcome of the game, such as a hundred and fifty dollars, we could double our money and the church furnace would be ours."

"Wait a minute," P.C. protested. "We always lose that game."

"You want to bet the church money on a hockey game?" Mel asked. "The women would have my hide if we were to gamble with the church's money. As church treasurer, I'm the one they'll come after."

"The only way we'd ever win is to bet on the other side," Frenchie pointed out. "With Olaf the Swede, there's no way they'll lose."

"Yeah, no one can beat Olaf," Mel said. There were nods of agreement. "The women folk won't stand for any gambling."

Silas sat back and puffed on his pipe while he waited for the dissension to dissipate. "Who's talking about gambling?" Silas asked. "Has anyone seen Rudy skate? He's faster than greased lightning—and he knows his way around the hockey puck."

Silas's audience was now listening with renewed interest. Everyone had seen Rudy on skates. His skill and finesse was the talk of the town. A match up with Rudy against Olaf the Swede would make for an exciting hockey game.

"OK. If we had Rudy up against Olaf, we might have a chance, but it would still be a gamble."

"What if Olaf were unable to play the whole game and had to leave the game early?"

"With Rudy on our side, it would be a sure thing," everyone agreed.

"Then it wouldn't be gambling would it?" It was obvious Silas had another trump card up his sleeve. Silas took a puff on his pipe and blew out a smoke ring that slowly rose above his head before dissipating.

"Well?" Mel interjected in hopes of a more expeditious explanation. Silas chewed on his pipe for a moment. He had no intention of being rushed.

"Olaf is strong as an ox." There were nods of agreement. "He also has the I.Q. of an ox, not to mention the hormones of an alley cat." Silas's audience sat patiently, totally confused by hormones and alley cats. "A hockey game can be quite strenuous, and a player can become dehydrated. If someone happened to be in the right place at the right time, Olaf could be encouraged to drink a lot of fruit juice—prune juice to be exact."

"That would slow him down," Frenchie chuckled, "but how you going to get him to drink it?"

"I'm not, the Widow Watson will. That's where the hormones of an alley cat come in. Olaf fancies himself as a ladies' man, although for the life of me, I don't know why." Silas waited for the laughter to subside. "The Widow Watson isn't all that bad looking and could charm the pants off Olaf if she were to put her mind to it. Look at the way she's been manipulating poor ol' Rudy."

"What makes you think she'll do it?" Mel asked.

"Because she wants that new furnace as much as anyone. She'll soon begin rehearsals for the children's Christmas Eve program. Without a new coal furnace, it's going to be mighty cold for those small children. Yes, she'll do it."

"What about Rudy? Can you guarantee he'll play?" Frenchie asked. "He may not be all that keen on the gambling part."

"Investment," Silas said as he corrected Frenchie. "This is an investment, not gambling. Rudy will play for the love of skating and hockey. I don't think we need to bore him with the financial aspects of our investment."

"OK, if you can get Rudy and the Widow Watson on the team, I'm willing to release the church funds," Mel said. He could appreciate a sure thing when he saw it.

"All right, that's settled. Now, whom can we count on to play?" Silas asked. "Can you cover the goalie position, P.C.?" P.C. nodded in agreement. P.C. wasn't fast on skates and lacked the peripheral vision for an aggressive hockey player, but he played to win and gave one hundred percent.

"Count me in," Frenchie volunteered. Frenchie had teethed on a hockey puck while growing up in Canada and, with the exception of Rudy, was by far their best skater.

"Don't look at me," Mel said. "Remember that old war wound I got as Teddy Roosevelt and I were riding up..."

"How about Red Weasel?" Silas asked, cutting short Mel's rendition of the Spanish American War.

"I think I can talk the Chief into it," P.C. replied. Weasel wasn't much of a conversationalist, but he could skate, having been taught by Jennifer during her winter visits to the Moose Lake Lodge. Like P.C., he was very competitive.

"Counting Rudy and me, we can field a team of five players," Silas calculated as he added up the total. "We would have to be on the ice the whole time."

"Maybe we could have six ten-minute periods instead of three twenty minute periods," Frenchie suggested. "It would give us some breathing time."

"Everyone in agreement?" Silas looked around; all heads were nodding in the affirmative. "P.C., you talk to Weasel, and I'll talk to Rudy and the Widow Watson. How about Saturday, December 1st? It won't give us much time to practice, but then the Pine Stump Economics Club won't have much time either. We need that new coal furnace as soon as we can get it." Again, there were nods of agreement. "Then it's all set."

***

The first of December came quickly as Silas had predicted, but not before the news of the big hockey game had spread throughout the county. That took less than an hour. Shops were closed, and the whole town assembled on the hillside overlooking the beaver pond to watch the match up of the decade as Rudy went against Olaf the Swede. The church women, having been given "kitchen privileges" at the parsonage, were selling hot cider on the side—a little extra money for the church wouldn't hurt. Of course, cider was free to the members of the hometown team.

Just to make things official, Toivo Rasmusson, circuit judge from Marquette, was procured to officiate the game, since the team from Pine Stump Junction didn't feel anyone with ties to Bear Creek could be impartial. To ensure the game ran smoothly—and to Bear Creek's way of liking—Mel provided the Judge with a twenty-dollar bribe, which was graciously accepted; Judge Rasmusson wasn't above a little gratuity. To prove his impartiality, he also accepted a twenty-dollar bribe from the Pine Stump Junction team. After all, he was an honest circuit judge with a reputation to uphold.

The entire pond had been cleared of snow and other debris. Any lumps in the ice were carefully removed and the ice smoothed over. This was the ultimate hockey game, and conditions had to be perfect. The net for the Bear Creek team was placed at the south end of the pond just in front of the hillside filled with the hometown crowd. The bench for the local heroes was located on the edge of the pond behind the net. A similar bench for the opposing team sat at the north end of the pond.

"Let's get the game on the road," Judge Rasmusson bellowed in his normal authoritarian voice. "All team members may now approach the bench." Five members from each team gathered around the judge for final instructions; although the rules had all been ironed out well in advance, and no one was paying attention to the detailed instruction. "Each team will field five players," the Judge continued. "The playing field is the entire pond, although the ice is thin at the far-west end near the entrance to the pond. You go there at your own risk. The game will consist of six ten-minute periods with two minutes of rest in between. There will be a two-minute penalty for any fistfights, whacking people with sticks, or other abusive behavior. Those are the rules, plus any other rules I might make up as we go. Any questions?" There were none. "If there are no questions, let the game begin."

Rudy stepped up to represent Bear Creek in the face off. As he expected, his opponent was the Swede. Standing at six foot four inches, Olaf towered over Rudy. Muscles bulged under his sweater in sharp contrast to Rudy's gaunt frame. Rudy estimated his opponent at over two hundred and forty pounds. On either side of Olaf were the Gustafson twins, Brett and Bart or was it Bart and Brett? Since Rudy couldn't tell the difference, he assumed it didn't really matter. He never did catch the names of the goalie and the scrawny defensive player.

The fans on the hillside expressed their displeasure in the face-off as the puck slid off to Brett's waiting stick, although it could have been Bart. The entire Bear Creek team descended upon the twin with the exception of Rudy who had been assigned to shadow Olaf. Despite his bulky size, Olaf was surprisingly fast, and it took all of Rudy's talent to keep up with him. Still, he was able to minimize the Swede's influence on the game, and after the first ten-minute period, the score remained at zero to zero. The team members returned to their benches for a well-deserved two-minute rest. This wouldn't be an easy game to win.

***

"Hello, Olaf. I couldn't help but admire the way you skate," the Widow Watson said as she approached the opposing team's bench.

"Olaf, good skater. Olaf score many points."

"My name's Alice. You'll have to excuse me, but I'm always attracted to men with muscles."

"Olaf have big muscles." To prove his point, Olaf flexed his biceps for the Widow to feel.

"Oh my, you do have big muscles." The Widow Watson seductively caressed Olaf's biceps. "You must get awful thirsty skating as fast as you do. Would you care for some warm fruit juice?" The Widow poured a large glass of prune juice from a thermos she carried.

"That's good fruit juice," announced the Swede as he downed the glass.

"Here, have another glass." Alice poured a second glass and passed it to the unsuspecting Swede. He guzzled it down almost as fast as the first glass. "Want another glass?"

"If Olaf drink too much, he slosh when he skates." Olaf laughed heartily at his joke.

***

"Well, I got him to drink two glasses," the Widow Watson informed Mel when she returned to the hometown bench. "I just hope it works."

"If it doesn't work, we might have to win this game fair and square," Mel replied. It was a scary thought.

The hometown team had returned to the ice, and the second of the six periods began with the home team getting the advantage of the face-off. Rudy carried the puck down the ice toward the goal until he was checked by the Swede. It was like hitting a brick wall.

Fortunately, Rudy was able to pass the puck to Frenchie before the collision.

From the far end of the ice, P.C. watched the puck slip back and forth between the two teams. As long as they stayed at that end of the rink, P.C. could relax. A goalie's job was mostly boredom punctuated by a few moments of sheer terror. They could stay at the far end the entire game, as far as he was concerned.

"Hello there," one of the twins said as he skated up to P.C.'s net. "All that skating tends to tire you out." He leaned on the net, pretending to catch his breath.

He's up to no good, P.C. decided, although his intentions were at the moment unclear. He didn't appear winded. The puck was at the far end of the rink, and if anything, the twin's absence was hurting their team. Just the same, P.C. would have felt better if the twin hadn't been on his blind side. It was harder to keep a watchful eye on him with his eye patched.

P.C. pulled his stocking cap down over his ears; he was beginning to feel a chill. It was his lucky cap. Jennifer knitted it for him many years ago when she was yet a child. He wasn't quite sure why it was lucky. He wore it at every hockey game, and every year they lost.

P.C. braced himself as he watched the events at the far end. Olaf had stolen the puck and was making a break for P.C.'s side of the rink. No one was between Olaf and the goal P.C. was defending. Rudy chased after him but wasn't closing the gap. Boy, could that Swede skate, P.C. thought as he prepared for the inevitable slap shot. Twenty feet from the goal, Olaf cranked back his hockey stick for a shot at the goal. P.C. crouched low when the puck began its course toward his net. Then the lights went out.

"Hey, you can't do that!" Frenchie cried out. "Judge, Bart just pulled P.C.'s cap over his eye."

P.C. extracted his head from his cap in time to find the puck resting comfortably inside his net.

"How could I've done that? I'm way over here," Bart retorted in his defense.

"Then it was Brett who did it." Frenchie wasn't willing to give up the argument.

"Did what?" the Judge asked. He had been shaking hands with the crowd and missed the incident. It was an election year, and it never hurts to work the crowd. "I didn't see anything. One point for Pine Stump Junction." The Judge looked at his watch. "End of the second period. You have a two-minute break."

***

"Hello, Alice." Olaf was pleased to find the Widow Watson waiting for him when he arrived at the bench. "Did you see that goal I made? We sure fooled them."

"You sure did. You guys aren't only strong, but smart, too."

"Olaf strong and smart."

"I think it was the warm fruit juice that gave you all that strength to make that goal."

"Yeah, it was that fine fruit juice of yours that gave me that extra strength."

"I still have some left. Do you want another glass?" Alice poured the Swede a large glass without waiting for a reply. "You should be able to make another goal easily after drinking this glassful," Alice said, passing him the glass.

"Olaf make another goal," Olaf downed his third glass of prune juice.

"You're a mighty big man. I think you should have another glass." Alice poured another glassful and handed it to Olaf, who drank it without hesitation.

***

"I got another two glasses down him," Alice confided to Mel. "If nothing else, there should be a lot of yellow snow around their bench."

"Yellow snow won't fetch any ribbons. We need that power play, or we may not win this game."

"I'll keep pushing the juice during the breaks. Something has to give."

The game was in its third of six periods, and still no team had a clear advantage. Rudy was able to negate Olaf's every move; but likewise, Olaf was there to foil all Rudy's opportunities. It was definitely a matchup of two superstars, and at the end of the third period, the score remained one to nothing in favor of Pine Stump Junction. The team members slowly returned to their respective benches. The enthusiasm of the earlier periods had faded.

"What is Alice Watson doing over at the Pine Stump bench?" Rudy asked Mel. "It looks like she's draping herself all over that Swede."

"I believe she's giving some Christian hospitality to our guests from Pine Stump," Mel replied. "Here, have some warm cider. That'll cheer you up."

"If you ask me, it looks more like she is giving aid and comfort to the enemy."

"Judge not, that ye be not judged."

Matthew 7:1, Rudy said to himself. He hated it when other people quoted scripture to him, especially when it was contrary to his current prejudices.

"It appears our primary strategy isn't working," Mel told the exhausted hockey players; that is, all except Rudy, who was more concerned about actions at the opposing bench.

"Isn't Olaf drinking the prune juice?" Frenchie asked.

"He drank four glasses, and the Widow Watson is pouring more down his gullet as we speak, but it doesn't seem to affect him."

"We're playing just as well as they are. If it weren't for their cheating, it would be a tied game," Frenchie noted.

"Losing because they outplayed us is one thing," P.C. said, "but to lose because they're better cheaters, that's humiliating."

"I have an idea," Silas informed the crew; that is, all except for Rudy, who was more concerned with activities on the opposing bench.

The fourth period started out routinely and the puck shifted between the two teams with, again, no team having a clear advantage. Defense was excellent, and the two goalies had little influence in the exchanges. Halfway through the period, Rudy skillfully extracted the puck from Olaf's stick, much to the Swede's surprise. They were still on the hometown's side of the pond, and the puck needed to be worked down to the other end before a scoring threat could be made. Rudy passed the puck across to Silas to keep it away from Olaf's hockey stick. As the opposing team descended on Silas, the puck was passed backwards to Frenchie. The puck slid past his stick, coming to rest behind the net. That was unusual, Rudy thought. Normally, Frenchie was flawless in such easy passes.

"I'll get it. I'll get it," P.C. announced as he skated behind the net to secure the puck. "I got it. I got it," P.C. said as he nursed the black disk out from behind the net. He continued to push the black disk away from the net while the opposing team descended upon him. No one noticed when Frenchie retrieved the puck from a small snow pile behind the net.

"I got the puck," P.C. continued as he trapped the black disk between the blade of his stick and the inside of his left skate. With the large crowd around him, it was difficult to see the black disk until Olaf grabbed P.C. by the waist and lifted him off the ice.

"That's not the puck!" one of the twins said.

"It's not?" P.C. asked incredulously after Olaf placed him back on the ice. Everyone was standing in a small circle staring at a thin black disk. "I must have dropped my black eye patch," P.C. said apologetically. He picked up the black disk that had been tied to the blade of his stick.

"That not hockey puck," Olaf decided, long after it was painfully obvious to everyone else. "You play good trick on Olaf."

"Oh, shut up and help us find the puck," Bart told the Swede.

Looking up field, only rear ends and elbows were visible as a three-man line consisting of Frenchie, Weasel, and Silas converged on the opponent's goalie. It was too late for any additional help; the goalie was on his own.

An unfettered, three-prong attack is a goalie's worst nightmare. How was he to defend against it? He would have to correctly guess which attacker would take the shot and put all of his effort into thwarting that one shot. Coming on his left was the publisher. He was up there in age and not one of the best skaters. He would be least likely to have the shot. In the middle was that Injun. He was also no spring chicken, but still agile and could be easily underestimated. Yes, he could be a threat. Then there was that French Canadian; he was definitely the best skater of the three and had the advantage of youth. His youth would be the key. The Frenchman had possession of the puck, and his youthful immaturity would prevent him from sharing any glory. Being the best skater, he could justify taking the shot. Yes, it would be the Frenchman.

The three attackers arrived in offensive territory in an even line. When Frenchie was within twenty feet of the goal, he pulled back on his stick in preparation for a forceful slap shot. This is it, the goalie decided. He would block the shot, but he assumed there would be some pain involved. Frenchie began the swing that would send the black puck screaming toward the left side of the net. The goalie, with clinched teeth, fell to his knees in front of the Frenchman. Half way through his swing, Frenchie gave a slight twist to his arm, realigning the hockey stick's angle of attack against the puck. He also swung low causing the stick to strike the ice before hitting the puck, robbing the stick of much of its energy. Instead of slamming into the net or goalie, the puck slid sideways to Silas's waiting stick. A small tap sent the puck into the unguarded side of the net, to the astonishment of the disheartened goalie.

"One point for Bear Creek," Judge Rasmusson proclaimed. "Score is now one to one."

"You can't count that goal," Brett protested. "They tricked us with that black eye patch."

"If ya can't tell the difference between a hockey puck and a black eye patch, my boy, that's your problem. Objection overruled."

The end of the fourth period found the Bear Creek team uplifted, except for Rudy who was more concerned with the activities at the opposing bench. There was no evidence their secret weapon was working, but there was a possibility of winning fair and square, or at least playing for a draw. That would, if nothing else, protect their money. Two more periods to go.

The fifth period was uneventful with the puck switching back and forth, but no real threat to either goal. At the end of the period, the score remained one to one, and the players returned to their benches for a two-minute rest. The next ten-minute period would decide which team would be victorious. Many were now willing to settle for a draw.

"Well, I did the best I could," Alice confided to Mel after the team members returned to the ice for the final period. "I think he drank over a gallon of that warm prune juice. I don't know how he did it. Other than peeing once behind a tree, it's had no visible effect on him."

"Maybe no one will score, and we can settle for a tie," Mel said wishfully. "If we lose that hundred and fifty dollars, the women folk will have my hide and burn my carcass to heat the church."

"Don't be so hard on yourself. We haven't lost yet, and we have a chance at a draw."

Indeed, a draw looked promising as the two well-matched teams battled through the first few minutes of the last period. Neither team could obtain an advantage. After five minutes of fruitless skating, the Pine Stump Junction team retreated to the security of their own goal for a conference.

"I don't like the looks of that," Silas told Rudy. "They're up to no good." The Bear Creek team had the puck, but there was no sense taking a shot with all five opponents in front of the goal. After a thirty-second consult the opposition scattered, and play resumed with again no team claiming a clear advantage.

"Watch for some shenanigans," Silas admonished his teammates. "They must have something up their sleeves."

After another minute of sparring, Brett, or was it Bart, stole the puck and disappeared behind his own goal. Once behind the net, the puck was stashed in a snow bank at the edge of the pond.

"What did you do with the puck?" Frenchie asked.

"It's over there," Bart said, pointing to Brett, or was it Bart?

Attention shifted to the other twin who, during the confusion, dropped a second puck to the ice and was now heading toward P.C. at the other end of the rink.

"After him," Silas directed his troops, although with Bart's lead, he was likely unstoppable. Rudy wasn't prone to such pessimism and took off in pursuit. If it had been Olaf, there would have been no chance of catching him, but the twins were slower, and Rudy gradually closed the gap. He was still eight feet behind the aggressor when the twin wound up for a shot at the goal. It was no accident he was coming in on P.C.'s blind side. Rudy was unable to stop the shot, but he was able to hook a piece of his opponent's stick with his own, reducing the force of the shot. The puck slowly slid toward the goal only to be intercepted by P.C.'s waiting mitt.

"Hey, they can't do that!" Frenchie complained to the Judge. "They used two different pucks!" A thorough exam of the offending snow bank failed to surrender the elusive puck. They would have been more productive if they had examined Bart's pocket.

"I know they had two pucks," Frenchie persisted.

"This is exhibit A," Judge Rasmusson said, holding up the puck. "Where is exhibit B?" His question was greeted with silence. "Case dismissed due to lack of evidence."

"There has to be a second puck," Frenchie argued. "I saw the puck disappear behind the net. There was no way the puck could have gotten to that guy." Frenchie pointed to one of the twins; he didn't know which.

"Are you challenging my decision?" the Judge asked.

"I think you're wrong," Frenchie replied, trying to hold his temper.

"Two minutes in the penalty box."

"What for?" Silas asked.

"Contempt of court."

"You can't do that. This is an ice rink not a courtroom."

"I'm a circuit court judge. I can do anything I want. You're out of here, too."

"You can't throw both of us out of the game."

"Out of my courtroom. Where's my bailiff? Bailiff? If I hear any more outbreaks in the courtroom, I will make a bench judgment and declare Pine Stump Junction the winner."

Blessed are the peacemakers, Rudy thought to himself. "Hold on, Silas, there's less than two minutes left. P.C., Red Weasel and I can stall for two minutes. We'll go for a tie. Against their better judgment, the two plaintiffs left the Judge's courtroom. That didn't sit well with the hometown fans, who expressed their displeasure with boos and cat calls, leading the Judge to wonder if he made the wrong decision. After all, it was an election year.

To everyone's surprise, the face-off went in Bear Creek's favor, and Weasel was able to secure the erratically moving puck. Skating around the ice, he made no attempt to head for the goal. When the mob descended on him, Weasel passed the puck to Rudy, who continued the game of keep away. Rudy could easily skate circles around the opposition with the exception of Olaf. Olaf might have been faster, but his large frame prevented quick shifts in direction, a flaw Rudy used to his advantage. To Rudy's surprise, it also reduced Olaf's playing field. As Rudy skillfully ushered the puck to the west side of the pond near the mouth of the creek with Olaf in pursuit, the ominous sound of cracking ice brought both skaters to a quick stop. Further cracking sounds confirmed it was only the ice under Olaf that was groaning from the stress. It was unable to hold his excessive weight. Olaf might be dumb, but he wasn't stupid, and he made a hasty retreat, leaving Rudy on thin ice but also in possession of the puck as the precious seconds ticked away in the final period of a tied hockey game.

"Olaf, you guard the Injun," Brett ordered. "Bart and I will get that preacher." The twins were able to flush Rudy off of the thin ice, but he was able to skate in and out of their midst unmolested. Only Olaf could come close to matching Rudy's skills. When Olaf went after him, Rudy returned to the thin ice. Seconds continued to tick away.

In utter frustration, the Pine Stump Junction team retreated to their goal for an emergency conference. Rudy skated over to his one-eyed goalie to confer with him and Red Weasel.

"What do you think they're up to?" Rudy asked.

"They ain't up to any good, that's for sure," P.C. concluded. Weasel nodded in agreement. He never was one for talking.

"They don't have much time left before it's declared a draw," Rudy pointed out.

"THEY'RE PULLING THEIR GOALIE!" Mel yelled from the sidelines.

Rudy looked down the rink to see a line of five skaters heading in his direction, leaving their goal unattended. The line was fifteen yards wide with two yards between skaters. Rudy assumed that gap would quickly close if he were to try to slip through. But he couldn't go around such a wide phalanx of skaters. If they were to get possession of the puck, there would be no way to prevent them from scoring, with their strength in numbers.

"Spread out," Rudy told Weasel, "and keep on your toes." Weasel spread out as ordered. He would have to break through their line, Rudy decided, as he headed for the advancing line. He would need all the speed he could muster to break through. Olaf was in the middle of the five; he must avoid him at all costs. On either side of Olaf was a twin, with the two skaters whose names he couldn't remember on the outsides. He would go for the outside of one of the twins. Yes, that would be his best bet. Rudy began picking up speed. A hush fell over the crowd as they watched the freight train heading for the brick wall. The wall passed Weasel who had skated out ahead of Rudy. Weasel wasn't their concern, and they allowed him to pass unmolested.

Rudy decided to go to the outside of the twin on his left, but wait…Olaf was dropping back! He didn't understand it, but if the Swede were going to drop back, he would take advantage of it. Rudy shifted his weight and headed for the center of the line. He had to get to it before the twins closed the gap. The twins, with their eyes fixed on Rudy, didn't notice the vacant spot between them until Rudy had his stick with puck through the opening. The twins rapidly closed the gap. With outstretched hockey stick, Brett, or was it Bart, caught Rudy's right leg, sending Rudy careening on one skate toward the thin ice to his left, but not before he passed the puck to Weasel. Rudy struggled to regain his balance, but his left skate, encountering a rut in the ice, sent his body sprawling against the thin ice. The ice gave way on impact, providing access to the cold water below.

Rudy surfaced in time to watch Weasel strut down the rink toward the unguarded goal. Standing tall with his black, broad-brimmed hat and single feather pushed low over the forehead, Weasel nursed his black, circular charge into the net for the winning score. In the distance, Rudy could see Olaf heading toward the outhouse. He was taking short, quick steps.

"Rudy, are you all right?" Silas caught Alice as she ran across the beaver pond.

"It won't help having you fall through the ice," Silas said. "We'll fish him out."

Extraction proceedings were already underway with Weasel crawling out on the ice to offer Rudy his outstretched hockey stick. Once Rudy had a firm grip on the stick, a crew of enthusiastic fans pulled on Weasel's feet, dragging the ensemble to safety. Rudy now understood the phrase "when hell freezes over." His beard was beginning to stiffen as the water turned to ice crystals, and his skates sloshed when he skated over to the bench.

At the bench, Rudy received a hero's welcome while other team members jumped around in ecstasy and patted each other on the back, all except Mel who was collecting money from the opposing team.

"Y-you b-bet on this g-game?" Rudy asked through chattering teeth.

"We now have enough money for the new church furnace," Mel proclaimed. "Thanks to you."

"Y-you g-gambled with the church's m-money?"

"I wouldn't call it gambling, not with you on our team."

"Enough talk. Let's get you back to the parsonage and into some dry clothes before you freeze to death," Alice admonished Rudy. She could see Rudy was already getting the makings for a good shiner on his right eye. He must have hit his head on the ice.

Rudy was in no position to argue and allowed the Widow Watson to herd him toward the parsonage like a lost child. Dry clothes did seem to have advantages.

At the parsonage, Rudy shed the wet clothes in the privacy of his bedroom while Alice added more wood to the wood-burning stove. Rudy was in no mood for formal attire and slipped into his red cotton underwear before seeking the comfort of the wood-burning stove. He hoped Alice wouldn't be embarrassed. He did check the trap door on his long johns twice, to ensure it was securely buttoned up.

Alice led Rudy to a chair by the stove. Rudy followed obediently, too cold to make a protest.

"Let me have a look at that eye. It looks like you whacked it a good one."

"Ouch!"

"Sorry," Alice said apologetically. "It doesn't look like it will need stitches, but you'll have a shiner by morning, I'm afraid."

"I can't believe they bet church money on the hockey game."

"Their hearts were in the right place, and it was for a good cause," Alice said, in defense of the men. "We really need that new furnace. Next week we will start practice for the children's Christmas Eve program. It'll be mighty cold without that new furnace."

"It just seems there could have been a better way of procuring the money."

"I'm sure we're better qualified to apply the money to God's work than the men of Pine Stump. Let me get something cold to put on that eye."

Rudy thought it was plenty cold already. "I'm surprised you're not more concerned about taking their money. After all, you did seem to have yourself draped all over Olaf during the breaks."

"Why Rudy, I do believe you're jealous."

"I AM NOT JEALOUS. It's just that I thought you could've given a little more support to the home team."

"I was just doing my Christian duty and providing him with a little fruit juice."

"They could have provided their own cider if they wanted it."

"It wasn't cider."

"It wasn't cider? What was it?"

"Warm prune juice."

"Prune juice! Doesn't that cause..."

"The Lord works in mysterious ways."

***

I am afraid it has been another depressing week in Bear Creek. What I thought was a friendly game of hockey with some men from Pine Stump Junction turned out to be a high pressured confrontation with church money wagered on the outcome. To make matters worse, there appears to have been cheating by players from both sides. I suppose their hearts were in the right place. They were trying to obtain money for our new church furnace, which we desperately need, but I cannot condone gambling, especially with church money.

As spiritual leader for the community, I feel I have failed to provide appropriate leadership. To make matters worse, half the community thinks the wager was my idea. I shudder to think of their opinion of my ethical standards. The only bright side is I am not Catholic; otherwise I would have to spend most of the day in confession. It seems the harder I try, the worse the situation gets. They definitely need a pastor with higher ethical standards. Spring cannot come soon enough.

Chapter Nine

Six days after the hockey game of the decade, a brand new coal-burning furnace was up and operational in the Bare Creek Methodist Church. The Bare Creek Economics Club graciously gave Rudy the credit for the new furnace, and Rudy received many compliments for the courage to bet the church's money on the outcome of such a tenuous match up. His persistent denials were taken as displays of modesty, which further enhanced the congregation's admiration; many people assumed Rudy would have been more averse to gambling. Still, the furnace was a welcome addition to the church.

The new furnace came none too soon, as the winter of twenty-three hit with a vengeance, creating a thick base of snow that covered the countryside. Temperatures plummeted to sub-zero levels, but those individuals taking refuge in the church remained warm and toasty. Among those taking advantage of the warmth was the Widow Watson and her menagerie of children as they prepared for their Christmas Eve children's program.

The annual event was the highlight of the Bear Creek Christmas season, and it was expected that every child would have an important role in the production. No child would be excluded. The theme was the same every year, as they portrayed the Christmas story with Mary and Joseph seeking out a place to stay in a crowded Bethlehem. There were roles for angels, wise men, camels, sheep, and other assorted animals. A collection of angel wings and shepherd costumes harvested from previous years softened the logistical problems. Still, trying to organize a score of small children was like herding chickens. This year, it seemed the children were younger than previous years with fewer older children to assign speaking parts, making it abundantly clear to the Widow Watson that she was over her head and could use additional help.

"I want to thank you for volunteering with the Christmas program," Alice told Rudy, once she cornered him after the Sunday service. "I don't know how I would've managed. Christmas Eve is only a few days away."

"I'm always willing to help," Rudy replied. The fact that Alice bribed him with a turkey and dressing dinner on Christmas Day didn't hinder the negotiations. Alice was a great cook. That was the part of life without a family that depressed Rudy the most: No one should have to spend Christmas alone.

"Your role is really quite simple," Alice explained. "All you have to do is read some Scriptures." Alice handed Rudy a list of Bible passages. "You start off with Matthew 2:1, where the Bible describes the three wise men. Then you pause while three of the children dressed as wise men walk down the aisle leading children dressed as camels. King Herod will already be at the front of the church. After that, you read Luke 2:8 while an angel descends upon some shepherds keeping watch over their flocks by night. All the extra children who don't have major parts will be shepherds or sheep."

"It seems pretty straightforward."

"Joseph will be played by little Joe Koski. I thought it was fitting, since they both have the same first name. Anyway, Joe is rather outgoing and should have no problems. He'll go from inn to inn and be turned away at all of them except the last inn, where they offer him the use of their stable."

"Basically, I just read the parts and wait until the action is over before starting the next scene."

Alice nodded in agreement.

"I think I can handle this."

"Mary is played by Becky Hakanen. She's cute as a bug, but only four years old and kind of shy. I thought it best if she waited in the back until Joseph finds a place to stay. He'll then wave to her from the front of the church, and she'll walk down the aisle. She'll have a pillow under her dress to make her look pregnant. When she gets to the front, she'll give you the pillow, which you'll hide under the pulpit. Mary will then kneel in front of the manger just after you place baby Jesus inside it."

"Are you using a doll for the baby?"

"We thought it would add a lot to the program if we used a live baby."

"A live baby? Where're you going to get a baby? We don't have any infants in the community. Jennifer isn't due until April."

"Well actually, we aren't using a human baby. We're using that church cat. I believe you call him Gomorrah."

"How'd ya get him to cooperate?" Visions of disasters floated through Rudy's mind.

"I must admit, he didn't quite have the Christmas spirit when we started, but he isn't much of a problem once we get him into his Christmas costume."

"You wrapped him in swaddling clothes?" This he had to see.

"No, that would never do. We got the idea from you. I made a burlap bag with a drawstring. Once we get him in the bag and tie the drawstring around his neck, he's no problem at all. He's really kind of cute with a frilly bonnet covering his head and those chubby little cheeks."

Rudy had a hard time imagining Gomorrah being cute even with his chubby little cheeks. Was she referring to his Gomorrah? He wasn't even sure he could put the cat in the manger without his allergies acting up.

"We'll sing a couple of Christmas carols before the program and maybe one after the program. There'll be a Christmas offering with the proceeds going to converting the heathens in New Guinea and feeding the starving children in China."

"When's the next practice?" Rudy asked as he studied the list of Scriptures he was to read.

"The next practice will be on the morning of Christmas Eve. That'll be a dress rehearsal to see if all of the costumes fit. The program itself starts at eight o'clock in the evening. I know it doesn't give you much time."

"I think we'll do O.K.," Rudy replied.

***

High in the heavens above Northern Minnesota, water molecules cooled in the frigid air. The molecules coalesced to form small ice crystals, which further combined to form six-sided, works of art. Each snowflake was different. Each snowflake was created for a special purpose. Each snowflake had a special mission. One snowflake, however, was more special than all the others. It had the most perfect structure and was a beauty to behold. This was the Christmas Snowflake. It had been given a mission far more important than all the other snowflakes combined, a mission that must not fail.

***

Becky Hakanen woke early on the morning of Christmas Eve. Today, she would wear her costume, and in the evening would be the program itself. At age four, she didn't understand the meaning of Christmas, but she did understand wearing a costume. That would be fun. Her parents were equally proud that their only child would have a leading role in the Christmas pageant. It was a good day for the Hakanens, and they would not allow the pending snowstorm ruin it.

The Hakanens lived five miles west of Bear Creek, a one-hour trip by horse and wagon—longer in foul weather. Jake Hakanen replaced the wagon wheels with skis. That would allow the wagon to glide over the snow's surface, but didn't guarantee an uneventful trip. He still might have to push the wagon occasionally to assist his team of horses. Due to the high winds and blowing snow, the Hakanens left early to compensate for the adverse weather. The icy wind bit into Jake's face, more so than he had anticipated. It was a necessary hardship while guiding the two horses toward town, but only one person needed to endure that discomfort. Jake suggested his wife take cover under a tarp in the back of the wagon, but she refused to leave his side. Becky wasn't given a choice; she was wrapped in a warm blanket and tucked under the tarp.

The storm showed no evidence of subsiding, and the snow began to accumulate. Visibility was down to twenty feet. At times, the travelers were engulfed in whiteouts with no features visible before them, except the white mist of their own breath. It took all of Jake Hakanen's expertise and vigilance to keep the sled on the road. In the back of the wagon, Becky relaxed under the comfort of the canvas tarp. The tarp softened the noise of the blowing wind, and the gentle motion of the sled rocked Becky into a sound, but not restful, sleep. She dreamed of the coming Christmas Eve program, as well as the many presents St. Nick would leave the following morning. Becky's body rolled and twisted in somnolent ecstasy.

It came as a shock when Becky rolled off the back of the wagon. It took a moment before she realized what had happened. She looked around; no wagon was in sight, only the whiteness of the falling snow. She cried out; but all she could hear was the blowing wind. In a panic, she began to run, running north, away from the road. Her feet plowed through the eight inches of fresh snow. The underlying crust of the old snow supported her weight, preventing her from sinking into the two-foot snow base, at least not until she reached the edge of the woods, where her left foot broke through the crust. She reached up for an overhanging branch of an aspen. The branch broke. She reached for another branch, which held and assisted her escape from the deep snow. With continued fear, Becky renewed her flight into the woods.

***

"The church bell's ringing," Maggie announced to P.C. and Jennifer as they ate their breakfast at the Bare Creek Cafe.

"It shouldn't be ringing now. Nothing special is going on at the church," Jennifer said. Jennifer's morning sickness had subsided, and she had returned to work at the cafe a week earlier. She was feeling fine, although her belly was beginning to swell.

"It must be an emergency. We need to head down to the church." Maggie began clearing the breakfast table, but not before P.C. stabbed another link of sausage with his fork.

***

Mel Barker was in the midst of his weekly inventory when he heard the bell ring. Could this be the long awaited invasion from Canada? If it were, they would find him ready, he decided, grabbing his metal helmet and flintlock rifle. With his powder horn strapped around his neck, he headed for the church.

***

Silas was running his printing presses and didn't hear the church bell. He wouldn't have been aware of it if Agnes hadn't shut down the motors and told Silas of the pending emergency. Agnes, with her camera and bag of accessories strapped around her neck, was ready to capture any historic event that might occur. Ringing the bell at this time of day could only signify disaster.

***

A good portion of the community was already at the church when Rudy arrived. He saw Mel Barker with his steel helmet and flintlock rifle. Perhaps it was another civil defense drill, Rudy thought; but if it were just a drill, why was Mrs. Hakanen crying?

"Rudy, Becky Hakanen is lost somewhere in that blizzard." Alice also had tears in her eyes.

"Where did she get lost? Out by her cabin?"

"No, she fell off the sleigh on her way into town for the morning practice. She could be anywhere along the five-mile trail."

"What are we doing about it?" A quick look at the bewildered townsfolk answered his question. No one had a plan of action except for Mel, who was convinced the missing child was a diversionary tactic by the Canadians. After all, what did we really know about the Hakanens?

The leadership void was filled with the arrival of General Maggie. It only took her moments to sum up the situation and arrive at a battle plan.

"We need two-man search teams to scour the roadside between here and the Hakanen cabin. No one is to go on his own, and everyone is to be back before dark. We don't need anyone else lost." Someone produced a local map, and Maggie assigned each team a section of the five-mile trail.

"I'm willing to help," Rudy offered. "Find me a partner."

"You may be more useful here."

Rudy was disappointed, but Maggie was right. A lost child in a blizzard like this could be devastating to a small community. His assistance might be needed at the church.

"P.C., find Weasel," Maggie ordered, but P.C. was already putting on his coat and heading for Moose Lake Lodge. Hopefully, Becky would be quickly found, and Weasel's talents wouldn't be needed. Jake Hakanen was retracing his trip into town and may already have his daughter safely wrapped in a warm blanket on his sleigh. If Becky were lost deep in the woods, her only hope might be the tracking skills of Red Weasel. Weasel wasn't noted for his common sense, but when it came to tracking animals or survival in the deep woods, no one doubted his abilities.

***

The jet stream's high winds urged the Christmas Snowflake eastward across Wisconsin and into Michigan's Upper Peninsula. The laws of physics eventually prevailed, and gravity slowly pulled the Christmas Snowflake downward, out of the influence of the lofty jet stream. The Christmas Snowflake was on a mission, and it would not fail.

***

Most of the men folk had already paired up and left in two-man search teams by the time P.C. returned with Red Weasel. Weasel was wearing his coonskin cap, heavy coat, and fur-lined moccasins; he was dressed for the elements.

"Which area of the road do you two want to search?" Maggie asked the two woodsmen.

"We'll search the section where the child is lost," Weasel replied.

"How will you know which section that is?" Maggie asked in bewilderment.

"I'll know it when I see it," Weasel answered. "May we borrow Charlie?" Weasel asked, turning to Jennifer.

"Frenchie is out searching for Becky, but I'm sure he wouldn't mind," Jennifer replied. "Charlie's already hitched up to the sleigh and ready to go."

"All we need is Charlie. The wagon will be of no use where we're going. When we find the child, we'll need transportation to get her back to the church. It'll be a long walk in the snow for a four-year-old."

Jennifer appreciated Weasel's confidence, she only wished she were that confident. The temperature was well below zero and dropping. A child couldn't last long in weather like that.

Weasel and P.C. unhitched Charlie from the wagon and strapped supplies to his back. It was difficult to know what they might need, but they settled on an ax, blankets, and a length of rope. A large thermos of hot chocolate was also added, since the child might need warming up after she was found. Strapping snowshoes to their feet, P.C. and Weasel headed down the road. Maggie and Jennifer watched the pair disappear into the snowstorm. Strange as it might seem, the community's greatest hope might depend on that pair of misfits.

***

The Christmas Snowflake continued its slow descent toward the earth. The downward progress was sporadic, as occasional updrafts would send the snowflake swirling upward, but the laws of physics must prevail, and the snowflake eventually returned to its downward trek. The Christmas Snowflake had a mission that could not be stopped by an updraft of air.

***

P.C. led Charlie down the snow-covered road, while Weasel inspected the snow along the sides of the road. Weasel frequently stopped to examine some invisible piece of evidence only to shake his head and move on down the road. The sides of the road were covered with tracks from other searchers, a fact Weasel found particularly irritating.

It took two hours to reach the halfway point, and P.C.'s optimism was beginning to wane. Weasel had found many interesting tracks, but after a moment dismissed them all. He had just stopped to examine another irregularity in the snow. P.C. looked out at the snow and saw only snowdrifts, nothing to indicate a small child had passed this way.

Weasel looked out across the snow and also saw snowdrifts. But his attention was drawn to two small ridges in the snow leading into the woods. The two ridges were a foot apart and parallel. Nature hates symmetry. An animal had shuffled through the snow toward the woods. The tracks had been filled in by the drifting snow leaving only the telltale ridges to mark the spot.

"Follow me and don't step in the tracks," Weasel said.

P.C. looked across the snow and saw nothing. "What tracks?"

"Just walk in my footsteps." Weasel walked to the right of the ridges of snow until he reached the edge of the woods. A broken branch three feet above the snow caught his attention. A deer or timber wolf was capable of breaking the branch, but they would have broken the branch by pushing against it as they plowed through the snow. The broken fibers should be on the side of the branch. These fibers were broken on the top. Weasel knew only one animal capable of reaching up and pulling down on the branch.

"These are human tracks."

P.C. knew better than to doubt the Chief when it came to tracking, but he still could see no evidence of tracks, let alone human tracks.

"Now we need to know if these are adult tracks and if the person was heading into the woods or returning from the woods."

P.C. nodded in agreement. That seemed like an appropriate next step.

"Weasel knelt beside the twin ridges of snow and gently brushed away the snow from the tracks revealing the undisturbed crust of the snow base. An adult would have broken through the crust. Weasel continued to brush away the snow as he worked his way toward the edge of the woods and the broken branch. Just in front of the branch, Weasel found a four-inch diameter hole in the snow crust. The defect had been filled by fresh snow, which was soft and fluffy. The defect was the size of a child's boot. The child must have broken through the snow base at this point. The hole in the crust was in front of the broken twig. The child had reached forward, grabbing the branch to help pull herself out of the hole. She was heading into the woods.

"This is where the child entered the woods," Weasel casually informed P.C., as if the conclusion were obvious to all. "You better get Charlie. We need to get going. At these temperatures, we don't have time to spare."

***

Becky ran for over an hour. The howling wind muffled her cries for help. Her crying decreased to occasional whimpers as her energy became expended. She had worked up a sweat with her initial panic, and now her damp clothes were robbing her of vital thermal energy. Her core temperature began to drop.

Becky slowed to a walk. Confusion overtook her mind. Where was she? What was she doing here? It must be bedtime; she was so sleepy. Becky wandered through the woods looking for her bed. Where was her bed? Becky pushed back a cedar branch revealing a small clearing in the forest. Could this be her bedroom? In the center of the clearing was a large stump from an old white pine. Could this be her bedpost? Yes, it must be, Becky decided as she curled up beside the stump. The unrelenting snow gradually covered the body of the young child. Within minutes, she was nothing more than a snowdrift.

***

One by one, the two-man, search teams returned to the church. The Hakanens looked up hopefully each time a team returned, but the search team members avoided their gaze. That told them everything they didn't want to know. The fact that the searchers were half frozen wasn't encouraging. The searchers sat around the new furnace in hopes of thawing out their frozen toes. Cups of hot coffee helped warm them from the inside. The women folk made sandwiches and hot soup, both of which were well appreciated. Talk was kept to a minimum by the cold, dejected searchers. If they were this cold, how could a four-year-old survive the storm?

By three p.m., all of the search teams had reported in with the exception of P.C. and Weasel. Every inch of the road had been scoured to no avail. It wasn't mentioned, but people were beginning to think the body wouldn't be found until spring. This wasn't the first time someone had been lost in a winter storm, and often they weren't found until the spring thaw. Sometimes the bodies were swallowed up by the forest and never found.

Water Lily arrived at the church with Weasel to offer assistance wherever needed. Occasionally her eyes met Maggie's as they began to worry, not only about Becky's fate, but also for the safety of their spouses. Would they know when to give up? Storms like this could also claim the lives of adults. P.C. and Weasel knew the woods better than anyone in Bear Creek, but even they had limitations.

***

Pulled by the force of gravity, the Christmas Snowflake continued its downward drift. The wind caused it to flutter and swirl through the cold frigid air. As it came closer to the earth, the air thickened and the air resistance slowed the snowflake's rate of descent. The Christmas Snowflake was in no hurry. The snowflake had an important mission, and timing was everything. If it arrived too early or too late, it would fail. Failure was not an option. The Christmas Snowflake must not fail.

***

"Still see the trail, Chief?"

Weasel offered no reply. The fresh snow covered all but the freshest tracks, and there were none of those to be found. The only clues available were the occasional disturbed branches, which were few in number and not specific; they could be broken by any of a number of woodland animals. Sometimes the snow brushed off a fir tree provided a clue—unless it was blown off by the wind. Weasel didn't want to admit it, but he had lost trace of the child an hour earlier. All they could do now was walk in enlarging circles and hope they would be lucky. P.C. and Weasel didn't have a history of being lucky.

Becky had been lost for eight hours, a long time for a small child in sub-zero temperatures. Without shelter, the strong winds would lower the effective temperature to sixty below. The wind-chill factor could be devastating, and a child didn't have sufficient body mass to retain heat. The chances of finding Becky alive were dismal, a fact both woodsmen were beginning to accept.

"Mayor, it looks like we're not going to find her."

P.C. nodded in agreement. "It'll be dark shortly. You think we should quit?"

"Christmas Eve is an important day for your people. You need to be with your family."

"What about you?" P.C. asked.

"It's just another day for me. Leave Charlie with me, and I'll search throughout the night. If I'm lucky, maybe I can find the body."

P.C. accepted the wisdom of his friend. He was cold, and there was little left he could do. No child could survive long in this weather. P.C. handed Charlie's reins to the Chief and started the long depressing walk back to town. He wouldn't enjoy admitting failure to the congregation back at the church.

***

Maggie took one look at the dejection in P.C.'s face and knew they had no success either. "Where's Weasel?"

"He's going to keep on looking." P.C. failed to mention they had found Becky's tracks. Providing false hopes would offer no one any good.

"Weasel's spending the night in this blizzard?" Maggie asked incredulously. Maggie's eyes met Water Lily's. A four-year-old had just lost her life, and now Weasel was perilously close to losing his.

"He thinks he is some kind of Noble Indian Warrior Chief," Water Lily said. "He has no concept of his own limitations."

"Chief will be O.K.," P.C. informed the two worried women as he shuffled over to the new coal furnace to warm his hands.

With the arrival of P.C., all hopes for Becky's safe return were quenched. P.C. and Weasel had been their last hope. Now hope was gone and people wandered about the church in silence, or they just sat in chairs with their heads in their hands.

"We need to do something," Maggie told Rudy.

Rudy had been sitting with the Hakanens. He didn't know what to say in such a situation, but he thought he should at least be with them. Rudy looked out over his flock of dejected followers. Children were the only active individuals in the church. They didn't understand the significance of Becky's absence, but they knew all was not well.

"It's almost eight o'clock, and it's still Christmas Eve. I think we should go ahead with our Christmas Eve program. If for nothing else, let's do it for the children who have worked so hard over the last several weeks," Rudy told the small group of church leaders who had gathered around him. He had no idea why he had suggested that. How could they have the Christmas Eve program without Becky? It was too late to change his mind. The congregation was mobilizing to match appropriate costumes to the correct child. What was he to do when it was time for Becky to come walking down the aisle?

***

The Christmas Snowflake continued its slow, downward descent. A great forest could now be seen below the snowflake. Everything was going as planned. The snowflake had a mission and would not fail.

***

Weasel shuffled though the snow. He didn't think he had any chance of finding the child dead or alive. He just had to be alone. It would take a miracle to find Becky in this snowstorm, and he didn't believe in miracles. Miracles were a part of White Man's religion. He believed in reality, and the reality was he had failed. People were depending on him, and he had failed. He was used to failure. He had been a failure all of his life. It was Chief Thunderhead who built up the Moose Lake Lodge, and it was his banker friend in Chicago who invested Weasel's money and sent him generous dividend checks every month. Weasel was where he was in life only because of the help from others. Everything he did on his own was doomed to failure. The only thing he was good at was tracking and hunting. Had he been born a hundred years earlier, he might have been a Noble Indian Warrior Chief. Today, even his tracking skills failed him. He couldn't think of a time when he more wanted to succeed. Not for himself, but for the sake of the poor child who had frozen to death in the storm. Weasel had always liked children. Water Lily never got pregnant. He was a failure at that also. Noble Indian Warrior Chiefs don't cry, but Weasel could feel his eyes begin to water.

It is best he keep moving, he told himself. If nothing else, just to keep warm. Weasel pushed apart some cedar branches to reveal a clearing in the forest. In the center was a large white pine stump. A small snowdrift rested at its base. Weasel stepped into the clearing. The snow was smooth without evidence of recent disturbance, but then any tracks in the snow would be obscured by the snowstorm within minutes. The missing child could be buried in the snow, and he could walk past her without ever knowing. Weasel walked past the white pine stump and entered the woods on the far side of the clearing. Above him, a snowflake was slowly drifting downward.

***

Two Christmas carols had been chosen to open the Christmas Eve program. The first carol was "What Child is This." It had been one of Rudy's favorites, but now it sounded like a dirge as the congregation began to sing. Rudy's mind wasn't on the Christ Child when they sang the opening verse "What child is this, who, laid to rest..." How could a loving God allow a four-year-old girl freeze to death in this blizzard? What about that passage in Matthew where it says if you have one stray sheep out of a hundred, you should seek out the missing sheep? Wasn't Becky one of God's sheep? How could this happen on Christmas Eve of all days? What kind of a God was he serving, Rudy wondered.

***

The snowflake twisted and turned with each gust of wind while it slowly descended. Timing was everything, and the Christmas Snowflake was right on schedule. It could not fail. It would not fail.

***

Weasel felt only slightly better after his short crying spell. It was another reason he wanted to be alone, Noble Indian Warrior Chiefs don't cry. It was time he faced the facts; he wouldn't find the lost girl. She was dead, and there was nothing he could do about it. He must now care for the living. He must find shelter for Charlie, who had followed him through the deep snow without complaining. It had to be cold for him also. He would have to provide shelter for both of them, or they wouldn't make it through the night.

Weasel found a tall spruce tree with large bushy branches that spread out all the way to the ground. Taking his ax, Weasel cut the branches off the lower six feet of the trunk. The remaining lower branches were notched until gravity forced them to bow to the ground, forming a small lean-to at the base of the tree. Weasel coaxed Charlie into the lean-to where he would be protected from the wind. He didn't bother tying Charlie to the tree. Charlie might be a dumb horse, but he still had horse sense and wouldn't leave the protection of his shelter.

Now he needed shelter for himself. A large drift next to a granite outcropping offered possibilities. With a piece of birch bark, Weasel carved out a small snow cave, punching a hole through the ceiling for ventilation. A generous supply of cedar boughs was placed on the floor of the cave to elevate him from the frigid ground. This wasn't the first time Weasel had spent the night in the woods on a cold, winter day, and he expected no problems.

***

Rudy found the second Christmas carol almost as depressing as the first. How could he sing "O Come, All Ye Faithful" when he was beginning to question his own faith? The faith of a real minister wouldn't falter, even under trying times such as this. What right did he have to be leading a Christmas Eve service? Why were they here giving praise to a God who would desert an innocent four-year-old child, lost in a snowstorm?

***

The trees of the forest were now clearly visible below the Christmas Snowflake as it drifted down. In the center of the forest, a small clearing was now visible. If the laws of physics prevailed, the snowflake would land in the small clearing. The snowflake had to follow the laws of physics. The laws of physics would help the snowflake complete its mission. The snowflake must not fail.

***

A hand gently pushed back a cedar branch as a pair of eyes peered into the clearing beyond. A large white pine stump could be seen in the center of the clearing, but the eyes weren't interested in the stump. The eyes were only interested in the small snowdrift at the base of the stump. The snowdrift loomed larger as the eyes approached. A gentle feminine hand reached out and brushed away some snow revealing the face of a sleeping child. The hand wore no glove, yet the hand remained warm. The eyes looked down at the child's face, now covered with a mask of death. The child would never again know the joy of childhood with its carefree games. The child would never grow up to marry and know the pains and pleasures of childbirth. The child would never be a devoted wife and mother. The child's death had been such a waste.

***

The Christmas Snowflake floated no more than a hundred feet above the ground. In the clearing below the snowflake, a small child was visible. The wind had stopped. Only the force of gravity pulled on the snowflake. Force equals mass times acceleration. The force of gravity was acting on the snowflake's small mass as it accelerated toward the ground. The snowflake must obey the laws of physics. It must float downward. It must complete its mission.

The snowflake was now fifteen feet above the ground. Still, there was no wind and the snowflake continued to follow the laws of physics. The laws of physics were directing the snowflake toward the child's head, and the snowflake must follow the law. At one foot above the ground, the Christmas Snowflake floated over the child's upper lip. Physics demanded the snowflake land on the child's upper lip. The snowflake must obey the laws of physics.

The Christmas Snowflake was now only an inch above the child's upper lip and prepared for a gentle landing, but wait—it drifted sideways. It landed on her chin instead! How can this be?

The laws of physics demanded that it land on the lip. The snowflake must obey the laws of physics. Without the laws of physics, the universe would fail. The snowflake cannot land on the chin. It must land on the upper lip. Unless...unless there was another force acting on the snowflake!

The erratic behavior of one small snowflake didn't go unnoticed. The gentle hand froze in midair as its brain contemplated the significance of the snowflake's errant path. It could mean only one thing. There had to be a spark of life still in the child. But it had to be rapidly kindled into a flame, or it would be snuffed out forever. The soft, gentle hand was joined by another, and they worked in tandem to remove the remaining snow. The hands then scooped up the child and pressed her against a warm bosom. The Christmas Snowflake, still clinging to the child's chin, slowly melted and disappeared forever—mission accomplished!

***

Now when Jesus was born in Bethlehem of Judea in the days of Herod the king, behold, there came wise men from the East to Jerusalem, saying, "Where is he that is born king of the Jews? For we have seen his star in the East, and are come to worship him." Rudy watched as three children dressed as wise men walked down the aisle leading their camels. The children in camel suits walked awkwardly behind the wise men. What will I do when it is time for Becky to walk down the aisle, Rudy wondered.

***

Charlie huddled in his makeshift lean-to, trying to keep warm. The shelter provided relief from the wind, and his body heat gradually warmed the small enclosure making life bearable. He could still hear the howling wind through the cracks in his lean-to. But what was that strange noise?

"Who's out there?" Charlie asked, but heard no reply. A moment later, a soft, gentle, hand reached out to caress his shoulders.

"Hello, Charlie."

"How'd you know my name?" Charlie asked.

The soft hand had no glove or mitten, yet it remained warm and comforting as it gradually massaged Charlie's neck. The hand slowly worked its way up the neck until it reached that secret spot just behind his left ear and below his straw hat.

"Scratch me there, and I'll follow you anywhere," Charlie confided.

"Charlie, I need your help."

"Just keep scratching, baby, I'm with you all the way."

"This will be your finest hour." The hand gently took Charlie's reins and led him into the storm.

***

The cedar boughs were three inches thick at the bottom of the snow cave before Weasel was satisfied. The pockets of air trapped within the branches would provide insulation from the ground. Without insulation, the ground would suck heat from his body, possibly causing death from exposure. Weasel didn't intend to let that happen. A wool blanket provided insulation from above. He had done this many times before, as his ancestors had before him. There was no doubt he would have a comfortable night. In the morning, he would return to the comforts of Moose Lake Lodge. It would, however, provide no comfort for his mind.

Before turning in for the night, Weasel decided to check on the comfort of his horse. The comfort of domestic animals took precedence over personal comfort, and Weasel would make no exception tonight. Weasel exited his snow cave and found the storm still in full force. He would quickly check on Charlie and return to his snow cave.

Charlie wasn't in his tree shelter! It was unthinkable that even the dumbest animal would leave shelter in a storm like this. What would force Charlie to take such action? He must quickly find the horse. How would he explain this to Jennifer and Frenchie? Charlie was his charge. He was responsible for him.

Weasel retrieved his snowshoes from a snowdrift where he had planted them. As he was strapping on the snowshoes, he heard horsy-type sounds in the distance. Was that Charlie or just an aberration of the howling wind? Weasel stared off into the distance. Visibility varied from second to second depending on the gusts of wind, but Weasel thought he saw motion within the swirling snow.

"Charlie?"

A definite horse sound was heard in reply. Weasel could barely make out Charlie's head with his broad brimmed straw hat as the plow horse plowed through the snow toward Weasel. On Charlie's back was a small child.

"Is your name Becky?" Weasel asked, after Charlie came to a stop.

"I want to go home," was the only reply.

Bending down, Weasel finished lashing the snowshoes to his feet and then reached up to take hold of Charlie's reins. "Come on, Charlie…it's time to go home."

***

And there were in the same country shepherds abiding in the field, keeping watch over their flocks by night. And, lo, the angel of the Lord came upon them, and the glory of the Lord shone round about them: and they were sore afraid. And the angel said unto them, Fear not: for, behold, I bring you good tidings of great joy, which shall be to all people. For unto you is born this day, in the city of David, a Savior, which is Christ the Lord. And this shall be a sign unto you: Ye shall find the babe wrapped in swaddling clothes, lying in a manger.

Alice herded the sheep and shepherds onto center stage. The sheep were mostly the small children who were apprehensive about participating in the program. Alice was also apprehensive about the program, but for a different reason. They would soon arrive at the part of the program where Becky was to walk down the aisle as the expectant Mary. How would Rudy handle that? Alice could only assume Rudy knew what he was doing.

I don't know what I am doing, Rudy decided. It was almost time for Becky to come walking down the aisle, and there was no Becky. Why had he insisted they continue with the Christmas Eve program? It's only going to rub salt into fresh wounds. He could think of nothing to do but continue.

And it came to pass in those days, that there went out a decree from Caesar Augustus, that all the world should be taxed. And all went to be taxed, every one into his own city. And Joseph also went up from Galilee, out of the city of Nazareth into Judea, unto the city of David, which is called Bethlehem, because he was of the house and lineage of David, to be taxed with Mary his espoused wife, being great with child.

Lord, we could use some help down here, Rudy prayed silently.

And so it was, that, while they were there, the days were accomplished that she would be delivered. And she brought forth her first-born son, and wrapped him in swaddling clothes, and laid him in a manger; because there was no room for them in the inn.

Little Joe Koski began wandering from inn to inn looking for a place to stay. He would soon be directed to the stable and call for Mary to follow him. Rudy felt a panic attack coming on, his head beginning to throb from his brain tumor. It had been in remission for several months. Rudy had almost forgotten about it. What was he to do now?

An innkeeper was directing Joseph toward the stable. All he could do was apologize, he decided.

"Mary, there is no room in any of the inns, and we will have to stay in a stable," Little Joe yelled out to the imaginary Mary. Little Joe looked down the aisle, but everyone else looked at Rudy.

Lord, we still need some help down here. At least give me a sign. You gave Noah a rainbow, and Moses was given a burning bush. Can't we have some help? Rudy stared out at the congregation who stared back at him. All he could do was apologize.

"I would like to..." But Rudy's apology was drowned out by a gust of cold, snowy air as a large, fur-lined moccasin kicked open the door at the back of the church. In the doorway stood a Noble Indian Warrior Chief. His coonskin cap was matted with snow, and ice crystals clung to his hairy eyebrows. His face was redder than a Red Man's face ought to be with the exception of the skin over the cheekbones that were pearly white with the first stages of frostbite. In his arms was four-year-old Becky Hakanen, snugly wrapped in a coonskin coat. On the back of the coat, the words "Northern Normal School" could plainly be seen.

"Isn't that your coat?" Agnes asked Silas.

"That is my coat!" Silas replied in astonishment. "I thought you said Abigail had that coat."

"Yes,—I believe I did."

***

Bear Creek had quite a scare over the holidays. It appears Becky Hakanen fell from the back of her parents' sleigh on the way to our Christmas Eve children's program. Unfortunately, it happened during one of the worst snowstorms I have ever seen, but then, this is my first year here in the North Country. We immediately sent out two-man search teams, but no one could find a trace of the missing child. After we had all given up hope of her safe return, she was rescued by Red Weasel. He is a rather amazing Indian fellow who is normally very quiet and tends to keep to himself. For my money, he is a real American hero, but he denies any part in saving the child's life. He gives no details of the search other than saying the lost child just showed up on Charlie's back. I am sure his modesty is preventing him from providing the heroic details. He seems to be changed by whatever happened out there in the snowstorm, as he is more quiet than usual. He has also started coming to church. He has never done that before.

Becky has been delusional. She keeps talking about this teenage girl with long dark hair. We had no women in the search parties, so she has to be confused. I suppose the cold can do that to you. Some of the church folk are taking her story as further support for the Abigail Farnsworth legend. I suppose we will never know what really happened out there. Maybe it was the work of an angel.

I am embarrassed to admit my behavior was less than adequate during the tragedy. I should have been providing spiritual leadership during the crisis, but my faith faltered, and I let the congregation down. My faith must be only skin deep, definitely not strong enough for a man of the cloth. I don't know if it is ethical for me to continue in this charade. Maybe it would be wise to quit now instead of waiting for spring even though it is only a few months off. When I do leave Bear Creek, I will give up the ministry. Maybe I can find a job on the assembly lines of one of those motorcar companies in Detroit.

Rudy closed the journal. Life in the ministry wasn't as he had expected.

Chapter Ten

The harsh winter of twenty-three extended well into the first three months of twenty-four, and was considered by many Yoopers as one of the worst winters in years. Cabin fever was rampant among those individuals of poor health or low motivation who were unwilling to brave the elements and venture outside the confinements of their homes. For those individuals who enjoyed the simple entertainment of skating at the beaver pond, the extended winter season was tolerable.

All good things (and bad) must eventually end; and with winter turning to spring, the snow began to melt, causing rivers to bulge as they removed the winter snow from the countryside. It was mid-April when the ice on the Bear Creek beaver pond began to break up; and the pond, deteriorating from lack of repair to the dam, began to shrink. Winter activities gave way to trout fishing, hiking, and the picking of wild flowers. It was a time of excitement and renewal. It was the perfect antidote for cabin fever.

Even Rudy Hooper was feeling invigorated with the warm, May temperatures. The prospect of a replacement at the Bare Creek Methodist Church lifted his spirits. Many times during the year, he had considered resigning his position; now if he could hold on for a few more weeks, a more qualified replacement would take the church's helm and provide the religious leadership so desperately needed in Bear Creek. Then, Rudy wouldn't be a quitter. He would have served a full year at the church, for better or for worse.

Feeling it would be nice to leave something behind, something he could pass on to the new minister, Rudy spent the evening of May second planting flowers around the parsonage. He chose perennials, since they would bloom every year. That might be the only legacy of his year in Bear Creek. Rudy was on his knees planting the last of the daffodils when he heard footsteps behind him.

"Good evening, Pastor Hooper. I see you're planting flowers."

Rudy looked up to see a very pregnant Jennifer. He couldn't imagine further expansion without bursting at the seams. It had to be difficult walking around with such a large watermelon sequestered in her belly, but Rudy had yet to see Jennifer without a smile, and this evening was no exception.

"Jennifer, this is an unexpected pleasure."

"I hope I'm not interrupting you."

"Shucks no, I needed a break. Why don't you have a seat on the porch swing and rest your legs while I get us both a glass of lemonade. I have some already made."

"Well, if it isn't too much bother." Jennifer sat down on the swing. It felt good to get the extra weight off her feet; they had been swelling of late.

Rudy returned with two large glasses of lemonade and sat on the swing next to Jennifer. "I hope this is sweet enough for you."

"It's excellent," Jennifer replied after taking a sip. "It's a good day for lemonade."

"So when's your baby due? You look big enough already." Rudy didn't want to say so, but Jennifer looked bigger than most pregnant woman he had known.

"Ma says it could be anytime. She says it's going to be a large baby, maybe a hockey player."

"We can use more hockey players in the town."

"I hope it's a boy. Frenchie is set on having a boy, I'm afraid he'll be disappointed if it's a girl. We're going to name him John."

"In that case, I'll pray for a boy. I have a fifty-fifty chance of having my prayer answered," Rudy chuckled.

"Actually, my pregnancy is the reason I'm here."

"Oh, I hope nothing's wrong." Rudy always assumed the worst.

"It's nothing like that," Jennifer reassured him. "It's just that Frenchie and I had promised to chaperone the church youth group on their annual canoe trip down the Two Hearted River."

"That sounds exciting. I've never been in a canoe. It must be fun."

"It is. They do it every spring."

"Where do they get the canoes?"

"They rent canoes from the Rainbow Lodge at the mouth of the river. The lodge transports the canoes twenty miles upstream, and the kids paddle back to the lodge."

"Twenty miles seems like a long trip." Rudy scratched his beard. "I suppose the current helps."

"It takes two days. Mr. Barker has some war surplus pup tents they use for camping."

"I suppose ten miles a day isn't bad. Should you be doing this with your pregnancy? Wouldn't want anything to happen to you."

"That's the problem. Ma says I could go into labor any time, and I have no desire to deliver my baby in a canoe while a bunch of kids watch."

"I agree. You shouldn't be canoeing in your condition, and I think Frenchie should be here with you also," Rudy said with conviction. Sometimes he had to voice his opinion.

"I knew I could count on you."

"You can always count on me."

"I'm sure you'll enjoy it."

"Enjoy what?"

"Chaperoning the youth group. Ma thought you might be reluctant, but you volunteered before I asked."

"I did?"

"Mrs. Watson said she would go if you went. I guess we're all set. We won't have to cancel the trip after all."

"But I've never been in a canoe."

"It's easy. Just point the canoe in the right direction and let the current carry you downstream."

Rudy wasn't convinced. "Does Alice Watson know anything about canoes?"

"I'm sure she's an expert," Jennifer replied. "But you'll have to be careful around those teenagers. They can be pranksters."

"I'm not worried about that."

"Don't underestimate them, or they'll get the best of you."

"What makes you say that?"

"I used to be one of them. At eighteen, I guess I'm still a teenager. The only reason I was picked for a chaperone was because I'm married and supposed to be above that kind of stuff."

"I'll keep that in mind."

"The important thing is ensuring members of the opposite sex aren't together in any of the tents. Even if nothing happens, it looks bad."

"That won't be a problem."

***

"Morning, Mel," Rudy said as he entered the Bare Creek Hardware and Feed store.

"Morning, Rudy," Mel replied, climbing down from his small stepladder.

"My monthly vitamin order didn't come in, did it?"

"Yes, I believe it did." Mel retrieved a small package from under the counter. "That'll be four bits. I understand you're chaperoning the church youth group."

"How did you hear that already? I only agreed to it yesterday evening."

"News travels fast in Bear Creek."

"Well, I do try to help out where I can."

"You're a brave man."

"It can't be that bad."

"They talked me into chaperoning those teenagers once."

"What happened?"

"It was easier riding up San Juan Hill," Mel replied. "Did I ever tell you about the time Teddy Roosevelt and I rode up San Juan Hill? It was in the year of 1898 and Teddy Roosevelt and I..."

"You said fifty cents?" Rudy placed two quarters on the counter and retrieved the vitamins. "I have to run. I need to pick up a copy of the Gazette." Rudy left before Mel had time to reenact the Spanish American War.

"Wait a second, Rudy. You have a letter. It arrived yesterday."

Mel handed Rudy an important looking envelope. Rudy checked the return address; it was from Bishop Samuel Johnson. This was the letter he had been waiting for. He would wait until he returned home to open the letter when he had time to savor the contents.

***

"I need a copy of the Bare Creek Gazette," Rudy told Silas.

Silas had been cleaning his presses, and his hands were covered with printer's ink. He didn't offer to shake hands. "Help yourself from the pile on the counter. They were hot off the press yesterday noon. The news shouldn't be too stale."

"Thank you, I will." Rudy retrieved a paper from the top of the pile and placed a dime on the counter. On the front page was a picture of Olie Olson with a forty-two-inch northern pike. "That's a good size fish."

"That it is," Silas replied. "Bet you wish you could have caught it. It came out of the beaver pond, you know. I haven't seen a fish like that in years."

But Rudy was no longer listening. His eyes were fixed on the article below the fish story. The caption read, "Local minister and schoolteacher to chaperone the youth group's annual canoe trip." "I thought you said the paper came off the press yesterday noon. Jennifer didn't ask me until yesterday evening. How can..."

"News travels fast in Bear Creek."

"Who normally chaperones the trip?"

"It varies," Silas replied. "No one's ever done it twice."

"Well, it makes me nervous. I've never been in a canoe before."

"Ah, there's nothing to it. Just paddle forward, and when you need to turn, use the paddle as a rudder." Silas took out his pipe and filled it with tobacco. It was obvious there was more wisdom to come. "What you need to worry about isn't the canoes—it's those teenagers," Silas said as he lit his pipe. "They can be a mite mischievous."

"That part doesn't worry me."

"Just keep the boys and girls appropriately separated and you'll do fine."

"It's just a matter of running a tight ship," Rudy replied confidently.

***

May 2, 1924

Dear Pastor Hooper,

I hope this letter finds you in good health. As you are aware, this office received your letter last fall requesting a replacement minister at the Bare Creek Methodist Church. At that time, this office was unable to grant your request and asked that you continue in that position if possible. It is our understanding you were able to continue at your post despite your medical and personal problems. For this, we are truly grateful.

We are pleased to inform you that a replacement has been found. This spring, I will be touring the Upper Peninsula Churches and will personally introduce the new minister to the congregation at the Bare Creek Methodist Church. Hopefully, I will be at Bear Creek in three weeks. If you have any further questions or concerns, please do not fail to write.

May the Lord be with you,

Samuel Johnson
Bishop Samuel Johnson

Rudy stared at the letter. This was what he had been waiting for. This was the light at the end of the tunnel. Only three more weeks and he would be done with his obligations at the Bare Creek Methodist Church. Then he could get a job at one of those Detroit motorcar factories. All he had left was an overnight canoe trip and three sermons. Two sermons—he would talk the bishop into giving a sermon when he arrived. Yes, it was a good day, and he wouldn't let it be spoiled by negative comments concerning the church youth. Those comments were made by individuals who had no training with young people. He just had to be stern.

***

The sun was bright, with only a few puffy clouds. Rudy estimated the temperature at above sixty, not bad for early May. The Farmer's Almanac was predicting dry, warm weather for the next several days.

Rudy tested the water with his finger, finding it cold. He expected that. The water from the Two Hearted River came from melting snow, didn't it? He would make a point to stay inside the canoe. Gus Sorensen from the Rainbow Lodge had a string of canoes lined up along the river bank with two eager teenagers standing by each canoe, ready to board should the go ahead be given. Rudy knew most of the teenagers from church, but that was only to say hello. They seemed like a friendly lot.

"You ready, Alice?" Rudy asked.

"I guess so," she replied. "I'm glad you know what you're doing. Otherwise, Jennifer never would've talked me into this trip."

"You've never been in a canoe?"

"No, I sat in one once, but it wasn't moving. I'm relying on you."

"It's not difficult." Rudy decided not to dwell on his limited canoeing experience.

"Are we set to go?" Matt Peterson asked. He appeared to be the spokesman for the group. Sally Sappanen stood quietly beside him, obviously his partner for the trip down the river. Sally had long blond hair that hung well below her shoulders and blue eyes—typical of the Finnish people. Her sweater was tightly pulled over a generous chest. Rudy wondered if all Finnish girls her age were that well-endowed. He would definitely have to keep the boys and girls appropriately separated. He didn't need any scandals in his last few weeks at Bear Creek.

"Yes, I guess we're ready."

"Let me help you." Matt offered his hand to the Widow Watson who gingerly tiptoed to the front of the canoe.

"Hop in, Reverend Hooper." Luke Hansen ran over to steady the stern of the canoe. "We'll shove you out?"

Matt and Luke gave the canoe a gentle shove, forcing the two chaperones into the center of the river before climbing into their own canoes. The other canoes were already disappearing down the river.

"Don't get too far ahead of us," Rudy yelled at the teenagers in his most authoritarian tone.

"We'll wait for you at Lookout Point," one of the teenagers yelled back.

"I think we'll have to paddle if we expect to keep up with them." Rudy dipped his paddle into the water. "You paddle on one side, and I'll paddle on the other." Under the encouragement of the two paddles, the canoe lurched forward. This isn't so hard Rudy decided as the canoe headed down the river.

Rudy's initial enthusiasm was a bit premature. The canoe's forward progress diminished, and then the canoe stopped. Rudy increased the power of his strokes. The canoe still refused to advance.

"I think we're hung up on a rock," Rudy said. But the water was plenty deep; Rudy was unable to touch bottom with his paddle. And if they were stuck on a rock, why was the canoe swinging side to side?

"Look behind you," Alice said. "They tied the canoe to a tree. I should have mentioned the kids can be mischievous."

"If that's the extent of their practical jokes, we'll survive." Rudy untied the canoe. Alice decided not to discourage Rudy with tales from previous chaperones.

Free from restraints, they headed down river. The canoe responded nicely to Rudy's paddle as he steered the canoe around bends in the river. Canoeing was easy. Rudy settled back to enjoy the scenery

On the riverbanks, the aspen were just coming into leaf, while down below on the forest floor, trilliums, and other assorted flowers proclaimed the advent of spring. Small birds flittered from branch to branch singing out their mating songs in hope of attracting a receptive partner. Occasionally, even a blue heron, mallard duck, or other large fowl graced their path. Rudy and Alice found a wide assortment of wild life, but there was no sign of the wild life they had been assigned to chaperone.

"Do you have any idea what Lookout Point is," Rudy asked.

"No, I've never been on the river before."

"Hopefully, it isn't too far downstream. I feel like we should be providing closer supervision."

Rudy took it as a good sign that no dead bodies were washed up along the riverbank, although there were no signs of live ones either after an hour and a half of paddling. The riverbanks were thick with aspen or, in the swampy areas, tag elders. Rudy wasn't sure he would see a body washed up along the shore even if there were one. Occasionally large outcroppings of granite loomed over the canoeists. Rudy could see why Yoopers referred to the Upper Peninsula as God's country.

Up ahead a large granite dome projected above the trees. Rudy estimated its height at one hundred feet. The river appeared to be winding its way toward the structure.

"I wonder if that could be Lookout Point?" It was a rhetorical question. He didn't expect a meaningful answer.

"AHOY DOWN BELOW," echoed a reply from the top of the dome as if Rudy's question had been audible from the large granite pedestal. At the top of the dome, Rudy saw several teenagers.

"IS EVERYONE UP THERE?" From what he could see, they were a few people short, although more heads appeared as others disappeared from sight.

"EVERYONE IS HERE EXCEPT YOU GUYS. COME ON UP, THE VIEW IS FANTASTIC."

"At least everybody is alive and well." Rudy steered the canoe toward the shore. "Do you want to climb the rock?"

Alice looked at the damp, black soil in front of the canoe. It extended outward ten feet where it was replaced by a dense thicket. Beyond that loomed the rocky pile of granite. "I think I'll wait here. That ground looks awfully soft."

"I'm sure it's solid. The kids made it."

"You go ahead, I'll wait here."

Rudy wasn't keen on climbing the rock, but he had to prove he was capable of keeping up with those teenagers; he was their leader. "I'll just go up for a few minutes and be right back down. I need to set a few ground rules."

Rudy stepped onto the moist, black soil. "The ground is a little soft." Rudy's feet and ankles were immediately sucked into the soft muck. His shoes were like suction cups as the black ooze reluctantly released its grip. Where were the tracks from the kids?

Rudy wondered. Surely, they had to walk through this muck. Rudy crossed the ten feet of mud in four large strides and stepped onto the dry riverbank. Mud continued to fill the crevasses and crannies of his shoes, creating sucking sounds with each step; at least he was now on dry soil. Between him and the granite dome was a twenty-foot stretch of tag alders laced with wild raspberry bushes whose thorny branches reached out to entwine Rudy's feet and scrape across his bare forearms. The tag elders rose before him like prison bars, slowing his forward progress. They were small and could be pushed aside, but they swung back like carriage whips when released. If teenagers can do it, I can do it, Rudy convinced himself as he thrashed through the undergrowth, but where was their trail through the brush?

After three minutes, Rudy reached the base of the granite dome. His forearms were scratched and bruised, and the beads of sweat on his forehead began to drip down his face while swarms of black flies circled his head like miniature vultures drooling over a potential meal. Some of the more daring black flies made kamikaze attacks on Rudy's eyes, nose, and ears. His feet still squished with each step. Three minutes and he had traveled only thirty feet. He couldn't quit now. If the teenagers could do it, he could do it.

Rudy looked up at the large granite rock while he waited to catch his breath. It wasn't a cliff, but it had to be close. He estimated the incline at about sixty degrees. Fortunately, there were cracks and toeholds to assist him in his ascent. He would need them if he were to make it to the top. Looking around, he couldn't see any plan of attack that was better than another. The only way to the top was to climb.

Rudy grabbed a handhold and pulled himself upward. The coarse granite handholds were like sandpaper and tore at the flesh on his hands and fingers. Several areas on his palms began to bleed, but the granite dust changed the droplets of blood into mud, and the bleeding ceased. Slowly he inched upward. Those teenagers were tougher than he thought. Rudy was developing respect for anyone capable or climbing Lookout Point. It wasn't as easy as it appeared.

Toward the top, the slope decreased, and the last twenty-five feet, Rudy was able to crawl like a dying man across the desert sand. With his last gasp of breath, he pulled himself forward to the top of the dome where he remained face down in a spread eagle position while he waited for his breath to catch up to him. Around him, a group of teenagers gathered in admiration.

"I told you he could do it," Matt said as he collected a dollar from Luke.

"You bet on whether or not I could make it up here?"

"We only bet a dollar. We didn't bet as much as you did on the hockey game. Now there was a risky bet."

"I WAS NOT THE ONE WHO BET ON THE HOCKEY GAME!" Rudy replied, loud enough for all to hear.

Rudy pulled himself to a sitting position once he was assured there was enough air to go around. He had to admit it was a beautiful view from the top. He was well above the trees, and he could see the Two Hearted River as it wound a path below him. He could see his canoe with Alice patiently waiting in the front.

"Wait a minute. Where are your canoes?" Rudy looked around. There was no sign of any canoes other than his own.

"They're all around the bend in the river," Luke replied. "We beached them at the canoe landing and walked up the trail." Luke pointed to a well-marked trail that casually traversed downward from the rocky dome. "The trail's a lot easier, but probably not as much fun as the route you took to the top."

"I guess we best get going if we're going to reach our campsite before dark," Matt said. The teenagers followed Matt down the trail.

"Don't get too far ahead of us."

"WE'LL WAIT FOR YOU AT THE DEVIL'S WISHBONE," Luke yelled back as he disappeared down the trail.

"WHAT'S THE DEVIL'S WISHBONE?"

"YOU'LL KNOW IT WHEN YOU SEE IT," someone said.

Rudy looked down at the river. His canoe was one hundred feet down a granite cliff, twenty feet through a virtual jungle, and ten feet across the quicksand. He wasn't looking forward to the return trip.

"Did you lay down the ground rules?" Alice asked when Rudy climbed into the canoe.

"Yep, I told them to go no further than the Devil's Wishbone and to wait for us there."

"What's the Devil's Wishbone?"

"It's a spot down river. You'll know it when you see it."

Rudy removed his shoes and washed his feet. His shoes were filled with black mud that had multiple crawly things wiggling across the surface. Rudy wondered if his shoes were salvageable. He threw the shoes into the canoe. He would deal with them later. Dipping his paddle into the water, he pushed the canoe toward the Devil's Wishbone.

After two hours of vigorous paddling, there was no sign of teenagers or Wishbone. The river was beginning to widen as more streams joined the march to Lake Superior, and the current was faster, the smooth surface of the river now replaced by gentle ripples as the water scurried along the riverbed. Occasionally, a protruding rock would agitate the water sufficiently to produce gurgling noises, breaking the otherwise silence of the day. At least all the waterways were converging and not diverging. There was no chance of losing their way along the river. Eventually they would have to catch up with the group.

"How much farther is this Devil's Wishbone?"

"It can't be too much farther," Rudy replied.

"What does it look like?"

"It's difficult to explain. You'll recognize it when you see it."

The faster current caused the exposed rocks to converge on the canoe at an increasing rate, forcing Rudy to devote his full attention to steering the canoe. He was able to avoid most of the rocks, but the canoe's aluminum sides still careened off some of the more aggressive boulders, jarring not only the passengers' aching muscles, but also their confidence.

"The current's picking up," Alice said. She hoped she sounded confident.

"Yep, we should arrive at the Devil's Wishbone in no time with the help of this current."

"It doesn't get any faster, does it?"

"I wouldn't think so." A large swirl of water lifted the bow of the canoe and slammed it back down on the water. "If this were a dangerous river, I am sure the church elders wouldn't approve the trip every year."

Rudy forced the canoe into a hard right turn to negotiate a ninety-degree bend in the river. The canoe straightened out in front of a hundred-yard gauntlet of swirling waves punctuated with gushers of frothy water. Granite walls confined the sides of the river, thwarting any thoughts of escape.

"Well, maybe a little bit faster," Rudy said. Attempts at steering were useless. The waves threw the canoe from side to side while sheets of water sprayed the voyagers with the melt-off from the winter snow. From the corner of his eye, Rudy could see teenagers lining the tops of the granite walls cheering them on while the water pulled the canoe rapidly down the ravine. Fortunately, the river narrowed, and the depth of the river hid any rocks under several feet of water.

"Is this really safe?" Alice asked. She no longer made any pretense of paddling but was hunkering low in the front with both hands clutching the sides of the canoe.

"The kids are up there on the rocks. They must have made it. If they can do it, we can do it." The first rule of chaperoning is never show fear, Rudy told himself as he pushed off from the granite wall with his paddle. He was no geologist, but he assumed a granite wall outranks a thin aluminum canoe.

At the halfway point, Rudy straighten the canoe and pointed it downstream. Fifty yards ahead of them, the river crashed into solid granite. Swirls had been cut into the granite over the years by the powerful water. It was hard to believe water was stronger than granite. The same water was now churning them down the ravine. What would happen if an aluminum canoe were caught between the water and the granite wall? Rudy had no desire to find out. Obviously, the river didn't end at the granite wall but had to bend to the right or left. At the top of each crest of water, Rudy strained to see the outlet. The river appears to curve to the left, Rudy decided. Yes, there was a sharp bend to the left. As the canoe got closer, it became obvious that it was a tight bend to the left where the river cut back on itself in the shape of a horseshoe—or a wishbone.

"Rudy, there's a sharp bend in the river. What're we goin' do?" Alice had come to the same conclusion about immovable granite walls and the flimsiness of canoes.

"Hang on and I'll steer the canoe toward the left side of the river as we go into the bend." Alice was listening, but hadn't released her white-knuckle grip on the canoe since they entered the gorge. Further advice wasn't necessary. The canoe bounced from one side of the river to the other, despite the wishes of its captain and entered the bend in the center of the river where the water was equally confused about its egress. It swirled around in a small whirlpool.

"We're spinning around," Alice said through clinched teeth from her vantage point in the front. The color of her face now matched the color of her knuckles.

"At least we haven't hit the wall—yet." Rudy made some feeble attempts to steer the canoe, but by the time he was able to alter the canoe's course, the canoe was pointing in a different direction. The whirlpool regurgitated the canoe on its third lap sending it and its crew downstream stern first.

"I think I'm going to get sick," Alice said. Her face was starting to look green. Rudy hoped this was a reflection from the water.

"Keep paddling. It'll keep your mind busy and help you forget your stomach."

Alice decided her mind was plenty busy, and if Rudy thought she was going to give up her grip on the sides of the canoe, he was crazy. "Are we going backwards, or is the water flowing uphill?" Maybe if she closed her eyes, it would all go away.

"I'm trying to turn it around, but it's hard to steer from the front of the boat." Rudy had obtained valuable experience earlier in the day, becoming fairly good at guiding the canoe through the water, but nothing prepared him for steering a canoe down a rapids backwards.

"Alice, the current is slacking. I think we made it." The gorge was beginning to widen, allowing the river to spread out and reduce the current. A probe with a paddle found the water only a foot deep. "It's shallow. We can walk to shore if we need to." Alice was not reassured.

"I'll hang onto the canoe. You walk it to shore."

"We no longer have to. Look, there're only small ripples on the water, and it's shallow. Open your eyes."

"If they're only small ripples, why do I still hear that roar of water?"

Good point. The roar did seem awful loud for such small ripples. "It must be temporary hearing damage from the noise back there in the gorge. The water here is so shallow we're even scraping bottom." The scraping noises continued for a few more feet before the canoe came to a complete halt.

"We stopped. Did you pull the canoe to shore?"

"No, we're stuck on a rock. Open your eyes."

"Not until you tell me we're on shore."

"We'll never get to shore unless we get free from this rock. I need you to push against the river bottom with your paddle." Rudy reached out to push off with his paddle, but it wasn't long enough to reach the river bottom. It wasn't long enough to reach the water. Rudy looked down at the Two Hearted River six feet below him.

"Alice, I don't want to scare you, but I think the canoe is hung up on a waterfall."

"Waterfall? I don't see any waterfall," Alice replied with eyes still closed, hoping that, if you can't see it, it'll go away. Go away it didn't, and the canoe continued to teeter with the posterior hanging over a six-foot waterfall.

"Don't move, Alice, or we'll be smashed on those rocks below."

Rocks below, we have to get off the rocks below. Alice was following Rudy's instructions to the letter, albeit one paragraph behind. With eyes still closed, Alice loosened her grip on the canoe and pushed off the rocks below with her paddle. Rudy watched as the background behind Alice changed from trees and rocks to clouds and blue sky. No longer hanging onto the canoe, Alice catapulted out of her seat, falling onto Rudy's lap. The waterlogged canoe, freed from its entrapment, slid down the falls into the quiet pond below.

"You guys were fantastic," Matt said as he waded out to pull the canoe to shore. Rudy wasn't sure if the sight of one chaperone sitting on the lap of another presented a proper image, but Alice had a death grip on his shirt with no indication of letting go, her eyes still closed.

"Did everyone make it through OK?" Rudy asked.

"We all portaged around the Wishbone. No one's ever tried going through the Devil's Wishbone—until now. And backwards no less. I really didn't think you would make it," Matt said as he gave back Luke's dollar. "Luke, let's go try it."

"NO!" both chaperones replied in unison.

"How much farther to the campsite?" Rudy asked after his feet were properly planted on terra firma. He wasn't looking forward to any more exciting canoe rides.

"Maybe an hour at the most," Luke replied. "The rest of the trip is rather boring." Rudy figured he could handle boring.

"Let's take a short break, and when we head out again, we all stay together," Rudy said. "No more surprises."

True to Luke's word, the rest of the day was uneventful. Rudy did all of the paddling, since Alice needed both hands to hang on to the canoe. Just prior to dusk, the group arrived at a grassy plateau. A dozen teenage commandos immediately assaulted the beachhead with youthful enthusiasm. Luke and Matt, being two of the older boys, assumed leadership, although the others didn't excel at followership.

"Make sure the tents are up before it gets dark," Matt warned the others who weren't listening—they were busy putting up their pup tents.

"I'm going to put my tent at the edge of the clearing," Matt informed Luke.

"I'm going to put my tent next to yours," Sally Sappanen informed Matt.

"Hold it," Rudy informed everyone. It was clearly time for chaperones to take charge. "We are not going to have tents scattered all over the clearing. The tents are to be placed in a single row with each tent separated by two feet. The girls will have the tents on the left, and the boys will have tents on the right. Your two chaperones will be in the middle with Miss Watson at the end of the girls' tents, and I will be at the beginning of the boys' tents. To make things easy, I have some pink ribbons that will be tied to the top of the girls' tents, and some blue ribbons that will be attached to the boys' tents. If you need either of us at night, you can find Miss Watson in the last tent with a pink ribbon, and you can find me in the first tent with a blue ribbon. Are there any questions?"

"Ah man, that's just like in the military."

"These are military tents. They're used to it."

Grudgingly, the teenagers set to work erecting the tents to the chaperones' specifications, and within fifteen minutes, a neat row of pup tents spaced exactly two feet apart stretched across the clearing. At the top of each tent, a blue or pink ribbon rippled in the breeze.

"Now we need a fire to roast our hot dogs," Rudy said.

"Let's get a lot of firewood."

"We can build a huge bonfire."

"A small fire will be sufficient," Rudy advised the eager teenagers.

"Ah man, can't even have a decent bonfire."

The fire still turned out larger than Rudy would have preferred, since the campers continued to appease the fire's insatiable hunger. A round or two of burnt hot dogs, plus a few marshmallows adequately satisfied the campers' hunger. At Rudy's insistence, the fire was allowed to burn down as darkness descended over the forest clearing. The campers serenaded the dwindling campfire with numerous campfire songs, some of which, Rudy thought, were a little too colorful for a church outing with women present.

"Every muscle I have is aching," the Widow Watson confessed. "I think I'll turn in and see if I can get any sleep in that pup tent." Sitting on the ground beside the fire was a mistake, Alice decided. Her muscles didn't want to move. She would never have made it to her feet, had two teenagers not come to her rescue. Why weren't they sore? She wasn't that much older than they were. Fortunately, a half-moon illuminated the night, and she was able to find her way along the row of tents. When she got to the last tent with a pink ribbon, she forced herself back to the ground and crawled into the tent.

"It's getting late," Rudy said. "Maybe we should all go to bed."

"Before you go to bed, do you think you can explain a few Bible passages that we find confusing?" Matt asked. "We were discussing them earlier in the day, and some of us are confused."

"I would be happy to explain them." Now, this is what church camping should be all about, Rudy thought, sitting around the campfire discussing religious matters.

"We have a question about Genesis chapter 34 verses one and two where it says: *And Dinah the daughter of Leah, which she bare unto Jacob, went out to see the daughters of the land. And when Shechem the son of Hamor the Hivite, prince of the country, saw her, he took her, and lay with her, and defiled her.* Does that mean he raped her?"

"Well, yes, I guess it does," Rudy agreed.

"That's not very nice," Sally said, curling her blond hair with her index finger.

"There are many sinners in the world both today and in history," Rudy said.

"But in verses three and four it says*: And his soul was clave unto Dinah the daughter of Jacob; and he loved the damsel and spake kindly unto the damsel. And Shechem spake unto his father Hamor, saying, Get me this damsel to wife.* Isn't that strange—raping a woman and then expecting to marry her?"

"She didn't really marry the scum bucket, did she?" Sally asked.

"You know there are better Bible stories," Rudy said, trying to change the subject.

"I want to know if she married him," Sally repeated.

"It sure sounds like she did," Luke said. "In verses fourteen and fifteen, it says: *And they said unto them, We cannot do this thing, to give our sister to one that is uncircumcised; for that were a reproach unto us: But in this will we consent unto you: If ye will be as we be, that every male of you be circumcised. Then will we give our daughters unto you.*"

"What's circumcision?" Lori asked. Lori felt cheated because she was born too late for the women's suffrage movement, but felt there were inequalities that still needed her special attention. "And why only the guys? That sounds sexist."

"You mean if all of the Hivites get circumcised, Dinah has to marry that rapist?"

"Is someone going to explain circumcision?"

"The New Testament has better stories we can discuss," Rudy suggested.

"I can't believe they consented to be circumcised," Luke said.

"Did the girls get to be circumcised too?" Lori asked.

"Nope, just the guys."

"I still think that's sexist if only the guys get to be circumcised. Reverend Hooper, can you tell me what circumcision means?"

"Well, ah, the word comes from Latin where, ah…circum means around and…cision means to cut. So it means to, ah…cut around…"

"Cut around what?"

"I think your mother can explain it better than I can."

"I still think it's sexist."

"Why did they consent to circumcision, Reverend Hooper?"

"I guess it was as a sign of friendship, like being blood brothers. Sometimes after a sin is committed, it is wise to forgive the transgressor."

"So did she marry that rapist or not?"

"No, that's the best part," Matt continued. "In verse 25 it says: *And it came to pass on the third day, when they were sore, that two of the sons of Jacob, Simeon and Levi, Dinah's brethren, took each man his sword, and came upon the city boldly, and slew all the males.*"

"Talk about military strategy, first they convinced them to have circumcisions, and when they're too sore to walk, the good guys kill them and take revenge," Luke said with a few slashes from his imaginary sword.

"Oh, that sounds gross," several of the girls decided, but not Lori who was trying to figure out why owning a circumcision should make it hard to walk.

In the heat of the discussion, Rudy didn't notice when Matt and Sally backed away from the campfire and disappeared into the night.

***

"Don't step on any twigs," Matt whispered to Sally as they walked along the row of tents.

"There it is," Sally whispered back. "That's the last tent with a pink ribbon. The pink ribbon was replaced with a blue ribbon, and the two teenagers returned to the campfire.

***

With discussion still going strong, Rudy didn't notice when Sally and Matt rejoined the group. He also didn't notice when the two teenagers gave a thumbs-up to the rest of the group.

"I think I'm getting tired," Luke said. "Maybe it's time we all went to bed."

"That's an excellent idea." Rudy was more than willing to end the discussion. "Maybe next time we could discuss something out of the New Testament like the Sermon on the Mount."

"If you want to go to bed, we'll put the fire out," Luke offered.

"That sounds nice. I'm really tired." Tired was an understatement. He didn't wish to admit it, but he was sore from head to toe. The second rule of chaperoning is: never let on that you're not as young as they are. "You guys are on your honor. Just make sure no boys are in tents with pink ribbons and no girls are in tents with blue ribbons."

"That sounds immoral. We would never do anything like that."

They're a nice bunch of kids, Rudy decided as he walked along the row of tents. Just the same, they need a stern disciplinarian to offer guidance. Much as the kids hated it, lining up the tents and keeping the sexes separated was for their own good. Someday they will be thankful. When they get to be parents, they'll understand. And the colored ribbons on the tents, now that was a stroke of genius. There it is, the first tent with a blue ribbon. That would be his. No sooner had Rudy bent over and crawled inside the tent when the blue ribbon on top was changed back to pink. A quick pull on a tent stake sent the tent collapsing down on the two writhing chaperones.

***

I am reluctant to make this entry into my journal without consulting an attorney, since charges may still be pressed against me. I have decided to admit my guilt, if it comes to that, and accept the punishment for my sins, whatever that might be. It appears I have assaulted the Widow Watson. Not intentionally, of course, but an assault is still an assault. The details are still fuzzy in my mind, but I distinctly remember climbing into my tent, which was the first tent with a blue ribbon on it. I must have had a blackout spell, as the next memory I have is lying on top of Alice Watson in her tent. Fortunately for her, the tent collapsed, and several of the alert teenagers came to her rescue. I don't think I'll ever be able to thank those teenagers enough for what they did. They may have prevented me from doing things I cannot allow myself to document in this journal.

I am sure my brain tumor was the cause of my blackout spell. It had been in remission for several months, and I had hopes it might have resolved. I should have known better; miracles never happen to me. Previously, I had hoped to work in a motorcar factory in Detroit; now I feel morally obligated to consider admitting myself to an institution where I can be placed under lock and key and not cause any more harm to society.

The Widow Watson has been very understanding and says she won't press charges. She is a wonderful Christian lady, and I, at times, even allowed myself to dream that someday we might share life together. This, of course, is now all for naught since I no longer have the courage to face her.

The rest of the community is treating it as a joke, and I am sure they are laughing behind my back. When I returned the tents to Mel Barker at the Hardware and Feed Store, he said he had heard the tents were quite cozy for two and then gave me a wink.

Three more weeks and then I can get that long period of rest.

Chapter Eleven

Tales of the spring canoe trip spread rapidly throughout the town, providing quality entertainment for Bear Creek residents. However, short attention spans soon drifted into other areas of interest, and the assault at the Two Hearted River was all but forgotten except by the perpetrator, whose conscience continued to torment his spiritual psyche. The rest of the Bear Creek residents focused on obligations that came with the warm, spring weather. Spring was the beginning of God's year when the world was renewed and fresh vegetation replaced the old. Spring was a time of hard work as local farmers prepared for the advent of another summer. The residents of Bear Creek were alive with activity.

Frenchie and Jennifer were particularly busy with Jennifer preparing for the slightly overdue family addition and Frenchie preparing the ground for his first crop of potatoes. A small, forty-acre section of the farm had been cleared of stumps the previous fall. Despite protests about being treated as a common laborer, Charlie, under Frenchie's guidance, had turned over the soil, and the forty acres awaited spring planting. A larger area of the farm still contained, well-entrenched stumps that defied routine attempts at extraction. The smaller stumps had been removed with shovel and pry bars, but the larger stumps required more forceful encouragement before they would relinquish their tenacious hold on the soil. Three cases of dynamite obtained from one of Northern

Michigan's many iron-mining companies provided that additional encouragement. Too old for safe use by the mining companies, the dynamite was obtained at discount and made short work of the most stubborn stumps.

Since P.C.'s assistance at the cafe was seldom needed and often discouraged, he had been quick to offer his expertise in stump demolition. Feeling P.C. shouldn't have all the fun, Weasel likewise volunteered his services. Their assistance freed up some of Frenchie's valuable time, allowing a head start on planting the back forty acres. With the short growing season in Michigan's Upper Peninsula, that was a major advantage. Frenchie, therefore, readily accepted their services over Jennifer's strenuous objections.

As P.C. suspected, the procedure wasn't much different than blowing up paint cans with cherry bombs; and after a few minor disasters, the proper amount of dynamite was determined. Too small a charge and the stump wouldn't budge; too large a charge and the stump was smashed into kindling wood. With the right amount of dynamite, a stump could be sent flying through the air in a graceful arc. P.C. held the record for height, having sent a large pine stump soaring fifteen feet into the air. Weasel, on the other hand, had best of show in the artistic class as one of his stumps flawlessly performed three somersaults in midair before firmly planting the trunk into the ground with roots sprawling out the top like angry tentacles.

"Ya know, Mayor, a couple more days like this and those stumps will be history," Weasel said during one of their many breaks. "What're we goin' do this weekend?"

P.C. stretched out in the shade of a large stump with a few sticks of dynamite for a pillow to give the question some serious thought. "If we have any dynamite left, I suppose we could try fishing at Moose Lake."

"That might be fun," Weasel agreed.

"Ever seen one of those motor cars?" P.C. asked after a few moments of silence.

"Saw some in Marquette once—give me a good horse any day." Weasel wasn't noted for embracing new ideas.

"Lot of motor cars in those big cities."

"Them big city slickers always have to have those new inventions." Weasel chewed on a piece of straw while he gave it some thought. "They ain't of much value."

"I'm goin' get me one."

"Get what?" Weasel hoped he hadn't heard right.

"A motor car."

"What you want one of them for? They ain't much good on the rough roads around here."

"I can drive it to church on Sunday."

"That's half a mile. You can walk that far." Weasel had visions of motorcars driving up and down Bear Creek's main street. It wasn't a pretty picture. "They won't run without that gasoline. Where you goin' get that?"

"Mel said he can special order it."

Weasel gave the topic some more thought. "You can't buy one around here."

"They have them for sale in Green Bay. Ma and I were going to Green Bay this weekend to pick up supplies for the cafe. I thought I could look them over then, but now she won't go until Jennifer has her baby."

"Suppose that sounds reasonable. Maggie's the best midwife in town."

"Of course, if Jennifer were to have her baby today or tomorrow, we might still be able to go. I'd like to look at one of those motor cars up close."

"Well, the baby comes when it comes. You can't do much about that."

"I suppose we could induce the baby."

"What's that?"

"Make the baby come early."

"You can do that?"

"Ain't much to it," P.C. said with his usual confidence.

"Is that safe?"

"Sure it is. We're just speeding up nature."

"I don't know."

"All we have to do is ride her around on these here bumpy roads to shake things loose a bit."

"We?"

"Well, you don't have to help if you don't want to. Anyone can drive her around the bumpy roads."

"What happens when she starts to deliver?"

"She won't deliver this afternoon. Women always have babies at night when it's most inconvenient. That's how they get back at us men for getting them pregnant in the first place."

"This afternoon sounds awful inconvenient to me. You sure she won't deliver this afternoon?"

"Of course not. All it'll do is shake things up. Maybe Ma will deliver the baby late tonight. Then there'll still be time to go to Green Bay."

"I suppose taking her for a ride on the wagon won't hurt any."

P.C. looked at his pocket watch; it was a quarter past one. "About time for a break. Let's head back to the cabin. I'm getting a bit thirsty."

"We need to get that extra case of dynamite anyway. These two boxes are about empty."

P.C. and Weasel found Charlie still hitched to the wagon. Charlie had made an executive decision and moved the wagon to the shade of one of the few remaining trees. The wooden boxes with the remaining explosives were tossed onto the back of the wagon, and Charlie was pointed in the direction of home. No further encouragement was needed.

***

Jennifer was returning from one of her frequent trips to the outhouse when the two explosive experts arrived. Her bladder didn't have the capacity it had in the past.

"We are powerfully thirsty," P.C. informed his daughter. "Got anything cold and wet?"

"How about some fresh lemonade?"

"That'll work for me," Weasel said.

Jennifer poured two glasses of lemonade. She would have poured a third glass, but she was tired of running to the outhouse. "Is it pretty warm out there?"

"Mighty hot out there," P.C. confirmed. "Feel sorry for Frenchie…slaving away in the hot sun while we sit here and drink cold lemonade."

"It's too bad he can't be here." Jennifer felt a moment of guilt.

"Yep, I'm sure he could go for a cold lemonade, the sun being so hot and all."

"If he were working closer to the cabin, I could take him a glass."

"That's an excellent idea," P.C. said. "Charlie's hitched up to the wagon. We could ride out and take him some lemonade."

"I'm not so sure that's a good idea."

"It's not far by wagon. You'd be there and back in no time."

"Ma says I should stay home until the baby comes."

"Frenchie's working on your property, so it's still home."

"I don't know if that would be wise in my condition. The baby could come anytime, you know."

"Have I ever led you astray?" P.C. asked.

Jennifer decided it best not to answer. "OK, I guess it won't hurt if we come right back."

The wagon wasn't in the front of the cabin where P.C. left it, but had wandered off to a shady spot beneath a tree where Charlie was munching on some grass.

"Come on, Charlie, we have a little errand to do." If Charlie hadn't had a mouth full of grass, he would've told P.C. what he could do with his little errand.

"Let me help you up on the seat," Weasel said, offering Jennifer his hand. The wagon seat was suspended on two "U" shaped pieces of spring steel placed on their sides that cushioned the ride over bumpy trails.

"Let me make sure these boxes don't bounce around." P.C. wedged the wooden boxes under the steel springs, rendering them useless.

"What's in the boxes?" Jennifer asked.

"Dynamite."

"Is that safe?"

"I think so."

"The boxes are almost empty. One stick of dynamite at the most," Weasel said.

P.C. urged Charlie forward with a slight tap from the buggy whip, and the wagon took off down the road a little faster than Jennifer had expected. With the wooden dynamite boxes wedged under the wagon springs, every bump in the road was transferred directly to the passengers.

"Can't we go a little slower?" Jennifer asked.

"Don't want this trip to last too long," P.C. replied. "We'll get the lemonade out to Frenchie and be back at the cabin in no time."

Jennifer hung onto the jug of lemonade she held firmly between her legs. "I don't think we need to be in that much of a hurry." Jennifer's back was starting to ache, a problem she had been having during the last several months.

"We're almost there. Shouldn't be much longer." P.C. steered Charlie over the bumpier parts of the road.

"I don't think this is a good idea," Jennifer said while holding her abdomen.

"Just hang onto the lemonade a little bit better," P.C. suggested. You're spilling it all over my leg.

"I'm not spilling any lemonade."

"Then why is my leg all wet?"

"It can't be my bladder; it no longer holds that much. I think my water may have broken."

This was starting to get inconvenient, Weasel decided. "Maybe we should head back." The suggestion was unanimously approved. Charlie was pointed toward home. That was fine with him. He never was enthused with this errand anyway.

The return trip was taken at a slower pace. Jennifer was encouraged to remain in bed upon arrival at the cabin. That might slow things down. P.C. checked the jug of lemonade hoping for a leak to explain his wet pant leg, but none was found. Perhaps his plan worked too well.

"How ya feeling?" P.C. asked once Jennifer was tucked into bed.

"I was having stomach cramps, but they stopped." Jennifer's smile turned to a grimace as a new wave of cramping began. "Maybe we should tell Frenchie what's happening," Jennifer suggested. "We have a signal: three shots from the shotgun. He'll know he's needed."

"I suppose I can do that." P.C. took Frenchie's double barrel shotgun from the gun rack on the wall.

"The shells are in the top cupboard."

P.C. found three shells and headed out the door. Placing two shells in the chambers, P.C. fired off the two rounds five seconds apart. He cracked open the gun, loaded the third shell, and fired into the air.

Click

P.C. muttered a few choice words when the gun failed to fire. Must be a bad round, he decided. Lowering the gun, P.C. prepared to open the breach. A loud blast attested to the integrity of the delinquent round as the gun discharged, sending buckshot into the side of Frenchie's wagon. A louder blast confirmed that some of the projectiles had found the dynamite.

"You were right, Chief. There was only one stick of dynamite left in the box," P.C. told Weasel upon returning to the cabin.

"Charlie OK?" Weasel asked.

"Aside from a rotten disposition and some wooden splinters in his hindquarters, he'll be OK."

***

Frenchie stopped to catch his breath when he reached the cabin. He figured he might be needed when he heard the first two gunshots, but when he heard the howitzer go off, he knew it was serious. The sight of the partially destroyed wagon wasn't reassuring. The sides and seat were gone, and there was a large hole in the floorboards. Charlie didn't appear happy either.

"What happened?" Frenchie asked when he entered the cabin.

"Aauhhh!" Jennifer replied.

"She said she thinks she is in labor," P.C. translated.

"I'm having a baby!" Frenchie shook hands with all present, including Jennifer.

"Do ya think we should send for Maggie?" Weasel asked.

"I want Ma."

"You wait here, Jennifer. Don't go anywhere. I'll get Ma…I'm having a baby." Frenchie shook everyone's hand again.

"You get Ma. Weasel and I'll stay here with Jennifer in case the baby comes early."

"Aauhhh!"

"We're going to have a baby," Frenchie told Charlie as he climbed onto the wagon. "We gotta fetch Ma." The axles and wheels were still in good shape, but with the bench seat blown off, Frenchie had to drive the wagon standing up, chariot style.

Charlie and the wagon took off with a jolt. Charlie galloped down the center of the road, assuming all other vehicles would yield the right of way.

"Did Frenchie go for Ma?" Jennifer asked between moans of pain.

"Ma will be here shortly," P.C. reassured her. "But don't worry, you always have Weasel and me."

"Aauhhh!"

"You know much about delivering babies, Chief?"

"Once watched some kittens being born."

"I want Ma!"

"We need to boil some water," P.C. said. "Have to have boiling water when delivering a baby."

"I can do that." Weasel set about boiling the water.

"I think the baby's coming. Aauhhh!"

"You can't have the baby until Ma gets here. Chief, help me tie her knees together with these towels."

"I want Ma!"

***

When Charlie, Frenchie, and what was left of the wagon arrived in Bear Creek, Charlie dug in his heels bringing the wagon to a halt.

"I'm having a baby," Frenchie told Maggie and the early afternoon patrons when he entered the cafe.

"Is she having strong contractions?" Maggie asked. Earlier in the week, Jennifer had experienced some false labor, and Maggie didn't want to overreact to another false alarm.

"She's howling with pain. It seems real," Frenchie said.

"Everyone out of the cafe, we're closing," Maggie informed her patrons.

"Can't I finish my pork chop?" one of the patrons asked.

"Eat it on the way out the door," Maggie replied without much sympathy. "Come on Frenchie. Let's go deliver a baby. You too, Water Lily; we can use your help." Water Lily was already grabbing her purse. She had been helping Maggie at the cafe in Jennifer's absence. She assumed that included delivering babies.

Maggie and Water Lily sat on the back of the wagon with their feet hanging over the side. It was no longer elegant transportation, but it still worked.

"How come there's a hole in the floor of the wagon," Maggie asked.

Frenchie shrugged his shoulders. "It didn't have the hole this morning when I loaned the wagon to P.C. and Weasel." That was enough explanation for Maggie and Water Lily.

Frenchie flicked the reins and Charlie took off at a gallop. The buckboard lurched forward, nearly throwing Maggie from the back of the wagon. She reached out for the few remaining sideboards in search of additional support. The ruts in the dirt road that constituted Main Street grabbed at the wagon wheels, tossing the buckboard from side to side like the tail of an angry alligator. Pedestrians, trying to cross the street, fled in terror in the face of the runaway wagon and the stampeding plow horse. Rudy, heading toward the Bare Creek Gazette to pick up the evening paper, would have been run over had Frenchie not pulled back on the reins, forcing Charlie to a momentary halt.

"Hop on, Rev. Hooper, we may need your services," Maggie ordered.

Rudy climbed aboard. He wasn't heading north, but an order is an order. He didn't think Maggie would accept no for an answer. All he wanted was a newspaper. The fact that he was addressed as Rev. Hooper instead of Rudy suggested this was more than a social event.

***

"I got the water boiling; what do I do now?" Weasel asked.

"I don't know. I suppose we could make some coffee." P.C. replied. "Jennifer, you want some coffee?"

"Aauhhh!"

"Jennifer's a little testy today," Weasel observed.

"Women get that way when they're pregnant."

"I want Ma!"

"She should be here shortly…Care for a sandwich, Weasel? I think there's some meat in the icebox."

***

Without springs to cushion the ride, every vibration of the wagon was transmitted up the passengers' spines, causing heads to bob and false teeth to chatter. This wasn't Rudy's favorite mode of transportation. Strange, he had never noticed the hole in Frenchie's wagon before. One would think that would limit the wagon's usefulness.

Rudy had only wanted a copy of the newspaper, and now he was privy to the local news as it was happening. From the conversations between Maggie and Water Lily, Rudy deduced Jennifer was about to deliver. It was refreshing to know he wasn't the one generating the news. A newborn baby in Bear Creek was always a source of excitement. Rudy looked forward to being a part of that excitement.

***

Moans of pain could be heard coming from the cabin when the wagon pulled up to the door. Maggie and Water Lily jumped from the wagon and headed for the cabin before the wagon came to a stop. There was little discussion concerning who was in charge when Maggie and Water Lily took command of the bedroom. No males were needed, thank you. Frenchie, assuming exceptions would be made for the father-to-be, found the bedroom door slammed in his face.

"Is there anything you want us to do?" P.C. asked through the bedroom door.

"GO BOIL SOME WATER."

"We already have boiling water."

"No we don't," Weasel said. "We used that for coffee, remember?"

"GO BOIL SOME MORE WATER."

"Why do you have to boil water when you deliver a baby?" Jennifer asked her mother.

"You don't, but those two don't know that."

The hardest part of the birthing process is the long wait, Rudy decided. It might have been easier if some positive action could be taken, or if there were some tool in which to gauge progress. Under the present circumstances, the most that could be done was to change cold water into boiling water, which was converted into coffee when no practical use for the hot water could be found. It was even more stressful on Frenchie, who paced the floor, unable to lessen the pain experienced by his wife behind the bedroom door. The moans were incessant, although they did wax and wane. The peaks of pain seemed to be coming at shorter and shorter intervals.

The only thing more tormenting than the shrieks of pain were the five minutes of silence when no noise or sign of life permeated through the bedroom door. The silence came suddenly and without warning, fueling the imagination of those individuals confined to the outer sanctum. The moans of pain, although unpleasant, had been accepted as the normal consequence of childbirth, but the silence left a void that gnawed deep into the pit of everyone's stomach. Nothing is more terrifying than the unknown. Everyone sighed with relief when Maggie appeared at the door holding a small object wrapped in a large towel.

"Is that John?" Frenchie asked, breaking the silence.

"No, it's a girl," Maggie replied.

Frenchie peeled back the edges of the towel to reveal a small, frail-looking child. "Why is she so blue?"

"She's a blue baby—born with a heart problem."

"Isn't there anything we can do?"

"Seen it before. It might be minutes, might be hours, but the baby's going to die."

"Can I hold her?"

Maggie passed the towel-wrapped bundle to her son-in-law. "I'm very sorry; Frenchie. You and Jennifer are young. There is plenty of time for more children."

Reaching down with his little finger, Frenchie touched the infant's small hand, but there was no response other than the labored breathing. It was as if the extremities were already dead.

This is when a good clergyman would say something to make everyone feel better, Rudy thought, but no words came to his mouth. He placed a hand on Frenchie's shoulder and watched the infant struggle for life, a fight she was rapidly losing.

Each breath the infant took was an effort, and the flesh around the base of her small neck retracting, distorting the tiny figure. The breathing gradually became shallower and less labored. Inspirations became irregular with frequent gaps in the breathing cycle. The periods of apnea increased until there were only occasional gasps of breath to document life. These, too, soon ceased, and the body lay still.

"I think that's the end," Maggie said after several minutes of lifelessness. "It's best if we put the old behind us." Frenchie didn't disagree, but neither did he make any effort to give up the baby.

Maggie nodded at P.C., who picked up a shovel and headed out the door. Weasel followed behind him.

"I don't have anything in which to bury her," Frenchie said, more to himself than anyone else. "I suppose I could use a shoe box. She's small enough to fit one."

She's so small, Maggie thought to herself. Something just doesn't make sense. "Rudy, do you think you could say a few words?" Maggie asked.

Rudy nodded, although he had no idea what to say. He didn't even have his Bible with him. All he wanted was the evening paper. What do you say at the funeral of a newborn infant? How does such a death fit into God's plan? Some things weren't taught in seminary.

P.C. had chosen a spot under an apple tree. That was a good spot, Frenchie decided. He would have to get her a headstone. Yes, his daughter needed a headstone. The hole was four feet deep, with the dirt from the hole piled to one side. It looked so cold, Frenchie thought. On the other side of the hole rested a small shoebox.

Rudy made a few awkward statements; what else can one say? He mentioned dust to dust and ashes to ashes, but his words were inadequate for the present situation. The shoebox was lowered into the depths of the hole, and P.C. began filling it with dirt. Maybe he should close with a Bible verse. It would have to be one he had memorized. The twenty-third Psalm...he could say the twenty-third Psalm. He knew that by heart.

The Lord is my shepherd; I shall not want. He maketh me to lie down in green pastures:

We are placing her below the green pastures. It's so cold down there, Maggie thought.

He leadeth me beside the still waters. He restoreth my soul:

I wonder if the wagon ride Weasel and I gave Jennifer had anything to do with the baby's death?

He leadeth me in the paths of righteousness for his name's sake. Yea, though I walk through the valley of the shadow of death, I will fear no evil:

That's a mighty big valley, Frenchie thought, as the dirt continued to pile up on his daughter.

for thou art with me; thy rod and thy staff they comfort me.

How can my few words provide any comfort at a time like this? Rudy wondered.

Thou preparest a table before me in the presence of mine enemies: thou anointest my head with oil; my cup runneth over. Surely goodness and mercy shall follow me all the days of my life; and I will dwell in the house of the Lord forever.

The mourners stood silently in a circle around the tiny grave for a few moments and then headed for the cabin.

"Can I see Jennifer now?" Frenchie asked Maggie.

"It was a hard labor since the baby was breach. Jennifer's tired, but I suppose it would be good for her to have you at her side."

Water Lily, who had remained behind with Jennifer, met Maggie at the door. "We have a problem," she whispered. "She's still in a lot of pain, and I can't get the bleeding to stop."

Maggie and Water Lily returned to the bedroom, and again, the door was slammed in Frenchie's face. It was back to waiting. He had lost a daughter and now he could lose his wife. Even with all of the advances in medical knowledge, women still died in childbirth.

Moans of pain were again heard from behind the bedroom door. This time the pain wasn't the pain of labor. This time there would be no benefit from the agony. Had there really been any benefit to the other pains? How do you stop the bleeding? Frenchie didn't know much about medicine, but he did know people die if bleeding can't be controlled.

Rudy sat in his chair with his head in his hands, his eyes closed. He wasn't good at tolerating someone else's pain. His body cringed with every moan. He prayed the Lord would stop the moaning, but then worried about how the Lord might do it. He hadn't forgotten the death of the baby. That was the first time Rudy had watched a person die. He prayed it wouldn't happen twice in one day.

As if an answer to Rudy's prayer, the moaning ceased, leading Rudy to wonder if his prayer was the cause of some unseen disaster. He was about to pray for forgiveness when a loud, screeching howl that only a newborn with an attitude can make, announced the activities occurring behind the bedroom door.

Within minutes, Maggie again appeared at the bedroom door holding another large towel. This time the towel was kicking and making plenty of noise.

"It's a boy," Maggie proclaimed. "They were twins; that was why the girl was so small." Maggie passed the bundle to Frenchie, who cautiously examined the contents of the towel. The baby was still covered with the white residue of a newborn, but was otherwise pink and healthy. The baby continued to cry, giving no indication he had any plans to quit. Frenchie placed his index finger in the baby's mouth. The crying ceased and was replaced by sucking sounds.

"Congratulations, Frenchie, you're the father of a fine healthy boy," Maggie said with pride in her eyes. She was now a grandmother. "You can go in and see Jennifer now if you want." P.C. and Weasel, following Frenchie into the bedroom, were cut off by Maggie and Water Lily. This was a time to be shared by husband and wife—and baby.

***

It has been a very exciting day. I was on my way to the Bare Creek Gazette when I was accosted by Frenchie, Maggie, and Water Lily. It seems Jennifer was in labor, and they were en route to deliver the baby. I was honored to be invited along. I have never been involved in the birth of a baby before. As it turned out, Jennifer was pregnant with twins, which was why she looked so big. Unfortunately, the first baby, which was a girl, was born with a heart problem. The baby was blue and lifeless. She died in Frenchie's arms. It was very sad. I don't think there was a dry eye in the cabin. We had to bury the baby beneath an apple tree, and I was asked to officiate at the funeral. Although I was glad to have been there, I don't think I had much to offer in spiritual support. It would have been nice if I'd had more time to prepare. I'm sure more qualified ministers could have done a better job.

The second baby came as a surprise. Not even Maggie suspected it. This was a healthy boy, which is what Jennifer and Frenchie had wanted. They are naming the boy, John. I like that name. It's a good Biblical name.

Next Sunday I will give my last sermon here in Bear Creek. Jennifer and Frenchie have asked me to baptize baby John. This is quite an honor, since they could have waited until the new minister arrived.

I haven't heard much more concerning my assault on Alice Watson, although I'm sure people are still talking about it behind my back. I'm fortunate Miss Watson has chosen not to press charges. Hopefully, no one will mention this to Bishop Johnson when he arrives. It would be so embarrassing. It would be nice if I could quietly slip out of town after my replacement arrives and get admitted to some institution where I might receive some help, or at least where they could prevent me from hurting anyone.

Chapter Twelve

May 2, 1923. Today is my first day in Bear Creek and the beginning of my journal. I am captivated by the beauty that is visible from my porch swing. The parsonage overlooks a beaver pond, and I can watch the engineering marvels of a beaver I have named Luther. Tomorrow, I will start work on a garden by the edge of the beaver pond. I expect an exciting year.

Rudy looked down at his journal. Did he really make the journal entry one year ago? Was he that energetic pastor so filled with optimism and hope? What had happened to him? Where did he go wrong? But then, he knew where he went wrong. He had exposed himself on the beaver lodge in front of men, women, and children; participated in gambling with church money; assaulted the Widow Watson; and worst of all, when Becky Hakanen was missing in the snow storm, he had lost his faith in the God he had sworn to serve.

Rudy now sat on the same porch swing he sat on one year ago. Then he had marveled at the beauty of the land before him, and he had been enchanted by the picturesque beaver pond with its overly energetic beaver. Without Luther's continuous repairs, that dam was deteriorating. Water was now leaking through a multitude of holes. The beaver pond was half its former size. In another six months, it would be just another segment of the river. There would be no more skating or hockey games to break the monotony of the long winters, and the townsfolk would no longer gather to observe the advent of the full moon. Were those summer gatherings really that bad? The beaver pond, which had been such a valuable asset to the local community, would be no more. It was a natural treasure that had existed for over twenty-five years, and Rudy had destroyed it in less than one. Was this the legacy he was to leave behind when he departed?

At least it would be over in a week. Sunday, he would give his final sermon at the Bare Creek Methodist Church, his last sermon anywhere. A short article in the Bare Creek Gazette had notified the community of his imminent departure. People would soon be dancing in the streets.

Rudy closed his eyes to make the world go away. With his eyes closed, he could create his own world, free of pain and disappointment. Lost in that darkness, Rudy didn't notice the approach of two visitors.

"I hope we're not interrupting your nap," Molly said as she climbed the three steps to the top of the porch. Her left arm was wrapped around the elbow of a tall, muscular man. His tanned skin and callused hands confirmed he worked hard for a living.

"Just resting the old eyelids," Rudy confessed with a bit of embarrassment. "I sometimes find it easier to think when I shut out outside distractions, but you're never a distraction."

"I want you to meet Al Peterson," Molly said as she introduced her friend. "We want to get married."

"Well, congratulations," Rudy said, shaking Al's hand. "I believe I've seen you at church the last several weeks." Al had a firm handshake and a large smile that radiated sincerity. His shoulder pressed tightly against Molly's arm.

"And when are you two going to make it official?"

"That's why we're here. We read in the paper that you'll only be here one more week. I know this is a lot to ask, but we would like you to marry us before you leave."

"I would be honored to perform the ceremony, but the church will have a new minister. You don't need to rush the wedding on my account."

"We would prefer you. You were the one who convinced me to terminate my prior occupation. We just want a simple wedding. It won't require much of your time."

Rudy never liked the way that men's magazine treated the Ollies. He had never mentioned it, but she must have sensed his feelings.

"Al is a farmer," Molly continued. "I'll be helping him on his farm."

"Well, Molly, if you really want to, I suppose we can do it anytime next week."

"Call me Nora Jane. I never did like the name Molly."

"Nora Jane is a nice name. What ever happened to Dolly and Polly? I haven't seen them around lately."

"Oh, they moved on to Pine Stump Junction at the request of a guy named Olaf.

Never would've thought Olaf would be interested in magazines for men, Rudy thought. He must have more culture than people give him credit.

Rudy watched the couple walk, hand in hand, down the drive. Hopefully, they would have a long, happy marriage. If he hadn't assaulted the Widow Watson, he might have had a happy marriage too. Rudy returned to his swing, closed his eyes, and allowed the world to disappear into darkness.

***

Trudy seemed full of enthusiasm as she coaxed a tune out of the old pump organ. Apparently, Sodom had destroyed a third reed. Trudy was now forced to orally replace F#, G and high C with the appropriate "La" or "Da" to fill out the tune. It didn't sound half-bad. As the congregation finished the last verse of *Rock of Ages*, Rudy stepped up to the pulpit. This would be his final sermon. Looking out over the sanctuary, he noted every pew filled and folding chairs were being set up in the back. Everyone in Bear Creek had read of his imminent departure, and the vultures had come to get one last look at the man who had assaulted the Widow Watson. Maybe he was being too critical. Perhaps they were here for the baptism of baby John. Jennifer and Frenchie were popular within the community. Just the same, the large crowd was unsettling.

The crowd looked normal. P.C. had his left eye closed in deep meditation. Al Peterson and Molly—that is Nora Jane—were holding hands, appearing more concerned with each other than with the coming sermon. Several small children were running up and down the aisles. In the far back, a young boy was chasing a large bullfrog that had escaped from his pocket. Yes, things were starting off normally.

Smiling at him from the second row was the Widow Watson. Rudy didn't know how she could appear so friendly after what he had done to her. She had to be a very forgiving Christian woman.

"Today's sermon is about Daniel and the lions." Rudy wondered if lions were any worse than a congregation of hungry vultures.

"In the first verse, chapter six of the book of Daniel it says: *It pleased Darius to set over the kingdom a hundred and twenty princes, which should be over the whole kingdom. And over these three presidents, of whom Daniel was first; that the princes might give accounts unto them, and the king should have no damage.* In other words," Rudy translated, "King Darius had divided his kingdom among one hundred and twenty princes who reported to three presidents, one of whom was Daniel."

"Verse three says: *Then this Daniel was preferred above the presidents and princes, because an excellent spirit was in him and the king thought to set him over the whole realm.* King Darius had noted Daniel was filled with the Holy Spirit." No one ever accused me of having an excellent spirit deep within, Rudy thought.

"The princes and the other presidents then became jealous. Verse four tells us: *Then the presidents and princes sought to find occasion against Daniel concerning the kingdom; but they could find none occasion nor fault; forasmuch as he was faithful, neither was there any error or fault found in him."* It wouldn't take long to find fault in me, Rudy was tempted to say. Rudy leaned to the left to dodge an incoming spitball; the Koski kids must be somewhere in the congregation. *"Then said these men, We shall not find any occasion against this Daniel, except we find it against him concerning the law of his God.* Daniel's enemies decided they couldn't find any fault in him, so they were going to use his faith in God against him, and they went to the king. In verse seven," Rudy continued, "they told the king: *All the presidents of the kingdom, the governors, and the princes, the counselors, and the captains, have consulted together to establish a royal statute, and to make a firm decree, that whosoever shall ask a petition of any god or man for thirty days, save of thee, O king, he shall be cast into the den of lions.* So Daniel's enemies convinced the king to sign a decree that couldn't be changed; and when they caught Daniel praying to God, they brought him before the king to be thrown into the lion's den." Rudy was thankful Bear Creek lacked a lion's den.

"Verse sixteen says: *Then the king commanded and they brought Daniel and cast him into the den of lions. Now the king spake and said unto Daniel, Thy God, whom thou servest continually, he will deliver thee.*" A truly merciful God would deliver me from Bear Creek, Rudy thought.

"And how did God treat his faithful servant? We find out in verse twenty-two where it says: *My God hath sent his angel, and hath shut the lions' mouths, that they have not hurt me.* The message from this story is: if you serve God faithfully, he will be there to protect you." If that were true, why am I having all these problems? Rudy wondered.

Rudy sat down in his chair behind the pulpit while ushers took up the offering. This was not one of his better sermons, but they hadn't come to hear his sermon. He was just the pastor who assaulted the Widow Watson. Baby John's baptism was the attraction. Newborns always draw attention in small communities. Rudy was even looking forward to the baptism. He would get to hold the infant. He liked children—even if they belonged to someone else.

Rudy accepted the offering plates filled with money, as well as a few empty gum wrappers and a toy soldier. It would go a long way toward converting the heathens in New Guinea and feeding the starving children in China. Rudy placed them on the altar after a short prayer of thanks for the gifts received. As his final ceremony, he would now baptize Bear Creek's newest citizen.

"Would those individuals wishing to be baptized please come to the front of the church." Rudy watched as Jennifer and Frenchie carried young John to the front. He was wearing a long white baptismal gown that extended well beyond his small feet. At least he wasn't crying. Baptisms aren't fun when the infant is screaming throughout the entire ceremony. Baby John was cooing and making the normal happy noises of infancy.

"And who presents this child for baptism?" Rudy asked.

"His parents, Claude and Jennifer D'Artagnan," Jennifer replied as she passed the lace-bound bundle to Rudy.

The infant continued with the happy baby sounds, and then reached out to touch the stole draped over Rudy's robe. Rudy felt a moment of jealousy. Why couldn't he have a family with children? Rudy reached into the bundle and offered his little finger, which the child eagerly grasped. The infant's little fingers couldn't encircle Rudy's smallest finger. It was moments like this he would miss the most when he left the ministry. Just holding the baby gave him a warm feeling.

"Sorry about that," Jennifer said, noting the dark water stain spreading out across Rudy's robe just below the baby.

"And what name have you given this child?"

"John Rudy D'Artagnan," Jennifer replied.

Rudy looked at Jennifer, wondering if he had heard right. Jennifer smiled back at him. Where is that Gomorrah? He must be close by, Rudy thought. His eyes were beginning to water. Rudy found Gomorrah sitting by the organ; beside him sat Sodom the mouse. That cat is totally worthless: *And the wolf will live with the lamb*, Isaiah 11:6

Rudy proceeded with the baptism, but his words sounded like echoes from some distant speaker. Did they actually name the baby after him? He continued to methodically perform the ritual until he heard himself say, "I now baptize you in the name of the Father, the Son and the Holy Ghost." He returned his namesake to the infant's smiling mother.

They named the baby after me, Rudy reminded himself while he shook hands with the worshipers leaving the church. The worshipers cheerfully wished him well. Maybe he had misjudged the congregation. Wasn't forgiveness one of the basic Christian principles?

"Excellent sermon," Mel said as he passed by Rudy. "We're going to miss you."

"It's been an interesting year," Rudy replied.

"You remind me of a chaplain I knew in the war. It was 1898 and Teddy Roosevelt and I were..."

"I'm really sorry about the baby wetting your robe," Jennifer said, interrupting Mel's monologue. "I'll be glad to wash it for you."

"Oh, don't worry about that. It's almost dry already." Examination revealed the wet spot still clearly visible. "I should be thanking you; I've never had a baby named after me. Do people often name their babies after ministers?"

"I can't think of any other time... but then no pastor ever lasted nine months," Jennifer replied. "For some reason, they never want to stay. No one's been able to figure out why."

"But we're not surprised you're leaving," Silas said, as he joined the conversation.

"You're not?"

"Shucks no, nothing good ever comes to Bear Creek; and if it does, it doesn't last long. We all knew it would be just a matter of time before one of those big Detroit churches scooped you up. I just wanted you to know we appreciate what you have done for us this past year."

Am I missing something here? Rudy wondered.

"Frenchie's not good at expressing thanks," Jennifer said, "but he has often told me how much your support meant to him when he thought I was dying with appendicitis and when our baby daughter died. You were always there when we needed you."

"You were the only one whose faith didn't falter when Becky was lost in the snowstorm," Maggie added. "You insisted we go on."

"Really?" A small crowd was gathering

"You showed us how to keep on going when all hope was gone. I don't know how we would have made it without your help. If we could have you for only one year, this would be the year."

Rudy felt a soft hand on his shoulder. He turned to find the Widow Watson dressed in her Sunday best. She looked as radiant as ever.

"I assume you know how I feel about your leaving."

"Yes...perhaps I do... I need your opinion on a certain matter. Do you think you could drop by the parsonage sometime this afternoon?"

"I'll be there."

Slowly, the worshipers dispersed to partake of their Sunday dinners, leaving Rudy standing in the doorway of the church. This wasn't what he expected. As he turned to reenter the church, he found Matt, Luke, Sally, and Lori standing in a huddle examining their shoes.

"And how are you kids doing today?"

"We're doing fine, I guess," Luke said, as spokesman for the group. It was obvious he wanted to say more.

"Is there something I can do for you?"

"Well, the youth group has sort'a asked us to let you know that…we're all very sorry."

"Sorry about what?"

"Sally and I, well…we kind'a changed the color of the ribbon on the top of Mrs. Watson's tent," Matt finally admitted.

"So that's how it happened." Rudy felt a wave of relief as a great burden fell from his shoulders.

"We didn't mean to cause any problems between you and Mrs. Watson."

"I suppose I can find room in my heart for a little forgiveness. Tell the rest of the group they're all forgiven."

"See, I told you so," Matt said as he collected a dollar from Luke.

"We know you'll be busy in that big Detroit church," Sally said, "but if you get any time off next spring and decide to come back for a visit, do you think you could chaperone us again?"

"That—I'll have to think about," Rudy replied. Christian charity only goes so far.

***

Rudy was sitting in his porch swing when Alice arrived. In her hand was a large plate of cookies; she seldom came empty handed.

"Hello, Alice, I'm glad you were able to come. I do apologize for the short notice," Rudy said as he visually inspected the large mound of cookies. It appeared to be chocolate chip, his favorite.

"Oh, I had nothing better to do, and it's quite likely I'll never see you again, with you leaving and all. Would you care for a cookie? I made them fresh after church."

Rudy plucked one of the larger cookies from the plate and chomped off a man sized bite. Alice's cooking had to be one of Bear Creek's major assets. With eyes closed, Rudy let the cookie linger on his tongue while the chocolate chips melted and bathed his taste buds with ambrosia. This was a moment to savor. "Excellent as usual," Rudy confirmed.

Alice had been standing while she waited for the verdict, but with a favorable edict, she took her seat on the swing. It was a wide swing with plenty of room, but Rudy found himself shoulder to shoulder with the Widow Watson. "You wanted to talk to me about something?" she asked after a few moments of silence.

"It sure is a beautiful day," Rudy said as he took another bite of cookie.

Alice looked up at the sky filled with dark clouds; it was threatening to rain. "If you say so."

"Did ya know the kids changed ribbons on your pup tent?"

"No, but I figured something like that happened. That's not the first time I've chaperoned that bunch. You should have seen your face. You were red as a beet, even in the moonlight," Alice said, as she tried not to laugh, but failed. Rudy didn't see any humor in it.

"The reason I asked you over here was to get your opinion on a letter I plan to send to Bishop Johnson. I have two letters, and I can't decide which letter to send. Rudy handed Alice one of the letters.

May 10, 1924

Dear Bishop Johnson,

We are eagerly awaiting your arrival in Bear Creek next week and pray you will have a safe and pleasant journey. It is our understanding you will be arriving sometime Saturday and will be with us for the Sunday service. The congregation of the Bare Creek Methodist church would be honored if you would be willing to conduct the Sunday worship service. We seldom have the opportunity to receive a sermon from such a theologically educated person as yourself.

It is also my understanding you will be bringing a replacement minister for the Bare Creek church. I feel this is no longer necessary. After giving it considerable thought, I have decided to remain at my post at the Bare Creek Methodist church. We would still appreciate your visit; and if you have time, I would be greatly honored if you would consider uniting Alice Watson and me in marriage—if she will have me.

I hope this late notice will not cause unnecessary confusion or hardships, and I apologize for the last minute change.

May the Lord be with you,

Rudy Hooper
Rudy Hooper

Alice read the letter and handed it back to Rudy. "I like this one."

"Don't you want to read the other letter?"

"No, I think this letter says all that needs to be said," Alice placed her hand in Rudy's hand, allowing the fingers to entwine.

Her hand felt natural in his, as if it belonged there. The couple sat quietly on the swing and looked out across the deteriorating beaver pond. Bear Creek would never be the same without that pond. The trees at the edge of the pond were in full foliage, although the leaves were still light in color testifying to the newness of the season. A lot had happened at that beaver pond. Twenty-six years ago, a teenage girl by the name of Abigail Farnsworth disappeared without leaving a trace. If she were, indeed, condemned to forever wander the forest, Rudy wished her well. He would keep her in his prayers.

"I hope you like lots of kids," Alice said, breaking the silence.

Rudy placed his arm around her shoulder and pulled her tightly against him. Some statements didn't need a reply. She laid her head on his shoulder. It felt good. He ran his fingers through her hair, and felt his heart racing. His whole body tingled with excitement. Was this love?

On the distant beaver dam, two dark-brown figures examined the dam, carefully noting the damage. The larger one was in front and walked with a limp as he planned for the needed repairs. The smaller one appeared to have a few ideas of her own; she had a shiny pelt.

And the Lord looked down upon Bear Creek from Heaven on high and said—"It is good!"

ABOUT THE AUTHOR

In 1999 Larry Buege was diagnosed with vocal cord cancer, making future speech questionable. His search for ways to earn a living without voice ultimately led him to fiction writing. Extensive surgery allowed him to return to his former employment, but failed to cure his newly acquired writing addiction. He now shares the fruits of his affliction with anyone willing to read his novels and short stories.

Larry is a former chemistry and physics teacher and a retired physician assistant. He currently lives with his wife in Marquette, Michigan along the southern shore of Lake Superior.

Made in the USA
Columbia, SC
28 May 2025

58515794R00148